May A Divine Awaken

Michael Tinsley

DEDICATION

This book is dedicated to my grandmothers, Julia and Hattie Sue, and to the coolest uncle one could have, Harold R. Tinsley.

ACKNOWLEDGMENTS

To my mother, father, brothers, and to my wife who believed in me, I love you. Most importantly, with God all things are possible.

The Doctrine of Divines

This testament on the day of solace solidifies unity across the eight Great Lands of Pyris. Under the authority of King Arius Ulta of Aypha, Queen Nandi Bonet of Amina, King Naasir Braven of Kamara, Queen Nitocris Sinfall of Zell, King Fate Everlast of Quinn, Queen Vanya Victoria of Dyna, King Dyren Linksan of Syren and Queen Lucia Karna of Tyna. By this signed Doctrine, all Divines shall live by these seven laws for now and forever.

ONE
No Divine shall be forced to fight for their land

TWO
Inhabitance in the Land of Beta is forbidden

THREE
Divines of opposite gender must live in separate lands, cohabiting only during the winter months

FOUR
The Book of Pure shall remain sacred and never to be opened

FIVE
Divines of opposite gender shall not engage in war unless under threat against the sacredness of the Book of Pure

SIX
Divines shall never use the soul as a source of power

SEVEN

Trials

MARCUS

Staring at my bathroom mirror, eyes twitching and bloody red, I splash cold water on my face hoping it wakes me. Too anxious or perhaps too scared, I slept not a second last night. Today is unlike any other; I must be focused or it shall be my last.

This morning sparks the beginning of Trials, an annual event where military squads from all across the Land of Aypha gather and compete for rank. It's here in the Village of Amarna, fifty squads will contend for the glory as best. In a few hours, the pride of many young men will be broken, and the grip of privilege will shift hands in usual fashion. But while pride and privilege can be restored, the same can't be said about life.

Inside my living quarters, the old wood floorboards crack under my feet as I stretch and release a heavy yawn. Having left my window open all night, a light coat of yellow pollen blankets my bedroom floor. Rubbing my weary eyes, I slip on a cotton gray jumpsuit and lace up my pollen-coated boots.

Before heading out, I grab my parents' portrait off a nightstand. Their painted image is all that remains. With each passing day, their faces become less familiar and my heart turns a little colder. Still, I kiss them for good luck and dash outside.

The morning sun is relentless as sweat trickles down my forehead and slides to the tip of my discolored nose. Packed alongside tattered wood cabins, a sea of young soldiers hurl insults and shove one another. Emotions run high as nearly everyone wants to move up in rank. The better your rank, the more perks your squad receives. Simple things like daily meals and better living arrangements. It doesn't sound like much, until you find yourself rummaging through garbage for an inch of food. This is the shame of being in Squad Fifty.

As a soldier in the worst squad across the land, we're prohibited from engaging in any real combat. Instead, we serve the role as the help. The lucky of us are cooks or farmers; I, on the other hand, manage waste. Every day my duty is to collect trash across the village and deliver it to a massive dumping ground. Decades of filth have piled so high, the rancid smell causes my eyes to burn and my throat to swell. For two years this has been my life. Today I rid myself of this putrid nightmare.

To move up in rank, our squad must compete in a Search and Destroy tournament. Better known as S&D, the tournament begins with two opposing squads setting up base camps in a forest. The objective is to locate the other team's base and destroy it without being spotted. Like last year and the year before, our squad stands no chance. To win S&D requires stealth and technique, a hopeless task for my squad mates. They've accepted their lives as servants, yet I refuse to do the same. I have to make a change, even if it comes at the cost of my life.

Proceeding through the raucous crowd of soldiers, I spot my fellow squad mates huddled in a circle laughing and joking. S&D is a serious tournament, yet they treat it as meaningless. None of them take their jobs seriously, and it's obvious why we're the clowns of the military. From their sloppy dress to their lack of motivation, the soldiers of Squad Fifty have always been known as bumbling idiots. But I didn't join the military to be mocked. I joined to become a true guardian of the land—not as a cook or a garbage man, but as a real soldier.

I wave to my squad mates, yet none respond. Instead, their laughter halts, and their eyebrows furrow at my presence. Admittedly, I'm a thorn to them.

"You guys should be preparing for the tournament. We're up first this year," I say.

"Ah, relax, Marcus. It's not like we can get further demoted," says my squad lead, Bamboo. A ten-year vet, Bamboo is by far the oldest and fattest of Squad Fifty. As a head cook, let's just say he eats more than his fair share. Pimples blister his oily face and his uniform is stained with grease—he cares nothing of his appearance and glorifies complacency.

"Yeah, Patches, Trials is pointless. We're going to lose as always," says another squad mate. Because of my discolored skin marks, my squad refers to me as Patches.

I roll my eyes in disgust and decide to break the news to them.

"Well, you guys will have to lose without me. Today I'm competing for the Elite Guard. This is the last time I'll see you."

A chuckle breaks out among the squad before they erupt into complete laughter.

Bamboo slings his thick arm around me. "You're right. It is the last time we'll see you because you're going to die. Take my advice, Marcus, the Elite Guard is not worth risking your life for." Bamboo squeezes my lanky arms. "Besides, it's not like you have what it takes to be an Elite."

I push away from Bamboo. His condescending grin kindles disdain in my heart. He thinks I'm like him—weak and lazy—but he's wrong. And soon, I shall prove it.

A loud bell rings as an announcer declares final call for the Elite Guard registration.

"I'm heading toward the pit. Good luck, guys," I say.

"Wish you the same, but you'll either be dead or back here with us. Same crappy duties, same crappy squad," says Bamboo. Right on point, rest of my squad mates chuckle and return to their silly jokes.

They're idiots.

Leaving my clown mates, I elbow my way through the sweaty crowd of soldiers and head straight to the competition grounds. The pit, as we refer to it, is a deep sunken quarry where individual competitions will be held. In the center of the red sandpit are a series of sparring rings where soldiers will compete in sword and hand-to-hand combat. Toward the back of the pit is a marksmen zone for archery and knife strike competitions. While I would love to test my archery skills, I'm here for something greater.

I descend into the pit and enter a large goatskin tent to register for the Elite Guard. As I add my name to the list, an enthusiastic voice curls up from behind me.

"Hey, there he is!" shouts my best friend, Asher. He jabs my shoulder unaware of his own strength. Though a squat in height, he's stocky like a bull and has piercing dark brown eyes.

"So, you ready?" he asks, wiping away sweat from his young face.

I nod. "Been waiting all year for this." Both of us have trained relentlessly for this moment. Becoming an Elite soldier is the highest honor Asher and I can achieve. More importantly, it's the only way to reunite with Darius—for he is a Divine.

The three of us were born in Eden, a vast village that sits between the Great Lands of Aypha and Amina. Separated by gender, males live in Aypha, while females reside in Amina. It's only in Eden where both genders can live. As children of Eden, we all played games and attended school together. At age twelve though, boys and girls of Divine blood are ripped from Eden and sent to defend their respective lands. As a Norm, that is, one without the blood, I had nothing to worry about. Many children feared being taken away, but I relished the thought. To me, becoming a soldier meant something worthy of life. A soldier has purpose—to protect and ensure their homeland has peace.

Like many with Divine blood, Darius was taken from Eden but Asher and I vowed to reunite with our friend. While he nor I were of the blood, we were permitted to join the Aypha military as Norm soldiers. It wasn't until later we discovered that Norms and Divines rarely interact. It's only in the Elite Guard that the two groups fight together.

"So, how many do you think are competing today?" I ask Asher.

"Irrelevant, we'll beat them all." Asher's assurance is larger than himself. What I'd give to have his confidence. "You worry too much, Marcus. Besides I've got your back."

I'm lucky to have Asher as a friend. Even though he's a hothead, I can always count on him.

"Glad I caught you two in time," whispers Darius as he slips inside the registration tent. Tall and fit, Darius is like a man among boys. We salute him with our fists over our hearts. As Norms, we're required to do so when in the presence of a Divine.

Darius slaps our hands down. "Knock it off guys. I'm not even supposed to be here." He partly slides back the hood of his black velvet cloak and reveals his close-shaven hair. "You all set for the Elite Competition?"

"Surprised we're even having it with all that's going on," says Asher. "Heard another Divine was found dead this morning. That's the second one this week. Any clue who's behind it?"

Darius shrugs. "Could be anyone."

"You're not worried?" I ask.

"Life's too short to live in fear. That's what my dad says anyway." Darius looks around the tent and waves for us to come close. "I have to run, but there's something I need to pass along. I'm not supposed to tell you but please guys, just take your time during the competition. Those who rush always fail. Think, don't panic, and most importantly, stay alive." Darius shakes our hands, slides his hood back on, and quietly departs.

I lean over to Asher. "Heard Darius was talented enough to join any Divine command. Why wouldn't he pick the assault command? They're the ones who get the most recognition."

Asher plucks my forehead. "That's the difference between you and him. You're eager to die for the glory while he's not. Besides, the assault command has the highest death rate among all Divines."

"That's a risk to be proud of. It's an honor to protect those who cannot protect themselves."

Asher chuckles and rolls up the sleeves of his gray jumpsuit. "No offense, Marcus, but you're a trash collector, and I'm not much better. Even if we become Elites, it's the Divines who really keep us safe. Without them, we'd all be dead."

He's wrong. Even as Norms, we can protect Aypha just as well as any Divine. Not all strength comes from sheer power.

From the tent, an official approaches us. "Hey, you two! The Elite Guard competition will start soon." The official hands us our registration papers. Asher and I quickly leave and hurry into the east woods where today's competition will be held.

An Elite soldier greets us at the bottom of a steep dirt hill. He laughs when we hand him our papers. "First time we've had anyone from such low-ranking squads compete. You sure about this? High chance you won't survive."

I gnash my teeth. "We know the consequences. No need to remind us."

The soldier concedes and dips his fingers into a copper bowl filled with black dye. He marks the number seventeen on Asher's forehead and prepares to write on mine, but pauses upon seeing the blemished marks on my skin.

"Is that contagious?" the guard asks while staring at the discolored marks on my face. It's a question I'm asked many times. Unusual stares from others is quite common. I try my best to ignore them, but the mind can be a fragile thing.

I shake my head, but the guard remains unconvinced and uses a brush to write eighteen on my forehead. The numbers are written on us as means to identify our bodies in the event something goes wrong.

Given the clearance to proceed, we head uphill where sixteen other contestants await. All the soldiers are from top ten Norm squads; only Asher and I are of lower rank.

"All right, the last of you Norms are here," says Rizen. Like Asher and Darius, I've known Rizen since Eden. He wears a black and gold jumpsuit and stitched on his shoulders are gold lion patches—the symbol of a Divine Aypha. Shrewd and arrogant, he treats Norms like underlings and abuses his authority just to remind us that we are not like him.

"This year, only five of you maggots shall make it into the Guard." Rizen slams his hand onto my shoulder and nearly breaks my collarbone. Because of our past, he finds a special joy in harassing me. "The Guard seeks only those with the greatest strength, intelligence, and mental fortitude. Today we'll see if any of you are worthy of such a role." Rizen points to a jagged mountain in the distance. "This year's competition is a gauntlet race. The objective is simple. You're to race from here to the top of Doom's Peak. First five to reach the top will become members of the Elite Guard."

A soldier from Squad Two raises his hand. "What are the rules?" Rizen grins. "There are none. Do whatever is necessary. I don't care if you cheat, steal, or kill your way to the top. Results are all that matter."

Victory

MARCUS

How insidious to kill just to win. I've made a terrible mistake if this is what it takes to join the Elites. But it's too late; quitting now would be a dishonor all unto itself. Asher and I exchange glances knowing the danger we're in. To survive we must partner up. Of the eighteen of us, there are five soldiers from Squad One, five from Squad Two, and five from Squad Three. Only Asher, myself, and a soldier named Gavin are outliers. Seeing our predicament, Gavin nods, agreeing to join us as well. My palms drizzle with sweat as tension among the group builds with each breath. This is now a matter of survival, yet am I the only one who feels this is wrong?

Rizen orders us to attention. We slam our fists to our chests as the leader of the Elite Guard arrives, Commander Claudius Royale. Alongside him is Darius, proud to stand with his father.

"At ease, everyone," orders Commander Claudius. "Just came by to deliver a message. Those of you who make it into the Guard will become a part of something special. The Guard is the only command where both Divines and Norms must work together. We're the shield and armor that protects Aypha. With pride, I tell you, this is a position of the highest honor."

"What is honorable about killing a fellow soldier just to join the Guard?" I ask.

Claudius frowns. "Who speaks?"

While the others look to their boots, I keep my head high and step forward.

Commander Claudius approaches. He stares down at me and unleashes a terrifying scowl. "You're my son's friend..." He motions for Darius to come forward.

Darius's jaw tightens upon approach. "Father, I apologize for..."

Claudius rests his hand on Darius's shoulder. "My son has a good eye for friends. Someone who values unity and life is rare these days. In the end, it is our character that defines who we truly are." Claudius gives me a nod, his scowl softens. "Good luck to you."

Relieved, I salute the commander and step back in line. Commander Claudius makes his way toward Rizen. He snatches him by the neck and forces him to the ground. Rizen immediately begins doing pushups.

"Contrary to what you've been told, killing your competition is prohibited," says Commander Claudius. He presses his boot into Rizen's back. "Still, today's challenge will test your resolve to survive. As members of the Elite Guard, our mission is to protect the borders of Aypha from our enemies. Out there you will encounter many hazards and must be prepared for anything. Today's competition is a taste of what you'll face on a real mission."

Commander Claudius orders Rizen back to his feet, he then scans the faces of all eighteen of us. "The odds of you all surviving is not high. Do any of you wish to back out?"

Rizen slides me a smug grin, but I ignore him. No one budges. We all want to be in the Guard. This is our only chance at becoming something worthy in life.

"Very well." Commander Claudius orders Rizen to await the winners at the top of Doom's Peak.

As Rizen departs, we're then instructed to remove our boots and strip to our undergarments. We're each given a dagger as our only tool for survival. Darius slips Asher and me a final nod for good luck. He then blows a horn and the competition begins.

Charging barefoot and half-naked, we enter a vast briar field of brittle thorns that slice across my flesh and burrow deep into my skin. Warm blood trickles down my elbows and kneecaps. As we jostle for position, a soldier from Squad Two shoves me into a bush, many thorns pierce my chest, but there's no time to think about the pain. I spring to my feet and quickly catch up to Asher and Gavin.

For two hours, we endure torture through the thorn-laced thicket, and it isn't until reaching a clearing we see the aftermath. All of us are coated in blood. Sweat drizzles into my wounds and stings without mercy. Along with us are the soldiers from Squads Two and Three; only Squad One lags behind.

Pressing forward, we arrive at a large lake. The water is murky, and there's a whiff of rotting flesh in the air. Soldiers from Squad Two immediately dive in while Squad Three heads farther up shore. Forced to make a quick decision, Asher, Gavin, and I each dive in. I'm not the greatest of swimmers, so the others quickly pull ahead.

I'm halfway across the lake when my soul spikes with terror. Gators that lie hidden within the marsh spring into the lake. The blood from our wounds sends them into a frenzy, and everyone panics. The gators swarm Squad Two first. Clamping their jaws onto the soldiers, they twist and roll their bodies, and rip off limbs. Painful screams fill the air, but the young men cannot be saved. Death is near and its net has cast itself upon us. As a gator swims toward me, I clench my dagger and prepare to clash. The gator targets my arm, I pull back just as its jaws snap tight. I thrust my dagger into the gator's snout, but all that does is piss the gator off. I shout for help. Gavin presses forward, but Asher turns back while I wrestle to keep the gator's mouth shut. The heavy weight of the gator presses me below the surface of the water. I hold my breath and my heart races. The silhouette of Asher swims over me. He grips his dagger and repeatedly stabs the gator in the eye; it hisses and retreats. Returning to the surface for air, I notice Asher's face is full of excitement. The thrill of this moment outweighs any fear that he holds. Thankfully, the other gators are so focused on the bloodbath of Squad Two they pay us no mind as we continue across the lake.

As Asher and I reach the lakeshore, I stare down Gavin. "You left me."

Gavin lowers his head. "I panicked, okay. Thought I was going to die."

Asher clenches Gavin's chin and turns his head to the bloody waters. "Look, if we don't help each other, we're all going to die."

Gavin nods and sinks his trembling fingers into the moist soil. It does nothing to calm his nerves. Nothing has prepared us for this. We knew the risk going in but seeing death has made this real. Of the five soldiers from Squad Two, only one survived. But he's done. Shivering and holding his mangled arm, he'll never be the same. To our surprise, Squad Three was able to avoid peril by swimming farther up shore. Strange though, Squad One is nowhere to be found.

"Let's move," says Asher.

Sprinting through a thick forest of pine trees, we travel up a hill until spotting a competition judge. As we approach, the judge jots down our numbers.

"Do any of you wish to quit?" he asks.

The judge seems surprise when the three of us refuse. He gives us a few seconds to reconsider before ordering us to spread out.

"Okay, to proceed forward the three of you must pass a defense challenge," says the judge. "You'll have sixty seconds to detain a soldier who will act as an assassin. If you fail to capture the assassin within the allotted time, you will be immediately eliminated from the competition." The judge drops smoke bombs at our feet, gray clouds fill the air and restrict our vision.

Asher screams in pain. "My arm has been cut," he yells. Seconds later, a sharp edge slashes across my arm. Gavin shouts as he too is slashed. An assassin lurks within the smoke with an unfair advantage. Somehow, we must disarm him, but doing so without vision is nearly impossible. Counting down in my head, we've got less than forty seconds to figure it out. The assassin slashes my outer thigh. The cut burns, I want to shout, but doing so will only distract the others. I tell everyone to be quiet and listen for the slightest of sounds. Thirty seconds left, the assassin's footsteps are near silent but as he strikes, his silhouette appears. I dive toward the shadow but miss. Twenty seconds to go, the assassin's silhouette disappears behind the smoke. The clouds will soon lift and desperation sets in. I can't see Asher or Gavin, but I can imagine their faces of frustration. Nearby, I can hear them blindly charging forward. The assassin again strikes one of them, but this time, he exhales and his faint breath carries through the smoke. Though I can't see him, I can almost trace his steps by the sound of his breathing. I stalk behind him in the smoke. Ten seconds remain, I just need him to strike one last time. He grunts as he lunges toward Asher or Gavin. I spring forward and tackle someone. A few seconds later, the clouds dissipate, and the soldier acting as an assassin gives a firm head nod.

The competition judge approves and gives us the clearance to proceed forward. Continuing through a dirt trail, we pick up the footsteps of Squad Three and arrive to a precarious sight. A soldier from Squad Three lies on the ground and is covered in blood. He moans in pain and nurses his leg. He appears to have suffered many deep cuts from the assassin exercise.

"Help me," he pleads. His fingers tremble as he reaches out to me. Blood streams down his leg, it's only a matter of time before he bleeds out.

"Should we?" I ask the group.

Asher scoffs and treats his own wounds by tying leaves around his arm. "If it, were you or I, would he? His own squad mates abandoned him. We must press on."

Without our help, the soldier will surely die. But Asher is right—this is a competition, one I cannot afford to lose.

Turning my back on the soldier, my stomach becomes hollow knowing his demise is near. As much as I want to win, I can't allow his death to be on my heart. I rip off a cuff from my underpants and tighten it around the soldier's leg. Creating a tourniquet, I successfully stop the blood flow from the soldier's wounds.

Propping him up against a tree trunk, we then press forward and trace muddy footsteps deeper into the forest. Eventually, we catch up to the remaining soldiers of Squad Three but they stand paralyzed. Before us is a massive field of jagged steel spikes. Impaled on the spikes are skulls and bones presumably of previous contestants. The only way to cross is over a dilapidated wood bridge held together by tattered ropes.

"What are you guys waiting for?" I ask.

"It's a trap," says one of the soldiers from Squad Three. His bottom lip quivers as he stares at the graveyard of bones.

"Oh please, those bones are obviously fake," jeers Asher. "It's just a ploy to intimidate us. Tell you what, since ya so scared, we'll go ahead and you guys can follow."

"Negative! We were here first; we'll take the lead." The soldier looks to his fellow squad mates, they nod reluctantly.

The soldiers' legs twitch and their knees buckle as they climb a ladder to the bridge. The rotted wood planks on the bridge are a breeze away from falling and the frayed ropes holding them together aren't much better. Still, the soldiers cautiously press forward, and are halfway across when a plank gives way. A soldier falls through and clings onto a frayed rope. He holds on with all his might as the fragile bridge swings back and forth. But the tension is too great, the rope snaps, and the soldier plummets to his death. The bridge begins to collapse, and the remaining soldiers attempt to sprint back. But it's pointless, the planks fall from beneath their feet, two soldiers fall onto the spikes below, only one makes it back before the bridge disintegrates. Tears fall from the surviving soldier's eyes. He plops to his bottom, tucks his head between his knees, and screams.

There were once eighteen candidates; only eight of us remain. While the last from Squad Three has given up, I refuse to do the same. This is it for me. I'd rather die here than return to Squad Fifty.

"There must be another way around," I say to Asher and Gavin.

Inspecting the field of spikes, I notice some are darker in color than others. Tapping an off-colored spike, it crumbles to ash. Among the real spikes are false ones that disintegrate upon touch. Slowly, we discover a trail of fake spikes allowing us to safely pass through. We breathe a sigh of relief, but it's fleeting as Squad One trails not far behind. Their strategy is fairly simple—take your time and let the competition kill itself. This is what Darius tried to tell us.

Still, we pick up the pace and begin our ascent up a series of forest hills. It takes us nearly an hour to reach a plateau and my heart pumps with excitement. Doom's Peak looms straight ahead. To reach the base of the peak we'll need to first leap over a mountain divide.

"What if it's another trap?" I ask the others.

Asher takes a hard swallow. "That's just fear talking. We've got this, Marcus!"

As we prepare ourselves for the final challenge, an enormous bear emerges from a nearby brush pile. It roars and charges full speed. Forced to fight or run, we sprint toward the mountain divide and leap over. Now it's just a matter of who reaches the top of Doom's Peak first. Digging our hands into the rocky cliff, we begin the grueling climb. While Asher is right with me, Gavin remains behind. He's still on the other side of the divide and cowers on the ground. The massive bear towers over him and sinks its bloodstained teeth into Gavin's arm. His scream of agony is deafening. While victory is only a few meters away, I can't leave Gavin behind. I snatch Asher's dagger, leap back over the divide, and sprint toward the vicious beast. With one swipe of its paw, the bear nearly crushes Gavin's skull. I shout to get the bear's attention; it turns to me and releases a nasty roar. Petrified, my hands and feet turn to stone. Legs planted firmly to the ground, I'm stuck by my own fear. The bear continues its vicious assault, mauling away at Gavin's face.

"HELP ME, MARCUS!" Gavin screams. Blood and tears fall from his eyes. I want to help but the fear of dying is real. Soldiers from Squad One run right by us. If I turn back now, I can still place in the top five but at the sacrifice of Gavin's life. *Do something, move*, I tell myself.

"GET OUT THE WAY!" yells Asher. He reclaims his dagger from my frozen hand and charges forward. Asher sinks his knife behind the bear's neck and slides it across its throat. The bear groans and dies within seconds.

Breathing heavy, a bloody Gavin shakes uncontrollably. His face is caved in and his lips are split in two. Still, he speaks firm. "Go! Finish the race."

By this point, three of the five soldiers from Squad One are near the top of Doom's Peak. However, the last two are just beginning their ascent.

Running back, we leap over the mountain divide and scale the cliff with absolute tenacity. We close the gap between the last two soldiers, and all four of us reach the peak simultaneously. There are only two spots left—now it's an all-out race to the finish line. I dig deep and run full speed with every grain of strength within my body. Warm air whistles past my ears as tears of determination fly from my eyes. Asher and I pull ahead with seventy meters to go.

Holding nothing back, I move ahead of Asher. Fifty meters left; my muscles begin to cramp. Pain shoots through the soles of my feet and legs. My sprint turns into a hobble. Asher moves ahead. Twenty meters to go, the others have caught up. Ten meters left, I'm now behind. I'm going to lose and all will be for naught. Desperate, I dive across the finish line and tumble to a stop at Rizen's boots. My knees and elbows scraped, blood and dust cover my skin. It's unclear if I've made the cut. As the others look on, we all hold our breaths and await a decision. Rizen sneers and shakes his head.

"Can't believe it. Asher and Marcus, you've earned the final two spots."

Agony
MARCUS

I slept well last night knowing life will soon change. Today I go from the trash heap of despair to the pinnacle of success. Days of trash pickup have come to an end. Today, in front of my peers, I'll be pinned as an Elite soldier. Soon, Asher and I will fight alongside Darius and the other Divines. Dreams are coming true and my purpose is beginning to take shape. No matter its imperfections, I pledge to defend my land and every last person within it.

Rolling out of bed, I spot my dingy work jumpsuit on the floor. Cleaned but once a year, its musty scent lingers heavy. Hot days of working in the village waste dumps have left permanent stains that no suds can erase. Yet with pride I slip on my rancid jumpsuit, for this is the last time I shall wear it. As part of today's pinning ceremony, we'll be stripped of our old garments and don a new uniform fitting for an Elite soldier.

Picking up my parents' portrait, I doubt they would be proud of this moment. I'm becoming exactly what they didn't want. My parents found no merit in war; they've seen its tragedies and desperately wanted to keep me from it. As explorers, their job was to locate rare jewels and artifacts from across the world. In the beginning, they would tell me enchanting stories of discovering temples of gold and majestic caves filled with jewels. As time went on though, their stories were of finding mass graves and vast lands burned to ash. Seeing such cruelty and devastation, my parents forbid me from joining the military. Yet here I am.

A loud bang rattles my door before Asher barges inside.

"Now that we're Elite soldiers, we can't be late, Marcus. Commander Claudius won't allow tardiness," says Asher.

I prop my parents' portrait back on the nightstand. "Guess I overslept."

Asher glances at the portrait and pats my back. "Don't worry. We'll find them."

It's been four years since I last saw my parents. Four years since they left for the northern lands only to never return. Some days I think they're still out there, lost in a foreign land searching for a way home; searching to return to their child. On darker days I wonder if they've abandoned me. As a child, it was common to go months without seeing them. Their obsession with the world's mysteries seemed to take priority over my basic needs. The thought of being abandoned stings like needles to the brain.

"Let's go," I say to Asher. I head outside as faint memories of my parents still linger.

Today's ceremony will take place in a nearby arena where soldiers across Aypha will convene and cheer on the winners from Trials. Along the way, we spot hummingbirds gathering nectar from a field of light purple tulips. I snag a flower and dip my nose onto its petals, the delicate honey scent reminds me of Eden.

"Don't know about you but I look forward to unity season." *It's been two years since I've been home, two years since I last saw her.*

Asher mocks me with kissy faces. "You going to finally confess? She won't be single forever."

I pluck Asher's forehead. "I suppose, as long as you don't ruin it for me."

Jogging our way through Amarna's square, I see my former squad mates picking up trash and washing the cobblestone roads. Their cold stares are like ice needles, but I press my lips tight refusing to mock them. I can only hope this moment will inspire them to change, to no longer just be subservient to others.

Asher and I round a corner and bump into my former squad lead, Bamboo. He gives me a hard look before returning a smile.

"Hate to admit it, but I'm proud of you, Patches." Bamboo clears his throat. "Sorry, I meant, Marcus." He stretches out his greasy palm. We squeeze hands out of faint respect. "Though you're no longer in Squad Fifty, you still have to represent us. Stay humble—that's the only advice I can give ya."

Accepting his words, Asher and I quickly sprint toward the arena where chants and roars of jubilation grow loud. Proceeding into an underground entrance, we enter a dimly lit room and find the other three Elite Guard inductees huddled in a corner. I walk over to congratulate them, but they ignore me as if I'm not there.

"Can't believe they let a freak into the Guard," says one of them to the others. Normally I'd ignore the comment, but who are they to speak ill of me?

"Amazing how this freak is better than all of you," I shoot back. "Test me if you want to."

Asher grins. He encourages malcontent and preferred if I did it more often. "You boys might as well get use to us," he sneers. "We survived the gauntlet just as you did!"

The three soldiers dismiss us and walk away. We're not even in the Guard yet and we've already made enemies.

A short time later, Rizen enters the room. We stand at attention and salute.

"Good. You're well trained in terms of respect in the presence of a Divine," says Rizen. "While you're about to become soldiers of the Guard, know that even the lowest of Divines still have authority over you. You're our subordinates; we are your leaders. Never disrespect a Divine. Doing so may cost you your life."

Rizen then rolls out a table, on it are five black and silver uniforms. Our ceremony garments are made of silk and have silver trim of leaves around the collar and sleeves. Patched onto the shoulders are silver wings, the symbol of an Elite Norm soldier.

"Some of you I expected to see here, others not so much." Rizen angles his eyes toward me. "Before the ceremony begins, there's one last thing I need to say. Beyond Aypha, there are other lands filled with Divines and Elite Norms like you. Out there, they will not hesitate to kill, and neither should you."

Overhead we hear an announcer congratulate the winners of the Search and Destroy competition. Squad Four has now become the top squad of the year.

"All right, get in line. It's time to get your wings," says Rizen.

Arranging ourselves in a single file, we proceed upstairs and down a corridor toward the arena's main stage. The screams and chants from the crowd have reached a deafening pitch. Excitement tingles my fingertips in anticipation of a crowd seeing a soldier from Squad Fifty become an Elite soldier.

"Follow me, everyone," says a stage coordinator.

As we march forward, Rizen yanks me by the neck and pushes me into a musty storage room. "Usually, I don't judge Norms, but I must when it comes to you." Rizen shoves me into a chair, his mood is as foul as the odor in the room. "Heard you froze yesterday at the sight of a bear. They tell me you watched a teammate of yours nearly die."

I stifle the urge to punch Rizen in his sack. "I was simply contemplating whether to save him or finish the race. Results are all that matter, right?"

Rizen strokes his chiseled chin. "Here's what I think. You got scared when you saw flesh being ripped off that boy. And instead of rising above it, you retreated…just like when we were kids."

Rizen's words cut deep like a well-edged blade. Past memories as friends play before me. A few months after my parents disappeared, Eden forced me to live with a man named Mr. Drew. He was a caretaker for troubled boys, and Rizen was one of them. While the old man was titled a caretaker, he didn't actually care; he simply loved the coin he received for bringing us in. He was a shrewd drunk and anytime we disobeyed his rules, he'd scorch our arms with hot steel and force us to sleep by his fireplace, just so our burns would sting through the night. Other times he'd have us take cold showers and force us to sleep outside. Being roommates, Rizen and I would share stories of the twisted things Mr. Drew did to us. Back then, we had a bond and talked about leaving Eden just to be free from Mr. Drew's terror. All we wanted was to be free, free from pain and nightmares. And while we both wanted Mr. Drew dead, it was only Rizen who acted upon those sinister thoughts.

Rizen's fingers snap before my eyes. "You hear me, Marcus? Timidness cannot be tolerated in the Guard. There's no room for weakness, whether Norm or Divine."

I stare at old scars on my arm, healed cuts once inflicted by Mr. Drew. His torture should've turned me colder. "Things have changed, Rizen. I'm prepared to kill for this land!"

Rizen's lips curl into a grin. "Prove it." From the corner of the musty room, Rizen yanks a sheet off a cage and unlatches a lock. A bear cub crawls forward and plays at Rizen's feet.

"Cute little thing, isn't she?" asks Rizen. "Found her yesterday whimpering beside her dead mother." Rizen places the cub in my lap and slips a knife into my hands. "With no mom, this cub will surely die in the wild. So, go ahead and put her out of her misery."

"What will this prove?" I ask, staring at the young eyes of the cub.

"You want to be an Elite, do you not? Kill the cub and prove you're not as weak as I know you are."

My hands turn moist as I press the knife against the cub's belly. She wiggles and yawns having no idea what's soon to happen. There is no fear in her eyes, only innocence. I hesitate, just as I did with the cub's mother.

"I'm not playing your silly mind game, Rizen." I fling the knife across the room. "This cub is no threat. To shed its blood would be cruel."

Rizen takes the cub from me and cradles her in his arms. "Compassion, something only a Norm possesses." With only his thumb, Rizen punctures the cub's belly, blood squirts onto his uniform. He tosses the cub at my feet. It's difficult to watch as the cub whimpers and cries before falling silent.

Rizen smears blood across my face. "If you can't kill a cub, how can you kill your enemy? You're not worthy of the Elite Guard. I'm revoking your passage."

"You can't do this!" I jump to my feet but Rizen slams me back into the chair. He whistles and two Norms enter the room. I recognize them from yesterday as the soldiers who Asher and I beat in the gauntlet race.

"Because of your antics, these fine soldiers were unable to join the Guard," says Rizen. "Two worthy soldiers were denied by a coward. Someone unwilling to do what is necessary to survive…how disgraceful."

Rizen exits the room and the soldiers approach. Before they can strike, I kick one of them in the shin and deliver a hard punch across his jaw. As we scuffle, the other soldier pins my arms back. Unable to break free, they take turns drilling heavy blows into my rib cage until I cough up blood. Tossing me to the floor, they pound mercilessly at my legs. In a final act of humiliation, they haul in waste buckets and douse me in piss.

"Enjoy life back in Squad Fifty, trash boy!" yells one of them.

The two high-five one another and leave me to soak in vile body fluids. Part of me wanted to lie motionless and cry until my tears could numb the shame. Still I crawl toward the door where I hear Commander Claudius introducing the inductees to the Elite Guard. I've endured too much pain to see my dreams fade away. Regaining my footing, I throw my body repeatedly against the door until the hinges break loose. Every breath I take hurts and though I smell like the bowels of a sewer, I hobble toward the platform stage to claim what is rightfully mine. That is until

Rizen orders his team to restrain me. I'm pinned down to the floor, and all I can do is watch as Asher and the others obtain their silver wings. As they don their Elite Guard uniforms, the crowd cheers while my heart dims for what was meant for me.

When the ceremony ends, Rizen's team releases me. I hobble on stage in search of Rizen but it's hard to find him in the large crowd of soldiers. Instead, I bump into Asher and Darius, they cover their noses instantly.

"Aw, you smell awful. What happened?" asks Asher as he takes a step back.

"Rizen…he denied my passage into the Guard," I say.

Asher's eyes ignite in anger. "Darius, you've got to talk to him."

Darius nods. "I will. Don't worry, Marcus. I'll make this right. Come, let's get you cleaned up and back to your quarters."

Seeing me walk with a limp, my friends act as crutches and help me leave the arena. We proceed down a cobblestone trail where passing soldiers brag about their accomplishments from Trials. Their grins of joy are torturous to witness.

"Let's take the back way," I say.

We veer off onto a dirt path and a slight drizzle falls just in time to mask my tears.

"Might be a big storm," says Asher as the gray skies grow heavy.

When we arrive at my quarters, standing at my front door is Rizen. "There you are, Darius. We have to go—an emergency meeting is being called." Rizen rests his hand on Darius's shoulder. "We lost another Divine."

Darius grinds his teeth and brushes off Rizen's hand. "Why did you deny Marcus into the Guard?"

Rizen's face turns sour. "Darius, do not have empathy for him. He's just like rest of the Norms. They're tools. By the blood—you're better than them."

"You shut your mouth!" shouts Asher as squares up with Rizen. "You talk as if we're trash. Our blood may be different, but we serve the same team."

Rizen smirks. "You just got in the Guard and you're already disrespecting your superior."

Asher rips the silver wings from his Elite uniform and grinds them into the dirt. "There's no honor in serving someone like you."

Rizen's eyes narrow. He cocks back to strike but Darius intervenes.

"Reinstate Marcus or I'm out as well," says Darius.

Rizen frowns and a hint of red flashes across his face. "You would really throw everything away and disappoint your father just for, Marcus?"

Darius picks up Asher's silver wings and hands one to me, the other to Asher. "No matter our blood differences, these are my friends. We will forever be friends. Disrespecting them is the same as disrespecting me."

"He's a coward," barks Rizen. "When the time comes to rise, Marcus will fail. Trust me, I'm a witness."

I can see my sorrow reflecting off Rizen's pupils. "As much as we hated him, killing Mr. Drew wasn't right," I say.

Rizen points to the scars on my arm. "He tormented us, Marcus! Killing him was the best thing that could've happened. The man was supposed to be our protection, instead, he was our affliction. He almost killed me that night, I needed your help, yet you ran when blood hit the walls."

The tips of my fingertips burn as I recall the gurgling screams of Mr. Drew. "We were just children, Rizen. Back then I wasn't ready for something like that."

"And neither are you today. On that night I realized you and I are not the same. Norms are timid and weak. A Divine's bloodline though is filled with rage and chaos."

I grit my teeth and approach Rizen. "You're wrong. I have just as much courage as any of you Divines. I worked too hard for you to strip this from me. The Elite Guard is where I belong."

"The bottom is where you belong," snaps Rizen. "This world is filled with haves and have-nots, and you have nothing to show the world. You're not a soldier; you're a servant. Don't ever forget that." Rizen slaps me, the weight of his heavy hand stings.

"JUST KILL HIM ALREADY," taunts a soft voice in my head.

Listening to her, I lunge at Rizen with such rage, blood vessels pop within my arms. Rizen evades my strikes and drills a blow to my chest knocking the air from my lungs. I gasp and drop to my knees.

"That's right, trash boy. Bow!" Rizen drives his fist to the back of my neck and I slam face-first into the dirt. "Feel the difference in strength between Divines and Norms."

"You're stronger than this," a woman's voice says. *"Show him who you really are."* Dark visions flash before my eyes and a kindle of fury burns within my heart.

I rise to my feet and a spark of wrath grows heavy inside my chest. Pain, hate, and anger all collide as rage ripples through my veins. Agony sets my bones on fire; blood fills my eyes and everything becomes darker than black.

Pain

MARCUS

The rain is cold across my scorching skin as I awake in a puddle of mud. Soaked in blood and grit, my bones burn as if they've been set on fire. Dark clouds eclipse the moon and a thick gray haze blankets the air. Asher, Darius, and Rizen are gone. The military barracks are empty and it's eerily quiet for a night in Amarna.

As I struggle to stand, an orange glow catches my eye. A line of fire burns in the distance and smoke rises in the night sky. A whiff of burned flesh causes me to gag. Before me, across a muddy field are many charred bodies. Among the massacred are Divines and Norms from the Elite Guard. My heart thumps fearing Darius and Asher are among the dead. Flipping body after body over, I search for my friends, but the faces of the dead are charred beyond recognition.

A roar of pain pierces my ear. Drawn to the screams, I spot several men in red cloaks circled around an Aypha soldier. On his knees, the Aypha's head hangs low and he shivers with each breath. The men in cloaks take turns stabbing the soldier with rusted daggers. The Aypha releases a blood-gurgling scream before a final dagger is sent through his temple. As the soldier falls face-first, I stifle my rage scarring the insides of my cheek. Tears of pain fill my eyes. I must do something. I must confront them but then I too will die.

Slowly backtracking, I tumble over a body and draw the group's attention. All eyes turn to me and the men give chase. Springing to my feet, I bolt across the murky field, and leap over many fallen brethren. Zipping through a cluster of barracks, I take shelter underneath a wood cabin and lie flat in a thin marsh. Two of the men stand above me on the cabin's walkway. Getting a closer look, I notice the sewing of black feathers on the back of their frayed red cloaks.

"Check inside," says one of them. Their footsteps shake loose wet sand from the wood planks above.

"He's not here," says the other. "Find him before this gets any worse." The two men then run off.

My skin prickles and my throat runs dry pondering what to do next. *Where is everyone? Surely, I am not all that is left.* Stifling my anguish, I emerge from underneath the cabin and peek around the corner. A firm hand latches over my mouth, I'm yanked back behind the wall.

"Not that way," says a man. Tall and slim, he's cloaked in all black and his voice is quite gruff. His face is covered by a mask painted half gold and black. Emblazoned at the top of the mask is a red lion emblem, indicating he's an Aypha Divine from our assassin command.

"Who are you?" I ask.

"Riki," says the man as he checks our surroundings. "We need to exit the village or else we'll be killed."

Not far from our position, several explosions erupt and the shockwaves ripple beneath our feet. Riki scrambles from the cabins and into a large field of cornstalks. I want to see morning, so I follow him and keep my head low.

Upon reaching the end of the cornstalks, we come to a halt before an open field. It's dark and I can see no more than a few feet ahead.

"I'll scout forward and signal with an owl call once it's clear," says Riki.

I say nothing, just nod nervously. Crouching in a low stance, Riki dashes with amazing speed across the field and disappears into the darkness.

Minutes go by before I hear a hoot. I dart across the field and reconnect with Riki, his black jumpsuit is covered in mud and bloodstains.

"You okay?" I ask as we enter into the woods.

Riki brushes himself off. "Yeah, just stumbled down a hill and cut myself."

I can't see his expression through his mask, but something isn't right. I'm only fifteen, but I know an honest man from a liar.

"Why are you helping me exactly?"

Riki cracks his neck. "It's my mission."

"Mission? What mission?"

Before he can respond, two men in red cloaks approach us. "Stop and give us the boy!"

Riki scoffs. "Marcus doesn't belong to you!"

The hair on my arms spike. How does Riki know my name?

"Leave him or you'll die," barks one of the men.

Riki slides off his gloves and tosses them onto the wet soil. "Neither shall happen." He shoos the men away but instead they throw daggers. Riki pushes me into a patch of berry bushes just as the daggers hurl past him. He stands firm as the men draw their swords and attack. With great precision and grace, he dodges their strikes.

"Stand down," Riki pleads, while evading their every move. His words though are pointless as the men have gone deaf in battle.

Strike after strike miss before one of them finally slashes Riki across his shoulder. Strange though, the men hesitate and slowly back away. They form bright yellow spheres into their hands and the heat emitting from them give warning of what will soon happen. I should run, but I can't keep my eyes off Riki. Even with death surely to follow, he stands as still as stone.

The men release their luminous spheres setting off a massive explosion. Dark dust quickly engulfs the area, and a gray haze simmers in the air. Riki is no more.

Peeping through the bushes, I brace to see a man lying in peace with flesh torn from his body. But when the debris settles and the air draws clear, Riki stands unscathed. His entire body is coated in an armor of diamonds.

As we stare in shock, one of the men builds the courage to utter a single word.

"Impossible."

The other man draws his blade. "I know you," he says. "You're from…"

A diamond shard shoots from Riki's fingertips and slashes the man's throat. Clutching his neck, the man staggers before collapsing to his death.

With his partner dead, the remaining cloaked man clenches the hilt of his sword and darts forward. Leaping in the air, he strikes Riki, but only his sword cracks.

"Who are you?" asks the man as iron shards from his sword litter the ground.

Riki sighs. "There are some things in this world your eyes weren't meant to see. Now leave us."

Instead, the man clutches the remainder of his fragmented sword and swings in defiance.

Emptied of patience, Riki touches the man's forehead and the air falls with pristine silence. Where a man once stood is now nothing but a sparkling shimmer. I stare in disbelief as dust dances in the air like soft snow in early winter. Riki has killed a man with the touch of his fingertips.

I slowly emerge from the bushes, unsure of Riki's intent. "Just what are you and what do you want?"

"Guess I can't deceive you forever," says Riki, his voice now much lighter. He removes his mask and what I see is nothing short of beauty. Riki is not a man, but a young woman. Her skin is silky tan and her eyes are light almond. Never would I have imagined a woman with such beauty to be a killer of men. "My real name is Rikari Niacin of Dyna. I was sent here to ensure your safety."

"Sent by who?"

From beneath her sleeve, Rikari unwinds an unforgettable piece of cloth I haven't seen in years. It's a yellow ascot laced with extremely rare pink diamonds. This wasn't just any ascot—this particular one belongs to a dead woman. Threaded into the silk fabric are the initials *S.B.*, confirming its hers.

"Where did you get that?" I ask.

"She gave it to me to show you. She's the reason I'm here," says Rikari.

I shake my head. "Sinclair is dead." A friend of my parents, Sinclair Bonet was assassinated years ago by the Aminas.

"You're wrong." Rikari stretches out her hand. "Let me take you to her."

I was ten years old the last time I saw Sinclair. A woman of opulence, Sinclair enjoyed traveling with my parents on their explorations for rare jewels. She also took an unusual liking to me. While my parents pushed for me to become a painter, Sinclair gave me my first dagger and told stories of past wars. *At any moment we could be erased from this world*, she used to tell me.

"I should go back," I say, unsure of Rikari's motives. "My friends need me."

Rikari shakes her head. "There's nothing back there for you. Something sinister is happening. Those men in red cloaks are assassins...very good ones too."

"But my friends—" I start to say. "I can't abandon them."

"They're dead, Marcus. Don't die trying to be a brave fool. Right now, our priority is to survive. In time, you can return and avenge the fallen."

I grit my teeth in anguish. Plumes of smoke and flames continue to rise throughout Amarna. Birds circle above my village; the smell of flesh and blood is too irresistible.

Nearby, we see a group of men in red cloaks scouring the woods. Rikari and I slip behind a patch of berry bushes, but it won't be long before we're spotted.

"You can take your chances with them or come with me," Rikari whispers.

Stuck between two terrible options, I leave with Rikari. But as we make our exodus, I can't help but wonder if Sinclair Bonet truly lives, what does she want with me?

A Reflection of Self

MARCUS

The rain has ceased but the air remains warm and moist as Rikari and I advance into a dense forest of pine trees. We've been jogging nonstop for hours and I need a moment to rest. Tired, I collapse on a bed of old pine needles which blanket the damp soil. Surprisingly, the ground provides better comfort than my raggedy bed back home.

Rikari stands over me, her hands on her thin waist. "How are you worn out already?"

Breathing heavy, I look at her incredulously. While I'm sucking down air, she hasn't even broken a sweat.

"Give... give me..." I wheeze. "Give me a few."

Rikari folds her arms and leans against a pine tree. "We really should keep going. At this pace, it'll be five moons before we reach Dyna."

"Five moons? Where are we anyways?"

Rikari examines the surrounding trees. "We're in the northern forest of Beta."

"There's no such place," I say.

Rikari's almond eyes light up. "How do you not know about this land? It's written in the Divine Doctrine."

I stand to my feet and dust pine needles off my soiled clothes. "The Divine what? Look, the Divines don't tell us Norms very much."

Rikari's eyebrows curl up. "You refer to yourself as a Norm...I suppose we do need to talk." She plops down on the trunk of a fallen tree. "First thing you should know is that Divines are anointed beings with unique abilities. The origin of our power is unknown, but many believe it was granted from the heavens. For centuries, Divine power has been passed down from one generation to the next. Meaning it can't be given to just anyone—it has to be in your blood, your heritage, your legacy! We are descendants of the greatest ancestral warriors to ever live. I am a Divine descendant—and according to Sinclair, so are you."

The roof of my mouth goes dry and my throat tightens. I am no Divine. If so, I wouldn't have ran from those men. "She's mistaken. As children, we're tested for Divine blood."

"Sinclair believes otherwise, and after what I saw, so do I."

Recalling the charred bodies of my fallen squad mates, I'm afraid to know. "What happened?"

Rikari grins. "You should know that across our world, there are many lands, but only eight are considered great. These are the ones ruled by Divines and as such we live by a set of laws known as *the Doctrine*. One law states every Great Land must be segregated by gender. The Lands of Kamara, Quinn, Syren, and Aypha are all ruled by Divine men. While the Lands of Zell, Dyna, Tyna, and Amina are controlled by Divine women. Although the lands are divided, each land partners with an ally land of the opposite gender. We call this our sibling land."

Rikari unrolls a tattered papyrus map. On it is a view of the world I've never seen before. There are islands on this map and other lands beside the Great Lands.

"Notice in the north are the Lands of Aypha and Amina. Your land and Amina are sibling lands. Likewise, in the west, Kamaras partner with Zells; in the south, Syrens partner with Tynas; and in the east, Quinns partner with Dynas. Combined, these form the Eight Great Lands."

On the map I notice a large land at the center of the Great Eight. "So this must be the Land of Beta?" I ask pointing to it.

"Indeed," says Rikari. "Beta is a sacred ground for Divines. It serves as the central point for each of our nations. The Doctrine states that Beta belongs to no one and is considered neutral territory. Still, many Divine squads patrol through here and hunt those who come too close to their territory." Rikari rolls up her map and scans the dense forest. "Speaking of which, we should move to a more secure location."

With the help of the moonlight, Rikari and I continue deeper into the forest until we reach a ridge overlooking a narrow river. The sound of flowing water and soft chirping birds provides a brief moment of peace.

"Here! Tie this rope around your waist," directs Rikari. Her piercing voice quickly cuts through my moment with nature. "We'll rest down by the river for the night."

As I tie the thick rope around my waist, Rikari wraps the other end around her fist.

"Well, hurry up and rappel down now, Marcus."

"Uh, shouldn't you tie the rope around a tree or something?"

Rikari playfully twirls the rope. "Nope, you'll be fine. My arms are sturdier than any tree in this forest." She nudges me to the edge of the ridge. "The sooner you get down, the sooner we can rest."

Taking a deep breath, I cautiously begin my rappel. About halfway down, Rikari yells from above, "You're taking too long. I'm letting go!" She releases the rope, causing me to plummet to the river basin. I'm uninjured but no thanks to Rikari.

"Okay, I made it! What do you want me to do next?"

"Just wait!"

Not thrilled with such a boring task, I return to my fascination with the tranquil river. I sit at the river's edge and notice several fish swimming by. Having not eaten all day, I figure I'll catch a few fish before Rikari returns. Removing my boots, I roll my pant legs up and enter the cool river. With so many fish swimming by, catching one should be rather easy, but after many failed attempts, I leave the river soaked and empty-handed.

Quite some time has passed since I last heard from Rikari. I call out her name yet the only response comes from the restless birds. Again, I call out. This time Rikari leaps from the ridge above and lands directly in front of me. Jumping from that height, Rikari's legs should've snapped, yet she appears unharmed.

"*Shh!* Are you trying to give away our position?" Rikari's soft face scrunches up. "Why are you so wet?"

I scratch the back of my neck looking for an excuse. "Well, actually, you see... uh... I was trying to catch us something to eat."

"Oh, yeah? What did you get?"

"Well, you see, I..."

Rikari laughs hysterically. "Couldn't catch one, could you? Oh, how disappointed Sinclair will be when she meets you."

"What's that supposed to mean?"

Rikari's smooth tan skin along her forehead briefly dents. "All Sinclair does is bring up your name. She's obsessed with you, so much so that she asked me to watch over you."

"For what?"

37

"Don't know for certain but I think it had to do with the attack on your village." Walking to the river, Rikari scoops water into a tin cup and takes a sip. "Strange times we're living in. Can't say I'm surprised though. The world is becoming very complex. Everyone is fighting for power and everyone has a lust for it."

The air breaks with a tinge of cold but it's Rikari's words that cause me to shiver. Shaking off thoughts of a cruel world, I notice Rikari has caught several fish using nothing but her bare hands.

"How'd you catch so many? What's your secret?"

"I'm starting to wonder if you're pathetically hopeless," Rikari says as she motions for me to come to the river.

"Look upstream—see that little one coming this way? Try and catch it."

As the little fish approaches, I reach with two hands and—

"*Missed!* Try again!" Rikari bellows.

Determined not to embarrass myself any further, I spot another fish, this one larger than the last. As it comes within reach, I dive for it and again—

"Whoops! Zero for two. Pitiful, Marcus, just pitiful. Oh well, time for me to cook my catch."

"Great!" I say. "Two for you, one for me?"

"No, no, no." Rikari wags her finger. "All of these are for me. I spent an enormous amount of energy on you today. Tonight, you'll have to earn your keep. Hurry, it's getting pretty late and we'll be on the move once the sun hits the nose."

I flip my hands up in protest. "But I don't get it—you haven't offered me any advice as to what I did wrong."

Rikari picks up her fish by their gills. "On the battlefield sometimes no one can help you. It's up to you to learn from your mistakes and adapt to the situation." She filets her fish with a makeshift diamond knife. "Be still, Marcus and observe your errors. Doing so will make all the difference in battle."

Why is Rikari telling me this? She's only a few years older than me yet seems so wise.

She heads upstream to start a fire and I return to fishing. I struggle for quite a while, and it isn't until the moon sets and the sun rises, I realize what Rikari was trying to teach me. All night, I've been doing the same technique and getting the same results. Suddenly, it clicks. Only I can observe my mistakes and must adapt.

As the next fish swims by, I know it is mine. I laugh, realizing what I've been doing wrong. Don't reach for where the fish is, reach for where it's going.

Divine Blood

MARCUS

With no breeze and under a blistering hot sun, Rikari and I press forward through the northern forest of Beta. I'm exhausted but at least my stomach is full of fish. Following behind Rikari, my thoughts drift to Sinclair.

She was once Queen of the Aminas, but somewhere along the way, she betrayed them. To this day, I don't know what she did, but when news spread of her death, everyone seemed happy, including my own parents. They acted as if she were nothing to them, like she never even existed. They say she was a traitor and a disgrace to the Land of Amina. To me, though, she was like a big sister. In the winter months, she would come to Eden and teach me the art of using a sword. Against my parents' wishes, she helped me hone my skills at throwing daggers with precision. She would even have me write poems where she would critique them, saying one day I'll fall in love with a girl and will need to know how to express myself.

"How much longer?" I ask.

Rikari continues to walk in silence, surveying the forest for traps and hazards. Whatever path we're on, it must be used often, for the grass has been worn and flattened by many feet. To our left, thorny pines soar to the skies; on our right are berry bushes and trees bearing green pears. Seeing my favorite fruit, I stuff a few in my pocket to save for later. Parallel to us is a major stream where young deer sip the cool waters. When the deer see us, they briefly freeze, before scattering back into the safety of the forest.

"Aren't they amazing creatures?" I ask. Rikari utters not a word. "Say, I thought Dynas and Aminas were rivals. What is Sinclair doing in Dyna anyways?"

Stubborn in her silence, Rikari seems more concerned with our surroundings than answering me.

Bored and in need of a laugh, I let Rikari walk a few steps ahead. Taking a pear, I throw it at Rikari's backside. In one swift motion, she turns and splits the pear with her fingers.

"No thanks, Marcus. I'm still full."

"You spoiled a perfect throw!" I huff. "How did you know?"

"My, oh my, so much to learn," says Rikari as she shakes her head. "It's called Oro Presence, a Divine ability to sense danger."

"Oro Presence?" I perk up. "Think you could teach me?"

"No!" snips Rikari. "First off, my abilities are distinctly different from yours. Second, some things cannot be taught. They must be learned on the battlefield. The more battles you survive, the greater the advantage you'll have over your opponents."

Once again, Rikari is giving me unwarranted battle advice. As beautiful as she is, she remains militant to the core.

We come to an open area where the trees break from our surroundings. In the distance, a set of mountains peak high into the clouds. The mountains are lush and green, there's many waterfalls, and arching over them are vibrant rainbows. Odd though, my skin prickles and a chill comes over me.

"That's the Valleys of Hope," says Rikari. "The Valleys separate the Lands of Amina and Dyna. Going through the Valleys is the fastest route home, but it's also the deadliest as Aminas are known to patrol this area." Rikari places her hand on the ground. The soil begins to shake and vibrate, exposing an underground stairway made of iron.

"Instead of going through the Valleys"—Rikari grins—"we're going underneath it."

"Okay, but that trick you just did, opening the ground... What was that?"

"It's my Divine Legacy, the ability to control metal and sand."

I think back to the fight against the men in red cloaks. This must have been the power she used to turn her skin into diamonds.

"Divine Legacy?"

"Yes. There's so much for you to learn but now isn't the time." Rikari gives me a slight nudge down the stairway. As we enter the dark tunnel, she strikes a torch that provides just enough light to see a few steps ahead. The tunnel is cold and silent like the dead.

"Now it's my turn to ask some questions," says Rikari. "Prior to the attack on your village, you were in a fight with a boy. Who was he?"

The shame of embarrassment crawls up my neck. "His name is Rizen," I say with reluctance. "And I hate him."

"Is that why you two fought?"

"He stripped me of my pride and denied me something special, something I worked hard for. During the fight I remember how angry I was. There was this uncontrollable and dreadful feeling in the back of my mind that I should kill him." I squeeze my eyes shut. "There was a rage burning inside me to the point I blacked out. When I awoke, there was this pain I felt as if my bones were burning."

"Burning bones? How odd," says Rikari, she strikes another torch just as the first one sputters out. "I've been watching you for weeks, Marcus. I must admit, at first, I didn't believe you were of Divine blood. You're not strong, plus you're clumsy. But during the fight with this Rizen kid, I realized something. The reason you're so weak is because you haven't had your Divine Awakening."

Rikari halts her steps and shines the torch over me. "Every Divine must awaken before they can use their power. During your fight with Rizen, you nearly awakened, but something stopped you."

I give Rikari a puzzled look. "Was it Rizen?"

"No, it seemed…internal." Rikari resumes her walk through the tunnel.

"None of this makes sense, Rikari. Divine Awakenings, Divine Legacies—it's all foreign to me. It's hard to believe you if I can't see or feel it."

Rikari doesn't respond. Instead, we continue silently to the end of the tunnel. As we pop our heads above ground, the warm sun tingles across my skin and soothes my weary aches.

Rikari crawls above ground and finally breaks her silence. "When you fall asleep at night, do you believe the sun will return in the morning?"

"Of course," I say, stretching my aching muscles.

Rikari looks to the sun. "Believe in yourself, Marcus, and just like the sun, you too shall rise! Now shut up and let me concentrate. We're almost home."

***

Almost home? Yeah right. It's several hours of silence before Rikari and I finally arrive at a security perimeter controlled by the Dynas. Shielding the Land of Dyna from outsiders is a massive iron wall that stretches high and wide. As we approach, molded iron figures protrude from the wall. Slowly, the strange figures transform into young girls dressed in all black. Their eyes are as white as snow and imprinted on their throats are white maple leaf tattoos.

"Commander, welcome home," grizzles one of the girls. While she's just a child, she has the voice of a demon.

"Return to your post and open the wall," orders Rikari.

The girl nods and smiles, exposing her gritty iron teeth. "Certainly, but may I ask who is the boy?"

"No," Rikari says coldly. "Now do as you're told."

The girls recede back into the iron wall and a large hole appears allowing us to pass through.

On the other side of the wall, beautiful maple trees now surround us. Brown and red foxes run wild and birds of all shades congregate within the trees.

"This is Dyna," says Rikari. "Across the entire land, you'll find maple trees. To us, the maple represents strength, beauty, and determination. It's a symbol of our identity."

Rikari rolls up her left arm sleeve and reveals a tattoo of a gold maple leaf on her shoulder. Below the leaf is a gold fox with the number seven, circled by a red ring.

"The girls from the wall had white maple leaves. Why is yours so different, and what's with the fox?" I ask.

"White leaves are for those who are a part of the defense command. Gold is reserved for those of highest rank," Rikari explains. "The gold fox means that I'm a commander, and the seven signifies that I am ranked seventh among the Absolute Commanders of Dyna." Rikari pauses before poking my chest. "You should be honored that someone of my rank was chosen to watch over you."

I smile. "Well, it's refreshing to know I'm in good hands."

"Not for long," chuckles Rikari. "Soon, we'll head to Village of Dink, but before we do, let's confirm something."

Following Rikari, she takes me down a pathway which leads us to an enormous gold monument of a fox. A young Dyna stands guard atop the monument's head.

"Welcome home, commander," the girl shouts as she slides down the fox's tail.

Rikari places her hand out. "Young lady, please draw our blood."

Doing as she's told, the young soldier pricks our fingers and places our blood into small vials.

"This test will prove you are of Divine blood," says Rikari, she sucks her finger to stop the bleeding. "In the northern lands grow Krysanthem trees. Their leaves react when in contact with Divine blood."

Rikari orders the soldier to find a Krysanthem leaf. After much searching through a burlap sack of leaves, the soldier finds an arrow-shaped green leaf with seven points. Rikari takes the Krysanthem leaf and drips her blood onto it.

Slowly the leaf's color transitions from green to yellow to red, before finally turning brown and disintegrating into dust.

"By exposing Divine blood to a Krysanthem leaf, it causes the leaf to go through its entire life cycle," says Rikari. "If I was a Norm, there would've been no reaction. If you're of Divine blood, the leaf should react the same way."

The young soldier finds another Krysanthem leaf and pours my blood onto it. Gradually, the leaf turns from green to yellow and then to a golden autumn color. However, instead of drying and shriveling, the leaf remains gold and radiates an unusual glow.

"Huh, that's never happened before," says Rikari. "Maybe it's an old leaf. Let's try it again."

The young soldier rummages through her sack for another Krysanthem leaf but after much searching, it's obvious none are left.

"Oh well," says Rikari. "Either way, Marcus, you get the point. If you weren't a Divine, the Krysanthem leaf wouldn't have changed colors." Rikari takes the gold leaf and examines it up close. "It's interesting that it never crumbled...You should keep it for good luck."

In awe of the gold Krysanthem leaf, I have no words to describe this moment. My own blood caused a leaf to transform colors and evolve. This was no trick or magic; this was proof that I am more than just a Norm. Fixated on the glowing leaf, I wonder how...

"How did she know?"

"Know what?" Rikari threads a thin string through the stem of the gold leaf and ties it around my neck.

"How did Sinclair know I was a Divine?"

"That's something you'll have to ask her. But don't get too excited. The test only proves you have Divine blood. Doesn't mean you're ready to harness the power of one. Right now, you're no different than any Norm. To obtain power you must achieve a Divine Awakening. But heed my words: the moment you awaken, there is no going back. Awakening means giving up your human side. It will make you ugly, ruthless, and above all, it will harden your soul."

Shades of Green Vines with Hints of Gray Skies

MARCUS

After completing the Divine leaf test, Rikari and I proceed to a village called Dink. According to Rikari, the Land of Dyna is comprised of three main villages. Dink is in the west, Dylark in the north, and Dono lies south. While there isn't much in Dink, it's an important village as it connects to the Dynas' central command. Standing on a rocky cliff, I can see most of Dink from my vantage point. The village is lush with maple trees and gold sculptures of foxes. In the distance a large waterfall shimmers from the reflection of the setting sun. Most of the shops are made of bronze and decorated with colorful ornaments. In the west, on a large grass hill are tiny limestone homes that are covered in moss but look quite cozy.

Beyond the homes, isolated from rest of the village, is a dense forest full of black trees with crooked branches. The trees reek of an ominous warning but before I can even ask, Rikari descends the cliff. Following behind her, we arrive at a giant bronze gate. Slowly, the gate melts and a short young woman appears. She wears a long sleeve white silk gown and tied around her waist is a silk red ribbon with stitching of gold foxes.

"Welcome back, Rikari. You look wonderful as usual," says the short woman, her voice is rather chipper.

"Yeah, yeah. You say that every time, Minnie," responds Rikari. "Has Sinclair returned?"

Minnie smiles. "Unfortunately, not yet." Minnie's big eyes twinkle like stars.

Rikari rubs her forehead. "Sinclair needs to hurry back. There's much to discuss."

"Indeed. And who is your friend?" Minnie leans closer to me. Laced on her sleeve is a gold fox emblem along with the number six, indicating she's sixth among the Absolute Commanders of Dyna. Minnie doesn't look at all threatening, but according to her rank, she's deadlier than Rikari.

"Minnie, he's not my friend," huffs Rikari. "But this here is Marcus."

Minnie's frizzy eyebrows arch. "Well, nice to meet you, Marcus. Aren't you handsome?" She pinches my cheek.

Now, in no creed should a young man ever blush, but I couldn't help feel my face flush with embarrassment.

Rikari chuckles. "Wow, kid. You have much to work on. Come, it's getting dark."

***

Walking through the heart of the village, we enter the shopping corridor. Built in long rows that face each other, the polished bronze shops have closed for the evening. Isolated on a corner though is a small wooden shack that appears to be open. The sign above the shack says "Sea Bound," and the smell of grilled fish wafts in the air. An old woman sweeps dirt from the entrance. Hungry, I run toward the shack and flag the old lady down.

"Hey! Any fish left?" I ask.

"My goodness!" yells the woman. "I haven't seen a boy here in many years! Why sure, I have plenty of fish. Already precooked and ready to eat."

"I'll take one!"

"Okay, that will be one Dripplet," says the woman. A Dripplet is a form of currency, but with all the excitement over the past few days, I completely forgot I had none. The little I had was back home. Embarrassed, I rub the back of my head and tell her of my misfortune.

The woman's pleasant attitude melts into annoyance. "Ah! I should've known you were a beggar. Scram!" The woman nudges me away with her broom.

With a growling stomach, I turn around only to see Rikari approach. While she's easy on the eyes, her walk is intimidating as her boots hit the soft gravel with much punishment.

"Hello, Denise. How did sales go today?" she asks.

"Not bad. Was hoping to sell more, but apparently I've attracted a scavenger boy." The old woman glares at me and clutches her broom.

Rikari slings her arm over my shoulder. "You should know this scavenger boy is my guest, and anything he requests, he shall have, mmk?"

Denise stutters out an apology and quickly grills two fish before wrapping them in corn shucks. She hands them to me and smiles nervously.

"Later, Denise." Rikari struts away without a smile.

Realizing she isn't going to get paid, Denise returns to sweeping.

"Hey, when I get the coin, I'll be sure to repay you," I tell the old woman.

"Oh, no worries. Commander Rikari protects us and we're forever indebted to her," says Denise. "Let me know if you need anything else."

I thank the woman and jog back to Minnie and Rikari, only to hear them arguing.

"Every time you come home, you always scare her," chastises Minnie. "You really should be nicer to Denise."

Rikari sucks her teeth. "She's greedy. Besides, Marcus could've caught his own fish if he had to." She nudges my side. "Might take him forever and a day, but he could've done it."

I ignore Rikari's slight jab. "Say, any other shops open?"

Rikari arches her long back and yawns. "Plenty of time to see them in the morning."

"Oh, c'mon! Don't tell me you're tired," I say.

Rikari frowns. "I'm not entertainment—that's more Minnie's thing."

Minnie giggles. "Forgive her, Marcus. Rikari isn't known for her hospitality. Tomorrow we'll check out the shops and I'll introduce you to Queen Valencia."

"Why punish him so soon?" asks Rikari.

Minnie places her hands over my ears. "Don't listen to her, Marcus. Rikari just wants to scare you like she does poor Denise."

"Humph. Think I'm bad, wait till you meet Valencia…speaking of, I need to give her my report." Clasping her hands together, Rikari grins. "Marcus is all yours, Minnie!"

Without waving goodbye, Rikari heads toward the black forest. As she leaves, I can't help but admire the cranky woman. She's beautiful, confident, and prideful. It's only been a few days together but I've grown to like her and hate to see her go.

"She might come off as rude, but deep down there's a sweet side to Rikari," explains Minnie. She then holds up two fingers. "But with me though, everything will be twice as nice. Come, let's get you to your quarters."

Traveling past the shops, Minnie takes me to a skinny four-story building made of bronze and colorful stained-glass windows.

"This is our visitors inn," says Minnie. "It's quite a nice accommodation plus you get a beautiful view of our Waterfall of Life." Minnie places her hand on her chest. "Rumor is if you stare at the waterfall long enough, it will inspire love within your heart."

I snicker, thinking Minnie must've stared too long to be so chipper. "Interesting. Well, right now I'm inspired to eat. Care to join me?"

Entering the inn, we're greeted by the sight of an empty lobby. There's dust everywhere and cobwebs in every corner and crevice.

"Apologies about the lack of upkeep. Been ages since we've had outside guests." Scrunching her nose, Minnie releases a cute sneeze. "Go ahead and pick any room you want. Once you're settled, meet me by the den."

I take the stairs to the third floor and see the dust here is just as thick as downstairs. I pick the first door on the right, and to my surprise, the room is spotless. The maple wood floors are polished to perfection, and there's a sweet aroma of lavender in the air. To my left is a small bed fit for one and in the corner on a tiny stool, is an old oil lantern.

As I open the stained-glass window, a rush of cool air flows into the room. I peer outside where a full moon shines brilliantly over the Waterfall of Life. Staring at the moon, I think of Asher and Darius. Somehow, I hope they've survived the attack on Amarna. The thought of losing my friends causes tears to form in my eyes.

Resting my elbows on the windowsill, I spot near the base of the waterfall a young woman with curly brown hair. She stares at the waterfall for quite some time before turning around. As she approaches the inn, her eyes cascade up to mine. Mystic eyes that I've never seen before. They aren't quite green nor are they gray; her eyes are like shades of green vines with hints of gray skies.

As she walks away, I rush downstairs to catch her. But by the time I make it outside, she's nowhere to be found.

"Hey there," Minnie says, startling me from behind. "What are you doing out here?"

"Oh, just looking around," I say, playing off my intentions of stalking the girl. "Say, does anyone else stay here in the inn?"

Minnie chuckles. "No, silly. I thought we already had this conversation. No one has been here for quite a while. C'mon back in. It's eating time."

Heading into the den, I see there's no chairs in the room, only a low table that requires us to sit cross-legged. Unwrapping the fish, I give one to Minnie and immediately eat the other.

"This is amazing!" I say, spitting out a few fish bones.

Minnie, on the other hand, hasn't taken a single bite. Instead, her big brown eyes give me a curious look.

"Hmm, you're not at all what I imagined." Minnie taps her cheek. "As much as Sinclair talks about you—and please don't be offended—I thought you would be a bit more…beefy."

I dig my nails into the dusty table. "Beefy? You imagined me to be a cow?"

Minnie giggles. "Oh no, no, no. I just thought you would have a little more weight on you that's all." She leans over the table and lowers her squeaky voice. "You see, the way Sinclair talks about you is quite obsessive, like you're some mythical legend. I didn't think you were real…but here you are."

Yup, here I am, sitting across from a strange lady talking about a woman I thought was dead.

"So, what exactly has Sinclair said about me?"

Minnie clears her throat. "Well, um…frankly, Sinclair believes you'll be important to us one day. She never says how or why, but we'll see it for ourselves someday."

I laugh to hide my nervousness wondering what Sinclair knows that I don't.

"Well, what do you see?" I ask.

Minnie reaches over the table, she cups my cheeks, and draws me closer. "I see a young man with eyes of ambition, but his soul has yet to be found." Getting up from the table, Minnie thanks me for dinner, though her plate remains untouched.

"Think I'm going to call it an early night." Minnie claps her hands together. "I've got a delightful day planned for us tomorrow. It's got me all excited just thinking about it."

Morning Glory

MARCUS

A loud bang at the door startles me. It's not even dawn, yet Minnie is eager to start the day.

"Up! Up! Up! Marcus, much to see, much to do." She pulls back my wool blanket exposing me to the cool air. "Meet you outside in five."

Getting dressed, I slip on the same musty work jumpsuit I wore back in Aypha. Thinking back, if Rizen hadn't denied me into the Elite Guard, at least I'd have on something more comfortable. I stumble outside and release a light yawn. To my surprise, sitting beside Minnie are two tigers, one white and the other gold.

My hands slightly tweak. "What is this about?" I ask.

"Meet my two buddies. The white tiger is Neptune, the gold one is Sphinx." Minnie caresses their heads and gives each of them a hug. "They're our transportation for the day."

What an odd woman. Of all the tame animals, she chooses tigers as pets.

"C'mon, it will be fine," says Minnie, she saddles the white tiger. "I'll ride Neptune since he's been cranky lately." From a woven sack, Minnie dumps out a collection of apples. The supposedly tamer tiger, Sphinx, sniffs the apples before devouring them.

"So, they just eat fruit?"

"No silly, they love meat, but since Sphinx has been such a good girl, she deserves a treat." Minnie scratches the back of Neptune's ears. "See, if you stop biting people you too could have a treat!"

Minnie tosses me a necklace with a tin bell. "You'll need this to ride Sphinx. She's trained to obey anyone wearing the bell."

As instructed, I place the bell around my neck.

"Okay, now slowly crawl toward Sphinx until you're face-to-face with her."

My head snaps up. "Are you crazy? She'll bite my face off!"

Minnie places her finger over her lips. "Shh! Marcus, please keep calm. She's only done that once...well, maybe twice, but have no fear. Just trust me."

I rub the temples of my forehead. "You're asking me to risk my life in order to gain approval of a tiger?"

Minnie nods vigorously. "Mmm-hmm, isn't this fun?"

Reluctantly, I crawl toward the giant cat, and as I do, the bell begins to tinkle and ting. Sphinx looks at me and licks her teeth as though she's about to savor the main course. She pounces and I immediately freeze. With her giant paw, she swings at the bell much to her delight. It isn't until she sniffs and licks the side of my face do I know I've received her approval.

"See, that wasn't so bad," says Minnie. "As long as you wear the bell, you'll be fine."

Around my neck is not only the bell but also the Krysanthem leaf necklace I received yesterday. Minnie says something about Sphinx, but I pay her no mind as I'm fixated by the beautiful leaf. Radiating a gold shine, it's even brighter than the day before.

"Do you understand, Marcus?"

"Oh yes, got it," I say, having no clue what Minnie said.

"Okay, then on to our first stop."

On the backs of Sphinx and Neptune, we quietly travel away from the shops and into a secluded field of rolling hills. As the sun rises, the hills transition in color from green to violet. Neither of us say a word, watching in awe as morning glory flowers open in full bloom bringing life to the day.

"I come here every morning just to see this," says Minnie as moths and bees spring from the ground. "These flowers only bloom for a few minutes before they curl up and fade. Though brief, they fill me with so much passion and inspiration." Minnie plucks one of the violet flowers and places it in my hand. "What gives you passion? What drives you each day?"

The flower reminds me of my days in Eden. There's something innocent about flowers, something precious that deserves preserving. While Eden had its flaws, it always felt safe, secure from violence and war.

"I've always wanted to be a protector," I whisper. "You know, someone people could depend on and trust." Recalling my failures, I bite down hard on my teeth. Gavin, Asher, and Darius. I failed them all. I ran when I should've fought those men in red cloaks. Perhaps Rizen was right—I'm not worthy of being a true soldier. I squeeze my eyes tight to fight back the sting of tears. "Honestly, I'm not ready to be a protector. Not certain I'll ever fulfill that promise."

"Such negative thoughts," says Minnie as she twirls a flower around the tip of my nose. "Don't give up on your passion just because of some adversity. There's no greater joy than fulfilling your dreams. Life is like a chain linked with success and failure. To keep the chain together you must always remember your passion, for it is our passion that keeps us alive."

What was I to say to this? Minnie's words hit me like a spark of lightning. Indeed, I may have let Aypha down, but I vow things will be different when I return.

"Thanks, Minnie. Much needed words."

Minnie twirls her finger around her long hair. "No problem. Morning glory flowers have that effect on people. Let us begin our day."

Hopping back on our feline friends, Minnie and I return to the village and stop at a shop called Cynthia's Cloths. The shop's door is painted red, and the frosted windows are stained with imprints of little hands.

"Now with our minds refreshed, let's address a greater issue," says Minnie while pinching her nose. "You desperately need clean clothes, and what better place to come to than the finest tailor in the known world!"

Entering the quaint shop, we're instantly greeted by delightful fabrics of all colors. The shop is a mess though with frazzled yarn and scraps of linen everywhere. Hanging from the walls, ceiling, and even piled on the floor are random materials and half altered outfits. Toward the back of the cluttered shop, wrapped around a polished wood pole, is a yellow silk scarf that reminds me of Sinclair. Gazing at it, I completely drift away.

"Can you hear me, Marcus?" Minnie snaps her fingers in front of me. "This is my sister, Cynthia. The greatest tailor in the world!"

"Hello there, Marcus," says Cynthia. She steps over a pile of fabrics and vigorously shakes my hand. "So nice to meet you." Her frizzy red hair matches the cluttered shop as does her chipped fingernail polish and red lipstick.

"I hear you're meeting Lady Valencia today." Cynthia presses her hands against my chest. "It is very important you look your best. Especially since her tolerance for males seems to have faded."

"Minnie mentioned her name last night. Um, who is she again?" I ask.

Cynthia grabs a sock from a pile of clothes and playfully whips Minnie on her shoulder. "Sis, how could you fail to introduce our queen?" Cynthia wraps her arm around my shoulder as if we're best friends. "The glorious Valencia Victoria is not only our Divine queen but also one of the greatest Divines to ever live." Cynthia strokes her double chin. "She can be intimidating, sometimes terrifying, but underneath her cold exterior is a sweetheart, I think."

"Okay, okay. I think he gets it now," says Minnie. "Marcus, later today feel free to ask the queen anything, just know though, she and Sinclair don't really get along. The two have been at odds ever since, Sinclair became second-in-command."

I scrunch my lips in disbelief. "Sinclair is the former Amina queen. She was your enemy. How can she become a leader of Dyna?"

"Ironically, it's actually Valencia's fault," says Minnie. "Years ago, Sinclair came here seeking refuge after betraying the Aminas. We could've turned her over, but Valencia allowed her to live here under the condition she reveal everything she knew about the Aminas. At first, we kept Sinclair in isolation but over time she was allowed to mingle with others. Personally, I hated her and wanted her gone, but that all changed after the Battle of Beta."

"Battle of Beta?" I ask.

Minnie unwraps the yellow scarf from the pole and ties it around her neck. "The Doctrine states no Divine shall inhabit the Land of Beta." Minnie's tone turns serious. "Two years ago, the Aminas violated the Doctrine by moving forces into the eastern edge near the border of Dyna. To assess the situation, Valencia ordered Sinclair to accompany me and my team on a recon mission.

"Unfortunately, our mission was compromised after being discovered by the Aminas. Outnumbered ten to one, the Battle of Beta was a great testament of our ability to endure. Our will was strong, we killed many Aminas, but as the battle progressed, it seemed inevitable we would perish. During the battle, Sinclair remained neutral. Certainly, her heart was in two places, but something caused her to move in our favor. In a beautiful sight, I saw why she was once their queen. Faster, stronger, and more powerful than her former subordinates, she slaughtered the Aminas, leaving not a single witness."

"My goodness!" Cynthia clutches her chest in dramatic fashion. "I can't imagine killing my own kind. What a tragic mind she must have."

Like a blade cutting through flesh, pain shoots through my chest. If Sinclair was willing to kill her own people, what trouble does she have in store for me?

"I don't get it. Sinclair helped you, still doesn't explain how she became a commander," I say.

Minnie looks out the shop's window, her warm breath fogs up the glass. "After that battle, Sinclair became sort of a hero to the people of this land. She was praised as a great defender of Dyna. She won us over with her loyalty." Using her finger, Minnie draws something on the moist window. "The praise Sinclair received infuriated Valencia. She became spiteful and grew a severe disdain for Sinclair. Valencia wanted her gone but couldn't just banish Sinclair after all she had done. Instead, she proposed an offer. If Sinclair could defeat her in a fight, she would be granted asylum for life. But if she lost, she would be forced to leave Dyna. Sinclair accepted, but Valencia wanted more; she didn't just want Sinclair gone; she wanted her dead. Raising the stakes, Valencia proclaimed that if Sinclair could survive their fight, she would become one of Dyna's Absolute Commanders. Sinclair agreed and like all of Valencia's obsessions, she recklessly sacrificed everything." Minnie moves away from the window revealing a broken heart.

"But both of them are still alive, so what happened?" I ask.

"Their fight occurred in the dark forest, so none of us actually saw it," says Minnie. "We did however hear the explosions and feel the cracking of the ground. For hours it was pure carnage until..." Minnie takes a deep breath. "They say lightning strikes before thunder. But it can't be true, because I remember the scream of thunder before the sky sparked a light so bright, it made the sun jealous. When the battle ended, Sinclair emerged from the black forest holding Valencia's lifeless body. To revive her, Sinclair threw Valencia into the river at the Waterfall of Life. If it wasn't for that, Valencia wouldn't be here."

Taking a piece of cloth, Minnie twists it repeatedly around her shaky fingers. "I think Valencia would've rather died that day. Ever since the fight, the queen has become reclusive and hasn't left her mansion. I think she's..." Minnie abruptly goes silent.

"Great job, little sis, not only have you frightened the boy, you've left him in suspense," says Cynthia. She squeezes my shoulders and slaps the back of my neck. "It's a shame you're friends with Sinclair. I was just beginning to think Valencia might actually tolerate you." Cynthia takes my measurements in preparation for her design. "Don't worry though, Marcus. At least you'll look good before the queen."

"Whatever you think works best," I say, not wanting to meet the miserable woman. "Can you do me a favor, Cynthia? I noticed Dyna Divines wear maple leaves on their clothes. Think you can stitch a Krysanthem leaf on mine?"

Cynthia gives me a bemused smile. "Sure thing, kid. I'll have it ready by this afternoon."

Leaving Cynthia's shop, Minnie and I head toward a small shop that booms with smoke from its limestone chimney. A long line of people impatiently wait outside. Many are unaccompanied children. Others are mothers with infants.

"Who are these people?" I ask.

Minnie ties Neptune and Sphinx to a pole just outside the store. "They're Norms from various lands who have been displaced from their homes as a result of past Divine wars."

I stare at their faces, thinking this could've been me. We then enter the little shop where the delightful smell of spices fills my nose. There's a counter up front, packed with children and women screaming for bread. From the kitchen, workers frantically try to process demands from the hungry crowd.

"Is it that good?" I ask.

"Greatest baked goods you'll ever have," says Minnie. "More importantly, it's free. These people have no coin, yet the manager sacrifices her own so others may eat. Come, let me introduce you to her."

As we head to the kitchen, the mob of people turn silent and politely move out the way for Minnie. My lips break in awe when I see the manager is the same gray-green-eyed girl from the night before.

"Marcus, this is Hazel. She and her aunt Denise operate this place," says Minnie.

I extend my hand, Hazel glances at my discolored skin and still shakes my hand without prejudice. "Nice to meet you," I say. "Believe I met your aunt yesterday. She cooks wonderful fish."

"That's her all right," says Hazel. Much like her eyes, Hazel's voice is soft and gentle. A beauty mark colors her right cheek, and as she whisks her curly hair back, I notice her wood earrings in the shape of diamonds.

"So, what brings you here?"

"He's a friend of Sinclair," interjects Minnie.

Hazel reveals a subtle flash of her teeth. "Oh! What a special guest we have."

I try thinking of a witty response, but only clumsy ones come to mind. "So, you really take care of all these people?"

Hazel places oven mitts on her hands. "Sure do. It's stressful but worth it." She unfastens a latch from a brick oven; heat laced with the aroma of cinnamon fills the kitchen.

"Ayphas would never do such a thing," I say. "It's hard to trust people who are not your own kind."

Hazel pulls a pan of cinnamon bread twist from the oven. "That's the problem. People are afraid of those who do not look like them." She glances again at my hand. "They fear what is different, blinded from the beauty of others."

Is Hazel talking about me or are we still talking about people in general?

"It's more to it than that," I say while gazing at the scrumptious baked delights. "Where I'm from we're taught only Ayphas and Aminas are allies, all others are enemies. Is that not the same philosophy in Dyna?"

"No, it is the same problem here." Hazel slides off her oven mitts and points to the hungry crowd at the front counter. "But these people are not our enemies. They mean no harm. They simply seek refuge from the carnage committed by Divines." Hazel's eyes turn stone gray as she stares at me. "Instead of unity among the Great Lands, there's division and distrust; I suppose it will always be that way."

Minnie clears her throat. "Hazel, can we speak in private for a minute? It's about your decision."

Hazel cringes and removes her apron. "Marcus, help yourself to whatever you like. That's if you trust me."

As the two step out, I take note of the tray of hot cinnamon bread twists and gobble down several of them. The twists are so good, I stuff a few in my back pocket for later.

Hazel and Minnie return a short time later. Their demeanor has changed and they avoid eye contact with one another.

Minnie however is not one to stay down for long. "Marcus, what's that on your lips? You eat like a heathen," she snickers.

Taking a wet cloth, Hazel wipes a coat of cinnamon off my lips. "Seems you like my cinnamon twists. You should stop by some other time, I've got a few treats you may like."

I smile and notice Hazel's eyes have returned back to their alluring color. "Sure, I look forward to you, I mean the treats."

Minnie's cheeks turn red as she grins at us. "All righty, well, come now, Marcus, onto our last stop."

We say goodbye to Hazel and head outside to find Neptune and Sphinx growling at the people in line. Minnie calls for them to settle down, which immediately they do. I try saddling Sphinx, but it's impossible as she's more curious about what's in my back pocket. Sniffing my rear, she nips me, exposing the cinnamon twist along with my right butt cheek.

"Marcus, I thought I told you not to have any sweets around her!" scolds Minnie while Sphinx devours my cinnamon twists.

So that's what Minnie was warning me about earlier this morning.

"Good thing Cynthia's preparing you some new clothes, until they're ready, you'll have to continue on as is."

With my cheek in the wind, we leave the bakery and head back to the morning glory hills.

"That girl back at the bakery. Tell me more about her," I say.

Minnie chuckles. "Ah, so you fancy Hazel? You know, you two actually have a lot in common. Like you, she struggles with her passion."

"Oh, how so?"

"Doubt, fear, plus maybe a traumatic experience or two."

I want to ask more but hold off upon arriving to an area void of grass. Before us is an odd sight—a round patch filled with sparkling black sand. On the fringes of the circle are large black crystals.

"We call this place Black Birth. This is where many Dyna Divines come to first learn their abilities." Minnie approaches the edge of the circle and breaks off a black crystal.

"Rikari tells me you aren't aware of basic Divine principles, so allow me to educate you. Of the eight Great Divine lands, each are separated by gender. Male Divines rule the lands of Kamara, Quinn, Aypha and Syren, while female Divines rule the lands of Zell, Dyna, Amina, and Tyna." Minnie takes a crystal and cuts the palms of her hands. "To pass down Divine blood requires a specific genetic pairing. Meaning, we must mate with those from our sibling lands to have Divine offspring." Minnie presses the palms of her bloody hands together. "This is why Dynas partner with Quinns, Aminas partner with Ayphas, Zells partner with Kamaras, and Tynas partner with Syrens."

For me to be a Divine, then so too are my parents. But why would they hide this and how were they able to do it? "So what happens when a Divine mates with someone from outside their sibling land?" I ask Minnie.

"Nothing. The child would be born a Norm. Also, even with the perfect pairing, there's no guarantee their offspring will have a Divine Awakening."

"Rikari told me. She says I need it to gain power."

"That's correct. Although you're of Divine blood, your power can only be activated through an Awakening. An Awakening brings a Divine's basic abilities to life, causing their body to evolve to see farther, think faster, endure greater pain, and even heal from wounds at an accelerated rate. Some Divines can even regenerate organs and limbs. You can do none of these things until you Awaken."

Minnie enters the black circle. "Once you Awaken, your next step is to learn your Divine Legacy. This is a specific power passed down by the blood of your ancestors. In other words, your Legacy abilities are tied directly to the land you're from. Allow me to show you a Dyna's Divine Legacy."

Minnie closes her eyes and touches the black sand, causing it to swarm around her like thousands of angry hornets.

"A Dyna's Legacy is the ability to manipulate metals, minerals, and sand. We can shape these properties into any object of our imagination." The dark sand shifts behind Minnie and forms large black wings. Sand from the circle swirls around and forces me in front of Minnie. No longer innocent, Minnie appears as a reaper coming to claim me. Sharp crystals rise from the ground and inch close to my throat before I yell out to Minnie.

She opens her eyes, the crystals shatter, and her sand wings diminish.

"Apologies, Marcus. When I use my Legacy, the urge to kill is strong." Minnie releases a strange giggle that leaves me unnerved.

"No worries," I say with a straight lie.

Minnie kneels on the ground and moves into a praying position. "I'll be more careful for this next demonstration." She whisks the black sand away but rising to the surface are mounds of gold. The gold then forms into a flight of steps and on the top one is gold replica of myself.

This is the Legacy of a Divine Dyna, the uncanny ability to shape metals into anything of the imagination. "What is the Legacy of a Divine Aypha?" I ask.

"It's irrelevant until you Awaken," says Minnie.

"So teach me."

Minnie chuckles. "Unfortunately, I cannot induce your Awakening nor teach you your Legacy. This is something only an Aypha or Amina can help you with. And guess who would be the perfect person…"

Sinclair Bonet.

The Book of Pure

MARCUS

As evening rolls around, Minnie and I return to Cynthia's shop. Much to my delight, Cynthia has tailored a splendid two-piece black outfit that even the most prestigious Ayphas would envy. The dyed black linen shirt and pants were woven with meticulous care. On the back of my long-sleeve shirt is the gold stitching of my last name in a vertical direction. It reads *AZURE*. Alongside my name is the stitching of gold and red Krysanthem leaves that appear as if they were being blown by the wind. Wrapped around the bottom of my pants are three gold stripes on each leg. Cynthia also fits me with a new pair of black boots with gold stitching around the laces.

"Sorry, Marcus. I'm afraid your old clothes must be burned!" shouts Cynthia from the other side of her cluttered shop. "Honestly, they reek of jungle musk."

Before she tosses out my belongings, I grab my old boots and pull out a special letter that I keep with me at all times. I slide the letter into my new boots before handing back my old ones to Cynthia.

"Well? Feedback please. What do you think?" Cynthia rests her hands on her hips, eyeing me up and down.

"Refreshing. Nicest outfit I've ever worn."

Cynthia tilts her head. "Sis, what do you think?"

Minnie nods. "Fantastic, sis! Absolutely amazing."

Cynthia walks around me for a final inspection. "A stunning outfit for a prestigious occasion! I must say, I went all out for you, Marcus. Now, I do have a favor to ask. Please tell Valencia I need more time. She'll know what that means."

"Sure thing."

After relieving Sphinx and Neptune for the day, Minnie and I leave Cynthia's shop and head toward the black forest. The sun has said it's goodbye, and as we approach the forest, Minnie utters not a word which is strange for such a loquacious woman.

At the edge of the black forest is Rikari and she too has a stern look. Both Dynas have turned dreadfully serious and the sign posted in front of the forest explains why:

AUTHORIZED DYNAS ONLY. All others who set foot beyond this point shall not return.

"Before we proceed, there's something I should tell you," says Rikari. "You're about to enter Valencia's domain. This is a privilege you should not take lightly. Understand that your connection with Sinclair will make it difficult for Valencia to trust you. Keep your emotions in check before the queen. Any questions?"

"Nope," I say with a hint of nervousness.

The moment we enter the deathly forest, the tree branches begin to twist and ooze a vicious white smoke.

"They're warning us that an outsider has entered," says Minnie. "Don't worry. The guards have been notified of your arrival."

As the tree branches continue to spew smoke, the three of us continue along an iron pathway where Dyna soldiers light torches and salute as we pass by. Upon reaching the end of the path, a cool breeze chills my bones. Revealing itself from the night, before us is a dark blue lake. In the center, an iron mansion with limestone pillars appears to float on the water.

There's no bridge or boat for us to take. Instead, Minnie places her hands into the lake forcing sparkling sand to rise to the surface. Slowly, a solid blue mirror forms over the water. We proceed across, and upon reaching the mansion, the mirror over the lake shatters like glass.

Rikari places her hands on the mansion's enormous iron doors, causing them to warp and compress until they're as thin as a strand of hair. We enter the mansion's foyer and before us is an onyx staircase draped with vines and purple flowers. Proceeding upstairs, we head down a dimly lit hallway where on the onyx walls are dead vines and brittle thorns that break as we brush by them. Also on the walls are portraits of women who appear regal and confident. In every portrait, the women are dressed in red and bestow a gold fox with the number one next to their name. They all have the same last name of Victoria and must be former queens of Dyna.

At the end of the hall, a guard stands by an onyx door with a gold fox emblem.

"Good evening, Commanders," says the guard. "Lady Valencia only wants to see the Aypha."

I look at Rikari and Minnie, but they say nothing as the onyx door dissipates. Taking a deep breath, I enter. The door resolidifies and locks me inside. Queen Valencia's room is damp and there's a hint of pain permeating in the air. The dim lights and cool mist gives the room a sense of depression. Proceeding further into the foggy room, I approach seven gold thrones placed in a straight line. Draped over the thrones are red velvet cloths with gold fox emblems. The seat cushions are also made of red velvet and the gold arm rests are carved with foxes.

"The thrones of the Seven Absolute Commanders," I say to myself.

Each throne looks the same except for the one in the middle. This one is much larger and stabbed into its cushion is a blade of iridescent colors. The blade's pommel is made of glass and swirling inside is a silver liquid. I want to grab the blade but there's something disturbing about it that restrains me. Looking beyond the thrones, attached to a stone wall are lush green vines with violet flowers. The vines extend across the walls and ascend high into the darkness above.

From somewhere in the room, faint footsteps approach. Each step is slow and harsh like an unforgiving tone of punishment to the floor. The steps echo across the misty room, making it difficult to tell which direction they're coming from. As the tormenting steps grow louder, my once cold hands begin to sweat.

When the tapping stops, the mist disappears and standing before me is a middle-age woman with black and silver strands of hair. Her long bangs cover her left eye; the other eye radiates emerald green. Her nose is long and sharp, and her body is covered in well-polished iron armor. The woman pulls the iridescent blade from the seat cushion and sits on the center throne. She motions with her blade for me to come closer, and as I walk along the green marble floor, vibrations of nervousness spring throughout my body.

"STOP," the woman orders. Her emerald eye cascades up to mine before she speaks with a slow drawl. "Already your presence annoys me. You smell like Cynthia's shop and you wear her tacky clothes."

The woman motions for me to step back, which I immediately do.

"I am Valencia Victoria, Queen of the Dynas," she announces with pride. "I understand you're Sinclair's pet—the one I've been hearing about for years." Valencia polishes her metallic blade. "Tell me, what is it that makes you so intriguing...Marcus Azure?"

Staring at her emerald eye, I pretend not to be intimidated.

"I haven't the slightest clue what Sinclair is referring to. To be honest, I thought she was dead."

"Nonsense!" shouts Queen Valencia. "She speaks of you with an obsession as if you're this glorious warrior. Everything from Sinclair's past she left behind, everything except you." The queen points her blade at me. "So why does she have such an affinity for you?"

Not sure why Valencia didn't believe me the first time, I speak louder. "I don't know what Sinclair is talking about. I've done nothing to warrant any acclaim."

Valencia frowns and taps her metallic blade. "It's important you understand lying has consequences...speak the truth."

What from the skies above has Sinclair been telling these people?

"Queen Valencia, I know nothing of what Sinclair has spoken. If I did, I would tell you."

Valencia grips her blade and approaches in a hostile rush. She thrusts the tip of her blade directly under my chin. The cold metal rests tight on my throat; I dare not move.

"There's something about you that reeks of repulsive lies," says Valencia. "Perhaps a taste of a blade will give you appetite to speak the truth."

I need to use my next words carefully, high chance this woman will slash my throat if I don't. But what else can I say? Even under her threat, lying is not a good option.

For the third time, I repeat myself. "I don't know what Sinclair is talking about."

Valencia slowly slides the cold iridescent blade down my chest, splitting my new shirt. Noticing the gold Krysanthem leaf necklace, Valencia whisks her black and silver hair away from her eyes.

Fixated on the radiant leaf, she places her blade onto it, causing the tip of her blade to frost and glow light blue. Slowly her entire blade glows blue before she pulls it away. Valencia turns her back to me and mumbles to herself. Her mumbles grow louder, and eventually, she enters a world of her own. "What a nuisance. I should've killed Sinclair on sight." Valencia vigorously scratches the back of her scalp causing thin strands of her hair fall to her shoulders. She paces back and forth and bites what little fingernails she has left.

From the odd scene before me, it's obvious Valencia's hatred for Sinclair has caused her to go quite mad.

"Perhaps it's best I go now," I say.

Valencia's muttering continues. "He doesn't belong here…You don't need him; you'll never need him… He isn't worth it…" Over and over, Valencia repeats the same gibberish. When she finally stops, she gives me such a stare of disdain that I have to say something.

"Lady Valencia, I come here with the upmost respect to you and your land. I'm honored to be here and I want to help you any way I…"

"I don't need you!" she snaps violently, her eyes now bulging. "I will never need you and I never needed her. You, young man, are a distraction, a nuisance. You've lied to me for the last time! Reveal yourself or I shall kill you!"

Fully enraged, Valencia's eyes show such malice it frightens my soul. I spin around and run toward the exit door, but as I do, a sharp pain spreads throughout my back. I stumble to the floor; warm blood now trickles down my spine. The crazy woman has stabbed me. As she towers over me, there's a look of confusion.

"Why do you not heal like a Divine should?" she asks as her blade once again radiates blue. Valencia heats her blade over a lit candle and seals my wound by scorching my skin. She helps me to my feet but frowns. "Perhaps you aren't a total liar. Have you not Awakened?"

"No, I tried telling you…"

I go silent as Valencia places her blade to my mouth. "Hush, little boy…earlier you said something intriguing. You honestly believed, Sinclair was dead?"

My hands shaking, I answer the psychotic woman as concise as I can. "I was told she was assassinated years ago for betraying the Aminas."

"Yes, Sinclair has done quite a few nasty deeds. Still after that, you and her never spoke?"

I shake my head. "Wasn't till I met Rikari did I find out she was still alive. Rikari was also the one who told me that I am a Divine and can awaken a power."

"Is that something you wish for?" Valencia points to a nearby wall, where mounted in a glass case is a tattered parchment with faded black script. "Before deciding you need to understand Divine Law."

Approaching the old parchment, I notice at the top are eight crests representing the Great Lands followed by several laws:

The Doctrine of Divines

This testament on the day of solace solidifies unity across the eight Great Lands of Pyris. Under the authority of King Arius Ulta of Aypha and Queen Nandi Bonet of Amina, King Naasir Braven of Kamara and Queen Nitocris Sinfall of Zell, King Fate Everlast of Quinn and Queen Vanya Victoria of Dyna, King Dyren Linksan of Syren and Queen Lucia Karna of Tyna. By this signed Doctrine, all Divines shall live by these seven laws for now and forever.

1. No Divine shall be forced to fight for their land.
2. Inhabitance in the Land of Beta is forbidden.
3. Divines of opposite gender must live in separate lands, cohabiting only during the winter months.
4. The Book of Pure shall remain sacred and never to be opened.
5. Divines of opposite gender shall not engage in war unless under threat against the sacredness of the Book of Pure.
6. Divines shall never use the soul as a source of power.

"These are the laws Divines are to follow," says Valencia. "Six simple laws our ancestors created to maintain peace."

"There's reference to a seventh law. What is it?" I ask.

Valencia shrugs. "It remains a mystery. Every known copy of the Doctrine is missing the last law. Regardless, what I'm about to tell you may be unsettling, but it's important you know before you pursue your Awakening." Valencia wiggles four of her fingers. "Law four states the Book of Pure is never to be opened, yet this is exactly what the Ayphas and Aminas are plotting to do. If they succeed, their efforts will lead to anarchy and destruction of all Divine life." Valencia pauses as she stares at the tattered Doctrine. "Peace has always been a fragile thing. To destroy it, all the Ayphas and Aminas need to do is open something as innocent as a little book."

Raising my hand to ask, Valencia shakes her head and continues.

"Tucked neatly in a pristine area, preserved and untouched by Divine hands, is the Book of Pure. In it contains a source of omnipotent power greater than any Divine has ever seen. To keep the Book sealed, our ancestral leaders known as the Noble Eight created eight keys and distributed them equally across the Great Lands. Each land is responsible for protecting their own key, as it is only possible to open the Book by combining all eight. This would be detrimental to the living—and it's exactly what your people seek."

Considering how manic Valencia was earlier, it's hard to tell if she is filled with lies or truth. Still, if Aypha and Amina are plotting to open the Book, it must be for a good reason. We must protect ourselves from our enemies. We cannot allow others to threaten our existence.

"How certain are you my people are doing this?" I ask.

Valencia firmly pokes my chest. "Never question a queen. The only reason I'm telling you is because Sinclair wants to put you in the middle of this mess. My advice? Leave here before she returns, otherwise she'll be your biggest regret."

I shake my head. "If Sinclair is alive, I want to see her. There are so many questions I need to ask. None more important than what she wants with me."

Valencia glances at my leaf necklace. "I think we'll both find out soon…this meeting is over." With the wave of her hand, Valencia shoos me away. But just as I'm about to leave, I remember Cynthia wanting me to relay a message.

"Don't know what it means, but Cynthia needs more time."

A slight smile almost spreads across Valencia's lips. "Show her your redesigned outfit. She'll know what that means."

Reflection

As Marcus awaits outside the mansion skipping rocks off the lake, queen Valencia, Rikari, and Minnie now stand together in the misty throne room. Designated for the Absolute Seven, the room is traditionally used for war planning and strategic meetings but it's been years since all seven commanders have come together.

"What do you think of the boy?" asks Valencia.

Minnie snickers and sits on one of the outer thrones. "He's just a lost boy seeking answers to the unseen."

Valencia glances at her blade. "He disturbs me. Sinclair speaks so mighty of him, but he's meek, soft, and not at all threatening."

"Even so, you must admit there's something more to him," says Rikari. From a bag, she dumps several bright gold Krysanthem leaves onto the floor. "First time it seemed abnormal, but every time I drop his blood onto the Krysanthem leaves, they turn gold and never fade away."

Valencia presses the tip of her blade onto a leaf; again it glows an icy blue. "The Aurora Blade reacts by color when it comes in contact with something of great force," she says. "Yellow, orange, and red are all moderate signs of power. Blue, purple, white, and black indicate a much higher level of strength." Wrinkles appear along Valencia's forehead. "He hasn't even Awakened, yet his blood holds something potentially devastating. Whatever he is, I need to know soon. While he's an ally today, tomorrow he may become our enemy."

Valencia picks up a gold Krysanthem leaf and holds it in her hand. "My instincts to kill him are strong, yet I find him intriguing. I can't help but wonder what will become of Marcus when he Awakens?"

"That's if he can," says Rikari. "I think something is suppressing him. Few days ago, I witnessed him fighting another Aypha. During the incident, his temperament exploded and he became uncontrollably wild. He was Awakening until something caused him to pass out."

"Maybe it's for his own good," Minnie softly interjects.

"Or maybe it's so he can be controlled," rebuffs Valencia. "Controlled by someone who likes secrets. Someone like Sinclair."

Rikari and Minnie exchange glances. "This is why you must leave this place," says Rikari. "Without your lead, Sinclair will continue to run things unchecked."

Valencia sighs and turns away from her commanders. "We've been over this. I can't leave here. I'm ashamed to be your queen."

Trapped in seclusion, Valencia hasn't left her mansion in years. Embarrassed by her loss to Sinclair, she fears her own women will mock her. Her heart remains empty and weak. Hollow is the best way to describe her soul. Years of reclusiveness have plagued her mind with paranoia. Her once youthful face has been sapped away leaving nothing but cracks of anxiety. While Valencia has won many battles, depression has kept her in ruin.

Minnie bows before Valencia. "You'll always be our queen. But if you stay confined to these walls, the others will lose hope in you."

Valencia lowers her head. "Have they not already? Do the halls of each home not ring of my failure?"

Rikari bows before Valencia. "No one would dare believe such a thing. Still, we worry about Sinclair. Look how she hides secrets about Marcus. For all we know she's plotting to use him against us."

"No, more than anything she wants revenge against the Aminas," says Valencia. "And she's going to use Marcus to obtain it." Taking her Aurora Blade, Valencia stabs it back into the center throne and walks toward a large mirror. "Keep an eye on Marcus. Probe his thoughts and continue to be friendly. If we can influence him enough, his thoughts won't be tainted by Sinclair."

"I have another idea," says Minnie in a timid voice. "Marcus has an eye for a young woman, but..."

"Great!" interrupts Valencia. "Ensure she befriends him as she can become our eyes and ears when the two of you aren't around."

Minnie fiddles with her fingers. "There's one problem. It's Hazel he likes."

Valencia's upper lip curls in distaste as she stares at her reflection. "Let my daughter know her duty is to this land, never to a man."

You Can't Kill Them All

"Sinclair Bonet, it appears the wrinkles of time continue to evade your face," says Annabelle.

Sinclair smiles, soaking in the compliment. "Likewise, Annabelle. It's been far too long since we've seen each other. And while never friends, I've always admired you."

The two women have gathered in secrecy near the southern border of Beta. An area perfect for clandestine talks— here no eyes can see and no ears can hear as they're surrounded by white brick walls covered in vines of honeysuckles. The only witnesses to their gathering are the buzzing bees.

"Rumor has it you were killed. So how is it I'm talking to the dead?" asks Annabelle.

Sinclair smirks. "That's an odd thing to say, coming from someone known as 'the Ghost.'"

Indeed, her name says it all. Annabelle the Ghost is as terrifying as her name. A bringer of death, the Queen of Zell is not to be crossed. A woman of short stature, she wears her traditional silk white robe with blue lotus flower designs stitched into the fabric. Underneath her robe she clutches a thin sword, ready to strike Sinclair if necessary.

Annabelle smiles in false kindness, searching for clues to Sinclair's motives. "So why are we here?"

Sinclair slides off her white gloves and briefly inspects her nails. "Don't be so hasty, Annabelle. Aren't you interested to hear my survival story first?"

Annabelle rolls her eyes. "I'm more curious of how you became a traitor. For the Aminas to claim they've killed you means you've been quite naughty."

Sinclair sits daintily on an ivory bench and crosses her long legs. "You have me all wrong, Annabelle. I'm no traitor. I simply ended an unhealthy relationship."

"When snakes and dogs lie next to one another, what do you expect?"

"Charming." Sinclair's lips part in delight. She plucks from the ground a yellow tulip and basks in its fragrance. "I know our relationship is as delicate as this flower. Fragile petals can only withstand so much before they wither."

Annabelle removes her white robe and holsters her sword. "Our relationship is more like a blade of grass. Thin and replaceable."

Sinclair pouts her lips. "Fair enough. But allow me to plant a new seed that grows stronger roots. I called you here to build trust. To do that, I'll answer all your questions, starting with my title as Traitor of the Aminas." Sinclair closes her eyes and her jaw tightens as she tries to find the right words to begin her story.

"When I was Queen of the Aminas, I worked hard to fix what my mother had left behind. There was a huge rift between us and the Ayphas, and it was my duty to restore trust between our lands. As you know, General X is now the ruler of Aypha and I worked with him for months to repair the bonds between his Ayphas and my beauties. Over time though, he became worried about being attacked by the Kamaras, so he came to me with a proposal to swap a portion of our land in the south in exchange for part of Aypha in the north. On the surface it made sense. But unbeknownst to me, General X was devising a trap." Sinclair scrunches her lips, a sigh of resentment funnels through her nose.

"Agreeing to the adjustment, I ordered my beauties away from the south, but not long afterward, General X accused me of committing a hostile act against a sibling land. He claimed I intentionally left the south border vulnerable so his enemies could attack Aypha. He argued I was doing this as retribution for my mother, and accused me of treason. He called for my execution, but only an Amina has the power to bring judgment upon me...Never thought my own sister would be so eager."

Annabelle clasps her hands. "Oh, how remarkable that Cynné would want you dead. And let me guess, you truly did nothing wrong to deserve death?"

Sinclair picks up another yellow tulip. As she holds its stem, a bumblebee flies within the caverns of the delicate flower. "I was tricked, Annabelle. I fell for the pollen but didn't see the trap." Sinclair squeezes the tulip, crushing its petals, along with the bumblebee. "Cynné and General X conspired against me when I no longer agreed with the agenda."

"What agenda?"

Sinclair's eyes fill with excitement. "I'll tell you, but first you must hear my story of survival."

A glimpse of annoyance flashes across Annabelle's face. "Go on," she mutters.

"Stripped of being queen, I was held for treason and sentenced to death by Cynné. But thank goodness for my talents as I escaped to the southern region of Beta. It is here, within these walls, I hid for months. However, when winter approached, the animals moved farther north and so too did I. Unfortunately, that's when I encountered my first death squad that was sent to assassinate me. Seeing the faces of the many women I once led, it wasn't easy killing that first squad, but over time I got used to it."

As Annabelle listens to Sinclair's overly dramatic tales, she's still unclear as to why Sinclair called for this meeting. Hearing enough, she interrupts.

"My, oh my, Sinclair. What an incredible story! Now tell me, what agenda does General X and Cynné have?"

Sinclair rests her hand over her chest. "Annabelle, how rude to rush me. I'm getting to that. Just let me finish my story."

Rolling her hand, Annabelle motions for Sinclair to continue.

"Okay, where was I? So, after several attempts at my life, I grew tired of constantly being targeted so I devised an incredible plan to fake my death. When the next death squad tracked me down, I eliminated all the poor girls except for one. She had approximately the same body size and height as me, so I kept her alive until the next death squad arrived." Stopping her story abruptly, Sinclair takes a moment to gather her composure.

"And?" asks Annabelle. "What happened?"

Sinclair releases a dramatic sigh. "I did something I'm not very proud of. I killed the poor girl and peeled off her face. Taking a knife to my own, I replaced her face with mine."

"How insidious," Annabelle says, her lips smear in disgust.

"Having my face on her, I hung the girl to make it appear as if I had committed suicide," says Sinclair.

"Thinking you were dead the Aminas claimed to have killed you."

"Correct, but to cover my tracks, I headed east, only to be captured by the Dynas. Pleading for amnesty, I made a deal with Valencia Victoria—a deal she surely regrets for I am now one of the Absolute Commanders of Dyna."

Annabelle's pointy ears perk at such an incredulous revelation. "Seems you've gone mad after all these years," she says. "You're delusional if you think Valencia would ever give you such an honor."

Taking off her silver silk robe, Sinclair exposes her arms. Tattooed on her shoulder is a gold fox with a red circle around it. Underneath the fox is the number two.

Annabelle licks her thumb and tries wiping away the permanent ink. "Unbelievable. How is this even possible?"

"I'm Sinclair Bonet. All things are possible with me."

Annabelle frowns and rubs her thin eyebrows. "This makes no sense. Why would Valencia allow you to become a commander?"

Sinclair walks toward a white lily patch and plucks a honeysuckle from a vine. She draws the sweet nectar to her tongue and swallows the flower whole. "Allow me to explain."

Sinclair proceeds to tell the story of her triumphant battle against queen Valencia and the deal made for her to become a commander if she were to win. Her ego satisfied, she looks to Annabelle expecting admiration, but the Queen of Zell remains indifferent.

"Very good, Sinclair. Enough of the stories. What is this agenda about?"

Receiving no looks of envy, Sinclair purses her full lips, but slowly relents. "To state this bluntly, General X and Cynné are plotting to acquire the eight keys to the Book of Pure."

Annabelle's eye lids widen. "How can you be so certain?"

Sinclair sucks her teeth. "Because I agreed to it before changing my mind. That is why General X betrayed me—I no longer believed in his vision. Therefore, he did everything he could to eliminate me."

Annabelle winces at the notion Sinclair might be speaking the truth. "Past few months, my Zells have been encountering Aminas on patrols of the west border of Beta."

"So, what does that tell you? The Aminas are testing you and preparing for war!"

Annabelle's jaw hardens. "If the Aminas think they can prevail, they're surely mistaken. I will not allow them to obtain our key."

Sinclair scoffs. "Don't kid yourself. The Aminas outnumber you five to one. With those odds, they can and will defeat you. General X and the Ayphas will then join with the Aminas to destabilize rest of the Great Lands." Sinclair holds Annabelle by the shoulders and stares at her with sincere intent. "Annabelle, we do not stand a chance if we fight independently. But united, we can defeat them. Instead of being plucked off one by one, I propose a true alliance between our lands. What do you say?"

Annabelle looks to the skies. With only speculation from a prolific manipulator, it's hard to trust Sinclair. Her mysterious motives and cunning tongue leaves Annabelle uneasy.

She shrugs away from Sinclair. "So, to protect my land, you suggest we align with the Dynas? Regardless of your newfound position, you're not one of them. Why should I trust you?"

Sinclair frowns. "It's a pity," she says while brushing her long hair behind her ear. "I'm coming to you because I believe a partnership is the only way to prevent anarchy. The Aminas know things aren't well between you and the Kamaras. As long as there's dissension between you and your sibling land, your enemies will use it to their advantage."

Annabelle sighs and plants the tip of her boot into the grass. "What are you offering?"

Sinclair's eyes light with glee. "Ah, finally, you're coming around! I propose supplying you with a squadron of Dynas to use at your disposal."

"And in return?"

"A simple request to help me when the time comes."

"Nothing is simple with you. I'd rather speak with Valencia than hear your cheap promises...no offense."

Sinclair crosses her arms. "Fine, but she won't come here, you'll have to come to Dyna."

Annabelle rolls her eyes and slides back on her white robe. "Fine, I'll be there in two months."

Agreeing, the women shake hands, but Annabelle's eyes remain fixed on Sinclair.

"What's your angle in all of this?" she asks.

"I simply want our world to remain balanced and equal," says Sinclair. "A day will come when your land is attacked—and when it does,

I would hate to see the remains of your flesh burned with regret for not heeding my words. When you return home, take a look at your Zells. Ask yourself, are you willing to risk seeing their existence forever erased? That will be your outcome. No prophet is needed to see even as powerful as you are, you can't kill them all!"

Intruder

Traveling north through the Land of Beta, Sinclair Bonet reflects on her discussion with the Queen of the Zells. Annabelle the Ghost will be in Dyna in two months and before she arrives, Sinclair must convince Valencia to partner with the Zells. But given Valencia's mind state, persuading her will not be easy.

It takes Sinclair nearly two days to cross the Land of Beta and arrive to the Valleys of Hope. She could have taken a different route home but curiosity has brought her here. She knows the dangers of traveling through the Valleys but ignores her instincts in a rush to get home.

Entering the lush green valleys, she covers her face with an ivory snow leopard mask with pink teardrops painted under the eyes. The mask is symbolic as it was once worn by her mother, Kissandra Bonet. Surrounding Sinclair are cliffs that leave her vulnerable to an ambush. Still she presses along a trail, knowing every step is a risk to her life. A life she no longer cares about. For her, there's only one goal left and she vows to see it through.

Upon reaching the lowest portion of the Valleys, Sinclair comes to a halt at an unusual sight. Ahead is a congested forest of trees. Its spring, yet many of the leaves have already fallen. Entering the forest, she heads to a warm spring to freshen up. Removing her silk robe, she enters the warm misty water and washes her soft skin with rose petals. While home isn't much farther, Sinclair believes in being flawless at all times.

After a relaxing bath, she continues through the forest but takes note that something is off—there's no birds chirping and a burnt smell of wood hovers in the air. Ahead of her are several smoking craters in the ground. Something violent has happened here. Examining the area, Sinclair follows a trail of fresh blood that leads up a hill and onto a flat plain. A dead Dyna Divine lies still. Her chest is torn open, her ligaments blown to pieces. Sinclair checks the woman's shoulder patch; the Dyna was a member of Rikari's reconnaissance command.

No longer intrigued, Sinclair turns around, only to be trapped by three young women in black. She doesn't recognize them but knows they're Aminas by the blood streaks running down their arms. It's common for Ayphas and Aminas to bleed along their forearms when they overuse their powers.

As the trio fans out around Sinclair, she wonders why couldn't she sense them. Were they masking their Oro, or was something else interfering?

"I am Rose Cross, leader of Team Six," announces one of the Aminas. Rose has soft violet hair and sprinkled across her cheeks are pink freckles. "No one walks the Valleys alone. Remove your mask and identify yourself."

Sinclair remains silent, still wondering why she couldn't sense them. Her lack of response frustrates the girls.

"Can you not hear? Answer her, dum-dum," says another Amina.

"Relax, Nova," orders Rose. She draws her attention back to Sinclair. "Speak if you wish to live."

Sinclair folds her arms in response.

"This is pointless," says Nova, her pale face flushes red. Like her stature, Nova's temper is short. "Let's just kill her so we can get home."

Under her snow leopard mask, Sinclair smiles, recalling how aggressive she was when she was their age. "You'll do no such thing," she finally says.

"So, you're not a mute," says the foul-mouthed Nova. She forms in the palm of her hand a bright yellow sphere of destruction. This is the power of an Orosphere, a concentrated sphere of energy that explodes on contact.

Nova clutches her Orosphere and rushes forward, but Sinclair easily dodges.

"Silly child." Sinclair grabs Nova's wrist, and with one tweak, the girl's forearm shatters causing bone fragments to erect from her skin. Before Nova can drop to her knees, Sinclair knocks her unconscious with a swift kick to the head. The third Amina of the team advances.

"Wait, Russina!" Rose orders. Yet her teammate remains defiant.

"You heard what Cynné said. Strike fiercely and show no mercy to our enemies," shouts Russina as she stampedes toward Sinclair.

Sinclair frowns under her mask, frustrated that her sister would teach such dangerous philosophy.

As Russina approaches, her hand sparks an Orosphere that sprays a ray of bright yellow light. Sinclair moves with absurd quickness and sweep kicks the reckless girl. Russina falls, her Orosphere connects with the ground and explodes. The force from the blast propels Russina into the air before she lands face-first into the ground. Her unconscious body rolls over several times before coming to a halt.

The lack of Amina discipline perplexes Sinclair. For them to provoke without cause and coordination shows things have drastically changed since she was queen.

With two Aminas incapacitated, only the lone Rose Cross remains. Her eyes cold and prideful, she fears no one.

"Whoever you are, I applaud your prowess, but this ends now," declares Rose as her muscles grow in tone. Orospheres illuminate from her hands and spark with wrath.

"Intriguing, most Aminas can only create one sphere at a time. The Oro you have is quite strong," Sinclair says. For the first time in ages, Sinclair is interested in fighting.

Rose grits her teeth. Her boots softly dance with the ground and caress the land with delight before she launches into a violent rush toward Sinclair. With the essence of quickness, Rose shifts toward Sinclair's right flank and releases her sphere. Sinclair avoids and counters with a swift kick, but Rose parries just in time.

"Seems you're faster than the others," Sinclair says. "I could use someone like you."

Rose frowns, confused by Sinclair's request. She steps back and unleashes a flurry of Orospheres. It will only take contact from one to deliver a deadly blow. Weaving around the Orospheres, Sinclair avoids many of them before one explodes at her feet. The force from the blast propels her into the air, she lands awkwardly on her back, and her mother's ivory snow leopard mask is now cracked.

Sinclair's spine goes numb and for the first time in a while, her life is in peril. Rose pounces on top of Sinclair and channels a final blast. This was nothing new for Rose. Killing her opponent was something she came to expect. While her young face contains traces of innocence, she's an assassin and a bringer of death.

"Goodbye, lady anonymous, you will not be remembered," she taunts.

Staring at destruction, Sinclair smiles as Rose releases her Orosphere. Death was supposed to arrive, but to the shock of Rose, her Orosphere does not detonate for Sinclair clutches it with her bare hand. She releases the sphere at the ground, triggering a small explosion that burns and damages Rose's legs. Unable to stand, Rose resets her dislocated leg and screams so loud it wakes Nova and Russina.

Sinclair now stands over Rose.

"How?" Rose's eyes pulsate and a glint of fear emerges. "How were you able to catch my Orosphere?"

Sinclair wipes dirt from her robe, angered she'll have to reclean herself before returning home. "While you're certainly more talented than your subordinates, you're just as foolish as them."

Realizing her peril, Rose tries to create another sphere but she's tapped of Oro.

"Oh my, after all those spheres looks like your arms have gone weak," sneers Sinclair. She kneels in front of Rose as her teammates stare helplessly from afar.

Depleted of energy, Rose breathes a heavy sigh. It was a breath of defeat, a breath she never thought she would feel. "Who are you?"

Sinclair caresses Rose's navel before placing her palm on the side of her stomach. She leans in and whispers. "I'm an Amina just like you. But let this be a testament—do not try me or I will annihilate you."

A bright shine illuminates from Sinclair's hand as the other girls scream in horror. Accepting her fate, Rose closes her eyes and in an instant it's over. Sinclair unloads a small yet unforgiving Orosphere directly through Rose. From the front to the back, a sizable hole can be seen in the lower half of Rose's fragile body. She gasps for air as part of her lower organs have been completely destroyed. Coughing up endless amounts of blood, she lies flat on her back in utter agony.

Admiring Rose's tenacity, Sinclair decides not to outright kill her.

"Aw, poor child," she mocks. "While painful, if you're strong enough, you'll survive."

Satisfied, Sinclair begins to walk away, but just before she reaches pass the sound of ear, she delivers a final message.

"Tell Cynné for her to send juveniles to battle is an act of a coward and the sign of a weak leader." With those parting words, Sinclair Bonet, traitor of Amina, graciously continues home to the Land of Dyna.

Before My Head Is Filled With Dreams

MARCUS

The next day after meeting Queen Valencia, Minnie and I return to Cynthia's shop to repair my new clothes.

"It's a shame what she did to your outfit," Minnie snickers. "At least Valencia was lively with you."

Lively was an understatement, more like hostile and terrifying. The fact that the crazy woman stabbed me shows how little she cares for life.

Entering Cynthia's shop, we see her sitting on a pile of clothes, while two Dyna soldiers yell at her.

"Calm down, calm down! Your uniforms are here somewhere!" Cynthia shouts to the women. "Come back tomorrow. I'll have them ready for you at no charge."

The women give Cynthia a final good fussing before leaving. She then hops off the pile of clothes and slips on a wrinkled red jacket. Patches of lint stick to it like strings of cobwebs. "Jeez, it's so hard to please people these days," she says, approaching a table stacked with bottles. "To be honest, I know exactly where their uniforms are, but I just can't stand those old prunes." Cynthia pops open a bottle of alcohol labeled "Ups" and guzzles it down in three gulps. She opens up a second bottle and is halfway done before noticing my shirt has been torn. Spewing out her drink, she rushes to me.

"Marcus, what happened?" she asks while inspecting my tattered shirt.

"Queen Valencia is what happened," I say.

Cynthia removes my shirt and holds it up to a mirror. "My, oh my, look at this! The queen has no regard for my hard work. She really needs to control her temper." Cynthia grabs her needle and thread. "Have a seat, y'all. This shouldn't take long." She slides onto her bench and starts to resow my shirt.

I swipe a pile of clothes off a velvet red chair and plop into the seat. Minnie continues to stand and shakes her head as I sink deep into the seat's cushion.

Struggling to wiggle out, I tilt my head back to the ceiling and notice streaming above are clotheslines of fleeces of wool, animal skins, and silk fabrics of all colors. In the back of Cynthia's shop are many leather-bound chests stacked to the ceiling in a very clumsy manner. Nothing appears neat as the dressers are just thrown up against one another with fabrics peeking through the creases.

"Sure is a lot of stuff you got here," I say.

"Why thank you," Cynthia responds to what isn't a compliment. "It's a great joy to collect and experiment with different fabrics. Which reminds me, were you able to tell Valencia I needed more time?"

"I sure did. She told me to show you what she did to my shirt as a response."

Cynthia halts sewing and springs from her table. "Oh dear, not good. I must get going, but before I do, tell me something, Marcus. What else did you and Valencia discuss?"

Minnie coughs obnoxiously and shakes her head. "Marcus, don't tell my sister anything. Cynthia is not only the greatest tailor, she's also the greatest gossiper."

But I don't mind. In fact I'm glad she asked for I don't know what to make of our conversation.

"Well, we discussed many things. The most intriguing was about a book that requires keys to open," I say. "Apparently, it's forbidden to open this book, but according to Queen Valencia, the Ayphas and Aminas are planning to do just that."

"It's not easy to believe, but it's true," says Minnie. "Your leader— the man they call General X, along with the Queen of Amina seek the eight keys to the Book of Pure. If they succeed, they'll have the power to destroy all living Divines."

Having such power may be a good thing. If we had it, my village wouldn't have been attacked. Asher and Darius would still be alive and our land would be at peace. "Have other lands not considered opening the Book?"

"Certainly, but none have ever acted on it. Opening the Book and using the soul are two laws Divines should never break. Putting that much power into the hands of few would only lead to destruction."

"Well what a gloomy and sad story," says Cynthia as she grabs her third bottle of Ups and takes a swig. She stands on top of her sewing table and tosses a bottle to Minnie. "Let's drink to jollier days!" Without hesitation, both women down their bottles and instantly become giddy. Smiling from ear to ear, their cheeks and noses turn red.

Cynthia hiccups several times before stumbling off her table. "Hey, Marcus, do me a favor and man the shop while Minnie and I run a quick errand."

As the gleeful pair leave, I wiggle out of the sunken chair and slip back on my semi-repaired shirt. Being curious, I head to Cynthia's back room where dressers of untucked drawers are propped up against the wall. Opening a maple wood drawer, I find inside a silk purple robe laced with gold threads. Slipping it on, I pose in front of a mirror as if I were a king.

"Hello, anyone here?" someone says from behind me.

Rattled, I whirl around and see it's Hazel. Her mossy green eyes and curly brown hair warms my heart.

"Is that you, Marcus?" Hazel chuckles. "Am I interrupting something?"

I quickly toss the robe back into the drawer. "No, just playing around. What brings you here?"

Hazel steps further into the shop and hops over several piles of clothes. "I'm here to pick up a collar necklace made of silver and silk from Cynthia."

"She stepped out, but maybe I can help you find it." Searching through Cynthia's cluttered drawers, I begin tossing fabrics everywhere.

"So, you do have a heart," says Hazel.

"What's that supposed to mean?"

Hazel comes closer. "What you said yesterday about the people at my shop. Do you really have no sympathy for them?"

I release a heavy sigh. "Honestly, I saw myself in them. I know what it feels like to be abandoned and lost. To be different but hoping people will still accept you." I glance back at Hazel. Her lips pressed tight, waiting for more explanation. It's best I don't. Best to keep my life's miseries to myself. Still I must confess, Hazel's heart is in the right place. "What you're doing is admirable. Putting others before self is a gift so few possess."

Hazel's lips part with a smile. "Sometimes we all need help." She joins in search for her collar necklace. Now beside me, Hazel's sweet aroma of cinnamon freshens the stale air of Cynthia's shop. We rummage through several unorganized drawers until our hands briefly touch. I quickly pull back when she stares at my discolored skin marks.

Hazel unfolds her wrist, inviting me to take her hand. "Mind if I?" she asks. Taking my hand, she glides her warm fingertips along the parts of my skin that were once filled with color. "Your skin, it is both beautiful and unique. Do not be ashamed of it."

"Seems your hands are as warm as your heart," I say. Our eyes connect and the subtle tension that was once between us dispels. I give her a smile, yet she looks at me with confusion.

"Is that your way of apologizing?" asks Hazel.

My eyes skate off as I give an awkward laugh.

"AW, LOOK AT YOU TWO!" shouts a drunk Cynthia as she stumbles back into the shop. After tripping over a pile of clothes, she wobbles back to her feet and leans against a wall for support. "An adorable couple in the making. Don't you agree, sis?"

Minnie, who is also drunk, can barely keep her eyes open. "Leave them alone. You're embarrassing them. Bad enough we barged in at the perfect moment."

"No, it's nothing like that," I say while waving my hands.

"Sure, sure, I know the making of a suave man when I see it." Cynthia struts and staggers around me before tapping the brim of my nose. "You're lucky, Marcus." She leans on my shoulder. "No offense to the other gals, but Hazel is like a swan in a pond filled with gawking geese."

Hazel coughs. "Um, Ms. Cynthia. Would you happen to have the necklace?"

"Oh, yes, my dear! Your mother is quite adamant I make this for you. I tried relaying to her that it wasn't ready, but you know how unreasonable she can be."

Putting it together, I should've known Hazel was Valencia's daughter as they both have the same alluring eyes.

"So your mother is the que…" As I speak, several bells ring throughout the village. We rush outside as does everyone else in Dink. Common villagers come down the slopes of their homes and form two parallel lines. They face each other and stand in complete silence.

Ding! Ding! Ding! A short pause from the bells occur before the chiming continues. *Ding! Ding! Ding!* Eventually, the bells ring nonstop creating a dramatic moment of anticipation.

Ding! Ding! Ding! Ding! Ding! Ding! Ding! Ding! Ding!

"She has returned," whispers Minnie.

With those words, we all witness Sinclair Bonet appear over the horizon. Sunlight has nearly faded, yet she's as vibrant as a spark of light. She looks exactly as I remember. Tall and full of beauty, hair wrapped in twists and big round eyes that sparkle. She wears a light blue ascot trimmed in gold, and a silk silver robe stitched with light blue and pink canaries.

As she strides into the village, her walk is upright, her chest is pushed out, and her full lips are held tight. She looks straight ahead acknowledging no one. Likewise, no one cheers or bows as she passes by. Everyone simply stands still, looking forward in silence.

While everyone else is quiet, I'm tempted to shout her name. She comes to a halt upon reaching me. She doesn't look or speak, but I know she sees me as a smile peaks from the crevice of her lips. She resumes her walk and proceeds to the black forest.

When the bells ring again, the crowd erupts into a raucous celebration. The village buzzes with life as the people chant and cheer for the return of Sinclair. A band of musicians play melodies with ivory flutes, and in front of a wine shop, Cynthia serves bottles of Ups to the crowd. Now I realize why it's called Ups as so many people begin to hiccup after a few sips.

Wiggling across the sky are tiny fireflies that flash vibrant lights of many colors.

"They're a gift from the Tynas as a peace offering between our lands," Hazel says while joining beside me. "There's a watchtower just north of here where you can see thousands of them. Care to see?"

"Absolutely!" I say with way too much excitement.

Minnie grins and her face turns apple red. "Well you two, guess Cynthia and I will relax here for the night."

Cynthia seems to have other plans though, as she's partying with the villagers drinking Ups and chanting ole time songs.

Minnie smacks her forehead. "Oh dear, please keep your clothes on this time." She scurries toward Cynthia and takes away her bottle. But it doesn't matter, as Cynthia quickly grabs another.

Hazel and I chuckle before proceeding into Dink's shopping corridor. Amber incense burns in the air as we walk by jolly villagers who sing and dance along an iron paved trail. Upon passing the villagers, Hazel and I are again alone and all I can think about is not blowing this moment. *Try to stay cool. Give her a compliment.*

"You smell amazing." I immediately cringe after saying something so stupid.

Hazel smirks. "Well that's an interesting observation. Do you have any more for me?"

I do, but I'm afraid they'll all come out just as awkward. "What I meant to say was those cinnamon twist you made the other day smelled amazing."

"Uh-huh," Hazel playfully rolls her eyes. "Well tell me something amazing about you, Marcus."

I ponder for a moment as we exit the shopping corridor, but nothing comes to mind. As much as I would love to be great at something, I'm simply not. The only thing I've ever been decent at is art painting, and that isn't saying much. "There's nothing special about me, I'm just...regular."

Hazel slides me a look of disbelief. "You're either really humble or you just don't know your gift yet...my guess is it's the latter."

From out of nowhere, Rikari slips beside us. "Marcus, where do you think you're going?" She must have been stalking me for quite some time. "Sorry, kid, but you have to come with me. Sinclair wants to see you immediately."

Clearly Rikari enjoys ruining perfect moments. I turn to Hazel and flash a subtle smile. "Perhaps we'll see the fireflies another time?"

Hazel nods. She doesn't speak to Rikari, instead she waves goodbye to me and heads back toward the shopping corridor.

Rikari shrugs her shoulders and escorts me up a dirt trail which leads to the edge of the black forest. She sucks her teeth as white smoke spews from the black trees. It takes a moment for me to remember that the trees smoke when a non-Dyna enters the forest.

"She doesn't belong here," says Rikari. "Our ancestors would be ashamed."

I turn to Rikari, her eyes remain dead-set on the trees. "What are your true feelings about Sinclair?" I ask.

Rikari grinds the tip of her boot into the ground. "Doesn't matter what I think. Come, let's get this over with."

Returning back to the iron mansion on the lake, Rikari takes me to the misty room where I first met Valencia. She walks up to the gold thrones and slides her long fingers across each one.

"These thrones represent pain, honor, and triumph. The seven of us who occupy them bear a tremendous burden. A seat here means more than a title of notoriety. Sometimes, sacrifices must be made when courage alone is not enough. Soon, you too will face these challenges. I just hope you're prepared."

Ever since I met Rikari, she's been telling me things as if she knows something I don't. I've never understood why, but clearly this moment with Sinclair isn't just a reunion—it's a call for something greater.

"Trust your instincts," says Rikari as she exits the room.

Now alone, I stare at Valencia's gold throne. Her iridescent blade is stabbed into the seat cushion and the swirling silver liquid in the blade's pommel is quite enchanting. Hypnotized by its elegance, I grab the blade, and a violent shock zips through my body. My arms go numb and sweat drizzles over my skin. Feeling sleepy, I lie down on the cold marble floor, and before my head is filled with dreams, I hear her call my name.

The Dark Raven

MARCUS

"You can't sleep forever," says a soft voice as my eyes break with piercing light.

Greeting me from my slumber is an alluring smile. Her lips perfectly complement her sensual voice, and her eyes appease the senses like the comfort of soft feathers. Holding me on the floor is Sinclair Bonet.

"My, my, Marcus. You've become quite handsome," she says, rubbing my back.

Not wanting to ruin the moment, I pause before speaking. "And you're just as elegant as I remember."

"Charming." Sinclair rubs my forehead. "Seems you're still hard headed, though." Glistening beside me is Valencia's blade. "Touching Valencia's Aurora Blade is a no-no." Sinclair helps me to my feet and measures me with her eyes. "You're a spitting image of your parents! How proud they must be of you."

Already Sinclair's assumption brings reality into focus. "Haven't seen my parents in years," I say. "They went on an expedition to the northern lands and never returned."

Sinclair frowns and her body goes limp. "I'm so sorry, Marcus. Your parents…" She takes a moment to gather herself. "You're parents meant a lot to me." She hugs me tight and her heartbeat is painful to my ear.

"Don't feel sorry for me, it's possible they're still alive. I came here hoping you would know where they may have gone?"

Sinclair sighs and looks to the misty ceiling above us. The black make-up around her eyes now stream down her soft cheekbones. "Afraid not, but what was the last thing you remember them telling you?"

I too look to the misty ceiling and recall their last words to me. "They warned me several times not to do it, but out of spite I did it anyways. They told me to never join the Aypha military."

Sinclair pats my back. "So, Gail and Saphron kept the Dark Raven within the shadows."

"Dark Raven?" I ask.

Sinclair strolls to a mirror by the front end of the room, and wipes black make-up clean from her cheeks. She then wraps her woven hair into a tight bun, patting and adjusting every strand into perfect position.

"It's an analogy," she finally says. "You, the Dark Raven, remain oblivious to what you really are. Your parents didn't want you in the military because they feared others would learn of your Divine Lineage." Sinclair's eyes meet mine in the mirror. "Remember how I would accompany your parents on explorations?"

"Of course. You always fancied the stones they'd find."

"That's right, and it was during those explorations your parents told me of their Divine Lineage and the need to keep yours a secret."

The tips of my fingertips turn cold. My parents, the ones I assumed loved me, did nothing to prepare me for this world. "I don't understand, why would they hide the truth from me?"

Sinclair motions for me to come closer. "Gail and Saphron had good intentions. They wanted you to live a normal boring life. But they've done wrong hiding the truth from you. As long as you remain in the shadows, you're hidden from your Divine power and any hope of becoming something."

Vicious memories of the massacre flash before my eyes. The blood stains, the smell of burned flesh, and the fear that Asher and Darius are gone causes my mouth to run dry. Revenge plays heavy on my mind.

"Rikari tells me I must Awaken to access my power."

"Indeed, but your parents didn't want that. They feared you would become like most Divines." Sinclair slides her dainty fingers together. "We Divines have a reputation of violence. Killing becomes natural, and empathy is nonexistent. This is what your parents feared would happen to you."

A hard knot forms within my throat. "Becoming a menace. Is that the penalty of having Divine power?"

"Of course not." Sinclair rests her delicate hands on my shoulders and positions me before the mirror. "Your parents couldn't see the other side of the moon. Many Divines use their power to protect. You can build instead of destroy. Unify instead of divide. It's all about controlling your lovely power."

I stare in the mirror, woe and wraith coalesce in my eyes. I vow to protect Aypha, and with my power I shall slay every last man who attacked my land.

My knuckles now red, Sinclair rubs the back of my hands. "You don't have to do this," she says. "I'm only opening you up to curiosity's maze."

"I need your help," I confess. "Several nights ago, men in red cloaks attacked Amarna and slaughtered many Aypha soldiers." I look down at my black boots ashamed of my actions. "I ran instead of fighting."

Sinclair raises my chin. "There's no shame in running from the Shadow Clan. Those who attacked your village are criminals of a Divine terror group. The Shadow Clan specialize in infiltration and assassinations—you wouldn't have stood a chance."

My heart pulsates thinking of Asher and Darius. Somewhere along the field of charred bodies they lay dead. "This terror group, what were they after?"

Sinclair glances at the Divine Doctrine displayed on the slick stone wall. "Who knows? They've caused havoc across many of the Great Lands for senseless reasons."

"Help me Awaken," I plead. "Help me so I will no longer be afraid of evil men."

Sinclair purses her lips. "A Divine's Awakening is normally a natural occurrence, but in your case, it's not so simple."

"It can still be done though, right?"

Sinclair releases a heavy sigh. "I think you should know something. When you were younger, your parents asked me to suppress your Divine power." Sinclair pokes my chest. "To Awaken, you'll need to break the suppression seal I've placed inside you. And the only way to break it is through pain." Sinclair presses her hands firmly on my shoulders. "Are you sure you want to do this?"

"I am!"

Sinclair smiles. "Very well. Soon you'll be reborn and the Dark Raven shall awaken!"

Alive and in the Flesh

Staring at the crashing waves on a black sand beach is Queen of the Zells, Annabelle the Ghost. Standing beside Annabelle is her second in command, Collen Que—or CQ for short. Though the crystal-clear sea is a beautiful sight, the women keep their distance as the sea is not of water but acid. Not far from the shore, across the toxic sea is a tropical paradise known as Chance Island. Its name comes from the rare occasions it's safe to travel when the acid levels drop. The hazardous sea hugs alongside the entire southern coast of Zell and provides a natural fortress of protection.

Annabelle hurls a tree stick into the sea, it dissolves on contact. "See, the acid levels are still too high for anyone to cross," she says to CQ.

"Still think it's best my command remains here to protect the border," responds the sleepy-looking CQ. Around her eyes are seriously dark circles due to chronic insomnia.

"You're paranoid, CQ. Nevertheless your command can stay, but I need you in the capital while I'm away. I'm going to Dyna." Annabelle unsheathes her thin blade and draws a plus sign in the black sand. "There may be an opportunity to form an alliance with the Dynas. Together, we can defeat the Aminas."

CQ tries skipping a rock into the sea, but it too dissolves. "Seems like an overreaction just because we lost a few fights against the Aminas."

Annabelle stabs her blade into the black sand. "This is different. They're coming for our key to the Book of Pure."

CQ's bushy eyebrows rise. "Are you certain?"

Annabelle sucks her teeth and stares at the acidic sea. "Not entirely. I was told this by Sinclair Bonet."

Wrinkles form across CQ's forehead. "Sinclair is…"

"Alive and in the flesh," finishes Annabelle. "It's a long story, but Sinclair appears to be working with the Dynas. She claims the Ayphas and Aminas are plotting to open the Book of Pure."

CQ scratches her thin black hair in agitation. "Don't take her bait. We don't need the Dynas, nor should we trust a traitor!"

Annabelle scoops up a handful of sand and lets it slip through her fingers. "The thought of losing just one of you troubles me. Last night, all I could see were your beautiful faces, faces I never want to let down. Partnering with the Dynas is our best chance of reducing casualties."

CQ grabs Annabelle's arm. "My lady, don't you see this is nothing but a trap?"

"Perhaps," Annabelle concedes. "Sinclair wears many faces. But this isn't about us; it's about revenge." Annabelle takes a deep breath; the warm sea breeze fills her lungs with clarity. "When I met Sinclair, I could feel the anger and disdain in her heart. She feels betrayed by the Aminas, more importantly by her sister. She wants revenge."

"I still don't like this. If Sinclair is telling the truth, we should take immediate action and strike the Aminas."

"Striking is not the same as annihilating. If we attack them now, we would be bringing unnecessary burden on ourselves. Committing now would be a pledge to eradicate all Aminas. Not only the Divines but Norms, children, and the unborn. That is the only way I will feel comfortable… is that something you're prepared to do?"

CQ's pale face tightens, and the dark veins along her neck begin to rise. "Yes, even if it takes killing every living specimen in Amina for us to survive. There's no reason we should hold back when we can light the flame now."

"Oh, CQ, your heart is as dark as your eyes. If this is a preamble to war, it will require patience. An alliance with the Dynas would be prudent."

CQ yawns. "Forget about them. That's why we have our sibling land. We should reunite with the Kamaras. They can help us."

Annabelle turns her back to CQ and scratches her thin wrist to the point she bleeds. "I'm afraid our differences with the Kamaras may be irreconcilable. Been two years since I spoke with Aikia. Seems he's pushing his men into a different direction."

CQ snarls. "The young prick needs to learn we're stronger together than apart."

Annabelle releases a heavy sigh. "In the end, we may have to battle alone and do what is necessary to protect our key to the Book of Pure."

CQ proudly places her fist over her chest and salutes her queen. "By the blood within me, I shall stand with you till the end, my lady!"

"As I expect all my Zells to do. But enough of that. Here are your orders. While I'm away, have Commander Nyree take control of the east border, while you take my seat at the capital of Zenith. I plan to be gone for a few weeks. If I do not return, it will be your mission to kill Sinclair Bonet."

Urgency

Returning home is the pitiful sight of three disheveled Aminas—Nova, Russina, and their wounded team leader Rose. They're lucky to be alive after their fight against the masked Amina. Never having encountered someone with such power, they had no clue their nightmare was the former queen, Sinclair Bonet. Their confidence shattered after nearly touching death's shadow. They enter the border gates of the Land of Amina in disgrace. Venturing into a garden of pink roses, the young women reflect on their battle.

"She could've easily killed us all," says Rose as she clenches the bloodstained bandages around her stomach. Rose's ability to rapidly heal surely has saved her life. "We need to work better as a team. You all disobeyed me."

"Pffft! It wouldn't have matter against that woman," says Nova.

"You're missing the point. You two lack discipline." Rose snatches Nova by the arm. "I'm your team lead and you're to do as I tell you."

Nova tugs away from Rose and snarls. "You're in a position of power by title only. You can act as tough as you want but I know the real you."

Rose's face turns sour. "What's that supposed to mean?"

"You're the same girl who was scared when the military pulled you from Eden. Scared to make your first kill. Your heart doesn't bleed for Amina. You're only in this position because the military felt sorry for you. Admit it, you don't even want to be a team lead."

Rose grinds her teeth but says nothing.

"Honestly, I don't think any of us wanted to be here," says Russina, she lowers her head and grimaces. "The military, they force us to become what we are."

"Speak for yourselves," says Nova, twirling a knife around her finger. "This is what I was destined to do. I was born to kill and die for Amina."

Rose glances at Nova with a solemn heart. "We're all in this together, Nova. We cannot defeat our enemies as individuals. Let us go see the queen and relay to her what we've encountered."

The trio proceed through a winding trail of pink roses which leads them to Queen Cynné's estate. Around the queen's manor is a well-polished gold gate and perched at the top of a lush green hill, is a three-story mansion made of white marble. Pink water streams flow down the sides of the mansion and trickle to a lake at the base of a hill. Amina is known as the land of love for all across the region are pink ponds and lakes. It's customary that nearly everything have a dash of the color.

An Amina guard wearing a traditional black linen dress with pink lettering approaches from behind the gold gate. "What do you want?"

"We need to speak to Lady Cynné regarding an incident," says Rose.

The guard shakes her head. "It'll have to wait. Lady Cynné is not to be bothered."

Rose rattles the gate's gold bars. "Listen, this is urgent. There's a rogue Amina out there who is far stronger than anyone we've ever seen. Lady Cynné needs to know this immediately."

"Stand down!" barks the guard. "I already told you, the queen is busy."

"Look, just let us in so we can speak to her," says Nova. "If we don't warn her, others will die."

The guard folds her arms. "Queen Cynné has instructed that no one is to interrupt her. The last guard who did that ended up in jail for a year."

Nova sucks her teeth. "Fine, I guess she doesn't mind having a little blood on her hands."

The guard relaxes her shoulders and releases an irritated sigh. "Wait here."

To Become Legendary

As Queen of Amina, Cynné Bonet has the potential to own the world. She commands thousands of Aminas and controls the largest of all Divine armies. Twenty years of age, she's the youngest to ever be queen. But that means nothing in the eyes of history. The daughter of the prodigious Kissandra and the younger sister of Sinclair Bonet, Cynné constantly lives in the shadows of her predecessors. Physically, she'll never be as strong as her mother, nor as witty as her sister; but if she can open the Book of Pure, she'll solidify herself as queen of all queens.

Buried deep inside her though lies a stubborn thought. To open the Book, Cynné needs unity among her Amina commanders. She is young and inexperienced, and her grip on her commanders remains worrisome. She trusts only one: her adviser, Loreen Lydon. An old guard of Queen Kissandra's reign, Loreen has been a trusted confidant to the Bonet family. It is only out of respect for the Bonet name that the other commanders follow Cynné. Unlike her mother and sister, the commanders do not fear her, and if she isn't careful, her life may end at their very hands.

Since usurping Sinclair's reign, Cynné has accomplished nothing worthy of a queen. To surpass those who are legend, Cynné knows she must achieve the impossible and open the Book of Pure. The power within will validate her existence, the betrayal of her sister, and grant her the one thing she desperately desires. To become legendary.

Behind her white marble mansion, Cynné sips tea in a garden of pink roses. Tall green hedges and gold statues of herself are conveniently placed throughout the garden. Nestled in the corners are marble water fountains where little birds flutter and chirp about. Like her sister, Cynné often indulges in vanity. She wears a gold lace cloak with a blush pink belt wrapped around her delicate waist. Her rose petal earrings are made of pink diamonds and her long-braided hair is sprinkled in flakes of gold. Inhaling the soothing aroma of blooming roses, Cynné contemplates if her Aminas are ready for war.

A lady of superstition, to increase her luck, Cynné wears a bracelet of rare turquoise stones found only at the bottom of Chance Sea. For protection, she wears a necklace containing a vial of her ancestor's blood. But of all her charms, the one she cherishes most is a gold coin from her mother. She uses it to make critical decisions, choices that could change her life for better or worse. On the top side, there's an engraving of Queen Nandi Bonet, one of the Noble Eight Divines and oldest known ancestor to Cynné. On the other side is the Bonet family crest, a wreath of roses wrapped around the letter *B*.

Cynné flips the coin. If it lands on Queen Nandi's face, it's a sign her Aminas are ready for war.

"Guess destiny must wait," says Cynné when the coin lands facedown. Taking a gold bell, she rings it calling for her guards.

A trio of guards scurry into the garden and bow their heads.

"Anything to report," barks Cynné.

A guard clears her throat. "Just one thing, team six requests to speak with you regarding an incident near the Valleys of Hope. They encountered an unknown but powerful Amina."

Cynné frowns, troubled with whom it might be. "Bring the team leader to me."

As requested, Rose Cross is brought to Cynné's rose garden. Still wounded, she clutches her stomach in pain and walks with a limp.

Cynné slides Rose's violet hair behind her ear. "What a sad sight to see a beauty in such an ugly state. What happened, my precious?"

Rose takes a knee. "During a patrol near the Valleys, we came across a masked woman who failed to identify herself. A battle ensued where we discovered she was an Amina. But not just any Amina...she was able to take control of my own Orosphere."

Cynné's left eye twitches. She pricks her finger against a thorn and drops blood into her tea. Oddly, the taste of blood soothes her anxiety.

"She controlled your Orosphere, that's impossible..." Cynné sucks blood from her finger, and her eyes drift toward a tall hedge covered in pink roses. "Anything else?"

Rose fidgets and looks to her boots. "Um, well, she said…sending girls into conflict was an act of a coward and the sign of a weak leader."

Cynné sips her blood infused tea to calm her hand tremors. "Only one woman would say something so audacious. Seems you've had the pleasure of meeting my mother, Kissandra."

Rose's eye lids widen in shock, believing she encountered the most infamous Divine since the creation of the Book. While Annabelle the Ghost and Valencia Victoria are notorious killers, there's no one like Kissandra Bonet. A legend above all, she's unequivocally the deadliest Divine of their generation.

"You're lucky to be alive," says Cynné. "Perhaps Mother has gone soft in her old age. Either that, or she hasn't fully recovered her power."

Rose's fingers tremble. "My lady, may I ask?" She waits for Cynné to nod before continuing. "What happened to your mother?"

Cynné pinches Rose by her cheekbone. "A beauty like you shouldn't worry about such things. Just know that Kissandra should be avoided at all costs."

Cynné pulls from her belt a shimmering piece of paper. She writes a letter and folds it.

"I'm sending a message to the field. All activities near the Valleys are suspended." Cynné flicks the paper into the air, and it transforms into a small pink canary bird. What Cynné is using is known as a Carrier. Special paper that can transform into live animals to relay messages.

"Seems we need to speed things up," says Cynné.

"In what way?" asks Rose as she watches the Carrier fly away.

Cynné grabs a handful of white dust from a pouch and takes Rose to a tall hedge of pink roses. "Every Amina queen is obligated to protect the land." Cynné blows the dust onto the hedge causing the roses and thorns to wither, and reveal a marble statue of Queen Kissandra. "But what good is it for a queen to leave behind a struggle for the next generation? All the queens of Amina have done wonderful things, but they lacked true vision. None of them achieved the impossible. Not even my mother."

Approaching the statue, Cynné touches her mother's forehead, which reveals a luminous pink crystal inside a glass case.

"This is our key to the Book of Pure," says Cynné. "It is the single most important thing to our land. By itself, it's nothing. But combined with the other keys, it can unlock the sacred power within the Book. One day, we shall unlock this power and with it solidify our place as the greatest above all Divines. Never again shall the Aminas worry about war for we will hold the power that ends all wars."

"My lady," Rose says hesitantly. "Isn't this against the Divine Doctrine?"

Cynné seals back the glass case and turns to Rose. "Of course. But our ancestors were foolish to think peace would be made by sealing power into a single source. It is inevitable, someday, someone will open the Book. We're just doing what was destined to happen."

Rose bows her head out of respect. "If it is your will, it shall be done. How may I serve you?"

As roses and vines grow back over Kissandra's statue, Cynné smiles. "Your sole job is to be a loyal soldier. One day, I'll call upon you, but for now you must rest."

Divine Dreams

MARCUS

Sinclair and I prepare for our first day of training by the base of the Waterfall of Life. While the morning sun scorches the back of my neck, Sinclair rests comfortably under the shade of a maple tree.

"These next few weeks will be the worst of your life," says Sinclair. "When it's over, you'll know the difference between pain and suffering."

"As long as I Awaken, it's worth it. Let's begin," I say.

Sinclair polishes dirt off an apple and takes a big bite. "Easy there, Marcus. First, let's rehash the fundamentals. Remember, Divines have two main stages of growth in their life. Stage one is a Divine Awakening; this is the birth of your initial power. It gives you the ability to run faster, jump higher, and rapidly heal. After Awakening, a Divine must work to master their Divine Legacy. These are special abilities inherited to you by your Aypha bloodline."

I crack a smile wanting to know more. "How long will it take to master my Legacy?"

Sinclair continues to chomp on her apple. "It varies. But let's not get ahead of ourselves. Instead, let's go back. Rikari tells me you almost Awakened during a fight. Tell me what happened."

The image of Rizen smirking as he stands over me still burns in my head. In that moment, I felt powerless, defeated, and ashamed.

"Well, there isn't much to recall," I say. "In the end, I just remember being alone and never wanting to experience pain again."

"Sounds depressing." Sinclair finishes her apple, seeds and all. "Tell me more about the pain."

"Um, well, there was this burning sensation in my chest and this intense pain that felt like my bones were on fire. That's when I blacked out."

Sinclair claps her hands with jubilation. "Wonderful! Just wonderful. Looks like my suppression seal still works after all these years. The seal works by inducing pain forcing your body to shut down in the event of an Awakening."

"Well, can't you just unseal it?" I huff.

"The only way the seal can be broken is by building up a tolerance for pain. Eventually, your body will learn to override it and thus break the seal."

A bead of sweat slides down my face. "So that's why I'm in the sun?"

Sinclair unfolds a gold lace fan to cool herself down. "You got it and our first test is to measure your resistance to pain. Each day, I'll induce more pain to strengthen your tolerance. My goal is to take you to the edge of death without actually killing you."

I scratch the back of my sweaty neck. "You're going to torture me?"

"Two for two," says Sinclair. "As we speak, the sun is slowly depleting your energy. The longer you stay out, the more your muscles will weaken and break down. How long do you think you can last?"

"This is nothing. I could do this for days."

Sinclair chuckles. "Just as cocky as your father. You're Saphron's son all right."

I flinch upon hearing my father's name. In Eden, many of the villagers referred to me as either Gail or Saphron's son, never by my first name. Shame to think others knew more about my parents than I ever did.

"What were my parents really like?" I ask. "I knew them but I really didn't know them."

Sinclair removes herself from under the maple tree and approaches. "Well, let's see. Your mom has always had a loving soul and is a woman of many talents. Singing, dancing, painting, she can do it all. Your dad on the other hand is a faker. He pretends to be stern but underneath that cold exterior is a jokester and man whose never seen a challenge too hard."

Warm memories rise within my mind. My mother's delicate touch guiding my hand as I learn to paint for the first time. My father's reassuring voice, promising me that I won't fall during a hike up Eden's mountains.

Sinclair pats my back. "So, Saphron's son, since you can handle this exercise for days, let's speed this up, aye?" Sinclair ties heavy weights around my ankles and places four bundles of wood around me. One by one, she lights the kindling. Sweat oozes from every pore of my body.

"How's this feel? You can do this all day, right?"

Shouldn't have run my mouth.

Sinclair lights two more wood bundles, the flames and smoke build around me causing my eyes to water and my chest to tighten.

"To endure pain, you must learn to calm your mind," says Sinclair. "That is key to this exercise—find a way to relax within the flames. Just yell if you need help." Sinclair disappears behind the smoke, leaving me to suffer within the circle of fire.

Staying calm is nearly impossible. As the flames flare, my skin cracks and peels. My heart pumps fast, and each breath becomes harder to take. Worse, the weights around my ankles make it difficult to move.

You can do this! Stay calm. But saying and doing are different things. The heat is relentless. The flames have sapped away my body's moisture to the point I can't swallow my own saliva. My eyes burn dry; it's painful to blink. My muscles cramp and my body breaks down.

I drop to my knees seeking mercy from the flames. "That's it, I'm done!" I yell, my throat burns with every word.

"Sinclair! Sinclair, that's enough!" I repeat. Smoke clouds my vision. I can't tell if Sinclair is coming to help. I try crawling away, but the weights on my ankles pin me in place. As the fire dances around me, I wonder, *Where is Sinclair? Why is she not coming?* Panic sets in as my legs and arms shake. Smoke engulfs my lungs; I can no longer call out for help. Unable to move, I curl up, close my eyes, and prepare for the other side.

So, this is what death looks like.

Upon opening my eyes, I'm no longer surrounded by fire, only shades of darkness and wickedly cold air. A bulb of light appears from above. Wiggling its way through the darkness, I follow the light until it hovers over a group of kids. Strange—it's my younger self along with other children from Eden. It's the first day of school, we're in a circle preparing to learn the morning pledge. The teacher calls for us to hold hands, and while many children lock hands together, my classmates ball their fists and shift away from me. They're afraid of the discolored marks on my skin and fear they'll become infected. The kids tease and call me wicked names. The pain of their ridicule forces my younger self to run away and race towards a pond where purple tulips blossom around. He stares at his reflection, and I know what he's feeling. Anger and sadness intertwine like rose thorns coiled around flesh. He curses himself wondering why he's this way. Thoughts of diving into the pond and never resurfacing cross his mind. As he stares at his discolored skin, a young girl approaches and stands beside him. She tells the story of her sister who had the same strange marks on her skin. Her sister too was once teased and came to the same pond in search of a purpose. She cups his hand, telling him to find his purpose and embrace who he is.

Everything then goes black as if the stars have fallen in sudden disappointment. I open my eyes and jolt back to reality. Staring at my discolored hands, I wonder if being here is my purpose. Sinclair stands over me and speaks but I can't hear her as my forehead throbs in severe pain.

"How did I do?" I ask as my voice echoes inside my head.

I read Sinclair's lips: "Terrible."

She grabs my wrist, drags me under the shade of a maple tree, and douses me with a bucket of water. Slowly my hearing returns.

"As suspected, your pain tolerance is below average," says Sinclair. "You also failed to stay calm. But don't worry, you'll get better. Drink some more water so we can begin the next exercise."

During my break, I take a cool sip of water and reflect on my dream.

"There's something I need to ask…the marks on my skin, do you know why I have them? Growing up I was teased for these marks and thought I was cursed."

Sinclair grabs me by the chin. "You aren't cursed, Marcus. Children can be unkind and you should pay them no mind. Your skin is unique and that's what makes you special." Sinclair helps me back to my feet. "Let's resume our training. Exercise one measured your pain tolerance and ability to stay calm. This next exercise is more about enduring physical pain and how well you focus."

Sinclair takes her diamond encrusted knife and carves a circle into the trunk of a tall maple tree. "Your objective is very simple: all you have to do is knock down five leaves from this tree. To knock them down, you're only permitted to strike the tree trunk. Shaking the branches are not allowed. Pretty simple, right?"

After being so arrogant during the last exercise, I bite my tongue.

"Here, let me soften the tree for you." Sinclair delivers a thunderous punch causing several leaves to fall. "Ah, I'm getting old." Sinclair examines her red knuckles. "Used to be able to knock down ten leaves with a single punch. Anyways, it's your turn. You have all day to complete this exercise, but there's a penalty if you fail. Every time you hit the tree and a leaf doesn't fall, I'll add a rock to a sack. If you fail to knock down five leaves, you'll have to complete another exercise."

Without thinking, I crunch my fist and strike the tree trunk. Pain shoots through my arm and not a single leaf falls.

"That hurts!" I shout in anger.

"That's the point," says Sinclair as she lounges under the shade of another tree. "Your body isn't used to traumatic pain, but the more you're exposed to it, the easier it will be to break the suppression seal. Free your mind to believe striking a tree is just like hitting a wall of feathers."

I give it another shot. Again, not a single leaf falls.

Beside Sinclair is a large pile of rocks, she adds two to a leather sack. "Keep going."

Repeatedly I strike the tree to the point my hand swells and my skin splits open. The only thing soothing is the warm blood that runs across my knuckles.

"That's twenty-five rocks in the sack."

Switching to my left hand, I try again to no avail. While the tree bark has peeled away, no leaves fall.

Determined not to quit, I spend the entire afternoon trying to knock down leaves. It isn't until dusk approaches that I consider shutting it down.

"That's one hundred and ten rocks. I'm going to run out soon," says Sinclair. "Why are you so afraid to hit the tree? It's like you're scared of the pain."

I frown at Sinclair's insult. "What are you talking about? I'm giving it my all."

"No, you're not. Every time you strike, your hand wavers because you're afraid of pain." Sinclair glances at my bloody hands. "Know why you failed the fire exercise?"

"Because it's impossible?"

"No, you failed because you panicked and lost focus. Everything a Divine does requires concentration. You cannot survive in this world if your thoughts waver." Sinclair pauses before snapping her fingers with an idea. "Here's what I want you to do. Close your eyes and think about what makes you the most upset. What's the one thing or person that causes anger and hate within? Whatever it is, I want you to focus and imagine destroying it. Let your emotions drive your strength. Once you're in tune with this sense, I want you to open your eyes and strike the tree."

Tracing so many thoughts of anger, the Shadow Clan flashes before my eyes only to be erased by the foul smile of Rizen. I gnash my teeth. I was supposed to become an Elite, I had proved myself worthy but he denied me any moment of joy. His arrogance and belief of superiority drives a deep sense of resentment in my heart. Visions of me wrapping my hands around his throat play within my mind. Channeling this anger, I open my eyes and strike without waver. As my senses return, my vision expands, and floating down the tree is a single leaf of appreciation for my hard work.

"Very good, Marcus!" Sinclair claps. "Finally!"

With both hands bloody and swollen, I'm relieved to have made progress. But I hate how I feel. As much as I despise Rizen, thoughts of killing him leave me uneasy. For all I know, he's already dead, and there's no good in hating the deceased.

Sinclair gazes at the horizon as blue shades of darkness spread across the sky. "You only got one out of five, but I think this is a good time to end. What do you say?"

"I am quite drained."

"Great. So, let's see—not including that last strike, there's a hundred and ten rocks in the sack. A new record, congratulations!" Sinclair laughs and slides the sack of rocks to me. "Since you decided to quit before knocking down the remaining four leaves, you'll have to carry the rocks back to your living quarters."

"But you were the one who suggested…"

Sinclair places her well-manicured finger over my mouth. "No one forced you to quit. You chose to on your own."

Accepting my punishment, I hoist the heavy sack over my shoulder and carry it back to my room. Just when I think of resting, Sinclair lies across my bed.

"What are you doing?" I ask.

Sinclair fluffs my pillow and makes herself comfortable. "I'm staying here for the night. How else will I know if you complete the next exercise?"

"Next exercise? I just lugged all those rocks back here."

"Ha! That wasn't part of the exercise. It was just a penalty for quitting. Hold on to those rocks. We'll use them tomorrow."

I groan in disbelief just as a knock comes to the door. To my elation, it's Hazel with two cups of hot maple tea.

"Here, have some," she says.

I reach for a cup, but Sinclair swipes it from me and pours it out the window.

"Marcus is only permitted to drink water." Sinclair takes the second cup of tea and sips it. She hands it back to Hazel in disgust. "Why are you here? Shouldn't you be baking bread?"

"Just wanted to see how Marcus was holding up...We all do." Minnie and Cynthia barge into my tiny room.

"Congratulations, Marcus! You did it!" slurs a drunk Cynthia. "Here, have some Ups."

Sinclair scowls and smacks the bottle from Cynthia's hand. "His training isn't over. It's just begun." Sinclair lightly flicks her wrist to shoo them from the room. "If you don't mind, we're about to begin our next exercise."

"Our apologies," whispers Minnie. She picks up the bottle and stuffs it under Cynthia's arm. "Sinclair, may I have a quick word?"

Sinclair releases a long and seething sigh before agreeing to step out with Minnie. Cynthia follows but not before giving me a wink.

"You got this, Marcus," she slurs and stumbles out the room.

Alone with Hazel, she comes closer to me and takes note of the blood trickling from my hands. "Sinclair's training must be brutal."

I nod. "It'll be worth it though."

Hazel dips her cloth into the teacup and wipes away my blood. "What are you training for?"

I try not to flinch as Hazel cleans my wounds. "A group known as the Shadow Clan invaded my village and murdered my people. When I Awaken, I'm going to kill these men."

Hazel wraps a dry cloth around my knuckles. "Then what will become of you? Once you kill, will you no longer care about life just as the men who attacked your village?"

A tinge of pain pricks my heart. Upon Awakening, will I really become as Rikari has said? Ruthless with a hardened soul? I head to my bedroom window and stare at the Waterfall of Life. "I made a promise to protect Aypha and to be there for my friends. The thought of killing

107

gives me pain but it shall bring joy for the sake of Aypha, for the honor of my friends."

Hazel joins me at the window and releases a heavy sigh. "You're right. It's inevitable." She presses her hand on the glass window causing it to rattle. Her eyes glow green. "I must do this."

"You must do what?"

"I…" The window cracks, Sinclair reenters the room, and Hazel's eyes return to normal before she scurries out my bedroom. I stare at the cracked window, wondering if Hazel's mind is just as fractured.

Unaware of what just happened, Sinclair unrolls a snow leopard fur mat. "Now that the distractions are out the way, let's prepare for tonight's final exercise." Sinclair sits on the mat and orders me to do the same. "This exercise is simple. All you need to do is put your mind at ease."

"Speaking of—earlier when I passed out, I had a dream about…"

"Don't tell me your dream!" snaps Sinclair. "Dreams are not reality. They're distractions to confuse the mind. Dreams will have you chasing unfulfilled ambitions for eternity. Ignore them and instead focus on reality."

Sinclair's harsh reaction gives me pause. Perhaps she's been burned by too many dreams.

"Tonight, you will practice the art of meditation." Sinclair lights two reeds of lavender incense and sticks them into a crystal vase.

Of all the exercises, this one has to be the worst. "Meditation is boring," I complain. "Can't we do something else?"

"Today's exercises prove you have a low pain tolerance, you're quick to panic, and you can't stay focused. Meditation will help resolve these issues." Sinclair lights another lavender reed. "Usually meditation takes months to master, but I've created a way to accelerate the process."

I rub my hands together. "I'm all for it."

"Good, because for the next few days you're prohibited from sleeping or eating."

"What! That's absurd."

"True Divines can go weeks without sleep or food, and tonight, so shall you. Meditation is your sleep; it is your healing and food. Meditation works by blocking out your surroundings and focusing only on yourself. I want you to relax and release all the tension within your body, starting from your head down to your toes. Focus on a pleasant thought and hold it tight in your mind. Block out everything else but this single thought."

I close my eyes and think of happy thoughts. My dreams are of her. The memories we share together dance in my mind. Slowly, I float away, forgetting everything but her.

***

For eight straight hours, I meditate under the guidance of Sinclair. There's a sense of peace where only thoughts of bliss flow through my mind. That is, until Sinclair smacks the back of my neck.

"Time to begin," she says and opens my fractured bedroom window.

There's a rumble in my stomach as I stand up and stretch. "We probably should eat something first."

Sinclair chews several mint leaves to freshen her breath. "Food is for those who don't quit." She points to the sack of rocks from last night. "Bring them with you."

I hoist up the sack and follow Sinclair to a grassy field near the base of the Waterfall of Life. She takes me to a cage made of sticks and unlocks the gate.

"Get in," orders Sinclair.

"For what?"

"Just do it or I'll make you regret it."

Begrudgingly, I enter the cage like a trapped animal. Sinclair grabs the sack of rocks and paces about fifteen steps back.

"Yesterday, we tested your pain resistance and ability to focus. We'll revisit these exercises, but before we do, let's conduct another test." Sinclair fiddles with a rock and gives me a creepy smile. "Even though you haven't Awakened, let's test your reflexes. On the battlefield, having quick reflexes can give you the winning edge."

Sinclair flicks a rock at me with such speed it breaks one of the wood sticks supporting the cage. Sinclair plays with another rock, tossing it back and forth in her hands. "Next one is for you. Hope you can dodge it."

"What!" A rock ricochets off my shoulder, instantly causing pain.

"This is the penalty for failing to knock down those five leaves yesterday. You can protest all you want, but there's still over a hundred rocks to go through." Sinclair flings another rock; this one skims the side of my pants causing a rip.

"They're moving too fast," I say. Another rock slams into the palm of my hand.

"I advise you to take what you learned yesterday and apply it to this exercise," says Sinclair.

109

Really? How is meditation going to help me? I can't just sit here and dodge rocks. Another rock sizzles across my arm and slices me like a hot knife. Something about warm blood on flesh causes one to quickly think. Be calm and stay focused.

As Sinclair flicks another rock, I follow its path yet can't move fast enough to avoid.

One by one, Sinclair pummels me with rocks until there's no more. Now bruised and slightly bloody, I'm glad the exercise is over.

"Very good," says Sinclair.

"I did terrible," I say while nursing my arm.

"At least you hung in there and didn't wimp out. You're building up a tolerance for pain. Yesterday, you would've given up." From under her gold silk belt, Sinclair takes out a small mirror and examines her face. She brushes her thin eyebrows and straightens her hair.

"Why are you so obsessed with your appearance?" I ask.

"Obsession is for the tawdry, Marcus. Now, if you would've said I'm meticulous I wouldn't be so offended. Subtle details make all the difference." Sinclair does one last check in her mirror before finally putting it away. "Let's go to the top of the waterfall for our next exercise."

After a short climb up the side cliffs to the Waterfall of Life, we head farther upstream until we reach a yellow flag pole.

"Okay, let's test your strength and endurance," says Sinclair. "Your objective is to swim from one side of the river to the other before reaching the waterfall cliff."

My stomach churns. Swimming isn't my specialty. "And what happens if I fail?"

Sinclair squeezes my arm. "Hmm, maybe a broken bone or two. So what do you say—ready for some fun?"

Sinclair's mind is more twisted than I thought. Taking a deep breath, I dive headfirst into the churning river and swim faster than ever before. Heavy waves crash against my thin frame and I swallow several gulps of warm water. Still, I push forward and it isn't until I'm halfway across when my arms weaken and each breath becomes harsh. Racing against time, I press through the choppy waters; the other side is only thirty meters away. I can barely keep my head above water as the relentless waves pound against me. Fifteen meters left. I'm nearly out of breath. The river picks up speed, and as I approach the crest of the waterfall, I try swimming against the current, but it's no use—I'm going over.

Plummeting into a freefall, I crash into the plunge pool. My body stings hitting the water with great force. Strange though, my skin tingles and a warm sensation grows within in my chest. The gold Krysanthem leaf around my neck shines brighter than ever, and a rush of bubbles flow all around me. A spark of excitement fills my veins, and just as it intensifies, Sinclair snatches me from water and drags me back to dry land.

The excitement I briefly tasted has now faded. "There's something special about the water, isn't it?" I ask.

"Indeed," says Sinclair as she wrings out her hair. "The Waterfall of Life has the ability to heal. Why do you think I've been making you drink so much water?"

Looking at my arms and hands, sure enough, the cuts I suffered earlier are now gone.

"When the time is right, this is where you shall Awaken."

"Am I not ready now?" I ask.

Sinclair chuckles. "Not even close. Instead, we shall repeat all five tests and monitor your progress. These exercises will improve your ability to stay calm, sharpen your mind, build strength, and endure pain, all so you're prepared to Awaken."

PART 2

The Incomplete Picture

MARCUS

I've trained with Sinclair for nearly two months but have yet to Awaken. With each passing day my tolerance for pain increases. Countless times I've been scorched by fire and thousands of rocks have pelted my skin. Every day Sinclair's training leaves me with busted knuckles and broken bones. Thankfully, the water from the Waterfall of Life heals me each day. However, without food or sleep, my body shows signs of wear. The headaches are nonstop, my fingers constantly jitter, and the slightest noises irritate me.

"You're getting better," says Sinclair as we stare at the Waterfall of Life. "As a reward, I offer you a choice. Today you can either sleep or eat. What will it be?"

"Eat," I say without hesitation.

Sinclair looks to a row of berry bushes. "Okay, you were right! Come on out."

Minnie, along with Sphinx spring from behind the bushes. "Marcus, I knew you would pick food!" says Minnie. "Your meal awaits you not far from the village. To get there, Sphinx will escort you."

"He's supposed to walk, but I'll allow it," says Sinclair, she licks her fingers and contours her eyebrows. "Good thing it's still early. Would hate for the others to see me like this."

Minnie rolls her eyes. "Sinclair tells me pears are your favorite fruit. You're in luck because just north of here is a vast field of gigantic pear trees."

Sinclair hands me a burlap sack with rope and string. "You can take as many pears as you want, but you can't eat them until you bring me back a purple pear," she says. "Purple pears are by far the sweetest and most coveted of all fruits, and I really would like to have one. They only grow on certain trees so you'll need to use some ingenuity to get to them."

I nod and hop on the back of Sphinx. We travel outside the village and into flat fields of farmland where crops of grain and corn grow. Further past the farmlands is the vast and lush field of pear trees. Sunlight shines over the trees and the pears appear like gold jewels hanging from branches.

The pear trees are unusually tall and none of the branches are within standing reach. Fortunately, a few pears have already fallen. Though I was supposed to wait, the temptation to eat is too strong. I quickly devour several pears; their sweet nectar is the perfect form of pleasure.

I rest under a tree with a full belly and my eyes grow heavy. Sphinx nudges me with her nose and roars.

"Alright girl, I don't want any trouble. Let's get this over with."

I need to bring back a purple pear for Sinclair, so we search the rows of colossal trees before finally spotting one at the top of the tallest tree in the orchard. Circling around the coveted pear is a swarm of black wasps. I scoop up a handful of rocks and try knocking the pear down, but it's no use.

"Well, this sucks. Got any other ideas?" I ask Sphinx.

Surprisingly, as though she understands, Sphinx taps the trunk of the tree with her paws.

"Of course! Just like the leaf exercise. I have to knock it down by striking the tree!" I scratch the back of Sphinx's ear. "You're such a smart cat."

Focusing, I block out everything and strike the tree with full force. While many green pears fall, the purple one doesn't budge. Worse, the wasps surrounding it are now in a frenzy.

"Guess I'll just have to go up there and get it," I say.

I quickly climb toward the top of the tree and pause just shy of the wasps. The purple pear is within arm's reach—all I have to do is grab it and escape. Without much thought, I snatch the pear and immediately fall to the ground, spraining both ankles. I mount Sphinx, and we bolt from the tree only for the vengeful wasps to follow and unleash a barrage of stings upon us. It isn't until we exit the orchard that the wasps break away.

"Well, that was stupid of me," I say to Sphinx. My arms, hands, and legs are now lumpy and my right eye is swollen shut. "But at least I got the pear!"

We return back to the village where Sinclair and Minnie await near the Waterfall of Life. Seeing our red and swollen bodies, they snicker before breaking into complete laughter.

"It isn't funny," I mumble, my lower lip too is swollen.

Sinclair continues to chuckle. "If you would've followed my orders and not eaten the pears, the wasps wouldn't have stung you." With a smug grin, Sinclair pulls out a purple pear and chomps on it with delight. "Want a bite?"

So angry, I throw my hands up in disgust. "Are you serious? What was even the point of all of that?"

"Tell me something, Marcus, are you in pain?"

While I've been stung many times, I don't feel any pain.

"Didn't think so," says Sinclair. "Which means it's time to Awaken! Minnie, do you mind? I want to share a story with Marcus in private."

"You got it," says Minnie as she whistles for Sphinx to come to her side.

As the two leave, Sinclair and I turn to the Waterfall of Life. It's enchanting view reminds me of what Minnie first said. *If you stare too long, it will inspire love.*

"What drives you more, anger or happiness?" Sinclair asks.

"Happiness of course. Happiness is peace," I say.

"Perhaps, but it's anger that brings about change. Anger alleviates fear and absolves the mind of pain. If you believe happiness is your true virtue, do you think you'll find peace?"

"I hope so…" I trail off, wondering where this is going.

Approaching the lower river, Sinclair leans over and stares at her reflection. "You know, when I first came here, I knew nothing of happiness. Used to be a lot of anger toward me. Anger that still exists inside of Queen Valencia." Sinclair cups her hands into the water and takes a sip. "You may have already been told, but she and I once fought to the death. If it wasn't for this water, Valencia wouldn't be alive today. The healing powers of the water saved her life and it will help do the same for you."

Taking a knife to her finger, Sinclair drips blood into the river, causing the water to sizzle and bubble. "Not only can the water heal the wounded, but if you stay in it long enough, it can spark the Awakening of those with Divine blood."

"So, all I have to do is stay in the water?" I ask.

"Unfortunately, for you it takes more than that. Remember, inside of you is a suppression seal designed to prevent your Awakening by inducing great pain. It's your job to resist this pain and break the seal."

Sinclair instructs me to undress, and as I do, she too dresses down to her undergarments. I slip her a couple of peeks as she wears nothing but a sheer silk undergarment.

"Focus on the task not my body," says Sinclair. She ties heavy sandbags around my ankles. "Once underwater, the Awakening process will begin and the suppression seal will activate causing pain. I'm confident if you stay calm and focused, the Dark Raven shall emerge from the shadows."

To think, it wasn't so long ago that I was nothing but a Norm. Soon, all of that will change, and when it does, I shall begin my hunt for the Shadow Clan.

"I'm ready to Awaken!"

Sinclair smirks. "Oh, one last thing. If you get the urge to sleep, fight it. Otherwise you'll die. Hope you find your happiness!"

"Wait! What?"

Sinclair clenches my hand and launches us into the river. With the heavy sandbags tied around my ankles, we quickly descend to the rocky bottom. Immediately, I panic and try to shake free only for Sinclair's grip to grow tighter. Trapped, I have no choice but to face fear and focus.

Calm down. Just focus on her. Think of the one who means everything to me.

Picturing us together reduces my anxiety. With each passing second though, the urge to breathe grows strong, but so too does my desire to Awaken.

Slowly, my body warms, and a shocking pulse inside me causes a rush of bubbles to flow toward the surface. The gold leaf around my neck shines bright. A force fills my body. I'm Awakening, just as Sinclair said. But like a bolt of lightning, pain explodes throughout my body. My bones burn with fire and I shake with a violent rage. I'm fighting against the onslaught of pain, the need for air, and the temptation to quit. As the pain intensifies, so too does the sensation of immaculate power. A tantalizing feeling of invincibility flows through my veins. This is Divine power, and for the first time ever, I truly feel alive!

But like a hammer to a nail, my euphoria vanishes and the urge to sleep grows heavy. Sinclair squeezes my hand, but I struggle to stay awake. Nearly two minutes have passed since I last took a breath and I'm reaching my limit.

Fight it, fight it. This is my life. I will not give in. I CAN'T, I CAN'T, I CAN'T!

But I do. The temptation to sleep is too great. Once more I drift to a place within my own mind. The water has faded. Sinclair is gone. Before me is my younger self. He sits next to her, and nothing but white surrounds them. A thumping sound grows heavy to the point I can feel it. It's my heartbeat, and the closer I get, the louder it becomes. Watching my younger self, I know he's nervous. He's scared to tell her how he really feels. He wants to thank her for giving him a purpose; for inspiration when pain was all he knew. Suddenly they disappear, and the whiteness around them shatters like glass leaving nothing but darkness. I don't panic or scream. I just imagine how life would be within a dream.

In a dark silence, two twinkling orbs of light appear above and scatter in opposite directions. Instincts drive me to the left, and as I walk toward the light, the allure of its beauty grows. Shining under the light is my younger self and the only girl I've ever cared about. He paints a portrait of her as a gesture of his feelings. Every stroke from his brush onto the canvas is painted with love. His all has been placed into her portrait, and as she smiles, a calmness comes over him like water flowing from a brook; there's no pain or worries, only peace. This is my happiness.

"Tell her how you feel. Tell her before it's too late!" I shout to my younger self. No weapon of pain is greater than love's rejection. But there's no torture worse than living with regret.

My younger self whispers to her, but there's dread in her eyes before—a piercing ear-bleeding scream jolts me from my dream.

I cough up water upon opening my eyes. Lying on my back, staring at the blue sky, I'm relieved to be alive. I try making sense of the dream, wondering why she keeps appearing. All those summer nights in Eden as we gazed upon the aurora skies, I regret not telling her. Perhaps it's a sign I'm too late.

Taking a knife, Sinclair grabs my hand and stabs us both through our palms.

"Are you crazy? What's wrong with you?" I yell.

She holds out her hand which begins to heal, yet mine remains wounded. I have failed to Awaken. Many weeks of grueling training have been for naught. The taste of failure lingers on my tongue.

"Looks like I'm—"

A tingling sensation grows within my hand, and slowly my wound heals itself. I jump in exuberance for I have Awakened! All of a sudden, my vision is sharper, smells are more distinct, and distant sounds are crisp and clear. My body hasn't physically changed, yet I can feel strength flowing through my veins.

I hug Sinclair yet she remains stoic.

"Congrats, Marcus," she says lethargically. "It's best you get some sleep."

Strange—Sinclair's mood has turned gloomy. This was a moment for celebration, but it feels depressing.

"Everything okay?" I ask.

Sinclair's eyes shine with unshed tears. "See you tomorrow," she says and retreats toward the black forest.

Confused by Sinclair's reaction, I stare at the waterfall. Before pushing me in, she asked about happiness and anger. Did she really think I would choose anger?

Leaving the waterfall, I return to the village shops, only to be caught by an irresistible aroma coming from Hazel's bakery. Stopping by, I see Hazel behind a linen curtain kneading a large lump of dough.

"Need some help?" I ask.

Hazel smiles. "Marcus, perfect timing. I'm experimenting on a new dessert I call Apple Fritas. It's a bread tart sprinkled with cinnamon and filled with roasted apples." Hazel raises the hot dessert to my lips. "Have some."

Of course I devour the treat and leave not a crumb. "This is amazing!" I say, wiping cinnamon from my lips. "You could sell thousands of these!"

Hazel's cheeks grow plum. "Glad you like. Have some more."

I scarf down several while Hazel rests her chin in the palms of her hands. "Something's different about you." She pauses. "You've Awakened!" Hazel wraps her flour-coated arms around me. Her warm touch is much needed. "Congratulations! Soon you'll be ready for the Shadow Clan."

I bite the insides of my cheek and plop onto a wooden bench. "I've been thinking about what you said. About what will become of me upon killing those men. To be honest…I'm afraid."

Hazel opens a drawer and blows dust off a portrait. "You and me both." She hands me the portrait, it's a painting of her younger self standing beside Queen Valencia. "It's a lot of pressure being the daughter of a queen. It's inevitable, one day, I will replace her. Unfortunately, that day may be soon."

"Oh?" I prop the portrait on a shelf only for Hazel to snatch it down.

"My mother isn't well. She's losing her mind, and the commanders fear she can no longer lead Dyna. They want me to take over, but I'm not ready." Hazel removes her apron and sits beside me. She stares intently at the portrait. "To become queen, a Victoria must go through a passage. One that involves life, death, and transformation."

I scoot closer to Hazel, her energy seems troubled. "That's a heavy weight to carry. Have you talked to your mother about this?"

Hazel slams the portrait facedown. "My mother and I don't have the best relationship. She may be queen but she's a tyrant to me. Very early in life, she made sure to strip me of my innocence. As a child, I wasn't allowed to have friends or any fun for that matter. While other children played games, I was practicing ways to kill. When other kids made arts and crafts, I was mastering the art of torture. I did all of this before the age of nine, and eventually it became too much. I needed an outlet, a way to reconnect and have empathy for people. Baking for others became my passion." From the back of the portrait, Hazel slides out a note. "Upon opening this bakery, my mother wrote this letter telling me that a queen must be wise, strong, and courageous. A baker is none of these things."

Hazel rips the note into pieces and her flour coated hands tremble. I rest my hand on hers, the light touch seems to calm her. "You can't live your life for others. You should follow your own beliefs."

"A Victoria doesn't get to choose their beliefs. Our sole purpose is to protect Dyna. Just like you want to protect your land, I must do the same or we shall perish." Hazel pulls back her hand from me and tightens her fist. "Baking isn't what I was born to do; killing is. But I fear upon doing so, I'll never have empathy for people again."

I lightly touch Hazel by the chin and guide her to face me. "Hey, we share the same doubt, but you have nothing to fear. From the first time we met, I felt your gentle spirit and could tell you had a genuine heart of love."

Hazel pauses and looks to the wood ceiling to fight back tears. "Hey, let's not drown in our fears. Tonight is your night. Let's celebrate."

As much as I want to, I can't. Something feels off about my Awakening. Sinclair's reaction, the dreams—it's far too strange.

"Something isn't right," I say, pressing my hand onto my chest. "Inside, I feel incomplete, like something is missing. I keep dreaming about a particular girl for some reason."

Hazel reties her apron. "Oh? Is she someone special?"

Hazel has just poured her heart out, yet I foolishly bring up another girl. *How clumsy of me.* "Eh, we've been friends since birth," I say. "But it's been years since I last saw her. In the dream I can see her face, but every time I try speaking to her, the dream abruptly ends."

"Maybe that's why you feel incomplete. Perhaps there's something you need to tell her or maybe it's something she doesn't want to hear."

Not wanting to talk about it any further, I change topics. "Say how about we go to the watchtower…"

"I should get back to baking," Hazel interrupts and returns to her kitchen table. "Tomorrow's going to be a busy day. I need to prepare some food for the others."

I stand beside Hazel, recognizing I've messed up. "This is why you're going to be a great queen someday. You always put others before yourself."

Hazel smiles and hands me tart. "Get some rest, Marcus. You've got a lot on your mind and plenty to dream about."

After saying goodbye to Hazel, I scurry back to my room, take off my boots, and pull out a letter I keep with me at all times. It was written months ago, but I've never had the courage to send it.

The letter was a confession to the girl in my dreams. Before joining the military, I promised to write her often. Which I did, but I always destroyed the letters fearing they would go unanswered. This letter is the only one I've ever kept. In it, I wrote about my struggles in the military, the frustrations of being in Squad Fifty, and the ridicule I received because of my discolored skin marks. I wrote about my envy toward the other squads and how inadequate I felt at the difference in our paths. I expressed that I sincerely missed her and yearned to reunite under the stars of Eden, where our minds would intertwine with dreams of endless possibilities. The letter was a confession of my state of mind, my passion, and heart.

Lighting a candle, I hover the letter over the flame, and just as I set to burn it, I notice a water stain at the bottom of the letter. The stain was an old teardrop next to the words: *"I love you, Rose Cross."*

I stare at those words, then slide the letter back into my boot as a reminder—my life is still an incomplete picture.

Revelations Aren't Always Great

MARCUS

Warm sunrays kiss my skin as the morning light fills my bedroom. Feeling restored after a great night of rest, fond memories of Rose play heavy in my mind. On many mornings, the two of us would wake up early just to watch the sun crest above the lush gardens of Eden. Back then, we would talk about our dreams and ambitions. While mine were goals of protecting the land, Rose's dream was to fulfill a promise to her sister, Scarlett. What first brought Rose and I together were memories of her sister, for Scarlett and I bestowed the same discolored skin marks. It wasn't until later that Rose told me, Scarlett was killed because of those marks.

On a cool summer morning in Eden, Rose told me the story of how her sister was once a soldier in the Divine Amina military. During the winter months, as tradition dictated, Scarlett and the other Aminas returned to Eden and reunited with soldiers from Aypha. A week into Scarlett's arrival, several people in Eden became ill and died after developing a mysterious skin rash. Troubled by what was happening, many of the villagers became paranoid and suspected Scarlett was the source, all because of her discolored skin.

At a very young age, Rose witnessed a mob set her sister on fire, a fire that incinerated Scarlett in a rage of flames. Days later, the villagers discovered that tainted river water was the cause of their illness and not Scarlett. A tragic mistake, the people of Eden apologized to Rose, and those who incited the mob were sent to prison. But after witnessing the cruelty of people, Rose promised no one would ever again suffer such a traumatic fate. Her dream was to create a safe haven in honor of Scarlett. The safe haven was to be for people who looked like her sister, like me, and anyone else who felt out of place. It was to become a place for children to live, free of stress for being different. I can only hope Rose's dream will one day become a reality.

Needing to release my rumbling thoughts, I get dressed to head outside only to find Sinclair sitting in the hallway. Her usually perfect hair is messy and gray bags sit under her poufy eyes.

"About time you got up," she grumbles while scratching her throat. "Must've been a long night."

Ironic, when she's the one looking so rough. "After you abruptly left me, I spent the evening with Hazel."

Sinclair yawns. "So there is something between you two. She's cute but boring, don't you think?" Sinclair brushes her untidy hair. "To me, her personality is just like her bread. Dry, flat, and forgettable."

"She's actually more complex than you think."

"Doubt it," says Sinclair as bristles past me and enters my bedroom. She sniffs the air and cracks a smile. "Smells like cinnamon in here. Someone did spend time with a certain baker!"

"No, no, no." I wave my hands in embarrassment. "It's the Apple Fritas."

Sinclair forms a heart with her hands. "Sure, I can keep a secret. But if Valencia finds out, she'll definitely kill you." Sinclair unfolds her pocket mirror and rubs away the weariness from her eyes. "Anyways, lover boy, now that you've Awakened, let's go test your new strengths."

Sinclair and I head to the top of the Waterfall of Life and scan the many village homes that rest on a grassy hill. Sinclair points to a home way out in the distance.

"What do you see in that window?" she asks.

It doesn't take much for me to see the details. "It's a coin of you," I say.

Sinclair smirks. "What do you think? Had a jeweler create it in my image. Isn't worth anything yet but it will be." Sinclair removes a gold coin from her pocket and palms it in her hand. "My mom used to be a woman of superstition and would flip coins to make decisions. But I never believed in such silly things." Sinclair frowns and tosses the coin into the river. "Anyways, before you Awakened, there's no way you could've seen such detail from this distance. Now that you've Awakened, you're physically stronger, faster, and can heal from serious wounds in minutes."

In a single pounce, Sinclair leaps from one side of the waterfall's river to the other. "Come," she beckons.

123

The idea of jumping over a river seems unreal, but that was before Awakening. Taking a deep breath, I run towards the river's edge and successfully leap over. As soon as I land, Sinclair pushes me into the river, causing me to plummet down the waterfall.

"Very good, Marcus!" says Sinclair who now stands at the edge of the lower river bank. She helps pull me from out of the water. "Now let's test your strength."

Soaking wet, I approach the same maple tree I've been practicing on for weeks. Without hesitation, I strike with such force, the tree trunk splits and every leaf falls to the ground.

"Impressive," says Sinclair, removing fallen leaves from her hair. "Let's do one final test." Sinclair unravels a set of twisted daggers and paces ten steps back. "You've proven you can dodge rocks, so daggers shouldn't be any harder."

"Have at it," I say.

Sinclair gives no warning before hurling the first dagger. Now able to react faster, I dodge the deadly weapon with ease. Sinclair launches another dagger, this one faster; still I evade. Increasingly, Sinclair throws daggers faster than what my eyes can follow until one sinks deep into my thigh.

"Got you!" says Sinclair with disturbing excitement.

Blood runs down my leg as I remove the dagger. Slowly my wound heals.

"Not bad, Marcus. You still need to work on your reflexes, but essentially our training is done."

I shake my head. "No, it's not. What about the next stage? I need to learn my Divine Legacy."

Sinclair chuckles and grabs a purple pear from her bag. "You're not ready for that. You've just Awakened." She licks the pear's skin before biting into it. "Your body needs time to adjust."

"I don't have time," I say in frustration. "I can't stay here and train forever. Aypha needs me. The sooner you teach me, the sooner I can help."

Sinclair finishes her pear and places the remaining core on top of my head. "Patience is a lost art. But okay, Marcus, I'll show you the basics. Recall that a Legacy is a unique power specific to Divines of each Great Land. Of the eight Divine Lands, there are seven main Divine Legacies. Ayphas and Aminas are the only Divines who possess the same Legacy, meaning you and I have the same power. Our Legacy is the ability to create energy by using Oro. As a Divine, Oro resides within all of us and is like blood. Oro is essential to executing your Legacy, which consists of several techniques."

"How many techniques are there?"

Sinclair flashes a subtle smile. "For your knowledge, there's three and the first is called Oroburn. This technique allows you to convert your Oro into a heat source giving you the ability to burn your opponents. Oroburn is useful in close combat, but is limited by physical touch. Our second technique is known as an Orosphere—a powerful ability useful for mid-range battles. To create an Orosphere, Oro must be concentrated and condensed into a central point. When properly harnessed, an Orosphere can set off an explosion...allow me to demonstrate."

Placing her hand out, a glowing yellow sphere forms in Sinclair's palm. As the sizzling sphere grows larger, ember flares spark from its core.

"Listen carefully: a Divine who masters their Legacy is entrusted with a higher level of responsibility. Divines have the ability to protect life or destroy it. I'm warning you Marcus, never abuse your power."

Sinclair forces the Orosphere into a nearby tree. The Orosphere explodes and all that remains is black smoke and splinters of burned wood.

My body stiffens upon seeing such devastation. So, this is the power of a Divine Aypha.

"Two of the Shadow Clan members were using this power," I say.

Sinclair winches. "I think it's time we talk about that. About the attack. This is about your..."

"*Yes, Sinclair!* Tell us how you've been lying to Marcus!" shouts Rikari from the top of the waterfall. She swoops down and lands before us. A sly smile spreads across her face. "Please, Sinclair, go on and tell us what you've known all along."

Sinclair's eyes twitch and her face turns cold. "This isn't your place."

"This place is more mine than yours," Rikari responds. "Go ahead and tell him the truth, tell him about..."

A bright Orosphere whistles past my head and explodes in front of Rikari, she shields herself by forming a small iron pyramid.

"Don't ever interrupt me again!" warns Sinclair, smoke fumes rise from her hand. "Return to the black forest. I'll deal with you there." For the first time ever, Sinclair doesn't hide behind vanity or dignity. Fury seeps through her pores.

"Tell him the truth," taunts Rikari as the iron pyramid around her disintegrates. "Tell him how you knew his village would be attacked."

Sinclair sparks another Orosphere. Rikari's eyes darken and she forms an insidious smile.

Knowing blood will soon spill, I tap Sinclair's arm. "It's okay, Sinclair. Just tell me what's going on."

Sinclair's menacing glare never leaves Rikari but she defuses her Orosphere and places her hand on my shoulder.

"My apologies, Marcus. That was unladylike of me." Sinclair turns to Rikari. "Since you're so eager to know the truth, take a seat and be quiet."

Rikari grits her teeth but places her hands on the ground and creates an iron bench to sit on.

"Marcus, can I ask you something?" Sinclair takes me by the hand. "What do you honestly think of me?"

"Uh, I think you're a misunderstood woman, but you have good intentions," I say.

Sinclair gently rubs the back of my hands with her thumbs. "Best compliment I've heard in years. It sounds awful, but trust me when I say I have your best interest at heart. It's an ugly truth, so it's best to be blunt. Those who led the attack on your village, the ones known as the Shadow Clan, they're commanded by your parents."

My mouth goes dry. Sinclair must be joking, but her face says otherwise.

"I KNEW IT!" shouts an ecstatic Rikari from her bench. "Someone loves keeping secrets."

"Lies," I say in disgust. "My parents are explorers. They aren't fighters, and they're definitely not criminals."

Sinclair rolls up her lacy sleeve and reveals a scroll wrapped around her arm. She hands me the scroll which is a painting of a group of men and women, each of them wearing the same red cloaks with black feathers I saw the night of the attack. In the painting are my parents along with a young Sinclair.

Hundreds of thoughts travel through my mind as I stare at the painting. I don't want to believe it, but if true…

"My parents killed their own people." It stings just saying it. "They killed my friends, all for what?"

Sinclair rests her hand on my shoulder. "What Gail and Saphron have done is noble."

I toss the painting back to Sinclair. "Mutiny has never been noble."

"It is if it prevents genocide," says Sinclair. "For years, Ayphas and Aminas have been plotting to open the Book of Pure. They seek the power within, and once obtained, they'll annihilate the Great Lands. This is why your parents never wanted you in the military. Your involvement just furthers a twisted vision—a vision that leads to your death and everyone you know."

My heart thumps heavy with despair. If true, there's no hope for a world that turns against itself.

"On the night of the attack, several members of the Shadow Clan attempted to break into a prison," interrupts Rikari. "What was that about?"

Sinclair unleashes a scowl at Rikari. "The Ayphas and Aminas need all eight keys to open the Book. It would be suicide to wage war against the Great Lands unless they had an advantage. That advantage is what Gail and Saphron tried to take away, and they must be within the prison."

"They?" I ask suspiciously.

Sinclair looks toward Rikari before speaking. "They're known as the Yazu. A tribe of Norms from the northern lands. They're the creators of the Spirit Weapons, and it is their duty to protect the most powerful of them: the Phoenixes of Ice, Flame, and Carnage. If the Ayphas and Aminas can obtain just one, it will be impossible to stop them from acquiring the keys to the Book. For months, the Ayphas have been holding the Yazu hostage, hoping to break them into revealing how to awaken the Phoenixes."

Rikari leaps off her iron bench and her eyebrows curl inward. "How long have you known this? Why didn't you tell us? We could have..."

"You would've caused more trouble than good!" Sinclair snips.

My jaw tightens. "You lied to me, Sinclair. You knew my parents were behind the attack, but you said nothing. Where are they?"

Sinclair's eyes veer off. "I should've heard from them by now...it's possible they failed their mission."

The back of my throat burns. "Are you saying my parents are—" I cut myself off not willing to believe it. "I need to go home. I need to know what happened."

Sinclair shakes her head. "Marcus, don't you see? Like your parents, like me, you're now a traitor. You can never go back home."

"Crow spit! I'm no traitor. I had nothing to do with the attack."

"The Ayphas will not see it that way. They'll think you've betrayed them. The best thing to do is stay here and continue to develop your skills. The war for Pyris will soon begin."

The audacity of Sinclair. She knows the plight of my parents yet is unwilling to help. She was supposed to be their friend, but in their greatest moment of need, she's abandoned them.

I snatch Sinclair's vanity mirror from her belt and shatter it with my bare hands. "You deserve misery," I say. "When I return to Aypha, everyone will know you're alive and hiding here like a snake!"

Rikari claps heartily. "Very good, Marcus! You're finally standing up for something."

"Have it your way, Dark Raven." Sinclair places her thumb on my lips. "Seems your mouth speaks with anger, not happiness." With an odd wink, Sinclair turns and walks away.

Happiness or anger? Why does she keep saying this?

"Sinclair, come back!" I yell. "What's that supposed to mean?"

Sinclair ignores me, I give chase, but Rikari grabs me by the arm. "Forget her," she says. "Now you see who Sinclair really is."

Indeed, it was naive of me to trust Sinclair, but she's an enigma. A liar and a deceiver. Yet I can't remove the thought she could be right. Are my parents truly noble or simply traitors? I swore to protect Aypha from its enemies but what to do when the enemy is of your own blood?

Wanting some time alone, I leave Rikari and head to the far outskirts of the village, where a watchtower sprouts high above many trees. I climb to the top of the tower and ponder my next move. I need to know the truth but returning home is problematic. If I've truly been marked a traitor, the Ayphas will kill me. I can't afford to be seen by them, at least not immediately.

Dangling my legs over the watchtower ledge, I sit back and fade away for hours. As dusk arrives, I can hear people calling out from the village in search of me. I'll come down eventually. For now, I just want to enjoy this moment of peace, for this could be the last time I'll ever experience it.

When the sun finally tucks beneath the horizon, flashes of fireflies illuminate the night, sparkling and glowing all around the village. Their lights cast hope on a night of great darkness.

"Told you they're beautiful," says Hazel as she climbs to the top of the watchtower. "Figured I'd find you here. You've got everybody worried looking for you." Sitting next to me, Hazel's cinnamon aroma puts me at ease.

"Just needed some time to clear my mind," I say.

Hazel scoots closer to me. "Rikari told me about your parents. I hope they're okay."

"They harmed Aypha, perhaps they deserve what they get."

Hazel pinches my shoulder. "Don't say that. There's more to this world than Aypha. Your parents' actions may have saved us all."

I think of Asher and Darius. Their lives weren't saved. Where is the honor in that?

"If my parents are alive, I want to hear the truth. I want to know if it was all worth it."

Hazel lightly rubs my back. "What's your plan?"

I shrug. "Well for starters, I need a covert way to return home. Once there, I'll figure it out."

"Doesn't sound like much of a plan." Hazel tries looking me in the eye, but I can't return the favor. Tears might just fall. Instead, I fixate on the beautiful fireflies that continue to flash along the night's sky.

"I know you're in pain, Marcus. I know you're lost and confused." Hazel plucks the side of my head. "That's why I'm going with you. Together, let's find your parents."

As much as I need help, I can't burden Hazel with my troubles. Besides, there's no guarantee I can protect her.

"Best I do this alone," I say. "No reason to drag you into this."

Hazel again plucks my head. "Don't be so stubborn. Let me help you." I finally relent and turn to Hazel, her smile is reassuring. She knows little of me, yet willing to risk her life.

"Why? You don't owe me anything."

"I'm worried about you. I don't think you trained all this time just to die at the hands of your own people. Sinclair believes in you for a greater purpose, and I want to ensure it happens." Hazel draws her lips to my ear. Hints of cinnamon sprinkle the air. "This world isn't filled with many good people, Marcus. Are you one of them or are you just another Aypha?"

I pause briefly, unsure of myself. "Come, help me discover who I really am."

Goodbyes Aren't Forever

MARCUS

Along with me, standing outside the giant iron wall at the border of Dyna are Hazel, Cynthia, Minnie, and her tiger Sphinx. It's time to say goodbye to Dyna. Beyond this point, I'm vulnerable to the world. The unknown awaits, but I fear not.

"Hey now, Marcus, why such a serious face?" asks Cynthia. She squeezes me with her hefty arms and smiles from ear to ear. "Got a special gift for you." Cynthia unrolls a gray-blue sleeve and slides it onto my arm. "Sinclair asked me to make this for you. It's a compression sleeve designed to reduce swelling when you learn your Legacy."

Snug and tight, the sleeve is embroidered with several gold Krysanthem leaves.

"Much appreciated," I say.

Cynthia hugs me by the waist and lifts me off my feet. "Don't leave us, Marcus. We haven't even had a chance to share a drink."

"Cynthia, put him down!" squeaks Minnie. "Seriously though, Marcus, you don't have to leave. Why don't you stay a little longer till we come up with a plan?"

I shake my head. "I'm thankful for everything you all have done but it's time to go home, and face the truth."

Minnie pouts. She knows I'm walking toward my death.

"I'm going with him," Hazel blurts out. She grabs my hand, much to my surprise. "We have to help Marcus."

Morphing from out of the iron wall, Rikari appears. "Negative! Your mother demands that you stay here."

Hazel squeezes my hand and draws me closer. "She doesn't get to dictate my life," she says. "Mother can't even leave her precious mansion to see me!"

Rikari rolls her eyes. "Don't make this difficult."

Hazel's eyes turn dark gray. "You all know my mother isn't well. It's time I begin my passage. If she can't lead us, then I will…"

Iron rods suddenly twist around Hazel's legs and torso, pinning her in place. "Sorry, darling," says Minnie while tightening the rods around Hazel. "You can't get involved in someone else's affairs."

Disappointment floods Hazel's eyes realizing she must stay behind. "Marcus, promise me you'll stay alive." Her eyes return to light green. "Stay alive so we may fulfill our passions."

"I promise." Seeing her pure face, I don't want to disappoint her, but in reality, we'll never see each other again. Our lives are bound for different paths. "I'm forever grateful for the experiences you've shared with me. I'm going to miss…"

Hazel breaks free from the iron twists, and we hug each other like it's the last time we ever will.

I slide back Hazel's curly hair and lean in to whisper in her ear. "Here, I want you to have this." I place my gold Krysanthem necklace around Hazel's neck. "Keep this near your heart and never forget me." *I know I'll never forget her.* She is the hope that the world will one day be as beautiful as her. She's the bridge between reality and dreams. Hazel is the sliver of light that remains between dusk and night.

Hazel rests her hand on the Krysanthem leaf. "Be careful, Marcus. Do whatever it takes to survive," she says.

Our arms lock together; neither of us want to let go. But we both know this moment cannot last forever.

Rikari taps my shoulder. "Well, kid, looks like this is it."

"If that's your way of saying you're going to miss me, I'll take it," I say. In usual fashion, Rikari remains stoic. She hands me a sparkling red map made of a strange, flexible metal. I notice the map is showing our current location.

"It's a dynamic map created by yours truly. It changes based on your location and shows where I've created underground tunnels. This may come in handy when you return home."

I give Rikari my thanks and tuck the map into my pocket.

"Oh! Speaking of travel, I have something for you too," says Minnie. She reaches for the bell necklace I've been wearing. "Sphinx will be your mode of transportation. I've trained her to obey you, so you shouldn't have any trouble." Minnie hands me a gold ball filled with jelly. "Give this to her once you reach near the Valleys of Hope."

"And with that, it's time for you to leave," says an eager Rikari.

Turning back to the iron wall, I take one last look, hoping to see Sinclair, but it's obvious she isn't coming.

Saddling up on Sphinx, I say my final goodbyes, and while everyone else waves, Rikari approaches and lays her hand on the back of my neck.

"Hope next time we meet, I won't have to kill you."

You Are My Friend

MARCUS

Riding on the back of Sphinx, we venture into the northern forest hills of Beta. Insects are buzzing and the fragrance of mint lingers in the air. The first few hours through the forest are quite ordinary, and I try to keep my mind off what is sure to come. Some form of tragedy awaits me, and I'm uncertain my heart is prepared for it.

Upon reaching a clearing, the sight of beauty unfolds before our eyes. Farther west are the Valleys of Hope. Recalling Minnie's instructions, I give Sphinx the gold ball filled with jelly to which she eats. Sphinx grumbles, her body glows, and magnificent wings of white and black feathers emerge from her sides.

Strapping myself tight to her, we soar into the sky and the air turns bitingly cold. The Valleys of Hope's lush green mountains and pristine waterfalls are majestic to the eyes. Countless rainbows arch over the valleys and a crystal-blue lake provides water to many tropical birds. As we fly over the lake, a strong shiver comes over me and my hands turn cold. The odd feeling quickly fades as we continue onward.

It takes us nearly a day to fly across Beta, and it isn't until night that we descend into a small tree patch for cover. We're just outside the border of my village. I'm shocked to see Amarna is no longer the same. The Shadow Clan's carnage has left many scars. Homes have been burned to rubble, bridges have been damaged, and a stench of death remains in the air. I thank Sphinx for getting us here. She licks the side of my face, and in an instant, she's gone, soaring back into the night sky.

All alone and wrapped in the darkness of night, I scan the village and spot several guards patrolling the eastern border. Undoubtedly, they'll arrest me if I'm caught. As the guards continue their rounds, I sprint pass

133

them with incredible speed. Shocked at my abilities, I'm still getting adjusted to my Divine power.

Needing cover, I lower my head and proceed toward my old quarters. "Traitor" is painted on my back door. Heading inside, I cringe as the rusted hinges churn and buckle loudly. My quarters have been trashed; my belongings tossed everywhere and shattered glass litters the floor. There's piles of dirty clothes, and many of my paintings have been ripped to shreds. Ignoring the mess, I pull up a floorboard and retrieve a few of my daggers. Just as I replace the floorboard, heavy footsteps approach.

"Hey, the back door is open!" shouts a man.

I quickly drop to the floor and wiggle underneath a pile of dirty clothes just as two guards enter. They light a torch and walk about my quarters causing dust to rise off the floorboards. Wrinkling and twisting my nose, I fight the urge to sneeze and dare not breathe.

"What's that?" a guard asks as he turns in my direction.

Clutching my dagger, my palms turn sweaty as I prepare to strike. *Am I ready to do this?* I ask myself. If the guard takes another step forward, I have no choice but to plunge this dagger into his chest. Sweat builds across my forehead, my muscles grow tense, and then…

"This isn't a bad piece of art. I'm taking it!" the guard says.

In the corner of my room rests a painting I did many months ago. It wasn't anything special—just an illustration of the sky pouring with rain.

"Might as well take it. Marcus ain't coming back," the other guard says.

As they leave, I relax the grip around my dagger. After counting down from thirty, I spring from the rancid clothes and peek my head outside. I scan the other quarters, and to my elation, there's a light coming from Asher's quarters.

I sprint into a field of tall wet grass and lie low. I toss pebbles at Asher's back door and breathe a sigh of relief when he answers. Emerging from the grass, I wave but Asher frowns before calling me over. As soon as I enter his quarters, he grabs me by my shirt and slams me against the wall.

"What the hell are you doing here?" he asks.

I slap away Asher's hands. "This is my land, isn't it? I have a right to be here."

Asher's ears turn red. "You arrogant prick! You betray us and now come back to gloat?"

My shoulders slump with disappointment. I thought Asher would think better of me.

"C'mon, you know..."

Asher grabs me by the collar. His eyes jolt uncontrollably. "You're a traitor, Marcus. I should kill you myself."

I break Asher's grip and shove him against a wall, rattling his tiny cabin. Dust from the wood ceiling falls on both of us. "Listen to me, fool—I'm not a traitor."

"Liar, then where have you been?" Asher tries breaking free from my grip, but surprised when he realizes he cannot. "Your parents were behind the attack, Marcus. You had to know something, but you said nothing."

I release my grip on Asher and draw his curtains closed. "You're wrong. But I do have a story to tell and its best you sit down."

Instead Asher reaches for a knife. "I swear, if you aren't straight with me, I'll kill you."

"Think, Asher, go back to the night of the attack. Last time I saw you, I was fighting Rizen. When I came to, the fires had already started and none of you were there. You abandoned me that night!"

Asher's jaw tightens. "We had to leave you. Your body, it was too hot to touch. Something took control of you. Wasn't long after, the red cloaks appeared."

"That's when Rikari arrived."

"Who?"

"The woman who saved me that night." I pause, wondering if I should tell Asher. "She took me to Dyna where I discovered Sinclair Bonet still lives."

Asher frowns. "Sinclair Bonet, the dead queen? Marcus, you take me for a fool."

"I've seen her with my own eyes. In fact, she's the one who told me that I'm of Divine blood."

Shaking his head, Asher tightens his grip around a knife. "Crow spit! You're no Divine and Sinclair is dead. Enough of this nonsense..."

I snatch the knife from Asher and stab myself through the palm of my hand. Asher's jaw drops as he sees my wound heal itself.

"Believe me now," I say.

Asher pulls up a stool and takes his knife back. "You've got my attention. Tell me what's going on."

I lean against Asher's mold-infested wood wall and release a heavy sigh. "It's true my parents were behind the attack, but at the time I didn't know. According to Sinclair, my parents are the leaders of the Shadow Clan."

"Marcus, you've just confirmed with your own lips that your parents are traitors…"

I shake my head. *Traitor*—the word stings like a thousand cuts. "Perhaps or they're heroes. Sinclair insists Aypha and Amina are plotting a war against the other lands. They seek ancient keys designed to unseal a book."

Asher shrugs. "What's so bad about opening a book?"

"Genocide. A cleanse of Divines and Norms. Only those who have the power within the Book shall survive. This means everyone—me, you, your family—will all die."

Asher stiffens his lip. "How do I know what you're saying is true?"

"You can't. I came home to find the truth myself. Sinclair tells me a group of people known as the Yazu are being held by the Ayphas. They hold the answer to unlocking Phoenixes—prodigious weapons Aypha and Amina will use against the other lands. This is what my parents have set out to prevent."

Asher's face turns gray. "You might be right about these Yazu people. Ever since the attack, there's been an increase of Divines patrolling the prison gates."

"My parents' mission was to free the Yazu, but it seems they've failed. The only way we'll know is by getting inside the prison."

Asher takes a hard swallow and rubs his temples. I know I'm asking a lot from him.

"You've never been a good liar, Marcus, and I pray you aren't now. If what you're saying is true, it's just a matter of time before we're all annihilated. Still, your parents are traitors. What they've done is unforgivable—but for the survival of Pyris, it may have been a necessary evil." Asher extends his hand. "Our entire lives, I've trusted you, Marcus. And it is out of faith that I will do so now. After all, you are my friend."

Fury

MARCUS

Asher and I stay up all night to strategize ways to enter the prison. Made of red stone, the prison sits on a hill and is surrounded by farmland. With so many guarding the prison, finding an entry won't be easy.

"Let's create a distraction," I tell Asher. "We could start a fire by the west entrance and then slip inside."

Asher releases a big yawn. "Okay, then what? There are probably more guards on the inside. We need a less intrusive way in. Too bad we can't dig under the prison."

I smack my forehead. "Of course!" Taking Rikari's map, I spread it across a table looking for any secret tunnels she may have created. Sure enough, there's one that runs from a barn directly to the prison.

"Looks like we found our way in," I say, grinning.

Peeking out the window, Asher again yawns. "Sun will be up soon. We'll have to make our move tomorrow night."

"Sure, but during the day gather some intel for us. Check out the barn and see what you find."

"I'm not your errand boy," snaps Asher. "Why don't you do it?"

"Have you forgotten already? Everyone thinks I'm a traitor. I can't be seen. Look at it this way, while you're in the barn, help yourself to some milk."

Asher's face turns red. "Not funny, Marcus."

Growing sleepy, I lie across Asher's bed. "Seriously though, just take a look at the barn and see if you can find the tunnel entrance."

"Fine, I'll do it, but just know you owe me for this."

"You got it. Now let's get some rest."

I sleep for what seems like a minute before the sun marches over the horizon. Asher is already up; then again, he probably didn't sleep seeing how I slept on his bed.

"Wake up, you little baby. Got you some breakfast," says a grouchy Asher.

He places a hearty loaf of bread on the table. The sweet smell of cinnamon instantly reminds me of Hazel. Her decadent fragrance and mossy green eyes I shall never forget. Yet as intoxicating as she is, Rose shall have my heart.

Asher rips off a chunk of the loaf. "Aren't you going to eat?"

Fiddling with my combat boots, I show Asher the old letter I wrote to Rose. "When I see her again, I'm going to give this to her."

Asher chuckles as he reads it. "Well, well. Look who's finally ready to confess his love. Shame you waited till you became an outlaw."

"Perfect timing, right? Doesn't matter though. Once this whole mess is over, we'll be together."

Snickering, Asher proceeds to a long mirror and puts on his uniform as best as he can. His Elite Guard jumpsuit is baggy and doesn't quite fit his short stature.

"Hate to bring you back to reality, but you're a criminal. It's just a matter of time before she finds out."

"Everything will work itself out," I say. "You think she's still in Eden or sent off to join the Aminas?"

Asher rolls up his pant legs and cuffs them into his boots. "My bet is she's still in Eden, maybe even found a new boy to keep her interest."

I punch Asher in his shoulder, though I'm terrified he could be right.

Asher rubs his shoulder. "Easy there lover boy, it was just a joke. I'll be back this afternoon and hopefully you'll have a plan for once we're inside the prison."

As Asher heads to the door, there's something else I need to ask him. Up until this point I've been reluctant to do so. "How's Darius? Did he survive the attack?"

Asher stops, one foot already out the door, his back is to me. "He's alive, but…let's talk later. I don't want to be late for roll call."

With Asher gone, I prepare myself for what may unfold tonight. Ugly thoughts come to mind. If my parents are alive, am I willing to kill to free them? Or turn against them and beg Aypha for forgiveness?

I swallow a dry piece of bread, my nerves too shot to even chew. Anxious, I catch myself tapping away at Asher's kitchen table. Unable to settle, I take some old paper and one of Asher's thin paintbrushes. Using some black dye, I paint a picture of a raven overlooking a village.

It takes a few hours to perfect the painting, and as the sun creeps across the sky, my anxiety returns. To calm my mind, I place a blanket on the floor and mediate. The practice does little to help me on this day.

When sunset nears, I begin to worry about Asher. He should be back by now, his shift ended hours ago. Something must've gone awry. Has he been caught? Is he being tortured? Has he been killed? Paranoia seeps in. I have to do something.

I grab Rikari's map, what's left of the bread, and slip out the back door into the night. Zipping behind the barracks, I head toward a stone bridge that passes over a river. Beyond the bridge is the barn. As two soldiers approach, I dip my head low and quickly turn around. Slipping under the bridge, I walk alongside the river and with one pounce, leap over it. I sprint up a couple of hills before reaching the barn.

I slip inside, and the repulsive stench of manure causes me to gag. Mooing and huffing, there's over a hundred cattle packed inside.

"Asher, you in here?" I whisper.

"Toward the back," he calls out.

Shoving my way through cattle, I see Asher waist deep in what I can only hope is mud.

"What happened?"

"Isn't it obvious? I decided to take a nap in cow crap."

"Really?"

"No! I'm stuck, you idiot."

I chuckle. "Did you at least get us some milk? I'm thirsty."

"Oh shut-up, Marcus. Lucky for you though I think I found the tunnel entrance."

I jump into the manure and help Asher out. In the corner of the barn, Asher has cleared away manure which reveals an iron door etched into the ground. When I give it a good tug, a latch gives way, sending Asher and me into a hole. It's dark, but with my Divine eyes, I can see we're in an iron tunnel. Asher, on the other hand is completely blind.

"Take my hand, Asher. I'll guide us," I say.

Asher smacks my hand away. "I'm not a child, Marcus. Just because you got a little power doesn't make you king."

"Have it your way, peasant."

Proceeding through the dreadfully cold tunnel, we reach an iron slab that blocks our path. Rikari must've put this here. Pressing my palms against the slab, I'm able to turn it just enough for us to slide by.

"Incredible," says Asher. "You have the strength of many men, yet your body remains lanky and unimpressive."

"Whatever."

As we continue onward, the tunnel becomes increasingly narrow to the point we have to crawl. Above us I can hear faint noises. The farther we go, the louder they become. The sounds of cries, screams, and moans of despair, are painful to the ear.

A strong stench of death catches my nose as we come to the end of the tunnel. We climb a flight of stairs and peep through a cloudy window. Below is a tiny prison cell, and balled into the corner is a woman and child. As the little girl weeps, her mother constantly wipes tears from her musty face.

"Hey, up here!" I call out to the woman.

Frightened, the mother drops to her knees into a praying position.

"Don't hurt us, please, please no more!" she screams.

"Shh! We're not here to hurt you, lady," says Asher.

Realizing the voices are coming from above, the mother looks toward the wall and wipes away her tears. She puts her ear against the wall and calls out, "Where are you?"

"In the window. Can't you see us?"

The woman backs away from the wall, pulling out strands of her thin hair. "It finally happened. I've gone mad."

Rikari must've created some sort of one-way window. Asher and I break the glass and climb through.

The woman shields her child. "I know you're not real! Go away!" she cries. Her hair grimy and her teeth gray, the disheveled woman shivers at our presence.

I extend my hand. "We're real. See for yourself."

Cocking her head to the side, the woman pauses and cautiously places her hand on my chest. "A familiar heartbeat. You are real! But how did you get here?"

"It's not important. Just know we're here to help," says Asher.

Wrong. Helping this woman is secondary. Finding my parents is my focus.

"My name is Marcus and this is my friend…"

"Hey, don't say my real name!" Asher interrupts. "Just call me Clover."

The woman looks at us in confusion. "Okay, Marcus and Clover. My name is Free." The woman calls for her child. "Yondi, come, come. Meet these young boys. This is Marcus, and, err, um, Clover, they're here to save us."

The little girl with long hair doesn't say a word. She just looks at me with an empty face. There's no hope in her eyes, only brown pearls of defeat.

"You'll have to forgive her. Yondi rarely speaks." Free's eyes brighten with excitement as she sniffs the air. "You have food! Please, may we have some?"

Somehow, through her own stench, Free could smell the cinnamon bread I stuffed in my pocket. They really could use it as their bones are showing and their skin is as pale as snow.

As they devour the bread, I notice the prison cell door is open.

"How many of you are here?"

"Used to be hundreds. Now only fifty-one of us remain," says Free, breadcrumbs fall from her mouth. "Many died from illness, some from insanity, and others were simply tortured to death. Every day I wonder when will it be my turn to die?"

Asher and I exchange glances. "Are you part of the Yazu?" I ask.

"Yes," says Free, with a slow, sad nod of defeat. The Ayphas have broken her.

"Mind telling us how you got here?" Asher asks.

Free sighs as she turns to Asher. "Surrounding our land is a barrier designed to prevent Divines from entering. However, a year ago, two powerful Ayphas broke through the barrier in search of the Eye of Truth. Threatening to kill us, we gave them the Eye. But we refused to tell them how to activate it. That's when the killing began." Free grinds her gritty teeth before holding her daughter. "Those of us who survived were brought here. Every day they torture, beat, and starve us, but no matter what they do, they shall never know how to activate the Eye."

"What happens if the Eye is activated?" asks Asher.

"Calamity. The Eye is the conduit to unleashing the Legendary Spirit Phoenixes."

Sinclair was telling the truth all along. "The men who brought you here, who are they?" I ask.

Free closes her eyes, trying to remember. "I can't recall the old man's name, but the younger one goes by Petune…strange though, ever since the incident, we haven't seen him."

"What incident?" I ask.

"Not long ago, there was some sort of fight above ground. Tons of explosions and men screaming. When the battle was over, a group of people in red cloaks were brought down here."

"My parents!" I interrupt. "It was them. Where are they?"

Free covers her dingy ears, the spike in my voice must've triggered her. "They're in the containment room. Upstairs on the main floor there's a red door on the wall only reachable by a ladder. That is where they were taken."

"Show me."

"You can't just walk upstairs. There's too many guards patrolling the floor," says Free. "You're going to need a plan."

"Help us and we'll free you from this place," offers Asher.

Asher's promise is foolhardy. It is impossible to sneak fifty-one people out of the prison.

Free smiles and turns to her daughter. "What do you think, precious? Think we can do it?" Yondi nods but with no emotion.

Proceeding down the damp prison hall, we round up all fifty-one Yazu and huddle tight around Free's cell. Many of the Yazu are gravely ill; the lack of sunlight has caused their eyes to become glossy. Many Yazu have bulging lesions while others have a constant cough.

Free stands on a wood stool. "Everyone, this is Marcus and Clover," she says. "They're here to rescue us. But in return they need our help. Marcus's parents are in the containment room, and we need a way to get him inside."

No one says a word. Everyone stares at us with little hope.

"I've got an idea," says a teenage boy with coarse red hair. He and I appear to be the same age. "The name's Roth, and it's best you remember it," he says with a grin. "Once a night, the guards do a shift in personnel. For a few minutes, there's a time gap where only one or two guards patrol the room. If we can distract them, it will give Marcus an opportunity to climb the ladder and enter the containment room."

"What do you say?" Free asks as she turns to us. "Sound like a plan?"

"Sounds perfect," I say.

An old Yazu man raises his hand. "What if you don't find your parents? Will you still help us escape?"

The man has doubts, and rightfully so. I have to be realistic with them.

"We'll find a way to save every last one of you," Asher promises.

Free claps her hands. "C'mon people, have some faith. Remain positive and trust that these two will guide us to freedom. Concentrate and be prepared for our exodus."

"The guard exchange is set to occur soon, so there isn't much time," says Roth. He stares at us with eyes of hope. "Marcus, Clover, we promise not to let you down. Please do the same for us."

It's hard to look Roth in the eye as I give him a nod.

After we thank them for their assistance, the Yazu leave while Free, Yondi, Asher, and I remain in the cell.

"Okay, so what's the plan?" asks Free. "This is so exciting! Aren't you excited, Yondi?"

Once again, the little girl looks directly at me but says nothing. She knows I have no plan.

Shaking off Yondi's cold stare, I pull out Rikari's map to locate an escape route. There's another tunnel north of the barn that leads to the eastern border of the village. The tricky part is we have to be above ground to get to the next tunnel. It's a risk, but it's the only option available.

To blend in with the Yazu, Asher and I change into some dingy old garments and cover our faces in dirt. As time nears for the signal to begin, my stomach churns and my hands become moist. A whistle blows and a wave of Yazu barge upstairs, they yell at the guards and bang empty pans. As they protest for food, a second wave of Yazu run upstairs. I hunker low behind them and spot on the far side of the dim room the red containment door. Instead of using the ladder, I leap onto the door's ledge and enter before the guards notice.

It's difficult to breathe inside the hot and muggy room. A torch provides the only source of light and all across the stone walls are chains connected to glass bulbs. Scanning the room, I search for my parents, but find only a man shackled to the wall. At his feet is a tattered red robe. His arms are stretched outward, and around his hands are glass bulbs filled with a liquid. Embedded in his wrists are tubes that also flow with the strange fluid.

I move closer, wondering if the man is dead.

"Hey, you there?" I ask.

Getting no response, I poke his chest. He bobbles his head and whispers low. I lean in and ask him to repeat himself.

"Kill me," he whimpers. "Please kill me."

My bottom lip quivers. "No, I can save you."

"Can't be saved. I am all that's left. Everyone's dead," says the man.

My heart pumps heavy, and my voice turns shallow. "So, Gail and Saphron were killed?"

The man's eyes slowly cascade open and explode with life. "Marcus? Son of Saphron! You shouldn't be here."

"I'm looking for my parents."

Breathing heavy, the man can barely speak. "Y-a…ya…your parents were never here. Different mission." Coughing and hacking up blood, he struggles on. "Their mission was to recover the Eye of Truth. My team was to free the Yazu. Unfortunately, we failed. I pray they did not."

"Where are they?" I whisper urgently.

He rattles his chains, looking at me with shameful eyes. "The plan was to take the Yazu to Chance Island. If your parents succeeded, that is where they are. You have to get some of the Yazu to the island. Once reunited with the Eye, they can destroy it."

"Come with me," I beg. "I need your help." I tug at the tubes in his arms only for my hands to burn.

There's a whistle from outside indicating my time is up. The Yazu can no longer stall the guards.

"It's pointless, son of Saphron." The man's eyes roll to the back of his head. "Petune killed my whole team. I'm only alive because he gets pleasure from torturing me."

This is the same vile man Free mentioned earlier. Only the twisted would enjoy seeing someone suffer and rot away.

"Son of Saphron, do me a favor and check my right sock," says the man.

Fiddling through his blood-soaked sock, I pull out a small gray pill. A poison pill.

"No, I can still free you." The pill rattles in my trembling hand. Again, someone whistles from outside.

"Do this for me, kid. Let me go on my own terms."

Staring at the pill, I hesitate. This man wants to die, and I'm the only one who can stop him. His eyes say it all. He wants to go; he's endured enough. My hands ooze with fear as I place the pill on his tongue and tilt his head back.

"Thank you," mutters the man after a hard swallow. "Don't worry about me. Just find a way to get the Yazu to Chance Island."

Suddenly, the man's body shakes and his eyes pulsate. Bile pours from his mouth and blood drains from his eyes—and then it's over. He draws his last breath but leaves behind a smile.

Witnessing a man die, there's no time to cry. Racing back to the door, I peek outside and see the Yazu lying on the ground. Many of them bleed from their backs after being whipped for their insubordination. There's now multiple guards in the room, making it difficult to cross without being seen. Roth looks up in my direction and smiles. He rises to his feet and tackles one of the guards. Pummeled to the ground, Roth is whipped repeatedly. My instinct is to help, but I can't squander this opportunity. I leap from the door ledge and quickly scurry back to the basement cellars.

Inside Free's cell, Asher awaits. "Well? Did you find your parents?" he asks.

I shake my head. "But I know where they are. A place called Chance Island. We need to get there immediately."

Asher raises his eyebrows. "What about the Yazu? We can't just leave them."

Grabbing Asher's arm, I pull him toward the secret window on the wall. "There's no way we can escape with so many," I whisper. "We just need to take a few with us."

Asher tugs away from me. "So, we should abandon the rest? Funny how they helped you but now you turn your back on them."

Chastised by Asher, I can't help but think of Hazel's words. Am I one of the good ones or just another Aypha?

One by one, the guards shove the Yazu back downstairs and lock the cellar latch behind them. The Yazu have suffered a terrible whipping. The guards spared no mercy as women and children drip with blood.

"Here's your defining moment, Marcus," Asher says harshly. "What are you going to do?"

"Everyone, follow me," I say.

They limp their way down the hall, and we cram inside Free's cell. Everyone is here except for Roth. I ask what happened, the Yazu lower their heads. Some begin to sob. The boy sacrificed his life for me. He did it so others may live. This is the true test of man's heart: to forfeit one's own desires is the true measure of a man. How awful of me to be so selfish.

"Let's go," I say.

With Asher leading the way, the Yazu are pulled through Rikari's secret window and into the tunnel. Only Free, Yondi, and I remain behind.

"Your parents?" Free asks.

I shake my head. "Don't worry about them. We must go now."

I help Free and Yondi to the secret window and follow them into the cold tunnel and up to the barn. Luckily, it's still dark. We need to head about a mile north to the exit tunnel.

Taking a deep breath, I slip from the barn and lead the Yazu down the slopes of the farmland. Freedom is only moments away. For the first time ever, I'm proud to have kept my promise to protect others.

Continuing across the hills, we halt upon reaching a river. I take a second look at Rikari's map. I've made a mistake confusing the river for a tunnel.

"Raise your hand if you can swim," I say to the Yazu. Only Yondi raises her hand.

"We're gawking crows out here," says Asher. "Let's get them back to the barn."

But as we turn around, two figures stand before us. It is my old friend Darius alongside Rizen.

"My, my," Rizen says. "Strange creatures do roam the night, and you know what they say, it's best to kill them on sight!"

Collision

MARCUS

In the absence of light, when all others sleep, only Darius and Rizen stand in the way of freedom. Our backs against a raging river, our only option is confrontation.

"What a mess we have here," Rizen says with a sly grin. "Marcus of the weaklings has returned to betray us again."

I bite down hard on my jaw. "You're wrong. I would never harm Aypha."

Rizen sneers. "Funny, looks like you're helping prisoners escape. If that's not treasonous, I don't know what is."

Asher steps before Rizen. "These are innocent people. They're not our enemies!"

Rizen slaps his knee and chuckles. "Innocence does not exist in this world. Do not have compassion for the Yazu. They are nothing but tools and should be treated as such."

"Tools? Is that all you think of them?" I ask.

"It's what I think of all you Norms."

Rizen has no idea what I've become. The urge to strike him builds. He will know pain just as I once did.

I spit at Rizen's feet. "You're disgusting. You've got no idea what you're talking about."

Rizen nudges Darius. "You hear this, Darius? Your friend here insults us not once, but twice. How do you think your father would feel?"

Confused, I look to Darius. His face is filled with malice; his stare poised with venom. There's pain in his pupils.

"Is it true?" Darius strains to ask. "Did you know Armana would be attacked?"

I shake my head. "No."

Darius steps toward me. "Are you sure? Because one of those killed was my father and witnesses say it was your parents who did it."

My stomach churns in disbelief. Darius's anger and pain are now dramatically clear. The back of my throat burns as if I've swallowed fire itself. I want to apologize, but what good will it do when there's so much pain in his eyes?

"Words of silence. See how a coward responds when confronted with the truth," says Rizen.

"Speak up!" yells Darius. He pushes me back toward the river.

"He didn't know. Tell them, Marcus. Speak up!" pleads Asher.

I can't. No matter how I rationalize it, my parents are murderers. Regardless of their intentions, this is a stain that shall remain forever.

"I…I…had no idea they would do this. I haven't seen them in years, Darius. You have to believe me!"

"You lying sack of filth! Then why are you helping the Yazu?" Darius jabs his fingers into my forehead, pushing me closer to the riverbank. "You're a coward, Marcus." Darius strikes me across the jaw. My head spins and again he strikes. His eyes radiate with death. I must defend myself.

I retaliate and strike Darius in the eye. His lips part, shocked by my strength. The two of us continue to exchange blows as Rizen, Asher, and the Yazu look on. With knots and bruises swelling across our faces, Darius slips his arm around my neck and pins me by the river's edge. He shoves my head into the river and nearly a minute passes before he lifts my head above water.

"I should tie you up and watch you drown," says Darius.

"Listen to me, Darius," I beg while coughing up water. "I can explain this."

Again, Darius shoves my head into the river. He then grips me by the neck and slams me into the ground. My spine goes numb. Darius unsheathes his blade and stands over me.

"Why didn't you speak up, Marcus?" Tears drip from Darius's eyes. "You were supposed to be there for me—for us. I'm ashamed to have ever called you a friend."

Darius cocks his blade back, but Asher runs full speed and tackles him. For a Norm, Asher is strong, but Darius is a Divine. He headbutts Asher and breaks his nose.

"Stay out of this, Asher!" Darius warns.

"Just kill 'em both!" cheers Rizen. "Put them out of their pathetic misery."

Darius gives me the coldest stare I've ever seen. His eyes murder me several times over, yet even with all his pain and hatred, he cannot kill his friends.

Rizen puts two thumbs down. "You cannot grow without letting them go, Darius. They are the weak link to your chain of Divine power."

My back aches as I struggle to stand. "He's wrong, Darius. Asher and I are the links that will keep you whole. Aypha is not what you think. We are all pawns to something evil."

"What's evil is betraying your land. To let your friends suffer and do nothing about it," says Rizen, he unleashes a devious smile and turns to the Yazu. "Now, what to do with them? These animals should've never been released from their cages."

"You're quite a despicable boy," says Free. Though she's as frail as a twig, she stands proudly before Rizen. "One day you will receive a triumphant death."

Rizen viciously backhands Free, causing her to slump to her knees. "Well, it won't be tonight. You animals are going back to where you belong."

Looking at the river behind them, many Yazu contemplate jumping in. They can't swim and know they'll die, perhaps death though is better than bondage.

"Don't do it," I plead, giving the Yazu hope. "Live for another day. Hold on and know one day you shall be free. That is a promise!"

Massaging her cheek, Free stands while her daughter Yondi holds her hand. "Listen to the young one," she says to the Yazu. "One day, true freedom shall come to pass."

The Yazu nod and—surprisingly—smile.

Rizen chuckles. "Such false words." He ties my hands together before returning us to the barn, through Rikari's tunnel, and back to the prison.

"Darius, take Asher and the others back to their cells while I deal with Marcus," orders Rizen.

"Stay strong!" I yell to the others. "We'll make it through this."

Rizen unloads a heavy punch to my gut, the blow causes my body to seize. "Pointless words," he says while dragging me to a cell. He straps me to a chair and places heavy shackles around my wrists and ankles.

Inside the room on the slick stone walls are needles and knives, likely used for torturing.

"You know, if I was Darius, I would've killed you on the spot." Rizen takes a needle from the wall and slides it down my forehead. "Unlike him, I won't hesitate."

"Killing a friend is never easy," I say.

"It is when you're a coward." Rizen pats the top of my head. "Sit tight. Your life is about to get much worse."

Rizen leaves, but shortly after, a thin man wearing a gold lion earring arrives to my cell.

"So you're Marcus Azure," says the man as he rubs his clef chin. The man's hair is perfectly combed, his face is without flaw, and his Divine black and gold uniform is pristine. He introduces himself as Commander Petune and speaks quite proper.

"Mr. Marcus, where have you been this whole time?"

Based on his flawless appearance, I would never imagine this is the man behind such brutal torture and killing of the Yazu.

"Quite rude of you to come home and not say hello," Petune says. He walks inside the cell and each step is silent like that of an assassin. "Rizen tells me you tried to free my prisoners. Pity you didn't succeed. Now, you too can enjoy their suffering." Petune rolls up his sleeves and brushes his honey-blond hair away from his face. "Usually, I'm not in the mood, but on this rare occasion, I'll be fair. You parents have taken something from us. Tell me where they are and I promise to let you live."

My skin crawls at Petune's words. Regardless of what I say, I know this man is going to kill me. His light brown eyes scan my face in search for a hint of weakness.

"I don't know what you're talking about," I say firmly.

"Oh my, not the correct answer." Petune taps my forehead with his long finger. "You know, there are several death squads hunting your parents and it's up to you to prevent their demise."

Petune slings a well-polished knife from his belt and slices off my earlobe. Warm blood trickles down my neck. The urge to fight rises, but there's nothing I can do while restrained to the chair.

Petune slides to my left and whispers in my ear. "Last time I'll ask— where are your parents?" His voice alters from polite to maniacal. Placing his knife to the back of my other ear, he saws deep into my flesh, the jagged steel grinds midway through before he stops. His evil eyes can tell his torture has no effect on me. He casually leaves the cell and returns with a young Yazu boy. He pushes the kid to his knees and places the tip of his knife into the boy's ear.

"You want to save these people, here's your chance. Speak up or watch him die."

The boy looks up at me with eyes of fear, his lips quiver and his frail body shakes in despair. I can save him; all I have to do is speak up.

"They're in the northern lands," I blurt out. I hold my face tight to conceal the lie.

"Are you sure?" Petune asks, his gold dangling earring sways back and forth as he tilts his head.

"Yes, now let the boy go."

Petune shrugs. "Okay." He drills the knife through the child's ear and as the little boy's blood runs toward my boots, I turn cold in disbelief.

Petune flicks blood from his knife onto my face. "You're a terrible liar." His knife is now pressed onto my temple. How he knew I was lying is anyone's guess. Does he have the ability to read minds? Perhaps he can measure the pulse of others or maybe he doesn't know and simply waiting to see my reaction.

Rizen approaches the cell in a rush. His eyes are wide open. "Sir! Commander Shomari is coming," he says.

Petune quickly throws a wool hood over my head. "Not a word out of you," he hisses.

Unbeknownst to Petune, there's a small hole in the hood giving me limited vision.

"Stand down, Petune!" shouts a stern voice. A muscular man in his twenties enters the cell. His shoulders are broad like boulders and his chest is of pure muscle. Strange bright red tattoos flash from his swollen arms.

"How many times has the general warned you not to kill any more Yazu?" the man asks.

Petune clasps his manicured hands together. "Are you my little babysitter now, Shomari?" He gestures outside the cell. "There's still plenty of them left."

Shomari's cold steel eyes ignite with fire. "You're unhinged. You've been at this for months, yet produced zero results." Unlike Petune, Shomari's black hair is uncombed, he's in need of a shave and wears a rugged combat uniform.

Petune smirks. "I love it when you get angry. This is why the general trusts me and not a belligerent beast." Petune cups Shomari's cheek. "Don't worry, when I become king, I'll keep you around."

Shomari slaps Petune's hand away. "Now isn't the time for your drivel. We need to…" Shomari turns to me and cocks his head. "Who do we have here?"

Petune calmly approaches me and presses a knife to my side. "I'm trying something different with this one."

"Well, it must wait. General X has called for an emergency meeting at the Crossroads of Eden. Come now."

Petune snarls. "Yeah, yeah, I'll be there soon. Just let me tidy some things up first."

Wrinkles run along Shomari's wide forehead before leaving the cell. Petune removes my hood and kicks my chair over. He smears my face into the blood of the dead Yazu boy. "When I return, you'll tell me everything or I'll paint every crevice of this cell with your blood."

As blood saturates my eye lashes, I nod reluctantly and prepare for death.

Sibling Rivalry

Outside the prison and away from the prying eyes of onlookers, Petune and Shomari arrive at the Crossroads of Eden. The Crossroads is a small bluegrass field that sits just outside the Village of Eden. It's here where the Aypha and Amina borders meet. Apple trees hug along the Ayphas' side of the Crossroads while young pink rosebuds bloom on the Amina's end. Shomari takes a knee in the wet open field and applies a clear oil over the red inked tattoos on his arms. His right forearm is tattooed with a lion, his left is inked with a fowl. Once a week the tattoos blister over forcing Shomari to apply oil on them to soothe an itch. Meanwhile, the colorful Petune returns to his delightful self, enjoying the cloudless night sky and basking in the fragrance of apple trees. He picks up a fallen apple and examines it's rotten spots.

"Not all trees produce good fruit," says Petune. "Just because you're King Rayne's son doesn't guarantee the general will anoint you as king." Shomari ignores him and continues to rub oil on his arms. "Aypha needs someone with poise and intelligence, not rage and brawn." Petune throws the apple at Shomari who pulverizes it with one squeeze.

"A title and authority means nothing to me," grumbles Shomari. His mind elsewhere, he keeps his rage reserved for the man who killed his father.

The young men disengage in further conversation and several minutes pass before figures emerge from the Amina border. As darkness behind their silhouettes recede, the moonlight reveals three women of impeccable beauty. The first is the Amina Commander Ophelia. Her wavy hair is pinned back and her nose is as pointy as a bird's beak. Next to her is Commander Loreen, a tall, lanky woman who's the oldest of the three. Her long face is etched with many wrinkles, but still holds much grace. Lastly, is their leader, a short slender woman whose skin is rich with color. The lines of her face and body seemed to have been sculpted from the mold of art itself. She defines beauty and bears a striking resemblance to her sister Sinclair. She is Cynné Bonet, Queen of the Aminas.

As the Aminas approach Petune and Shomari, they immediately roll their eyes. There's an awkward pause before Cynné eventually speaks. "Care to explain why we're here?"

"Good seeing you as well," says Shomari. "We're here under the general's orders."

"Oh, that's right. I almost forgot you two are lapdogs for the old man. Always doing what the master tells you."

"Ah, Cynné, it's great to see you're still a thorn of annoyance buried beneath fingertips," quips Petune.

Civility will be sparse tonight. While Ayphas and Aminas are sibling partners, it's rare they get along. Years of backstabbing and in-fighting have caused a major rift between the two lands. Meetings are held infrequently, and when they occur, they usually turn into grand arguments.

Loreen brushes her silky gray hair behind her back. "May I remind you all, no matter our feelings toward each other, we must remain united if the Book of Pure is to be opened."

"Loreen, you're always the voice of reason," says Petune. He walks behind Loreen and licks his lips. "You know, if you were half your age, we could've been quite the couple." Petune rests his hands onto Loreen's shoulders and lightly squeezes.

Loreen runs her delicate fingers down Petune's chest and onto his crotch. She squeezes tight, and Petune's face lights red.

"When I was half your age, I devoured pups like you." Loreen gives a final twist before releasing her grip.

Petune licks the front of his unblemished teeth, tantalized by Loreen's ire. While the two continue to trade insults, Ophelia mumbles to herself. She's a mercurial woman, triggered by the slightest disturbances. She twitches often and talks to herself frequently. Second in command to Cynné, Ophelia is one of the strongest and most terrifying Aminas. Unfortunately, her strength is countered by her unhinged mind. In all cases of life, Ophelia prefers fighting over diplomacy.

"Shut up! Shut up! Shut up!" she shouts at Loreen and Petune. A strange woman, Ophelia's head is permanently cocked to the side. "This is stupid. Shomari, why are we here? Why has the general called us?" Hearing nothing, Ophelia flicks a pebble that hits Shomari's forehead.

Lucky for Ophelia, Shomari is uninterested in foolishness. His mind is elsewhere focused only on revenge. As the son of King Rayne, Shomari was born into Divine prestige. His father was a man of charisma who once led the Ayphas to victory in Great War II. A man of much knowledge and charm, the Ayphas practically worshiped King Rayne, that is until his life was ended by the hands of a Divine prodigy. Shomari has endured much tragedy, suppressing his rage, he holds onto a deep obsession to kill the legendary, Aikia of the Wind.

Ophelia claps her hands. "Ah, here comes the general now," she announces.

The Ayphas and Aminas place their hands over their hearts in respect for the ailing man. A survivor of three Great Wars, he too possesses much knowledge and wisdom. But with war comes consequences as the general has become a rugged and angered warrior. He is a Divine of apathy and has the patience of a bull, but his gruff persona shows why he is the leader of the Ayphas.

Once a formidable Divine, the general is now weak, and a strange illness has turned him sick and frail. His body is covered in red blotches that eat away his muscles. His time is near and what better way to close than by opening the Book of Pure.

Leaning heavy on his crooked cane, he limps toward the others as they form a circle around him.

"I take it everyone is reacquainted," the general says to the group. "Remember, as Ayphas and Aminas, we are like brothers and sisters. As kin, we will have our disagreements, but the common goal of opening the Book comes before all." Exhausted from just a few words, the general takes several deep breaths before continuing. "I've called this meeting because our plans are being threatened. Several weeks ago, the Shadow Clan attacked Armana in an unsuccessful attempt to free the Yazu. Unfortunately, they were successful in stealing the Eye of Truth."

Veins pop up along Cynné's temples. "What do you mean it was stolen?" she snaps. "We can't obtain the Phoenixes without the Eye!"

"That's why we're here." General X releases a wet cough and black phlegm oozes from his mouth. "Shomari, give us a status update."

Staring at the moist blades of grass at his boots, Shomari remains aloof, his mind still elsewhere. Plagued by the face of Aikia, he desperately wants to see it erased.

"Shomari give us your"—the general's voice turns hoarse— "give us an update."

"We believe the Eye is in the possession of a family," Shomari finally says. "A husband and wife named Saphron and Gail Azure are said to have killed one of our top commanders who secretly guarded the Eye. Intel suggests the Azures are the leaders of the Shadow Clan. Their son, Marcus Azure, is also suspected of being involved. Their whereabouts are currently unknown."

"So, what are you going to do?" asks a perturbed Cynné.

"We have death squads searching for the Azures, but so far they've turned up nothing," admits General X. "It's possible they're in the Valleys, and since you control the area, I need you to search for them."

Cynné scoffs. "You've lost the Eye and now need our help to find it. Even if we do, what good is it if we can't activate it?" Cynné fiddles with the gold decision coin her mother gave her. "The signs haven't told me yet, but I could move now and capture the Zells' key, with or without the Phoenixes."

"Ah, Cynné. So quick to speak without full thought," says Petune. "Concentrating your resources to fight the Zells leaves you vulnerable to your rivals. Who's to say once you start the war, the Dynas or Tynas won't come for you? You'll need the Phoenixes to defend against them."

Cynné sucks her teeth at the notion, but Petune is right. War always results in mass casualties, and Cynné will need to preserve her resources.

"Starting the war without the Phoenixes is unwise," says General X. "We must be prepared to take on all the Great Lands. The Eye is the key to everything. Without it, the Phoenixes are lost, and so too our plans for the Book."

"Fine, I'll help find the Eye but on two conditions," Cynné insists. "First, the Yazu must be handed over to me. It will do us no good to recover the Eye without knowing how to use it."

"You know that's my area," Petune protests. "Stick to what you're best at…killing off family."

Cynné grins. "You've had the Yazu in captivity for months, yet you have nothing to show for it. No leads, no new information, not a single clue of how to activate the Eye."

General X strokes his frizzled gray beard. "Hmm, Cynné's criticism is valid. Petune has failed to deliver. Perhaps it's time for a change."

"But, sir! They're resistant and beyond strong-minded people. They're like cactuses, unrelenting no matter how oppressive the drought."

"Colorful words don't make up for failure," snips the general.

"But, sir…"

"Enough! Cynné, you get your request. The Yazu are yours."

"I'm not done," says Cynné. "If I uncover how to activate the Eye, I want the first pick of a Phoenix."

General X taps his cane and briefly pauses before agreeing.

"But, sir!" pleads Petune. "You're giving her too much control."

"Time is precious, Petune. My legacy is at stake."

Ophelia leans against General X. "Seems you're relying on us a lot more now," she taunts. "It's almost as if we should be the ones dictating the plan."

General X whispers something so dreadful in Ophelia's ear, her silly smile fades and the color in her face drains to the soles of her feet.

"Here's the plan," announces the general. "The Aminas will join us in the search for the Eye. Cynné, you work with Shomari to transition the Yazu from our prison to one of yours."

Petune raises his pointer finger. "Sir, may I propose a slight alteration? Give me a couple more days with the prisoners. I'm on the verge of something special."

"No," rebuffs General X. "Effective immediately, you're relieved of your duties."

Petune bows his head. "Absolutely, sir…you are the general after all."

Reunion

As Cynné and her commanders return to Amina territory, a messenger approaches and bows before them.

"My lady, Defense Squad Four reports seeing two cloaked individuals traveling east through the Land of Beta. How do you wish to proceed?"

Cynné smiles with glee. "See that?" She grabs Loreen by the arm. "Destiny is already in our favor. I bet it's the Azures. Loreen, quickly prepare a team for an intercept mission."

Loreen frowns. "You know my squads are best suited for defensive ops, not search and destroy."

Cynné kisses her teeth. "I'm aware. That's why you'll use one of Ophelia's teams."

Mumbling at first, Ophelia breaks out in protest. "Then why is this not my mission?"

Cynné waves off Ophelia. "This mission is more about finesse than death." Cynné snaps her fingers calling for the messenger. "Have Rose Cross gather her team and report to my mansion."

Bowing to her queen, the messenger leaves in search of Rose.

"I should be leading this mission," repeats Ophelia. The veins along her forehead pulsate with anger.

Cynné runs her fingers through Ophelia's gritty hair. "Your time will come. For now, you are to stay here and watch over the capital."

Ophelia grinds her bloodstained teeth. "Fine, my lady, but you shouldn't give me such boring tasks. You know you can trust me."

"I do," says Cynné. "Still, Loreen is better suited for a specific reason."

Stretching out her crooked neck, Ophelia cocks her head sideways. "Guess being old has its privileges."

Ophelia breaks away and heads home while the others proceed to the pink rose garden behind Cynne's mansion. A short while later, Rose, Nova, and Russina arrive.

Having the girls stand in a row, Cynné caresses their faces, admiring their luck. In her mind, surviving against Kissandra makes them special.

"My beauties, I want you to accompany Commander Loreen on an intercept mission. Your targets are likely Gail and Saphron Azure of Eden."

Rose's ears perk when she hears the name Azure.

"The Azures have stolen a precious item from us, and I need it back. Your objective is to recover what is known as the Eye of Truth."

Loreen pulls Cynné to the side. "You're not serious about using these girls, are you? They're novices and ill-prepared for such a critical mission."

"Fear not, these girls will bring you good luck," boasts Cynné. "I can feel it in the atmosphere."

Loreen's cold stare could freeze a cauldron of flames. "I don't believe in your superstitions and I'd rather do this on my own. These girls could get themselves killed."

"Nonsense!" snips Cynné. "These girls are destined for greatness. I know it."

Loreen's gray eyebrows rise. "Destined?"

"Indeed. These young ladies have fought my mother and have lived to tell about it. If that's not a sign of destiny, I don't know what is."

Loreen leans closer to Cynné. "Why didn't you tell me about Kissandra?"

"I'm telling you now. Not too long ago, these girls encountered her in the Valleys of Hope. It's possible she's still there, and that's why I need you for this mission." Cynné examines one of her most delicate pink rose bushes. "If there's anyone she won't kill, it's you."

Loreen sighs heavily. "More reason I should do this alone. These girls lack experience."

Cynné cuts three roses from her bush and strips them of their thorns. "What better way to gain experience than this?" She slides the roses behind the ears of the young Aminas.

Loreen grimaces at having to lead such novices. A tactician, she's a survivor of war not because of her strength but through wisdom and logic. She knows this is a bad idea, but Cynné is queen and she's just an old lady.

Loreen turns to the girls. "Alright you three, pack a bag we head out in thirty."

"I have to bow out of this mission," says Rose while grabbing her stomach. Though her wounds have healed some pain is unforgettable. "I'm still a little rattled from my last mission."

Loreen nearly scratches out the last of her gray eyebrows. "Great, anyone else a liability?"

Nova sneers at Loreen's jab. "Russina and I are prepared to go," she says with eagerness.

"That's what I like to hear!" shouts Cynné. "Use this opportunity to learn from one of the best." Cynné places her hand on Loreen's shoulder. "Be cautious. You aren't as young as you use to be."

Loreen stares at Cynné's hand with disbelief. "To think the girl I helped raise is giving me advice is a sign of the times. Don't you worry. This old lady will be fine."

Given their orders, Loreen leaves with her team while Rose Cross stays behind. Her head lowered, she stares at the creases along her leather boots.

"I'm disappointed in you," says Cynné as she tends to her rose garden. "Last time we spoke, you said if it was my will, it shall be done. Yet when the opportunity arises, you cower."

Rose's feet curl inside her boots. "I've failed you already my queen, please forgive me."

Cynné snips a red vine off a bush and approaches Rose. "When a queen tells you to do something, it's not an option it's an order." Cynné wraps the vine around Rose's arm, thorns break into her flesh. "You owe me one. Don't ever disappoint me again."

The Mission

Within the northern forest hills of Beta, Loreen hunkers high atop an oak tree. Alongside her is Nova, Russina, and a Divine Amina named Sky who was from Ophelia's command. The four Aminas are camouflaged in green leaves that perfectly match the tree canopy. From their aerial vantage, they can monitor the winding trails that lead to the Valleys of Hope. It is here the team plans to intercept the Azures and recover the Eye. Soon to go completely silent, Loreen provides her final instructions.

"Listen up, our objective is very simple. Once our targets arrive, we'll neutralize them using clear water rose petals."

From her sleeve, Loreen reveals several twisted rose petals with sharp tips. "These petals can knock out anyone upon direct contact. We'll use them to immobilize our targets. Once they're incapacitated, we'll move in and recover the Eye, understand?"

The girls nod. Loreen gives Nova a few clear water rose petals and a wooden shooter. "Since there's multiple targets, we'll need to launch a synchronized attack. I'll be on the other side of the trail. When I raise my hand, that's the signal to strike. Got it?"

"Absolutely," says Nova. Her eyes light bright in hopes of impressing Loreen.

"We'll only get one chance, so don't miss." Loreen turns to Russina and Sky. "You two, your job is even easier. In the event your position is compromised or something goes awry, you are to flee and alert the other Aminas."

Though not exactly the roles they were expecting, the two nod in unison.

With the mission set, Loreen leaps to another tree on the opposite side of the trail. Positioned directly across from Nova and the others, she conceals herself within the leaves and settles on a sturdy branch.

For hours, the Aminas wait patiently in silence. Bugs crawl along their skin and sweat stings their eyes. It isn't until the sun shines above them that a short woman wearing a blue silk mask appears around the bend of a dirt trail.

Seeing the woman's stature, Loreen is relieved it isn't Kissandra. Still a dilemma exists. Is this a target or not? There was supposed to be two of them.

Across the trail, up in the canopies, Nova salivates. She wraps her hand around the wooden shooter, the clear water rose is primed for release. She waits for Loreen's signal, but it never comes. As the masked woman passes by, Nova inexplicably unloads the clear water rose petal. A perfect shot. But the petal goes straight through the woman. Thinking Nova missed, Loreen shoots her petal, yet it too passes through the woman.

The masked woman comes to a halt and scans the trees.

"I know you're there!" she shouts. "Why hide behind leaves and cower within branches? COME FACE ME!"

Shaking her head from the other side, Loreen orders the girls not to engage. She knows that voice—it's a familiar one, from a distant past. But in her old age, she struggles to remember who.

"Are you afraid? Shall I come up there and hang you?" taunts the masked woman.

"Russina, Sky, back me up," Nova whispers.

"We're to retreat," responds Sky. "That was our order."

Nova weighs the risk but thoughts of glory tempt her to lean closer.

"Cowards!" mocks the masked woman. "Only the weak hide."

Nova cannot resist such taunting words. On impulse, she springs from the trees and lands before the short woman. Like sheep, both Russina and Sky follow, leaping from their positions. But while the three girls reveal themselves, Loreen remains hidden. Something about the woman's voice stops her from doing anything irrational.

On the ground, Nova, Russina, and Sky form a triangle trap around the woman.

"You call us cowards, yet you hide behind a mask," says Nova. "Who are you?"

The masked woman chuckles. "I'm just an imagination, one you shouldn't have bothered."

"Real or fake, you're trespassing on Amina territory."

"Trespassing? The Land of Beta belongs to no one."

"It does now," says Nova.

Underneath her robe, the masked woman grabs the handle of her blade. "Typical Amina arrogance. Disgracing the Doctrine like that! You all should be burned and forgotten."

Nova grinds her teeth, she can sense the threat. "Oro release!" she yells, her arm violently shakes before a bright yellow Orosphere forms in her hand. She rushes forward, but the woman zigs around her and sprints toward Russina. The woman unleashes her thin blade but Russina leans back just enough to avoid her throat from being slashed.

Sky releases an Orosphere, but the masked woman quickly leaps away and lands in front of Nova. Nova releases her Orosphere only for the woman to absorb it with her hand.

"You're a Zell!" says a stunned Nova.

"Indeed, and you three are dead."

Realizing what they're up against, the Aminas charge their Orospheres with so much energy, the spheres cause the atmosphere to become unstable, and the ground itself begins to crack.

The masked woman darts into the forest. As she weaves around trees, the trio follow in pursuit, cornering her at every turn. Converging around the woman, the girls trap her from different angles. In unison they release their hot Orospheres, and just as their strikes connect, the woman disappears, leaving nothing but a trace of white smoke in the air.

Perplexed, the Aminas scan the area. Behind them, stands the mysterious Zell. Before they can react, she reappears behind Russina decapitating her with a single slash. Fresh blood is still in the air when the woman appears behind Sky, the Amina is split evenly in half. The ruthless woman then spawns in front of Nova, and swings at her throat, only for Loreen to intervene. While Nova is safe, a deep cut now stretches across Loreen's back.

Nova hyperventilates. "Who is she? I—I—I couldn't even react." Her teeth won't stop chattering.

Touching her bloody back, Loreen examines her injury. "She is Queen of the Zells, Annabelle the Ghost."

"Loreen, you old biddie. Has the sun touched you with a ray of insanity?" says the prideful Annabelle as she removes her mask.

"Nova, get back," orders Loreen.

"Yes, little girl. Run for your pitiful life," echoes Annabelle.

Nova's legs fearfully shake to the point she must crawl away. Passing by the headless Russina and the divided Sky, she tries her best not to cry.

Annabelle wipes Amina blood from her blade and points it at Loreen. "So, are you here to kill me?"

Loreen doesn't respond. Her eyes fixed on Annabelle, she calculates her odds of survival.

"What is this about? You're too old not to speak," taunts Annabelle.

"You were not our intended target. The girls made a grave mistake," says Loreen. "You've proven your point. Now continue with your travels."

Annabelle chuckles. "Loreen, you and I both know this is where you shall die."

Streams of Oro suddenly swirl around Loreen as a burnt-orange hole appears in her chest. Like a spark of fire, an orange mist of Oro covers Loreen's body. Her eyes are the color of the sun, and dark orange Orospheres fill her hands.

"I'm warning you, Annabelle, I will not simply lie down and admit defeat."

The Ghost smirks. "What a hollow threat. Who said I'd even allow that?"

Loreen's Orospheres intensify. "Walk away. There's no need for this. As you can see, I have a mess to clean up."

"Don't worry. I'll clean up after you." Annabelle vanishes and reappears beside Loreen, stabbing her in her stomach. Instinctively, Loreen's devastating Orospheres ignite and explode, ripping Annabelle's body apart. There's a smile on Annabelle's face as her remains fizzle into white smoke.

"You did it, commander! You killed her," says a relieved Nova.

"No, child," says Loreen as she clenches her bloody stomach. Feeling lethargic, she contemplates retirement recognizing her step isn't as quick as it once was. As her wounds heal, she approaches Nova and slaps her with great force. A purple bruise instantly appears on Nova's cheek.

"If you ever disobey me again, I swear, I will kill you myself!" shouts Loreen.

Nova cradles her cheek. "Sorry, commander, I was just going off instincts."

"What did instincts get you…two of our own are dead, and if I hadn't intervened, you too would be a headless corpse."

Looking at her deceased teammates, tears threaten to spill from the corners of Nova's eyes. Not out of sympathy for her teammates, but she knows she's lost her chance at becoming a team leader.

"By the time I blinked they were already dead," says Nova. "Never have I seen power like hers."

Loreen nods. "Scary, isn't she? I've fought many Zells in my lifetime but none like Annabelle. Most Zells have three distinct Legacy techniques: the power to absorb raw energy, the power to control water, and the ability to perceive time in slow motion. But Annabelle is different. She's taken time perception to another level where she can fool even our perceptions of her existence."

Nova rubs her forehead, confused.

"We were fighting a past image of her," says Loreen. "Attacking her in the present is no better than striking air itself. That is why she is called the *GHOST*!"

"If that's true, how can a past image kill in the present?"

Loreen shrugs. "Some say she's a dead woman with a soul that refuses to die. True or not, what I do know is her Legacy is uncanny, for she has single-handedly slayed entire Divine armies. That woman will be our biggest challenge when the time comes to battle the Zells."

Nova shuffles her feet hoping to shake out her unease. "What now?"

Loreen scoops dirt from the ground and passes it to Nova. "First, you're going to give your teammates a proper burial. Their deaths shall not be in vain. When you're done, we'll return home and regroup…war may be coming sooner than we think."

Crow Spit

"CROW SPIT! I should've never trusted you!" shouts an angry Annabelle. Pissed off at being discovered by the Aminas, Annabelle is none too pleased with Sinclair.

"Honestly, Annabelle, I had no idea they would be there," says Sinclair. "Besides, why would I want them to kill you? If anyone should have the honor of killing the Ghost, it shall be me."

Now in the Land of Dyna resides Sinclair, Valencia, and a furious Annabelle. The three gather beneath Valencia's mansion in a cavern where stalagmites and stalactites appear like milky icicles. The air is damp and restless red-eye bats hover above.

"You're a liar," shouts Annabelle. "This was a targeted attack led by Loreen Lydon. Why would she be in the Valleys unless she knew of my travels?"

Sinclair examines her polished fingernails all to avoid eye contact. "Pure coincidence," she says. "Either way, you're here and so are we. All of us seek the same goal of stopping the Ayphas and Aminas."

Annabelle stands nose to nose with Sinclair. "Have you forgotten, you're an Amina yourself?"

With Annabelle's lips inches away, Sinclair considers kissing her. Not out of attraction, just to infuriate her.

Sinclair steps back. "Seems you've forgotten my title as the traitor of the Aminas. As I've said before, it's not about me or you—it's about keeping balance in the world. Let us settle our past differences and work together. It's the only way we'll survive."

"It's amazing, now that you're no longer a queen, you advocate for unity," scoffs Annabelle.

While the two continue to bicker, Valencia Victoria says nothing. Frustrated by the two, she regrets agreeing to this meeting. The old

Valencia would never have put up with this, but her lack of confidence forces her to rely on others.

"We're willing to loan several Dyna Divines to help protect your land against the Aminas," offers Sinclair.

"At what cost?" asks an incensed Annabelle. "Generous offers have consequences, especially when dealing with you."

"In exchange for our help, all we need you to do is protect a young boy."

Annabelle's eyebrows curl at the odd request. "Valencia, what do you really want?"

"We need you to protect the boy. It's that simple," repeats Sinclair.

"I'm not talking to you," snaps Annabelle. "Valencia?"

Valencia wraps her hand onto a stalagmite. "You know, I don't particularly care for either of you." She breaks off the tip of the stalagmite and crumbles it into her palms. "But facts are facts. The Ayphas and Aminas are a threat to the sacredness of the Book. We must work together or risk being dismantled one by one. I know its unusual, but you should hear Sinclair out."

Annabelle grumbles and turns to Sinclair. "Who is this boy?"

"His name is Marcus Azure, a Divine Aypha. His parents are close friends of mine and have asked me to protect him. Unfortunately, I no longer can."

"Why?"

Sinclair purses her lips. "He doesn't trust me."

Annabelle grins. "As no one should. But surely you could find someone else to protect him. Why me?"

"You're the best fit. He needs to be in the hands of someone we can trust. Beyond that, it's a simple and fair agreement."

Annabelle places her fingers over Sinclair's lips. "Your greatest weapon has always been your mouth. Saying it's simple and fair are words you should never utter. Nothing is such with you."

Sinclair licks Annabelle's fingers. "You're salty," she says and spits on Annabelle's boots. "Like I said, it's a simple and fair exchange. You protect him, and we'll give you what you need to defend against the Aminas."

Annabelle stares at her reflection off a mud puddle. Her options are limited. She desperately needs help to protect her Zells, but dealing with the unscrupulous Sinclair is unsettling.

"Fine, we have a deal. For a hundred Dyna Divines, I'll protect this young boy."

"The great seas will dry before I allow that," interjects Valencia. "I refuse to place so many women in harm's way. I'll loan you twenty-five Divines."

"Twenty-five isn't sufficient."

"Indeed, it is. A single Dyna can handle what three of your Zells can do."

"At a minimum, I need seventy-five just to protect our borders," concedes Annabelle. "The Aminas are constantly looking for weaknesses in our defenses."

Valencia draws her lips tight. "Twenty-five is all you'll get."

"How about fifty," proposes Sinclair.

Valencia slams her hand into the ground causing multiple stalactites to descend all around Sinclair. "Be mindful of who rules who," says Valencia.

Weaving out of the cluster stalactites, Sinclair claps in admiration.

"This is the Valencia I know! Forgive me, my lady. I'm simply proposing something temporary."

Disdain crawls across Valencia's face. "Annabelle, why are you here? Why don't you just announce an alliance with the Kamaras? I'm sure Aikia and his young men would love to go to war with the Ayphas."

Annabelle stares at the bats above. "Things are complicated between us. Aikia doesn't see the need for partnerships."

"Pity," says Valencia. "I'll make you an offer. I'll loan you a hundred Dynas on the condition you protect the boy *and* you give me your key to the Book of Pure."

Annabelle laughs at the audacious request. "Why would I do such a silly thing when the intention of defending my land is to protect the key?"

"No, your priority is to preserve common life in Zell, and I'm willing to help. But I need assurances that if you do fail, the Aminas gain nothing."

Annabelle huffs having to choose between her people and her pride. "You've always been honorable, Valencia, but Sinclair is not of similar cloth. She's a dingy and mangled rag. How can I entrust you with my key when everything coming from Sinclair reeks of deception?"

"I can hear you," says Sinclair. She grabs one of the frenzied bats from the air. "You know, after studying these creatures, I've noticed that they lack good vision. Kind of like you, Annabelle. You can't see beyond today. In the long run, where will you be if we do not unite?"

Annabelle snatches the squirming bat from Sinclair. "You forgot another observation." She rips off the bat's wings and tosses it at Sinclair's feet. "If a bat has no wings, it becomes nothing but a blind rat willing to do anything to survive. Fitting of you, wouldn't you agree?"

"My, you two could trade wit for wit all night," says Valencia. "But enough nonsense. Annabelle, you can trust me with your key. Besides, if Sinclair steals it, you're more than welcome to kill her. Deal?"

"Deal," says Annabelle. "For a hundred worthy Dyna Divines, I will temporarily relinquish our key as well as protect this Marcus kid. Now where is he?"

"Unfortunately he's not here, but don't worry, I'll get him to you," says Sinclair.

With cold stares, the three know their partnership is as strong as a dying dandelion on a windy day. But they don't have a choice; they all need each other. Their commitments will either lead to unity or treachery. War with the Ayphas and Aminas is approaching, and with it comes pain and sorrow. In this world, war has always been a necessary evil, but one must be careful for allies do not always stay the same.

Valencia extends her hand to break the tension, and as the trio shake hands, a sense of relief comes over them. They work out the details of their agreement, and as Annabelle prepares to leave, she delivers a final shot.

"Oh, Sinclair, one last thing. I know there's something you're not telling me about this boy. Just so we're clear, if you cross me, I'll kill him no matter who he is."

Sinclair smiles. "Annabelle, I'm hurt you still don't trust me. That's nothing but paranoia getting to you. Please be careful on your way home. I hear there's a ghost on the loose."

Forever Friends

MARCUS

Cloudy water drips from the ceiling of my prison cell while hairless vermin squirm on the floor and nip away at my ankles. Chained to a chair, I tug away, but the heavy shackles won't break. Time isn't on my side. Soon, Petune will return. He seeks my parents, he wants the Eye, but he shall not have it. I will die here before giving in to that man.

Staring at the rusted cell bars; the thought of dying in such a decrepit place turns depressing. Again, I tug at the shackles but to no avail. Even with Divine power, there's limitations to my strength. Trapped in solitude, separated from Asher and the Yazu, I pray their spirits are in a better place than mine.

Hours pass before Darius arrives to my cell. Not saying a word, he uses a jagged key and removes the shackles from my bruised wrists and ankles.

"Thanks," I say.

Grief pollutes Darius's eyes. He slides down in the corner of the cell and asks me to take a seat.

"I'm going to miss him," he says, referring to his dad. "We were just starting to become close, ya know." Darius, like other Divines from Eden, rarely saw their fathers. Most fathers were too busy fighting for Aypha leaving them little time to bond with their children.

"I remember how excited he was, when I first came to Aypha," continues Darius as he stares at the slick stone ceiling above. "He taught me how to fight, how to use my Legacy, and showed me what a true Divine is all about." From his pocket, Darius reveals a black mask with a gold lion pattern stitched into the satin fabric. "Before his passing, he gave this to me. He told me it's a lucky mask that has been passed down from one father to the next." Darius examines the mask. "I wonder if he had this when your parents attacked, would he still be alive?"

A heavy sigh seeps slowly from my mouth. "Your father was a great man, Darius. You are his legacy and I'm certain he's proud of what you've become." A knot of guilt burns in the back of my throat as I struggle to continue. "I'm sorry for what my parents have done. But please, don't take this out on me."

Darius taps the metal bars on the cell gate. He seems dissatisfied in my response, but he deserves to know the truth.

"Listen, Darius, there's something you should know about Aypha. There's a plot being led by people like Petune to use the Yazu for evil. My parents tried to stop this evil and as a result blood has been spilled."

Darius tightly squeezes his father's mask. "Unbelievable. You're still trying to justify your parents' actions. One of the last things my father said to me was to always honor Aypha. It is a Divine's mission to protect this land till the last drop of blood leaves our body." Darius ties the mask around his neck and slips it over his nose. "I will honor his wishes and protect this land from threats like you."

Darius rises to his feet as do I. Rolling up my sleeve, I show him my inner bicep. Tattooed on it are the initials *FF*. "Remember the day you were called to join the Ayphas? Remember what we agreed to no matter what?" The same initials are inked on Darius and Asher.

Darius looks away. "We made a pact. Forever friends."

"That's right. You, Asher, and I agreed to always have each other's backs. I'm still honoring that pact, but you have to trust me." I extend my hand to Darius. "What if I told you your allegiance to this land leads to the death of thousands? Would you still follow the path?"

Darius leans closer and slaps my hand away. "Not only would I follow, I'd lead the way." Darius's voice is pure ice. "We vowed to protect Aypha and bleed to keep it safe from foreign and domestic threats. No matter how you twist it, your parents are criminals. They've taken away the tree of my life and for that, I will kill them."

My jaw tightens in alarm. "I can't let you do that. I can't allow you to harm my family."

Darius rips off his shirt and flexes his muscles. "When we fought earlier, I held back, thinking you were weak. It didn't dawn on me till afterward that you're no longer a Norm. Somehow, you've become a Divine, and knowing this, my conscience is clean."

Darius lunges forward, tackling me onto the slick stone floor. We wrestle, thrash, and bash one another until our fight empties into the prison hallway. Regaining my footing, I catch Darius with a hard-right hook causing him to stagger.

"Your anger blinds you from the truth," I say, hoping my words still have meaning to my friend. "The Ayphas have enslaved, tortured, and killed innocent people. Wake up, Darius, this isn't right!"

Darius spits blood from his mouth. "You still speak like a broken Norm. Sometimes, evil must be done. Doesn't matter how heinous we become—allegiance to Aypha is above all. Those who break this pledge must be eradicated."

"Then eradicate me first!" says a familiar voice.

Standing behind Darius is the beautifully crafted Rikari Niacin. She wears a black cloak and possesses an eerie smile laced with death.

Darius turns and sizes up Rikari. "And who are you?"

"A dream killer." Rikari unties her cloak, revealing a gold fox symbol on her tightly woven undershirt. She sidesteps Darius, but he snatches her by the wrist.

"Stay out of this or I shall dig two graves tonight." Darius tightens his grip on Rikari.

Her insidious smile widens. "Be careful, kid. You're about to reach the same destiny as your father." Her savage words spark the ugly in Darius. But before he can act...

"Impressive!" claps Petune as he and Rizen approach from the end of the dim lit hallway. Petune takes note of Rikari's gold fox emblem. "What an honor to meet an Absolute Commander. Seems you're out of place though."

Rikari scans Petune's meticulous appearance and perfectly combed hair. "You must be the dandelion Commander Petune," she says. "Intel books describe you as a man of immaculate self-absorption. Appears the report was accurate."

Petune releases a haughty laugh. "Oh my, you're a gem. Seems you know much about me, yet I know so little of you." He snaps his fingers. "Rizen, Darius, please handle Marcus while I indulge with this adorable Dyna."

As Petune and Rikari clash, Rizen and Darius dash toward me. Doing an about-face, I bolt down the hall, and zip around a few corners until reaching a dead end.

"C'mon, coward, at least go out like a soldier," says Rizen as they catch up to me. He nudges Darius. "End him."

Darius looks me in the eye and hesitates. Beyond the hate and anger, perhaps he still sees his old friend.

Rizen frowns. "Darius, what are you waiting for? Punishment must be delivered." Rizen moves into a fighting stance. "If you don't kill him, I will. Just hope this fight won't be as pitiful as the last one."

He thinks I'm weak. The same arrogant grin Rizen flaunted on the day of trials he shows now. I was pathetic back then. Powerless. But I'm no longer that person. I have Awakened and will show him what I've become.

I swing at Rizen to erase his face. While my punches are swift, Rizen avoids them with ease. Frustrated, I release a fury of strikes and catch Rizen with a shot to his chin.

"Lucky one," says Rizen as he checks for blood. He counters with a barrage of swift strikes; each I avoid much to his surprise. All the training Sinclair put me through has made me agile and elusive. But Rizen is relentless. He strikes me in the chest causing my lungs to collapse. Wheezing, I bend over and catch a knee to my nose. Blood splatters on the cold stone floor. Two swift jabs cause the vision in my right eye to vanish.

Countering his strikes, I connect with a combination of punches. Rizen stumbles. Now's my chance to finish him. I release an uppercut, but Rizen catches my fist mid-swing.

"You've Awakened, but you're still weak," says Rizen. "To know that you have Divine blood brings shame to the Aypha name. You don't deserve such power." Rizen squeezes my fist, popping and breaking my fingers. I drop to one knee. My face burns, blood collects before me, and everything around me begins to swirl.

"What a disgrace." Rizen clamps harder onto my fist.

Have some pride. Don't go out like this, I say to myself. I think of Asher, Free, and Yondi. They need me. If I die now, what shall happen to them? By my resolve, I will protect them. I pry my hand loose from Rizen's grip, and there's an incredulous look on his face as I proudly stand tall before him.

"No longer am I a garbage boy. I am your equal!" I yell.

With all the wraith of pain within me, I unload a thunderous kick and break Rizen's jaw.

Rizen smiles as blood spills from his lips. "Like I said, a disgrace." He palms me by the head and shoves me into the wall. Immediately, I enter into an oh-so-familiar place.

From the darkness, Rose calls out my name as a shimmering ball of light appears over her. For the first time, I can see her beautiful face. I reach out for her hand, but her image disappears and is replaced by a silhouette of Sinclair Bonet.

"WHAT DO YOU WANT?" I shout.

"Happiness will only get you so far," she says. "With anger, you can be so much more. Become who you are." Sinclair plucks my forehead, sending my body into shock. Awakened from my dream, I'm filled with vigor, my body is healed and my eyesight has been restored. Rizen is shocked as I rise to my feet, his eyes nearly pop from their sockets.

"Embrace the anger," Sinclair's voice echoes.

I clutch my temples, squeezing my eyes shut. "Get out of my head!" I yell.

Rizen grabs me by the throat. "Who are you talking to?" He pounds away at my face...yet his strikes have no feeling.

"Become who you are, Dark Raven," says the voice of Sinclair. "Kill him."

Balling up my fists, rage fills my veins. With a single punch, I send Rizen backward into a wall.

"This ends now," wheezes Rizen. "ORO RELEASE!"

A magnificent yellow sphere gleams in Rizen's hand like the light of a boiling sun. This is the Divine Legacy of the Ayphas and Aminas. The ability to destroy flesh and bone on contact. As his Orosphere shines with blinding light, I brace myself. And then it happens. Rizen's Orosphere explodes...

A thunderous boom ripples through the hallways. Yet, I'm alive. There's a huge smoking hole where a prison wall once was. Darius is clenching Rizen's forearm.

"Marcus is not your battle," says Darius. "Do not take away my vengeance."

"Then kill him now," says Rizen. "Otherwise, you'll regret it."

Darius looks at me. Hate burns in his eyes. He wants to kill, but something pulls him back.

"Commander Petune needs him alive. Once he's done with him, Marcus is mine," says Darius.

Suddenly, alarm bells ring from above. Rikari races down the hallway. Her right arm is wounded and her face is bruised. "Marcus, we must go!" she shouts.

Still in shock of nearly dying, it takes a moment for me to gather my words. "No, we can't, not till we save Asher and the Yazu."

Rikari places her hand on the smoking hole in the wall and forms a metal tunnel. "There isn't enough time. We'll come back for them."

"DARIUS, RIZEN, COME WITH ME!" A bloody Petune shouts from the end of the hallway. "YOU THERE, MARCUS. Return the Eye or I'll kill them all!"

Grabbing my arm, Rikari shoves me into the tunnel, and as the hole closes, the last image I see are the cold stares of Darius and Rizen. Swiftly, Rikari and I race through the tunnel, and as we hit the surface, fresh air fills our lungs. It's still dark but dawn is approaching. We quickly sprint across open farmland and disappear into the nearest forest. Scrambling through a patch of sticky plants and tall trees we run nonstop until reaching an area of divergent paths.

"What's wrong?" I ask as we come to a halt.

Rikari's hand latches tight around my arm. "I can feel them," she says. "Aypha Divines are coming from every direction, and they're closing in."

"Which way should we go?" My pulse now beats like a steady drum.

Rikari cracks her neck. "Doesn't matter. Prepare yourself for battle. Your life is on the line."

I Shall Return

MARCUS

The Ayphas are on the hunt. Rikari and I feverishly sprint through a lush forest trying to outrun them. Soon the sun will rise, making us easy targets. As we hurdle fallen trees and splash into mud puddles, nostalgia comes over me. Once again, I'm running away from everything I know and love. Then again, everything I once loved is no more. My parents are traitors, Asher is as good as dead, and Darius will forever despise me.

We halt at the edge of a steep cliff and wait for dawn. Somewhere in the forest below is a hidden tunnel that will lead us across the Aypha border.

Life begins anew as the morning glory sun shines over the misty treetops. Birds chirp and tiny creatures chatter among themselves. The sound of life is refreshing yet my spirit feels terrible having to leave Asher and the Yazu.

"I can't do this again," I say, clenching my teeth. "I have to go back for them."

Rikari scans the trees below. "We will. But right now, I'm just trying to keep us alive." Rikari slides onto a protruding rock that overlooks the forest. She points to an area where the treetops are already in a fall bloom. "The tunnel is right there," she says. "But before we can claim it, there's something we must handle. YOU TWO CAN COME OUT NOW."

Behind us, emerge two Aypha Divines from the forest.

The Ayphas form Orospheres. Rikari thrusts her hands into the ground causing silver spikes to erect at the feet of the Ayphas. They dodge the spikes and launch their Orospheres. Rikari forms a silver pillar shielding us from the explosion. Smoke gathers around us. Something wraps around my leg and drags me from Rikari. One of the Ayphas has pulled me into the forest by wrapping a shiny rope around my leg.

Digging my hands into the dirt, I try to slow down the momentum, but it's no use. I fiddle with my belt, reach for my dagger, and slice the rope. There's a hiss. The rope uncurls and reveals itself to be a snake. Oddly, the snake has the ability to reconnect to its severed body.

I spring to my feet, but blood rushes to my head causing me to stumble under my own weight.

The Aypha approaches with his snake coiled around his arm. He towers over me with a devious smile. I scoop a handful of dirt and throw it in his eyes. He rears back, and I stab him in the foot with my dagger. I hobble to my feet but take no more than five steps before his snake strikes my leg. After collapsing on the ground, I try prying the snake away, only to realize something.

The irritated Aypha pulls the dagger from his foot and limps toward me. "Let's not do this the hard way," he says as his wound begins to heal. "Soon your whole body will begin to swell, and you're going to die unless I give you an antivenom. If you want to live, tell me why is the Dyna helping you?"

Coughing and dry heaving, I can only whisper.

"Speak up," says the Aypha.

I whisper again, but the Aypha cannot hear me. He moves closer, a mistake, for I shove the snake's fangs into the side of his neck. Stumbling backward, the Aypha screams and begins convulsing.

Now it is I standing over the soldier. I'm unscathed by the snake's bite as it had only bitten into the leather of my boot. While the Aypha's face and neck swells, I pick his pockets for the antivenom.

"You win, kid. But what now?" gurgles the man. "You really going to let me die?" Tears moisten in the corners of his eyes. I should but he doesn't deserve it. He's an Aypha like me, just trying to do his job to protect the land. I toss him the vial which he quickly drinks, stopping the spread of the poison.

"Thank you, thank you for your mercy." The Aypha breathes heavy. He lies on his back, broken of pride. I start my walk back to Rikari, but stop when I hear the spark of Oro.

Turning to face the Aypha, he clutches a dreadful Orosphere.

"Fool," he hisses as the yellow sphere intensifies. "A battle is never over until one is dead." Laughing, he aims the sphere at me. But his eyes suddenly go dark and his Orosphere dissipates. A silver spike protrudes through the back of his head, and as his body slowly slides down the spike, footsteps approach from behind.

"Hope you've learned a lesson," says Rikari, wiping blood from her forehead. "In the Divine world, compassion and mercy are strangers to us all. Never show empathy to an opponent. Not only is it weak, it's a death sentence."

Staring at the bloody man, I'm at a loss for words. To survive, must I become this ruthless?

"You lack natural killer instincts," Rikari says with displeasure. "You're a pup with no bite."

"If I had to, I would've killed him," I say, trying to convince myself.

Rikari approaches the dead Aypha and lifts up his bloodstained head. "You certain? Remember this face. It's death, and you'll see it many times if you want to survive. You're a Divine now. Everyone is your enemy. The path you walk will not be filled with sunshine and blue skies. Ahead lie dark clouds and raindrops of red."

"I understand," I say while turning away from the Aypha. I take out Rikari's map in search of Chance Island, spotting its location off the coast of Zell.

"You don't need that; I know how to get us home."

"I'm not going back to Dyna. I've seen what evil looks like and I understand why my parents stole the Eye of Truth."

Rikari gives me an incredulous look. "Your parents... have the Eye?"

"Yes, and with them are other members of the Shadow Clan. Together, we can devise a strategy to free Asher and the Yazu."

Rikari frowns. "Think we should tell Sinclair?"

I pause, uncertain of Sinclair's motives. "No, something tells me my parents don't trust her."

Rikari shrugs. "No one would argue that."

PART 3

The Hunt

Alarm bells continue to ring inside the Ayphas' prison. Petune, Darius, and Rizen tip around puddles of blood as several prison guards lie scattered across the halls.

"The Dyna killed them," says Petune.

Soon an Aypha response team will arrive, but they won't find Rikari or Marcus, just three Ayphas standing among the dead.

"What should we do?" asks a worried Rizen.

"Relax." Petune presses a sequence of stones on the wall, causing it to unhinge and open. "Go and wait for me in my quarters."

Darius and Rizen scuttle into the tunnel. Just as the wall closes, additional guards arrive. Flooding into the basement, they see Petune surrounded by the dead.

"Commander, what happened?" asks a horrified guard.

Petune dips his fingers into a puddle of blood. "It appears a reaper has come to visit us."

Though his hands tremble, the Aypha presses for clarity. "Did, did you—did you do this?"

Petune places his hand over his heart. "What a despicable thing to suggest. Who do you think sounded the alarm? You and your men should return upstairs while I continue to investigate what happened here."

The guard salutes. He and his men return upstairs. Straightening his hair and wiping his face of sweat, Petune does his best to clean himself up before Cynné and Shomari arrive.

Barreling down the hall, Shomari grabs Petune by the collar. "What did you do?" he asks.

Petune flicks a smile of deception. "I just arrived a few moments ago and saw this mess before me," he says. His hand is still healing from his fight with Rikari, but he covers it well. Nodding to the dead guards, Petune continues his farce. "Seems while we were away, someone infiltrated the prison."

Cynné scowls. "What a great coincidence. Soon as General X strips you of your power, the guards responsible for watching the Yazu suddenly die." Cynne places her hand on Petune's chest. "You're breathing hard for someone who just happened to walk in."

Petune caresses the back of Cynné's hand. "Surprisingly your touch isn't as awful as your mouth." Petune then kneels over the dead bodies. "In all honesty, I'm a little distraught. I handpicked these men and sad to see them go."

Shomari scans the prison corridor and notices fresh blood farther down the hallway. He enters the cell where Marcus was being interrogated.

"What happened to the Yazu you had down here?" asks Shomari. "The one you said was on the verge of cracking?"

Petune strokes his chin. "You know, suddenly I'm having memory issues. And seeing how I'm no longer in charge, guess you'll have to figure it out yourselves."

Shomari points to the exit. "Leave. Cynné and I will take it from here."

As Petune sets out to depart, a soldier approaches the trio and bows.

"Sirs, my lady, our perimeter teams are tracking two unknown individuals heading toward the southern border," says the soldier. "We suspect it's connected to tonight's incident. Several teams are in pursuit, as well as Commander Ophelia."

"Ophelia? I told her to wait for the transfer of the Yazu," says Cynné.

Petune sneers. "Great job of keeping your women in line. You know, Sinclair never had this problem when she was in charge."

Cynné grits her teeth and snaps back. "This coming from the man whose handpicked men are all dead. You really have no place to talk." Cynné shoos Petune away. "Your services are no longer needed."

Petune gleefully exits while Cynné and Shomari make their way to the prison cell holding the Yazu. As they do a head count, Free and her frightened daughter Yondi move to the corner of the cell.

Combing through the group of soiled faces, Cynné and Shomari notice one of them stands out. His face isn't nearly as dirty as the others, his cheeks are full and his hair is closely shaven.

For Asher, he knows nothing but trouble lies ahead.

***

While Shomari and Cynné interrogate Asher, Petune returns to his quarters where Darius and Rizen anxiously await. Petune's quarters are well appointed with rabbit fur flooring and lavish artworks stolen from other lands. Desperate to find Marcus before Ophelia, Petune calls the young Ayphas to his living room.

"Shame Marcus got away," says Petune, he pours himself a glass of red wine and indulges in the sweet aroma. "He was our only lead to finding the Eye."

After Claudius was killed, Petune took over for the Elite Guard but had a soft spot for Darius. The goal wasn't to replace his father but to shape Darius into a loyal soldier. Knowing what it feels like to lose a parent, Petune has taken Darius under his wing, hoping to guide him onto a better path.

"It's my fault," says Darius, he stares at a half-filled decanter on Petune's mahogany wood table. "My emotions got in the way."

Petune smiles, elated to see Darius embrace his failures. "Here's your chance to redeem yourself." He sips his wine and rests his hand on Darius's shoulder. "Intel suggests Marcus and the Dyna are heading toward Beta. Following them is Commander Ophelia of the Aminas. It's important you intercept Marcus before she does. Ophelia is a woman of bloodthirst and on a hunt to kill."

"And what about the Dyna?" asks Rizen. "How are we to handle her?"

Petune enjoys another sip and places his eyes on a spotless shelf of books. He grabs a book wrapped in gold film and skims through it. Written by the Ayphas and Aminas, the book contains intelligence on other lands—information on vulnerable defenses and profiles of leaders. After thumbing through, Petune drops his pointer finger on a particular page.

"Rikari Niacin, what a beauty," he says as he caresses her portrait. "Says here she recently became one of the Seven Absolute Commanders of Dyna. Strengths and weaknesses currently unknown." Petune combs his fingers through his hair.

"You'll need to separate Rikari from Marcus. I'll assign a couple of others to help you."

"And once they're separated, then what?" asks Darius.

"Just track him. It's likely he'll lead you right to his parents. Once you find them, send me a Carrier message, and I'll take it from there."

Darius and Rizen nod. As they prepare to leave, Petune provides a final message.

"At the end of this mission, Darius, I expect you to kill Marcus. Whatever emotions or feelings you have for him, destroy them now."

Darius rolls up his sleeve, on his inner bicep are the same *FF* tattooed initials that Marcus has. Darius heats a knife over a candle and filets the initials off his flesh. "Marcus means nothing to me," he says. "He and his parents are dogs who deserve to be dragged through mud and pissed on. When called upon, I shall kill Marcus in the name of my father."

Petune smiles knowing he has Darius's heart. "Time to begin the hunt."

What Is the Price of Your Soul?

After a perilous encounter against Annabelle the Ghost, Commander Loreen and Nova return to the Land of Amina. Their mission was a complete failure and the lost burns across their faces. Two Aminas were killed and they failed to obtain the Eye of Truth. Their only lead was now gone, and Queen Cynné will not be pleased. As the two approach the first Amina security perimeter, they stop before a giant wall of pink roses. While the roses are beautiful, touching them will turn bone and skin to mush.

Loreen unfastens a pouch from her belt and takes out a pinch of shimmering white dust. She blows the dust across the wall, roses and vines wither away, and create a large opening for them to pass through. Proceeding along a winding trail with rosebushes on each side, Loreen ties blood-stained ribbons around Nova's wrist. The satin ribbons were once pink and worn by Russina and Sky, that is until they met their demise at the edge of Annabelle's blade.

"Their deaths are not on me, but you," grumbles Loreen. "Your selfish actions caused this."

Nova stares at the bloody ribbons of her fallen teammates, while the ribbons can be unraveled, their deaths will always be tied to her.

"I'm sorry, commander. I take full responsibility," says Nova, a hint of guilt lingers on her tongue. She has apologized several times but Loreen remains furious.

"Diving on a bloody sword is pointless! Owning responsibility isn't the same as learning from your mistakes." Loreen blows dust on second wall of roses. "Our mission failed because you lack discipline and maturity."

As the roses wither away, Loreen releases a discreet sigh. "I suppose it's not all your fault. These are the consequences when we let children fight our battles. The queen...her belief in signs are...misguided."

The two proceed through the second wall and enter a maze of well-manicured hedges. Getting lost in the maze would surely lead to disaster for any intruder. Lethal traps and poisonous spiderwebs are hidden throughout the maze.

Following behind Loreen, Nova continues to stare at the ribbons of her fallen teammates. "We aren't ready for the Zells are we?" she asks.

"Not at all." Loreen blows dust across several hedges, translucent spiderwebs in front of their path are now visible to the eye. A few seconds pass before the spiderwebs dissolve. "Annabelle alone would destroy us in our current state."

"You seemed to have held your own against her." Nova briefly pauses. "Commander, how can I become like you?"

Loreen scoffs and picks up the pace through the maze. "You've got many scars to earn and deaths to see to become like me."

"What I mean is, I want to become as strong as you. When you fought the Ghost, I noticed your Oro was different. It was darker and more intense than anything I've ever seen." Nova takes a hard swallow. "Commander, were you using the soul?"

Loreen comes to a halt. She snatches Nova by the throat causing her face to turn blue. "I used it so we could survive. It was my only option." Loreen releases her grip and drops Nova to the ground.

Nova massages her tender neck and it takes a moment to regain her breath. "So it's true, the soul gives us greater power. Then why is it forbidden by the Doctrine?"

Loreen places her palm on her chest. "The soul briefly allows Oro to be more potent but it comes at a consequence. Over time using the soul causing mental instability and body deformities. Still, that's not the ultimate reason why using the soul is prohibited..."

"What is then?"

Loreen looks to the sky and sighs. "Do not become fixated on using the soul for strength. Focus on refining your skills and become a more tactful soldier. Only through time and patience can you become as great as me."

Nova nods absently, but her curiosity about the soul remains. "Understood, commander."

When Loreen and Nova arrive at Cynné's mansion, they find the queen out back trimming rosebushes in her garden. A bed of pink rose petals rest at the queen's delicate feet.

"Please tell me you recovered the Eye," says Cynné as Loreen and Nova approach.

"Negative, the mission was a failure," reports Loreen.

Cynné clenches a vine of thorns, causing blood to run down her wrist. "What happened?"

"It's my fault," blurts Nova. Her head is lowered and she stares at her combat boots.

Loreen squeezes Nova's wrist to quiet her tongue. "We encountered the Ghost and two of those girls you assigned to me were killed." Loreen notices the teardrops sprinkling Nova's boots. "These girls are too inexperienced. They're not mentally or physically ready for war. They need proper training."

"Nonsense!" Cynné takes a seat at a glass-stained breakfast table and pours hot water from a kettle into a teacup filled with rose petals. "Our beauties are ready for anything. Aren't they, Nova?"

Nova is silent and wipes her tears away using the blood-stained ribbons from her fallen teammates.

"They lack discipline, patience, and skill. If we continue on this path, many more will die," warns Loreen. "Your signs may say one thing, but as your adviser, I'm telling you, they aren't ready."

Cynné gathers a sip of her rose tea. "Wrong, Loreen. My spirit is telling me—" she pauses and sets her teacup down. "Wait, why was Annabelle near the Valleys? First Mother, now her. Are they working with the Dynas?"

Loreen sits beside her queen and slides her long gray hair behind her ears. "Kissandra may be weakened, but she hasn't lost her dignity. Annabelle could be a different story. With so many altercations between us and the Zells, maybe she's getting spooked."

Cynné frowns and orders Nova to leave the garden. Nova nods and quickly exits.

"If the Zells are forming an alliance, it's best we attack them now." Cynné taps her teacup with a silver spoon. The pressure to act spreads across her young brow. "You may disagree, but we can't risk losing this chance to acquire their key."

Loreen unfastens her leather boots and slides them off, relieving the pressure in her aching old feet. "Defeating the Zells without the Phoenixes will not be easy." She strips off the arm guards shielding her frail wrists. "Annabelle is getting stronger. We need to focus on interrogating the Yazu. How did the transfer go?"

Cynné's face turns red. "It's been delayed. There was another incident on the Ayphas' side. Ophelia is in pursuit of whoever breached the prison."

A thick vein rises on Loreen's forehead. "You let Ophelia lead a search mission?"

Cynné bites her lip. "No, she disobeyed my orders."

"Seems we have discipline issues from top to bottom. Cynné, she's a problem. She abuses the soul, and she's already talking to herself. It's only going to get worse."

"It's fine, Loreen. I'll find a way to keep her in check."

Loreen looks to the roses, knowing it's too late.

I Need You

MARCUS

As Rikari and I travel through the south region of Beta, surrounding us are nothing but red sand desert hills. We've lost the Ayphas who were tracking us but we're drained, dehydrated, and in desperate need of sleep. The sun beats across our backs and our pace has come to a crawl. Still, the journey to Chance Island must continue. Reconnecting with my parents and rest of the Shadow Clan is the only way to save Asher and the Yazu. But upon seeing my parents, what will I say to them? They've abandoned their only child, leaving me to the heinous wolves and pit vipers of this world. Then again, they tried to shield me from this life. The life of a Divine and the cruel weight it supposedly carries. The faint line between love and hate of my parents has become indistinguishable.

Rikari and I reach a patch of desert where the sand draws flat and brittle. In the distance are red clay plateaus and signs of vegetation.

"Lucky Caverns is that way," says Rikari, pointing toward the plateaus. "There's underground springs in the caverns where we can recover and escape the heat."

As we travel toward the caverns, a black and orange bird approaches at a rapid pace. Hovering over us, the bird glows and oddly transforms into a scroll.

"It's called a *Carrier*," says Rikari as the scroll drops into her hands. Rikari unfolds the scroll, her eyelids widen upon reading it. "This can't be a coincidence." Rolling up the scroll, she shoves it into her sleeve. "It's a message from Valencia and Annabelle. They want me to take you…"

Rikari's eyes catch with fire as she places her hands on the ground.

"We've been spotted!" she yells.

Sure enough, two Aminas appear from the direction of Lucky Caverns. As they move closer, I recognize them from home. Blanche and Cassini, blonde-haired sisters who were pulled from Eden two years before I joined the military.

"Just when I thought we're all alone, Marcus the traitor stands before us," says Blanche.

Cassini snickers. "I knew following the Carrier would pay off. Never thought it would be him," she says. "Queen Cynné's going to promote us to captains after this!"

The girls giggle. There must be a significant bounty out for me.

"Who's your friend? She looks scary," says Blanche. The two Aminas move closer and smile, their teeth shine with delight.

Rikari regresses to her cold ways. "Just go away and return to whatever hole you crawled out of."

Laughing, the girls ignore Rikari's warning.

"You know, we get double the reward if we keep him alive," says Cassini to her sister. "Marcus, dear, why don't you be a good boy and come with us? We promise to be gentle."

I straighten my back and press out my chest. "I'm not the same boy you remember from Eden. Its best that you leave us," I say.

"Doubt it. Your voice may have gotten deeper, but you're still the same scared kid," mocks Cassini. "Look at you, you're shaking."

I glance down, and sure enough, my hands tremble not from fear but with rage.

"Enough chatter," says Rikari. "You're in our way." Rikari steps forward.

"Oro release!" Cassini and Blanche yell. As they charge toward us, Orospheres form in their hands.

Rikari turns to me and releases a heavy sigh. "I hate Aminas. Vain and stupid, they're all quite repulsive… forgive me, Marcus."

Rikari pounds her fist into the sand and forms two gigantic hands made of iron. The massive hands snatch up the girls and squeeze them tight. Wiggling and squirming, Blanche and Cassini struggle to free themselves.

"Zealous idiots! Why attack a Dyna? Let alone one of the Absolute Seven," announces Rikari. Removing her cloak, Rikari shows the girls her gold fox patch.

Realizing their foolishness, Cassini and Blanche turn gray.

"Oh, c'mon now. Don't kill us. We were just trying to have some fun. Have a little mercy," says Blanche.

"Mercy? Such a word should never be uttered," sneers Rikari. "There was no mercy when the Aminas slaughtered my sister, so why would I show it now?" The iron hand squeezes Blanche even tighter.

"Okay, okay, okay. Please, forgive us." Sweat beads along Blanche's forehead. "We'll go about our way just as you requested."

"Too late." Rikari's iron hand squeezes Blanche, splattering her blood across the desert sand.

Cassini releases an Orosphere blasting herself out of the other hand. She bolts toward Rikari, but in a heartbeat, her movement halts. Her feet now burn and grow heavy. Unbeknownst to her, she stepped in liquid iron that quickly solidifies around her legs. This is Rikari's genius. The moment Cassini freed herself from one trap, another had already been set.

"Why won't they learn?" mocks Rikari as she approaches Cassini. "Certainly, you should know better than to foolishly rush toward me without thought. How many of you have lost the art of war?"

Cassini goes limp. "Just end this quickly."

Rikari pauses. She sees the defeat in Cassini's eyes; killing her now would be cruel. But when her eerie smile appears, I know what's coming.

"Don't," I plead, dreading to see another death. "She's just a kid."

Rikari pierces me with her eyes. "Indeed but I shed no pity nor allow death to discriminate."

Rikari slams her hands to the ground, causing iron spikes to impale Cassini through her lower body. There's a soul-shattering cry from Cassini as tears and blood stream down her freckled cheeks.

"*STOP IT, RIKARI!* You've done enough," I yell.

But Rikari is ruthless. She rubs the back of Cassini's hands causing them to harden and turn as black as coal. Cassini's hands shrink and appear like dry twigs aged by winter's cold. Brittle to the touch, they crumble to a shimmering dust.

"What I've done to your hands is everlasting," says Rikari. "I've sealed them with diamond dust so they'll never grow back. While you'll never be able to use your Legacy again, at least you're alive."

Going into shock, Cassini struggles to keep her eyes open before eventually passing out.

"That wasn't necessary," I say.

Rikari slips her cloak back on. "Agreed, an iron spike through her skull would've been much cleaner, but you still believe in sympathy. Haven't you learned your enemies deserve no mercy?"

I look away as blood trickles down Cassini's iron-covered legs. "The way you fight...it just seems so cruel."

"There's no victory for a Divine who remains noble..." Rikari stops. For the first time ever, she looks worried. In the distance, a fleet of thirty Aminas rapidly approach us.

Rikari places her hand on the ground. "Spit! There's not enough metal to fight so many. Marcus, how fast can you run?"

"Probably faster than you now."

"Prove it to me. I want you to run and don't stop until you reach Zell."

Rikari is out of her mind if she thinks I'm going to leave her. I've abandoned Asher and the Yazu; I refuse to leave behind another friend.

"No." I shake my head. "We do this together."

"Negative!" Rikari barks. "You cannot die here." She tosses me the scroll she received from the Carrier bird. "Take this to the Zells. It explains everything. Now go!"

Before I can reply, blood flows from Rikari's pores. Her skin transforms into diamond scales of armor. She thrusts her hands into the sand causing a fault within the ground. As the fault expands and deepens, magma geysers erupt from the cracked surface. What was once a fault has now become a massive lava river.

The Aminas charge forward. Four of them break off and speed toward us at an alarming rate. Three leap over the river successfully, while a fourth falls short, plunging into the lava. The Amina screams in agony. She tries climbing out, but her flesh melts away and her bones turn to ash.

"Leave, Marcus!" Rikari yells as more Aminas arrive.

In an onslaught, they pummel her with Orospheres. Her diamond armor protects her, but she can't sustain this state forever. She's buying me time to escape. But I refuse to abandon her. Outnumbered by many, Rikari needs me. Pulling out my dagger, I charge the Aminas.

"Rikari, I've come to....*AARRRGGHHH!*"

A hand made of sand crafted by Rikari, grabs my legs and flings me far away from the battle. I tumble to the ground and twist my ankles, the pain will wear off shortly but the shame will linger. Why would Rikari try to fight so many by herself? I can help her; I know I can.

Dusting myself off, it takes me several minutes to return to the battlefield. But when I arrive, Rikari is nowhere in sight. The lava river has receded; only the scent of burned flesh lingers in the air. On the ground lie many silent Aminas. Their bodies pierced with iron spikes. A few feet away from them are solid statues of Aminas encased in iron.

Everyone here is dead, except one.

"So, you came back after all," says Cassini. Her lower half is drenched in blood, and her face is lighter than snow.

"Where is she?" I ask.

Cassini's eyes bob heavy. "She's in the caverns. But you shouldn't follow. There's even more fighting her now. Just a matter of time before it's over."

I look to the caverns and the trail of blood along the way. "You're wrong. I can save her." As I walk away, Cassini wraps what's left of her arms around me.

"Marcus, wait!" Cassini's clutch is weak and cold. "From one child of Eden to another, I just want you to think for a second. If you go to the caverns, you'll be killed. That woman is sacrificing herself for you. Don't let her death be in vain."

I grab the hilt of my dagger and squeeze it tight. "I can't live with myself if I don't help her."

"You won't be living at all if you do." Unable to move due to the spikes in her body, Cassini leans against me. "What are your dreams, Marcus? If you die today, would you be satisfied with your life?"

"No," I admit. "I was supposed...I wanted to be a protector of Aypha, a champion, someone people would look up to. That dream can never happen when everyone thinks I'm a traitor."

Cassini rests her cold head against my chest. Her lips are now gray from the loss of blood. "I know you're not a traitor. You've never had the heart of one. We're just following orders."

I nod, saying nothing.

With her arms wrapped around mine, Cassini begins to tremble. "You know, this isn't how I expected my life to end. I had a dream too. Blanche and I had plans to explore the northern lands and escape this life. But when they pull you from Eden and force you into the military, all your dreams are destroyed."

Tears flow from Cassini's eyes as she lowers her head. Moments ago, we were enemies, but I can't help but feel sympathy.

"Help me down, Marcus."

Against my better judgment, I pull the iron rods from her body. Immediately, she collapses into my arms.

Cassini releases a shallow chuckle. "See, Marcus, that weak heart of yours is going to get you killed. The Dyna is right—there's no mercy in this world."

"Everything isn't as simple as malice and mayhem," I say. "Compassion overrules both."

Cassini coughs up blood. She's lost so much of it that her Divine healing will not activate. She's dying and it's a miserable thing to witness. "Maybe you're right, Marcus. Kindness is greater than destruction, but we've gone too far. Divines are taught to hate each other. But what sense does that make? There should be more unity among us. If only that were so."

Cassini closes her eyes. Her body becomes icy to the touch. I wrap my arms around her to provide some comfort.

"Stay awake," I beg.

"You know that dream of yours, Marcus?" Cassini whispers. "Maybe it isn't lost. Maybe you just need to dream bigger. Go and live so you may fulfill that dream."

Cassini's body goes limp within my arms. She's now free from this world. The tears I've been holding back finally slip out. In the last few months, I've seen more people die than ever before, and none felt good. Death has become common, and the more I see it, the more it troubles me.

Taking a moment to gather myself, I look east toward Lucky Caverns and west toward the Land of Zell. As much as I want to help Rikari, I cannot. There's a dream I have to fulfill. A dream that brings unity and protection not just to Aypha, but to all of Pyris.

The Zells

MARCUS

Two days have passed since separating from Rikari and thoughts of her demise rip at my heart. Guilt seeps into my veins knowing this woman has sacrificed everything for me. Faint hope of Rikari's survival carries with me as I continue across the Land of Beta. Having gone days without water, the dry warm air has long ago wicked away what little moisture I had. My tongue bleeds upon licking the blisters on my lips and with each grueling step, my vision becomes hazier.

When evening approaches, relief is in sight. Ahead lies a wetland filled with mossy trees of all shapes and sizes. The letter Z is carved into the light bark of many trees, indicating I'm in Zell territory. I stumble into the wetlands and there's a dramatic shift in the atmosphere. The ground is damp, warm fog hovers low, and the air is thick. Perched on the branches of mossy trees are many yellow-eyed crows that gawk at my presence. Sloshing forward, the murky water rises to my knees and every step I take becomes heavy. While I'm desperate for water, the rancid smell coming from the wetlands deters me from drinking.

Needing a break, I lean against a tree only to watch as crows gather above my head. Guess they can sense I'm near death, but I refuse to allow birds to peck away my flesh.

"YOU ALL MIGHT AS WELL GIVE UP!" I yell to the crows, but they remain unfazed by my insane outburst.

I close my eyes for a few minutes but awaken when the swamp water begins to bubble around my legs. The crows squawk and scatter in a mad frenzy. Something has spooked them and I can feel it in the air. A shadow figure from my peripheral weaves between trees. I unsheathe my dagger, and pressure builds through my veins. Eyes watch me but I can't tell from where. In the distance, a strange orb of water appears. The orb hurls forward and explodes causing mud to splatter all over me. Wiping the thick black mud from my eyes, I'm now surrounded by several young girls. Some swing from trees, others have emerged from below the swamp waters. They all stare at me in a silent anger. Their faces are light green, and their hair matches the color of the surrounding mossy trees.

As the girls whisper to each other, a woman wearing a cloak of sticks and leaves approaches. Her hair is mossy green like the others, but she is much taller and slightly older. Her skin is striped with light green and brown, she blends perfectly within the wetlands.

"You're trespassing. Leave here immediately," the peculiar woman says.

I've trekked across an entire desert; there's no way I'm turning back. "I'll do no such thing," I say in defiance.

The young girls gasp and again whisper to one another.

"Little boy, you're confused," responds the older woman. She places her hand into the swamp water, causing it to swirl around me. "That wasn't a request."

Slowly I reach into my pocket and pull out the scroll Rikari gave me. "This is for you."

The woman retracts her hand and the swirling water quells. A short girl with long curls approaches and takes the scroll from me.

"It's a signed pact between Queen Annabelle and Queen Valencia of Dyna," announces the little girl. "The pact states that the two queens have reached an agreement of an alliance between our lands. In the coming days, one hundred Dynas shall arrive. In exchange, Marcus the Aypha is to be protected at all times."

After the girl speaks, the edges of the paper glow and burn until it is no more.

I'm to be protected? Protected from who? I wonder.

The older woman approaches. "So, I take it you're Marcus the Aypha."

I nod but the girls release a strange sigh of disappointment.

The woman shakes her head and calls for the girl who read the letter. "Zyniah, you know what to do."

The little girl grabs my hand and massages it. The pleasant feeling lasts briefly as she pricks my finger.

"What did you do that for?" I ask as Zyniah drops my blood into a vial. Giggling, the little girl hides behind the older woman.

"Zyniah, apologize to him!"

Zyniah pouts. "Sorry," she says reluctantly.

The older woman clears her throat. "Forgive us. It's been a long time since these girls have seen a boy. As you can tell, they don't know how to act...I am Commander Nyree Trust and these are my girls." Nyree takes my blood and pours it into a black bowl with a snake head. "Before I let you pass, we need to run a test." She places my hand inside the bowl. "This is a truth test. For every truthful answer, the eyes of the snake shall light up. Lie and the snake will come to life and deliver a fatal bite."

Having nothing to hide, I give Commander Nyree the go-ahead to ask me any question.

"Is your name Marcus Azure?"

"Yes."

The snake's eyes light up.

"Do you have any ill intentions toward us?"

"No."

Again, the snake's eyes light.

Zyniah approaches. "Commander, I have a question for him." Her eyes remained fixated on mine. "Are you of Aypha blood?"

"Yes," I say.

As before, the snake's eyes light up.

Zyniah's eyebrows rise as she touches my forehead. "Hmm, seems you're telling the truth."

Nyree snaps her fingers. "Okay, that's enough, Zyniah. Escort Marcus straight to Commander CQ and inform her of the alliance with the Dynas." Nyree turns to the other girls. "The rest of you, return to your post."

The girls nod in unison and vanish on the spot.

"Okay, Marcus! Come with me," says Zyniah. Grabbing my wrist, she leads me farther into the swamp where the rancid water rises to my waist and nearly up to Zyniah's neck. In the canopy of low hanging trees, yellow and black snakes dangle from the branches. Many hiss while others expose their fangs as a warning.

As we continue onward, something coarse rubs against my leg. Bubbles pop on the surface and multiple gators crest above the murky water. Zyniah remains unfazed and hums to herself.

"Sooo, you don't find this uncomfortable?" I ask.

"Huh? Oh, these guys...you know I never really pay them much attention," says Zyniah. "They protect us from outsiders...must be your

196

blood that's got them all curious." She continues to hum, oblivious to the danger I'm in.

Meanwhile, the gators remain at my side until we reach dry land. Taking a knee, I'm completely exhausted and need a few minutes to rest. Oddly, Zyniah's long hair begins to shed, and her skin tone transitions from mossy green to mahogany brown.

"Uh, what..."

"It was camouflage." Zyniah brushes fallen hair from her shoulders. "Our bodies can blend into any environment by absorbing energy from our surroundings. It's one of our Legacy abilities." Zyniah tosses me her water canteen, I drink every drop. My feet throbbing, I take off my boots to relieve the pressure.

Zyniah sits across from me looking rather annoyed. She wears a dark-blue leather dress plated with scales of iron, and her arms are crisscrossed in white and blue ribbons. "You act kind of old for someone my age," she says while playing with the curls in her natural, amber colored hair.

From the looks of it, Zyniah and I are several years apart, but I don't bother to question her.

"You would act old too if you had traveled days without rest."

Zyniah shrugs and murmurs something.

"Say, I got a question. How far are we from the coast of Chance Island?" I ask.

"Not too far. Why you ask?"

"It's a secret."

"Ooooh! Tell me." Zyniah's eyes fill with curiosity.

"Nope, then it wouldn't be a secret."

Zyniah crosses her arms, showing her age. "Just like an old person, keeping secrets for no good reason. You know, Lady Annabelle keeps secrets too and I can't stand it. Especially in a time like now. Everyone is acting tense, afraid war is on the horizon. The adults say things haven't been this bad since Kissandra's reign."

"Well, rest easy. The Dynas will be here soon," I say.

Zyniah plucks a blade of grass from the field and lets a warm breeze carry it away. "I hope you're right. Maybe I'll have time to play games again. I miss having fun, but I guess war will make anyone grow old..." Zyniah briefly frowns before perking up. "Hey, is that why you act so old? Have you been in a lot of wars where you're from?"

197

I chuckle. "Nope and hope to never see one. Just like you, I'd rather go back to playing games."

Zyniah grins, showing all her tiny teeth. "Looks like we got at least one thing in common, old man. Let's keep moving."

Zenith, the capital Village of Zell, is nothing like the swamp that surrounds it. Cherry blossom trees are everywhere, and their sweet scent provides a refreshing welcome. Most of the homes in Zenith are made of bricks and painted blue and white. On a cliff by the eastern edge of the capital, towers a bronze statue of a woman looking to the sky.

"Who is she?" I ask in admiration.

"The Reaper, Queen Zora," Zyniah says proudly. "The elders tell me she ruled before Queen Annabelle. We pay homage to her for the sacrifices she made during the Last Great War. We are all indebted to her for she is the reason my people are alive."

Continuing into the capital, we pass by many shops and the young women can't help but stare. Their jaws drop and their eyes brighten as Zyniah escorts me to a white castle overlooking a lake. Behind the castle's marble gate, a female guard approaches and frowns.

"What is a Kamara doing here?" asks the guard.

"I'm not a Kamara, but my name is Marcus." I smile, the guard blushes, and Zyniah steps between us.

"Is Commander CQ around? We have orders from the queen to protect Marcus."

"No," says the guard as she continues to stare at me. "She's investigating something out west."

"She needs to hurry back," Zyniah huffs. "We just received word of an alliance with the Dynas." Zyniah looks behind the guard and toward the white mansion. "Well, since she's not here, what should I do with Marcus?"

"Commander CQ has put Charlotte in charge. Take him to her."

Zyniah shivers. "Never mind, we'll wait till CQ returns." Zyniah tugs me away before the guard can even say goodbye.

Leaving the gates of the castle, we venture away from the heart of Zenith to a forest of dead trees with twisted trunks and branches. Among all that is dead here, a pretty path of white lily flowers leads to the only living tree in the forest. The tree is five times the height of the surrounding canopy and is made of vibrant white leaves that provide shelter to the birds playing about its branches. At the base of the wide tree trunk is a rickety door. Dusting silk cobwebs off of it, we enter the tree and light a few candles. Inside the tree is a home complete with two beds, a kitchen, and a bathing room. Hand-carved pieces of wooden furniture are in the foyer and little stairs wrap around the inside of the tree walls up to a loft.

"This is where you'll stay till Commander CQ returns," says Zyniah. "There's a lot of history in this place, so take care of it. This is where Queen Zora once lived."

Next to one of the beds is a portrait nailed to the wall. I recognize her face from the statue in the village.

"So, this is the Reaper, Queen Zora. What happened to her?" I ask.

"The elders tell me she died not long after her battle against Kissandra. Defeating her must've taken a toll."

This is the second time Zyniah has said this woman's name.

"Who is Kissandra? You speak as if I know her."

A blank stare falls upon Zyniah. "How does an Aypha not know who Kissandra is? She was Queen of the Aminas, and unquestionably the strongest Divine of modern time. Somehow, Queen Zora defeated her. She couldn't kill Kissandra, but she diminished her power, preventing her from taking over our land. Since their battle, no one has seen Kissandra and we can only hope she has met her demise."

I stare at the Reaper's portrait, amazed at her accomplishments. "Well, I've had a long journey. I need to rest." I plop onto a bed, the feather stuffed pillows cradle my weary head.

"Aw, it's still so early. Why don't we play a game for a bit?"

As much as I need sleep, Zyniah's innocent eyes are too much. "Okay, but just for a little while. My eyes are getting heavy."

Promises Are Like Shadows

MARCUS

Who knew Zyniah was so obsessed with playing games? Oblivious to my red eyes and obnoxious yawns, Zyniah insists we continue to play a game called Pebbles.

"I win again!" she says as little rocks spill to the ground. Pebbles is a simple game where the goal is to pull rocks from a constructed pile without knocking it over. Whoever causes the pile to collapse loses.

We've played the game now well over fifty times, and Zyniah has won them all. My hands are shaky due to lack of sleep, and I'm frustrated that I can't beat a kid. While it's against the rules to grab a pebble with two hands, there's nothing against using one hand to steady the other. Changing my strategy, one by one we pull pebbles from the tall stack. As the stack becomes wobbly, Zyniah begins to fidget. When it's her turn to pull a pebble, the stack comes crashing down.

"Yes! I finally won!" I shout.

Zyniah pouts. She scoops up the pebbles and tosses them into her wooden box. "You know what you did was unfair," she says.

"Was it against the rules?"

"No, but it just seems odd to do that. Why are you so odd, Marcus?"

Seeing I've frustrated little Zyniah, I try to lighten the mood. "Well, I'm sure you'll beat me next time."

"Yeah, until you find another way to cheat." Zyniah crosses her legs and clenches her teeth. "Got to pee. I'll be right back."

As Zyniah heads to the bathroom, I slide into the covers of my bed and close my eyes. Rikari lingers in my mind, if she survived the Aminas' onslaught she should've been here by now.

"I'll be right back, going to get us breakfast," says Zyniah as she returns from the bathroom. She opens the front door letting sunlight in.

"It's best you stay inside, you don't want the other girls to know you're here. They'll kidnap you and use you for their own pleasures."

"I'm coming with you," I say. Although I'm sleepy, it couldn't hurt to meet the other girls. Besides, Zyniah is driving me insane.

"Okay, don't say I didn't warn you." Zyniah hands me a blue cloak which I slip on and cover my head.

We leave the forest and return to the capital of Zenith. Zyniah takes me to their mess hall, which is a large white stone building covered in blue ivy vines. Up top is a large bronze bell used for announcements. Inside the building are several rows of long wooden tables. While the hall is empty, someone is in the back preparing breakfast. Peeping our heads into the kitchen, an old thick-skinned woman is stirring something in a pot over a fire.

"Hi, Ms. Stussy!" shouts Zyniah. Her outburst startles the heavyset woman causing her to knock over the pot and spill hot oats all over the kitchen floor.

Ms. Stussy shrieks. "Zyniah! What did I tell you about surprising me like that?"

Zyniah looks down and presses her pointer fingers together. "I'm super sorry, I was just excited to introduce you to someone…"

Smiling from ear to ear, Ms. Stussy approaches and gives me such a big hug, it takes my breath away.

"Welcome, Marcus. The young girls have been talking about you since last night. So what brings you here?" she asks.

"The queen wants us to protect him," interrupts Zyniah.

I clear my throat and look to Zyniah, she's full of wonderful energy but her mouth moves faster than she can think. "Um, yes. But I'm actually on my way to Chance Island."

Wrinkles appear across Ms. Stussy's forehead. "The island is off limits. Why are you interested in such a place?"

Grabbing a handful of towels, I help clean up the mess on the floor. "Rather not say at this time."

Ms. Stussy's bushy eyebrows rise.

"Same thing he said to me," blurts out Zyniah.

Ms. Stussy chuckles and her belly jiggles. "That's okay. I'm sure he's got his reasons. Let me just say though, getting to Chance Island isn't easy. You'll have to cross over acidic water. Sometimes the water levels are safe, sometimes they're not."

Just great. If my parents are on the island, who knows how long before I can reach them?

Ms. Stussy strokes her double chin. "Say, Zyniah, why don't you take Marcus to Charlotte. She'll be able to help him."

"Uh, I'd rather wait till Commander CQ returns," says Zyniah with a nervous twitch.

"Still afraid of her aye? She's not as mean as you think."

Zyniah rolls her eyes. "Uh-huh. Say, you got any food, Ms. Stussy? We need to eat before the others arrive."

Ms. Stussy rubs her giant belly before reaching into a cabinet. "Well, seeing how you caused me to spill my hot oats, all I have left is some pea soup from last night."

Ms. Stussy pours a hearty scoop of cold pea soup into a bronze cup. Pinching my nose, I gulp the soup down in one breath. Instantly, I feel queasy.

Zyniah grabs my wrist. "Okay, thanks Ms. Stussy. We gotta go."

"Nonsense, child, patience is time's best friend you know."

"But we really should before the others…"

Upstairs, Ms. Stussy's assistant rings the bell for breakfast call. Moments later, a group of young Zells who wear white and blue combat uniforms rush into the mess hall. Spotting us in the kitchen, the girls scream and rush toward us in excitement. They bat their eyes and blow kisses at me. I've never felt so awkward in my life. Being the center of attention, I should be enjoying this, but the girls poke and rub me as if I was part of an art exhibit. As a second wave of girls come in, they too rush over. Many grab my cheeks and touch my lips. One even has the nerve to pinch my butt.

"Easy, girls, easy," says Ms. Stussy, she beats the girls back with a broom. "Leave Mr. Marcus alone. You're overwhelming him. Breakfast will be ready shortly so please have a seat."

Instead, the girls gather around me to ask more questions.

"Why is your skin discolored? How old are you? Do you have a girlfriend?"

Apparently, many of these girls haven't seen a male in years. According to them, the Zells and Kamaras haven't had a reunion season in nearly five years. The questions from the Zells continue until Zyniah stands on top of a table.

"Girls, Marcus is tired and needs a break. We'll see you all later." Zyniah grabs my hand and rushes me out the mess hall.

"What a relief," I say.

"Told ya. This is why you should've stayed inside. Let's get you back to your quarters."

Zyniah takes me through a trail and into a field of cherry blossom trees. Their pleasant fragrance could keep me here forever. The allure of the pink and white petals is intoxicating and a sense of calmness comes over me. Admiring the blossoms, I pluck off a few petals and smell them with delight. The moment of bliss is cut short when I hear metal scratch against metal. Curious of the source, Zyniah and I weave through the trees and spot a woman sharpening a leaf shaped knife across a grinding stone. When done, she plucks a strand of her hair and drops it onto the knife's sharp edge, splitting the hair in half.

Zyniah leans next to me and takes a big gulp. "That's Charlotte," she whispers.

Charlotte wears a white suede tunic and her wrists are shielded by scales of iron. Strapped to her back are five black swords. Two of the swords face downward crossing in an X. The other three are strapped upward with the tips meeting at the center of her back. Circled around Charlotte are straw-man targets. She closes her eyes and throws her knife, striking a target's heart. She unsheathes two of her swords and slashes the targets, cutting off their arms. Without looking, she launches her swords at two other targets and strikes them dead in the face.

"NICE!" I say out loud.

Charlotte turns in our direction. Her cat like eyes give me pause but I smile and wave. In return, she frowns and huffs in annoyance.

Strands of Zyniah's curly hair shed and her hands tremble. "P-p-please forgive us, Commander!" Zyniah looks to the ground and tugs my pants legs as a hint to walk away.

Zyniah stands on her tippy toes to whisper in my ear. "It's best we leave her alone. She's always grumpy."

"If she can get me to Chance Island than I need to speak with her," I say.

"She won't help you; she doesn't help anyone really. Just wait for Commander CQ."

I pat Zyniah's head. "I know you're scared of her, but you can't be a wuss forever."

Zyniah folds her arms and wrinkles her nose. "Hey! Just because you're old doesn't mean you can talk to me any kinda way."

Chastised by a kid, I'm embarrassed to have scolded her. Besides, who am I to talk? We've all got fears.

"Forgive me, Zyniah, I promise to never talk like that again."

Zyniah uses her forearm and wipes tears from her eyes. "Promises are like shadows. They're only good when it's sunny."

I lightly squeeze Zyniah's shoulders. "I'll keep mine regardless of the weather, mmk?"

Zyniah nods and returns a smile.

When we look back up to speak with Charlotte, we realize she's no longer here. Thankfully, Zyniah has an idea where to find her and takes me to Charlotte's home which sits isolated on the western green hills of Zenith. Charlotte's home is made of black and white stones and her slope roof is constructed of brass tiles. Out front is a pond with lush green leaves and white lotus flowers.

Taking off our boots, we quietly enter Charlotte's quarters and note everything inside—from the wood floors to the ceiling—is black and white. Sitting cross-legged with her back toward us, Charlotte stares at a large painting of a sun, half black and half white. Even though her back is to us, she's aware of our presence.

"What is he doing here…Zyniah?" asks Charlotte.

Zyniah fiddles with her fingers. "F-f-forgive me, Commander. We didn't mean to bother you." She takes a deep breath. "Lady Annabelle has asked us to protect Marcus. As our guest, he is asking for your help to get to Chance Island."

"Why does an Aypha need to go to such a place?" Charlotte spares me no glance. Her stark voice reminds me of Queen Valencia. She rolls up her hair and sheaths five swords into her back holsters. According to Zyniah, these are the Seven Blades of Might, but I see only five.

"I'm looking for something," I say.

"And what is that?"

I clear my throat. "Prefer not to say. But it's something extremely important to me."

Charlotte finally slides her eyes toward me, she can't be older than twenty and when she stands her curvy figure is quite pronounced. Her hair is a dark shade of purple and her skin is like toasted olive oil. "I'm certain it is since you're willing to risk your life. Chance Island is filled with perilous traps and many strange creatures. Many who visit the island never return."

"I'll be fine. Just get me there and I'll do the rest."

Charlotte frowns before her full lips spread. "You'll die."

I pause and scratch my forehead. "How do you figure?"

Charlotte looks at Zyniah, who places her hand on my forehead. "Um, Marcus, there's something I should tell you. I can sense your Oro strength and...well... you're not very strong."

"There you have it," says Charlotte. "You're weak, and the island is not for the pitiful. If it is our job to protect you, then I cannot allow you on the island in your current state. All is not lost though, while I'm not an Aypha, I can surely help...if you're willing."

I bow before Charlotte. "Whatever it takes."

Secrets

On the outskirts of Lucky Caverns, Ophelia approaches an immaculate scene of beauty and destruction. More than thirty lifeless Aminas are scattered across the battlefield of blood and iron. Ophelia's cruel heart sinks heavy. The Dyna who killed these Aminas showed no mercy, and neither will she.

"This was done by a single Dyna?" Ophelia says to herself. "If so, her blood must taste delightful."

Due to abusing her soul, Ophelia's insatiable desire for blood is quite uncanny. Obsessed with its sight and taste, she carries the color throughout her attire. Her choker, boots, and silk belt are all dark red even though Aminas are to wear a dash of pink.

Following the massacre's trail, Ophelia arrives at the mouth of Lucky Caverns and finds a flustered soldier checking the pulses of fallen Aminas.

"What happened here?" Ophelia asks.

The Amina stands to attention and salutes. "Commander, we encountered the fugitive, Marcus Azure, and a Dyna Commander named Rikari," says the soldier. "Marcus escaped, but we have the Dyna trapped inside the caverns."

It isn't long afterward, Rizen, Darius, and two other Ayphas approach the caverns. Although traveling on the backs of stallions, they've arrived too late.

"Why are you young pups here?" Ophelia cocks her head sideways. Her grin is as eerie as her scratchy voice.

"We're here on behalf of Commander Petune and searching for any Yazu who may have escaped," says Rizen.

"You're not lying to Ophelia, are you?" Ophelia presses her knife to Rizen's chest. "She doesn't like being lied to."

Unaware how unstable Ophelia is, Rizen continues to lie. "No, commander. We're just following orders."

Ophelia's eyes twitch, the tip of her knife breaks Rizen's skin. A vicious explosion rattles the ground, causing her to stop. Dark clouds of smoke spew from the caverns.

"Looks like I found my target," Ophelia says, retracting her knife. Her eyes gleam a malevolent red. "Your real target is not here, but I hope you find him before I do."

Rizen and Darius share a glance. They quickly leave while Ophelia races inside Lucky Caverns. More victims of Rikari's onslaught are scattered within the cold hollows.

Ophelia bites down hard on her finger. "This is what I need," she says in excitement. "It's been so long since I've had a good fight."

Farther into the cave, several Aminas stand in front of a thick iron slab.

"Commander, the Dyna is trapped behind this barrier," announces a wounded Amina.

Ophelia sniffs the air, the smell of fresh blood delights her senses. "This moment is meant for me. My beauties, Ophelia will take revenge for all the harm this Dyna has done to you. By heaven's design, I will take back your pain and heal it through the demise of this woman!"

The Aminas roar. Ophelia's hand sparks, forming a powerful gold Orosphere. She launches the sphere which destroys the iron slab. Inside, an injured Rikari lies propped up against a cave wall. Trapped inside, her strength depleted, she's lost too much blood to heal. Unable to stand, she takes a knee.

"What a letdown," complains Ophelia. "This was supposed to be an auspicious moment. You killed many of my beauties and deserve a painful death. But seeing how pathetic you look, I'll do you a favor. Tell me why you helped Marcus Azure and I'll end you properly."

Lightheaded, Rikari isn't fully coherent as Ophelia's torturous voice rings in her ears.

"No answer? That's fine, I'll still enjoy draining the last of your precious blood." Ophelia releases a tiny Orosphere hitting Rikari in the shoulder. The Orosphere ignites and blows off Rikari's right arm.

Another sphere hits Rikari and mangles her right leg. Though missing limbs, Rikari remains poised. She's going to die here, but it seems she plans to take one last victim with her.

As Ophelia unleashes a third Orosphere, Rikari uses what strength she has to dodge it. The sphere explodes along the cavern wall. Adjacent to Rikari is now a hole and trickling below is a spring. Rikari's blood filled eyes light up. She searches for traces of metal and smiles.

"Since when do Dynas smile before death?" asks Ophelia. She doesn't notice the iron slabs forming above her head.

"The dead should not talk!" shouts Rikari as she drops the slabs onto Ophelia. Pointless though, as Ophelia counters with her Orospheres, sending iron fragments everywhere. Rikari releases a diamond arrowhead from her finger which strikes Ophelia in the throat. The Dyna then leaps through the hole and plunges fifty feet below. Blood quickly fills the water spring.

With one good arm and leg, Rikari weaves underneath a set of boulders and through a channel. There's light ahead, and as she reaches the other side, she pops her head above water for a quick breath. Guided by a gentle spring, she's escorted toward the back end of the cavern where her only chance of survival fades as she's carried directly toward an entire squad of Aminas.

Unable to fight, Rikari is dragged from the water and tossed to the ground. When Ophelia catches up, she removes the diamond arrowhead from her throat and stabs Rikari repeatedly. Toying with her, she shoves Rikari's face into the gritty black dirt. The Aminas look on with pleasure.

"Behold, young beauties, before you is the pathetic and the weak," proclaims Ophelia. "This is the sight of defeat and a testament that no Divine is invincible. It is us that shall be the ones to emerge as the Queens of Pyris."

Ophelia grabs Rikari by her hair. "Look at these faces, you despicable Dyna. These are the faces of beauty and perfection. We are the ones to fear." Ophelia then rolls Rikari on her back and sparks an Orosphere. "And I am the face that will haunt you in the afterlife." Ophelia releases a maniacal laugh. To watch the last breath of the dying gives her the greatest joy.

"Kill her and I'll kill you, Ophelia," says a voracious voice.

Behind the group of Aminas, standing in the spring is a woman wearing a blush pink robe. The crystals woven into the robe's silk fabric sparkle and on the sleeves are white circles, embroidered with the names of former Amina queens. Only one woman is allowed to don this robe—Kissandra Bonet. Her face though is covered by her iconic snow leopard mask, leaving Ophelia to wonder.

"How badly did Queen Zora hurt you? It's been far too long since I've seen your face," says Ophelia.

Kissandra charges an Orosphere so massive and powerful, all who see it turn white with fear. "Do not kill the Dyna," she warns.

Ophelia cocks her head sideways. "What does this filth mean to you, my lady?"

"Nothing, but if you kill a commander, they will want revenge. Revenge leads to battles, which lead to war and you cannot defeat the Dynas without the Phoenixes."

Ophelia's nostrils flare as she tilts her head further sideways. "This woman killed over forty Aminas. She deserves death."

"In time you will get your revenge. For now, let her go. Your focus should be on the Zells."

Ophelia snarls. "You're no longer our queen. I don't take orders from you!"

Kissandra's gold Orosphere intensifies, causing the water within the spring to boil.

Ophelia grits her teeth and discharges her Orosphere. "Fine, Kissandra. Have it your way. But do not interfere with me again." Ophelia orders the Aminas to vacate. As they do, Kissandra offers one last bit of news.

"I hear you need help activating the Eye of Truth."

"Rumors are nasty things," says Ophelia, secretly wondering how Kissandra knew. It's been years since anyone has seen the former queen.

"I have what's needed to activate the Eye." Kissandra unveils a vile of blood. "Have Cynné carry out my wishes and it's hers."

"Your wishes?"

"Cynné knows." Kissandra passes Ophelia a gold Carrier letter as a means to keep in touch.

Ophelia shoves the gold paper into her dark red boots. "Very well, I'll relay the message. But I'll also tell her how you've aligned yourself to the Dynas."

"Think what you will," says Kissandra. "But you should be thanking me. I'm stopping you from doing something you'll regret."

Ophelia flashes her middle finger. "Goodbye, Kissandra. Till we meet again."

Upon the Aminas' departure, Kissandra turns to see Rikari lying still beyond the dead. Most of Rikari's blood has soaked into the grainy sand and there's a gaping hole where her shoulder once was. Kissandra wraps her torn sleeves around Rikari's wounds but it's pointless.

Removing her mask, it is not Kissandra but Sinclair who takes a moment to reflect on Rikari's accomplishments. Rikari was the youngest to ever become an Absolute Dyna Commander. Her sacrifice will not be forgotten. It is with her life that Marcus can fulfill the promise.

"Oh, Rikari. If only I had arrived sooner," says Sinclair. Shedding a tear, Sinclair looks for a place to bury Rikari. Beneath her feet though, grains of sand move toward Rikari and cover her body.

"Guess I'm not the only one holding a secret...that Minnie is something else."

Oro

MARCUS

In a desolate and dilapidated mansion of crumbled stones and ash is Charlotte, Zyniah, and myself. Within the archaic structure, brown vines cling to the remaining gray stone walls. Weeds and dirt blanket the floor. Its ceiling is no more, giving us a great view of the blue sky above us. Located northwest of the capital, the old worn-down mansion sits secluded in a forest of young trees. Charlotte insists I practice here to avoid being bothered by the other Zells. Only Zyniah is allowed to watch me. The sooner I get through this, the sooner I can get to Chance Island.

"As a Divine Aypha, I'm amazed you don't know how to use your Legacy abilities," says Charlotte. "No wonder Annabelle asks that we protect you."

"Wasn't till recently I Awakened," I say while leaning against the remains of a damaged stone statue.

Charlotte rubs her forehead. "Guess we'll have to start with the basics."

Where the mansion's foyer once was, Charlotte rummages through a pile of old books and picks up one with a purple cover. Blowing dust off the book, she thumbs to a page and hands it to me. Written in red ink is the word "ORO" along with a brief definition.

"Oro is the source of power within all Divines and is the basis of all Divine Legacies. Oro resides within the body and has the same vitality as blood itself."

"When you first Awakened, Oro was released throughout your body," says Charlotte. "It's what gives you incredible enhancements to your sight, strength, and healing. But Oro can be used for much more…"

Zyniah places her hand on my forehead. "Your Oro levels are almost unnoticeable; however, I do feel like there's…"

Charlotte pinches Zyniah's shoulder. "Zyniah, I'll do the talking, you be quiet," she says. "Now, Marcus, this is important. Each Divine bloodline uses Oro in a different manner, and it's this difference that makes each bloodline Legacy unique. No matter our abilities, they all rely on Oro."

"And that's why we're here to help you as much as we can," interrupts Zyniah.

Charlotte takes a deep breath. "Thank you once again, Zyniah. Every Divine Legacy has multiple techniques. Do you know yours?"

"Yup, Oroburn and Orosphere," I say. *This was according to Sinclair.*

"You're forgetting one." Charlotte flips through the purple book and hands it back to me only for Zyniah to take it and read to herself.

"Zyniah, read it out loud!" shouts Charlotte.

Zyniah fidgets and snaps to attention. "My mistake, commander. It says an Aypha has three basic Legacy techniques. Oroburn, Orosphere, and Oromanipulation. WARNING: Ayphas must be careful how much Oro they expend, as once they exceed their limit, it may result in permanent body damage and in some cases death."

"Death!" I shout. "Dying from using Oro?"

"Calm down," says Charlotte. "Your body naturally knows its limits. Only a hardheaded fool goes beyond them. Okay, let's get started. The first step you need to learn is how to release Oro from the body. To do so, you simply need to call for it."

Thinking about my encounters with other Ayphas, I remember them saying a particular phrase before creating an Orosphere.

"Oro release!" I shout. Upon speaking, my left hand begins to warm and white smoke rises from the pores of my skin like a thick fog.

"That's Oro in its purest form," says Charlotte. "Initially, you will have to call for it, but over time, you'll be able to release it through sure will. To deactivate it, simply say, 'Oro Yield.'"

Upon saying the phrase, the Oro around my hand disappears.

"Now that you can activate and deactivate Oro, let's focus on your first Legacy ability of Oroburn." Charlotte sticks a straw-man target into the ground and directs me to burn it.

I call for my Oro and wave it over the straw-man, thinking it would magically burn it.

"Don't know what I'm doing," I say.

Zyniah shrugs her tiny shoulders. "The book doesn't explain either. Says it should be a natural occurrence."

Charlotte runs her fingers through her purple hair and removes the iron arm guards from her wrists. "Looks like this is going to be harder than I thought. Seems your body needs a boost to heat up Oro, and I've got the perfect idea."

Charlotte's idea is actually torture. I'm now standing half naked in a barrel filled with cold water, and my teeth are chattering.

"They say the old sages could boost their internal body heat through meditation," says Charlotte as she drops another cold stone in the water barrel. "I bet with a little bit of practice you can too." Charlotte squeezes my hands. "I want you to call for your Oro and picture heat flowing from your mind into your hand. Think of only this flow and block out everything else. I'll be back in a few...Zyniah, keep him company, okay?"

As Charlotte leaves, I close my eyes and picture a small flame. The more I focus, the larger the flame becomes.

"You doing okay, Marcus?" asks Zyniah, breaking my concentration.

"Yes," I say slowly.

Zyniah lies down on a cracked stone bench. "Okay, let me know if you need anything. I'm going to take a nap."

Again, I close my eyes and picture a flame growing in my hand. Unfortunately, Zyniah's snoring breaks my concentration.

"Zyniah! Wake up. I can't focus with you sucking down air like that."

Zyniah sits up and wipes drool from her mouth.

For the third time, I close my eyes and meditate. An hour goes by with no interruption and I've made zero progress. I open my eyes only to see Zyniah directly in my face.

"Were you this close to me the whole time?" I ask.

Zyniah says nothing.

"You can talk now. The meditation isn't working."

Zyniah pretends to unzip her mouth. "You know when I was first learning my Legacy, I would intentionally bite my lip or stub my toe. That little shot of pain would really help me focus."

While it sounds simple, it's worth giving it a try. Still inside the barrel of cold water, I bite down hard on my finger until I draw blood. Closing my eyes, I'm strangely calm. Each breath I take is controlled, and each thought is of balance and harmony. Everything surrounding me becomes mute, heat builds within my mind. Channeling this feeling into my hands, my Oro begins to heat the barrel of water. To Zyniah's credit, I can now burn objects with my hands.

213

When Charlotte returns, I demonstrate for her my Oroburn technique by burning down a straw-man with a simple touch from my hands.

"Very good, Marcus," says Charlotte. "You've already mastered your first technique. Let's begin the next one."

Charlotte orders Zyniah to read the purple book of how Ayphas create Orospheres.

Flipping through the pages, Zyniah's eyelids widen. "The Orosphere technique is the preferred form of attack for Ayphas and Aminas. This technique is performed by concentrating and compacting Oro until it converts into an explosive form of energy. When an Orosphere turns yellow, it becomes explosive. Orospheres can range in size and strength depending on the amount of Oro used. With practice and training, Ayphas and Aminas can propel Orospheres."

"Basically, all you have to do is squeeze and compress your Oro repeatedly until it's primed," says Charlotte. "Why don't you give it a try?"

"Oro release!" I yell, causing Oro to cascade across my hand. Squeezing the Oro into my palm, I can feel its flow and rhythm. The more I squeeze, the heavier and warmer the Oro becomes. Slowly the Oro takes the shape of a deformed sphere. As the sphere wobbles in my hand, a sharp zing splinters through my veins causing the sphere to break form.

"Not easy to maintain, is it?" says Charlotte.

"I almost had it on the first try!" I say proudly.

Charlotte shrugs. "Almost does not equal absolute. Try again."

"You're doing great, Marcus!" shouts Zyniah as she claps from her chair.

Charlotte cups her hands. "Ah, with such a great supporter you don't need me here. I'm going to check on the others. I'll be back later on."

The second Charlotte leaves, Zyniah instantly gets off track. "Hey, let's play a game before we start."

I shake my head and turn to a straw-man target. "No, I need to practice. Now's not the time to play your silly games." Again, I try creating an Orosphere, but it breaks down before reaching its explosive form.

For hours, I try unsuccessfully to create an Orosphere to the point my hands throb and cramp up. Needing to take a break, I lie down and stare at the sky above. Zyniah immediately hovers over me.

"Ready to play a game?" she asks.

"Can't you see I'm resting?"

Zyniah sucks her teeth and lies beside me. For a few minutes, we stare at the clouds and count the birds that fly over. Unfortunately, Zyniah is quite an antsy girl.

"This is boring. Let's play a game," she says with anxious eyes.

"Okay, but only for a little while. I have to get back to training."

"Oh yes. Absolutely!" Zyniah pulls out a large clear jar filled with crickets of all sizes and colors. "Let's play Crickets!"

"Never heard of it."

"How dull are you, Marcus? Surely everyone has played Crickets before. Jeez, I guess I'll explain as best as I can." From the jar, Zyniah pulls out three crickets. One black, one green, and one yellow.

"Okay, Crickets is a game of strategy and reflexes. The purpose of the game is to capture as many crickets as possible within sixty seconds. The tricky part is to collect the crickets without losing the ones you've already caught. As you capture one cricket, another may slip out, therefore it requires quick reflexes to maintain your cricket collection. The small black ones are worth three points, the medium green ones are worth two, and the big yellow ones are worth one. Also, within the lot are two tiny clear crickets. They're very difficult to see, therefore, if you collect one, they're worth ten points. At the end, we'll tally up the cricket scores, and whoever has the most points wins."

I raise my hand. "Just one question…how many points if I squish a cricket?"

Zyniah kicks me in the shin. "Don't even consider the thought! These are my friends." She pours the remaining crickets onto the ground. None of them move or chirp. "They're trained to respond to whistles. One whistle they move, two they halt, and three they return to the jar."

Zyniah is a quirky little girl, but what would possess her to train crickets is beyond me.

"One, two, three." Zyniah then whistles and the crickets begin to hop and chirp in every which direction. Scrambling in a frenzy, we try grabbing crickets as they spring and hop all over the place. Focusing on the smaller ones, I try to collect as many as I can, but as I grab one, another slips out. Changing strategies, I go for the larger ones, but they too slip from my hand. When Zyniah whistles for the crickets to halt, I have just one.

"Okay, show me what you got," says Zyniah.

Revealing a yellow cricket, Zyniah pauses before snickering with delight.

"Hey, it's my first time playing!" I say.

Zyniah has captured five black crickets in one hand and a mixture of many green and yellow ones in the other.

"I WIN!" Zyniah gloats and dangles the one cricket I caught in front of my face.

I snatch the cricket and toss it as far as I can. "What a stupid game."

"If it's so stupid, why can't you beat me? Mad you can't cheat this time?"

Why am I arguing with a little kid? I should just let it go...but I can't.

For ten games straight, Zyniah whoops me hand over fist. By the eleventh game I don't even bother to play. I just watch Zyniah's technique. Somehow her little hands can open and close fast enough before the crickets can escape. As I watch Zyniah scoop up the jumping insects, a clear cricket lands on her shoulder. If I could just grab it and a few others, I could beat her. I reach for the cricket, but it springs from Zyniah's shoulder. I chase after it. One, two, three scoops I miss. But then again catching crickets is similar to catching fish. Don't strike where it is, but where it's going. Eventually I get the technique down and scoop up not only the clear cricket but many others without losing them.

When the game ends, we tally up the score. While I have fewer crickets, I have a clear one, which surely will be enough to beat Zyniah.

"It's a tie!" she says.

"A tie? No way! Count again."

"I triple counted, Marcus. Twenty-five to twenty-five—it's a tie."

"Then we need to play again."

Zyniah whistles three times for the crickets to return to their jar. "Sorry, the crickets are tired now. Plus, it's getting dark."

"No, wait! One more game."

Zyniah chuckles. "Ah, for such a stupid game, you seem to really enjoy it. We'll play again tomorrow. It's time to resume your training."

Training? I had forgotten all about it after playing Crickets. I was so focused on trying to beat Zyniah, I got sidetracked.

"Well, show me what you've mastered," says Charlotte as she returns to the mansion.

"Show her, Marcus! Create an Orosphere just like we practiced," says Zyniah.

The nerve of her. She knows I can't do it.

As Charlotte looks on, I call for my Oro and rapidly begin to squeeze and compress it. To my surprise, the Oro feels heavier and more concentrated than before. My reflexes have improved as I'm compressing Oro much faster and with greater control. I watch in excitement as the Oro becomes dense and hot until it transitions from a white cloudy ball to a shining yellow sphere of pure explosive energy.

Success! I have done it! In my hand, I clutch power, strength, and devastation. Staring at Zyniah, who is all smiles and giggles, I realize her stupid little game helped improve my concentration and ability to speed up the compression process.

"Release it!" says Zyniah.

Running toward a straw-man target, I release the wobbling Orosphere and then…

POP!

The Oro dissipates back into mist.

Emotional Ties

MARCUS

Falling short of releasing an Orosphere, it's an embarrassing moment for me.

"Looks like you need more practice," says Charlotte. She examines my hand and takes note of the discolored marks on my skin. Strange though, more marks have appeared since I started training.

"Give it a few more days and you'll have it together," says Zyniah.

But I don't have a few days. I need results now. Every day that passes brings Asher and the Yazu closer to death. Petune is not a man of patience and I can only imagine the horror he's putting my friend through.

"Just take me to the island," I say in frustration. "Don't need to create an Orosphere to protect myself. I can deal with whatever is on the island."

Charlotte lights a few torches inside the dilapidated mansion to break the cool night's air.

"An Orosphere is a basic ability every Divine Aypha possesses," she says. "If you cannot learn this technique, you're not ready for Chance Island." Charlotte approaches and pokes me in the chest. "An Aypha's emotions are connected to their Oro. Ayphas draw strength from their emotions, whether a pleasant feeling of happiness or a dark emotion of anger."

"Wait, what did you just say?"

Charlotte slides on a white robe with a blue lotus flower emblem on the back. "I said your emotions are tied to your Oro."

"No, specifically you mentioned happiness or anger. Someone else once said this."

Charlotte rolls her eyes. "Okay, well you should've listened to them. You need to draw from one of these emotions to maintain an Orosphere."

Closing my eyes, I think of pleasant memories of Rose and the comfort of her soft voice. The memories quickly fade though, and my mind wanders to thoughts of Rizen. His savagery toward the Yazu and his disregard for life draws anger from my pores. I call for my Oro and squeeze it into the palm of my hand. Slowly my Oro transforms from white to yellow. Hot and heavy, the Orosphere is difficult to control. Clenching my teeth, I tighten my grip around the sphere. I'm shaking and my veins rapidly pulsate. My heart races, and raw Oro spews uncontrollably from my arm.

"Oro yield," I command, but the Oro doesn't dissipate.

"He's losing it," says Charlotte.

"Oro yield!" I repeat but Oro continuously spills from my arm at an accelerated rate.

Zyniah clamps her hands onto my arm, shutting off the flow of Oro. "Thanks, Zyniah."

She says nothing—her skin is now bronze and her eyes crystal blue. Raising her hand, she releases a massive stream of blue Oro into the sky. Tears flow from her crystal-blue eyes, her body shakes violently and she collapses.

Charlotte rushes to Zyniah's aid. She checks for a pulse, but there isn't one. My heart seizes in fear the little girl is dead.

Suddenly, Zyniah coughs but shivers nonstop.

"She absorbed too much Oro, but she'll be okay," says Charlotte as she wraps her robe around Zyniah, the shivering stops but she falls into a deep sleep.

Relieved, I plop to the ground and close my eyes, only for Charlotte to shake me.

"Stay awake. You expelled nearly all of your Oro. If it wasn't for Zyniah, you would be the one in a coma right now."

Looking at Zyniah as she sleeps, I have a new appreciation for the annoying girl.

"How did she stop it?" I ask.

Charlotte takes one of the lit torches and waves the flame over Zyniah. "It's our Legacy. We have the ability to absorb energy as well as liquids. In a way, you could say we have opposite Legacies. While Ayphas and Aminas release their inner Oro, a Zell uses Oro to absorb energy.

Once absorbed, we can amplify the energy and do all sorts of things with it."

"So, the energy Zyniah released was my own Oro? Why was it blue then?"

"When a Zell absorbs another's Oro, it is natural for it to be blue," says Charlotte. "What's also of note, we can see and sense things faster in real time than other Divines. Like Ayphas, we have other Legacy abilities, but they're rare to specific Zells."

Zyniah wakes, her eyes have returned to normal but frost remains on her eyelashes.

"Thanks, Zyniah. I owe you." I squeeze her tight and her body is cold like a winter's night.

Zyniah places her frosty, tiny hand on my cheek. "Marcus, I felt your pain and anger. There's a rage inside of you that is volatile."

I hadn't noticed before, but running down the sides of my arms is blood. A side effect of expelling too much Oro.

"Whatever you have resentment toward must be pretty strong," says Charlotte. "But this rage inside of you must be controlled to master your Legacy abilities."

"Anger. This is what she wanted me to feel," I say.

"She?"

BOOM!!!!!

Sparkles burst across the sky before burning embers rain down across the land.

"Come, something has happened in the village!" yells Charlotte.

The three of us rush back to Zenith where a large group of Zells gather in front of Queen Annabelle's mansion. Many candles are lit on the steps of the mansion and standing on a platform is a group of women wearing black cloaks. While their faces are covered by hoods, the maple leaf symbols on their sleeves indicate they're Dynas.

Seeing them gives me hope Rikari is alive. Next to the Dynas is Nyree, the Zell commander I encountered in the swamps. Raising a blue and white blade, Nyree gets the attention of the crowd.

"All that can hear my voice, I have great news to report from our magnificent queen. Lady Annabelle brings forth a message." After unsealing a letter, Nyree reads the note to the crowd.

"To the valiant women of Zell, today we begin anew with an old rival. As a new threat looms, we must strengthen our alliances. Queen Valencia and I have worked through our differences in hopes of forming a fruitful bond. As a pledge to our new sisterhood, Queen Valencia offers her support to defend our borders. Behold and welcome, the unconquerable women of Dyna!"

Instead of clapping, the young Zells whisper to one another and the older Zells frown upon the announcement.

"*Clap!*" Charlotte orders as she makes her way through the crowd and onto the platform. The Zells snap to attention and clap with hurried enthusiasm.

One by one, the Dynas remove their hoods and announce their names. After ninety-nine have done so, only one Dyna remains. Turning to the crowd, she removes her cloak. It's not Rikari, but it is a familiar face.

"Hazel Victoria," she announces and the crowd goes silent. There are no whispers from the Zells, only jaws dropping and stares of awe at Valencia's child.

"Hazel! It's me," I yell, waving from the back of the crowd. She spots me and a crooked smile spreads on her lips.

Charlotte shakes her head at my ridiculous outburst. She then escorts the Dyna's inside Queen Annabelle's mansion. Before entering, Hazel turns to me and rests her hand on the gold Krysanthem necklace I gave her.

"Somebody's in love," Zyniah giggles while pressing the tips of her fingers together. "I saw the way you looked at her. Your whole voice changed, as did your body temperature. She is very pretty…"

I roll my eyes but impressed by Zyniah's ability to read me. "We should go now. Let's get back to training."

"No, let's wait." Zyniah parks herself on the steps of the mansion. "It's not every day I get to meet a Victoria."

I sit beside Zyniah and notice the excitement in her eyes. "Why are you so giddy? She's a girl just like you."

"What an insult, Marcus. There's nothing normal about a Victoria. It's a name to fear and admire at the same time. The elders say Victorias have ruled Dyna since the beginning. With such a strong bloodline, no other Dyna can rule their land. Having the future heir in our presence is a true sign of their commitment to protecting us."

An hour later, the Dynas exit the mansion and we wave Hazel down. Before I can even speak, Zyniah takes over.

"Hi, I'm Zyniah." She vigorously shakes Hazel's hand. "You're sooo pretty! What do you use for your skin? What fragrance are you wearing?"

221

Hazel smiles and introduces herself to the impressionable Zyniah.

"Wow, even your voice is amazing…I see why Marcus likes you."

I feel my face turning red. "Hazel, pay her no mind. It is great to see you though." I give Hazel a warm hug, a hug I thought would never happen again. Seeing Hazel's light green eyes and curly bronze hair makes all the difference tonight.

"Bet you didn't expect to see me again." Hazel slides her hands down my arms, our hands cup together. The sweet scent of cinnamon still clings to her.

"So, the Dynas and Zells have truly formed an alliance."

Hazel shrugs. "Seems so. In a few days, we're to report to the northern border of Zell."

Realizing our time together will be limited, I know I need to make the most of it.

"Have you heard from Rikari?" I ask. Hazel's eyebrows rise. She must not know and telling her won't be easy. "Rikari and I were in Beta when we encountered some Aminas." I take a hard swallow before continuing. "She sacrificed herself so I could escape. That was several days ago and I haven't seen her since."

Hazel doesn't even flinch. "Commander Rikari put herself on the line as any Dyna would. If she has perished, I'm sure her last breath was glorious. She fought to ensure your purpose could be fulfilled. Which by the way, why are you here?"

"It's a long story. Let's talk about it over dinner."

"Ooooh, Ms. Stussy makes the most amazing food," interrupts Zyniah, she slides in-between us.

Hazel leans down to Zyniah. "Is that so? Well, I look forward to meeting her. I too am sort of a chef." Hazel glances up and sees rest of her Dyna teammates awaiting by a stone water well. "Unfortunately, it will have to be some other time."

Zyniah pouts. "Okay. But before you leave the village, will you spend some time with me?"

Hazel rubs Zyniah's shoulder. "Absolutely." She hugs the two of us before connecting with the other Dynas. Tonight they will be staying at a nearby inn, while I'm stuck another night playing games with Zyniah.

Where Snakes And Elephants Are One In The Same

"What do you mean she's gone?" screams a hysterical Valencia from her red velvet throne.

A petrified guard looks to the green marble floor inside Valencia's war room. "We looked everywhere, my lady. Hazel has left the land." The guard looks up to Valencia. "She must've slipped out with the Dynas traveling to Zell."

Valencia swipes an apple from her fruit tray and calls the guard toward her. "You all had one simple job to do." Valencia crushes the apple over the young guard's head. "You're dismissed, tell Minnie to come in."

Soiled in fruit juice, the guard leaves and a few moments later, Minnie slips inside. She notices Valencia's trembling hands and decides to sit beside her.

"She's okay, my lady."

"What's happened to me?" Valencia stares at her unsteady hands. Her volatile behavior is due to years of neglecting her health. "I once commanded thousands, now I struggle to control one."

"She's a teenager, my lady. Don't you recall being rebellious?"

A rare chuckle escapes from Valencia. "Haven't seen my daughter in over a year. You would think she would come visit me."

Minnie shakes her head. "This place isn't filled with the most pleasant memories. This is where you broke her, remember?" Minnie holds Valencia's hand. "If you want to reconnect with Hazel—or anyone else—you must leave this place, my lady. The women need to see their queen and know everything will be okay."

Valencia slouches deeper into the cushion of her throne. "I hate this place, yet I cannot escape it. It's safe here, away from judgment and eyes of disappointment. I've lost the respect from my commanders and even my own daughter."

"You're wrong. We always have and always will honor you, my queen. Your name is forever sealed among the greatest."

No matter how many times Minnie reassures Valencia, there's no getting through to a woman stuck in a pendulum of depression.

"Yet I failed against Sinclair," Valencia sighs. "My ancestors and successors shall forever be ashamed of me."

"That's your pride talking. Even the greatest lose sometimes." Minnie's words draw a blank stare from Valencia. "Besides, there's something more pressing." She clears her throat and leans closer to her queen. "War is coming, and we'll need you, her, and him to win."

Valencia stabs her Aurora Blade into the marble floor and rests her head on the blade's mercury pommel. "Sinclair is playing with fire when it comes to Marcus," she says. "If she's not careful, the flame will consume her and burn us all."

As the two discuss what to do with Marcus, the petrified guard from earlier returns.

"My lady, I just received word that an Aypha Divine wants to meet you outside the west wall."

Valencia straightens her back and her hands no longer tremble. "Who is he?"

"His name is Petune, and he has Commander Rikari."

"Rikari? But Sinclair was to…" Valencia dismisses the guard. She tugs at her thin silver hair causing several strands to break off.

"This is your moment," says Minnie. "Something like this requires your attention."

"I'm not ready yet." Valencia's jaw tightens and blue veins rise on her forehead. "The others…they'll laugh at me… they'll mock me behind my back. I know they will."

Minnie sighs and looks to the front door. "These thoughts are only in your head. You're the valiant Valencia Victoria! Please, do this for us. We need you."

Valencia takes the hilt of her Aurora Blade, unscrews the mercury filled pommel, and tosses it to Minnie.

"No, Minnie, it is the other way around."

***

Charged with saving Rikari, Minnie arrives outside the western wall, where more than fifty Dynas stand guard opposite of Petune. He holds Rikari's lifeless body and displays a devious smile.

"Looks like I have something that belongs to you!" Petune shouts and drops Rikari like a sack of potatoes.

A silhouette of tears form under Minnie's eyes as she stares at Rikari's gray skin. Dried blood stains run along Rikari's forehead and her wounds are filled with sand.

"What did you do to her?" asks Minnie.

"Me? I found her like this after receiving a Carrier message. Can't say I wasn't looking for her though." Putting his foot on Rikari's stomach, Petune rolls her over. "You see, this woman illegally entered Aypha and stole one of my boys. I'm here for him."

"There is no boy here."

Petune sparks an Orosphere. "You're too sweet of a woman to lie." He hovers it over Rikari's head. "She's alive, but won't be if you don't give me Marcus Azure."

Clutching Valencia's mercury bulb, Minnie contemplates breaking it. While what's inside the bulb guarantees Petune's death, it doesn't mean he won't kill Rikari first.

"No one by that name is here," says Minnie.

"Oh? What about Gail and Saphron Azure? You wouldn't know about them either, would you?" Petune's Orosphere grows brighter. "Hand them over. I'd hate to make a mess of your new commander."

Minnie shakes her head. "None of these people you seek are here."

Petune inches his Orosphere closer to Rikari, causing her skin to burn. "If you have nothing to offer, then I see no reason to keep her alive."

"You'll die," says Minnie, her nails press tight on the mercury bulb. She's one squeeze away from unleashing carnage.

Petune licks his teeth, admiring the innocent-looking Minnie. "For your sake, sweetie, I hope you're right."

"Kill him, commander!" yells one of the Dynas. Rest of the crowd joins in, encouraging violence.

Minnie's fingertips harden on the mercury bulb. If she shatters it, the full wrath of Dyna will fall upon Petune. The bulb is only for the most dire of situations, but to Minnie, this is it. Rikari's life is on the line, and she means everything to Minnie.

Relaxing her grip on the mercury bulb, Minnie slowly cracks open her lips. "I cannot help you with the ones you seek, but I can offer someone greater...Sinclair Bonet."

Loyalty

The pink glass-stained doors shatter as Ophelia barges into Cynné's rose garden. Her eyes blaze with anger as she stampedes toward Cynné who rests beside a pink rosebush.

"Unbelievable," rants Ophelia. She rattles the rosebush, causing petals to fall. "Your mother had no business interfering in my kill."

Accustomed to Ophelia's weird outbursts, Cynné is unmoved. "Calm down. What's this about my mother?"

Ophelia shoos birds away from a water fountain and takes a quick sip. "I was in Aypha when the prison breach occurred and went in pursuit of the suspects."

"You disobeyed my orders to stay put," Cynné interrupts.

"I'm your second-in-command, Cynné. I should be hunting and killing not leashed as a dog."

Cynné snatches Ophelia's wrist and twists it until it breaks. The pain means nothing to a woman who has been stabbed and burned hundreds of times.

"Your insubordination is going to get you killed," says Cynné. "You're a commander. Act like one."

Ophelia drops to her knees and kisses Cynné's hand. "I was just bored, my lady. Every now and then I need a rush. Otherwise, I'd die of sheer boredom."

Cynné proceeds inside her mansion and into a well-lit dining room where porcelain plates and meticulously polished silverware are in perfect order atop a table. Positioned around the long table are gold painted chairs wrapped with pink bows. Hundreds of delicate pink rose petals are spread across a white marble floor, and along the walls of the dining room are glass cases displaying crystal figurines of leopards, lions, and ballgown women. Cynné sits at the head of the table, a butler places a satin pink napkin onto her lap and pours her a glass of rose water. From a silver platter, the butler unveils an assortment of figs, cherries, and almonds. As the platter is neatly placed in front of Cynné, Ophelia attempts to sit beside her queen but stops upon observing Cynné's scowl.

"Cynné, I know I disobeyed you but it was with merit," says Ophelia, she takes a seat several chairs away from her queen. "I pursued the suspects and located them near Lucky Caverns. By the time I arrived, Rikari Niacin, the newest Dyna Commander, had killed many of our beauties. Before I could kill her, your mother intervened and ordered me to stop."

Cynné slides her trembling hands under the white tablecloth and away from Ophelia's view. "Why would my mother care about the Dyna?"

"I wondered the same. She said killing Rikari would've caused an immediate response from the Dynas...true or not, it wasn't her call to interfere."

A solemn look passes over Cynné. "Mother's right. Without a Phoenix, war with the Dynas is problematic."

"Kissandra claims she can help us with that." Ophelia shows Cynné the gold Carrier paper she presumed was from Kissandra. "Your mother thinks we still have the Eye of Truth. She's offering to give you what's needed to activate it on the condition you carry out her wishes— whatever that means."

Cynné stares at the gold paper and huffs. "The bad blood between them is endless. She wants me to kill General X. Guess she doesn't know he's ill and soon to die anyways. But the longer he lives, the better. He's the only one keeping the Ayphas in line. Once he's gone, the monkeys will be set loose."

Ophelia picks up a dinner knife and twiddles her tongue around it. "Killing the general would be fun though." She stabs the knife into the dining table. "Speaking of which, it was Marcus Azure who was inside the Aypha prison. He and Rikari were together. I don't know his whereabouts, but Petune's young men are in pursuit."

Cynné's hands no longer tremble and instead turn cold. "I should've seen this sooner. When Shomari and I arrived at the prison, there was an

Aypha Norm among the Yazu. Seemed strange at the time, but now that I think about it, he must be connected to Marcus."

Ophelia approaches Cynné and twirls the queen's long hair. "What do you want me to do, my lady?"

Cynné smacks Ophelia's hand away. "I want you to round up any Amina who knows Marcus and have them report to me immediately."

Shortly after their discussion, Ophelia returns to Cynné's dining room with Rose Cross. Cynné has just finished her desert and orders Rose to sit beside her.

"I understand you are friends with Marcus Azure?" asks Cynné.

Rose carefully nods. "Yes, we grew up together," she says with caution.

Cynné clasps her hands over her stomach. "That's good. And how would you describe your relationship?"

Rose straightens herself up on the dining room chair. "In Eden we were very close."

Cynné grins. "Is that why you chose to bow out of the mission with Loreen? You know he and his parents are traitors, correct? By taking the Eye from us, the Azures have weakened the Lands of Aypha and Amina, leaving us vulnerable against the other lands." Cynné places her hand on Rose's chest to measure her heartbeat. "As long as the Azures are alive, they're a threat, wouldn't you agree?"

Rose nods. "Indeed, my lady."

Cynné keeps her hand on Rose's chest, the heartbeat remains steady. She then motions to Ophelia, who brings in a shackled Amina. The young girl is covered in soot and bruised from weeks of torture. The restrained girl is brought to her knees before the queen.

"Tell me, Ms. Rose, what is the Amina Oath?" asks Cynné.

Rose clears her throat and slaps her fist over her heart. "At all times I will honor and be loyal to the queen. I will defend her against all threats and obey her every command. With my blood, I will sacrifice my life, for it is my duty to forsake all others in the name of protecting Amina. Not family, not friends, not sibling shall come before my land. If I break this oath may my death be dishonorable."

"Very good," says Cynné. "This girl before you has broken her oath of loyalty. She betrayed us by sending messages to the Zells. Her execution was to be public, however I've decided to make it more intimate." From under Cynné's robe, she unsheathes a gold blade and places it on the girl's shoulder.

The shackled Amina weeps knowing she's breaths away from death. With her arms shaking, she raises her head and apologizes to Cynné…useless words. Cynné curls her blade around the Amina's neck and as the young girl's head rolls to a stop, Ophelia smiles, oblivious that the message was meant for two.

Cynné's eyes are as cold as winter. "Which is more important to you—Ms. Rose, your land, or your friends?"

Rose takes a harsh swallow. "The land always, my lady, the land is above everything."

Cynné smirks. "Good. Those who remain loyal to me shall be rewarded." She tosses her bloody blade onto the table and orders Ophelia to hand her a book. The book is wrapped in linen and contains portrait drawings of many young Aminas. Cynné thumbs through it and stops on a particular painting. The portrait is of a teenage Amina, her violet-colored hair is draped to her shoulders and her brown skin contains traces of discoloration. "I understand your sister, Scarlett was killed a few years ago." Cynné hands the portrait book to Rose. "What would you give to have your sister back?"

Beads of tears trickle down Rose's cheeks as she stares at her sister's portrait. "Anything," she says softly.

"I can bring your sister back." Cynné wipes Rose's tears away. "All that's required is your loyalty."

Defiance

Commander Shomari is a young man in need of a heart. Twenty-three years of age, his mind wanders endlessly on ways to kill. His fury is not of carnage but of precise vengeance against a single man. He was just a boy when his father, King Rayne was killed in the last Great War. Word quickly spread that a young prodigy from Kamara had slayed the mighty King Rayne. With the king's death, the last Great War came to an end but it also renewed the cycle of vengeance. Ever since his father's passing, Shomari has trained relentlessly for the day he encounters the King of the Kamaras, Aikia of the Wind.

Customary to his daily routine, Shomari travels to his father's hand-built temple, which sits atop a plateau overlooking the Village of Armana. It was here, King Rayne once taught Shomari many life lessons of honor, respect, and pride. Here he showed his son the art of meditation and the key to using their Aypha Legacy abilities. It was also here where Shomari first learned about the cruelties of battle and the everlasting scars of war. King Rayne was a man who had seen much in his lifetime, he dedicated his life to understanding the world all to prepare his son for the inevitable.

Sliding back the red painted doors of the temple, Shomari enters and stands before a gold shrine of a lion. Removing his boots, he proceeds along the lacquered wood floors and rubs his broad hands across the shrine. It was customary for King Rayne to touch the shrine for good luck, his son now does it out of tradition. Shomari proceeds down a corridor where the interior walls are constructed of papyrus sheets and decorated with hand drawings of flowers. Entering his father's training room, he removes his shirt and reveals an unsightly scar across his chest. He stretches his muscular limbs in preparation for his daily training routine. As a warm-up, he completes a set of a thousand push-ups and sit-ups. He then blindfolds himself and throws knives at designated targets on the walls. He repeats this process until striking each without fail. To stay nimble and calm, he unrolls a bed of spikes and runs across it repeatedly without puncturing his feet. With no break in-between, Shomari releases nearly all his Oro and submerges himself into a barrel of water. Mentally strong, Shomari holds his breath for nearly twenty minutes before needing air. He does this to prevent fatigue as he knows his battle against Aikia will require great endurance.

Wrapping up his training for the day, Shomari takes a wool towel and dries off his broad chest and thick arms. Though he's a young man, his iron-tight jaw and prickly facial hair make him appear older. He approaches the front of the training room where his father's light armor is showcased on a table. King Rayne's chest armor is made of thin black iron plates tied together. Chain mail woven with gold silk threads shield the arms, and malleable shin guards made of pressed paper and iron shavings protect the legs. Shomari straps on the light armor, his father's scent still lingers. This is the armor his father died in and it will be the same armor he wears when he faces Aikia.

Shomari proceeds to his father's study where a portrait of a rising sun rests above a wood desk. Sliding back a chair, he sits at his father's desk which is covered in old books and drawings on papyrus paper. Though the study is empty, it is here Shomari speaks daily to his father. Somedays he reflects on past times between them. Other days he writes letters to his father vowing to avenge him in the most beautiful of ways. Shifting through his father's papers, he pulls out a drawing he's seen many times. His father's sketch of a fowl, lion, and scorpion. The three images match exactly to the red ink tattoos on Shomari's arms and tongue. Strangely though, the tattoos didn't appear until after his father's death. Unfortunately, the drawings have no words so the meaning of the tattoos remain a mystery.

As Shomari continues to stare at the drawings, a Carrier enters the room and lands on the desk. The bird glows and converts into a letter. The message is from Cynné who requests the transfer of the Yazu per General X's orders. Shomari scribbles a note on the paper and folds it. The paper glows, converts back into a bird, and flies away.

Leaving his father's temple, he immediately returns to the prison holding the Yazu. He directs the guards to shackle the prisoners and to take them outside. Oblivious of what's going on, Asher, Free, and her mute daughter Yondi, grow suspicious as they're ordered into a line.

When darkness falls, Cynné arrives a short time later and is accompanied by ten Amina guards. She stands beside Shomari but neither speak to one another. The Aypha and Amina guards pair up alongside the Yazu and begin their walk toward the border of Amina.

The night's air is warm as the group proceed along a lumpy dirt trail and into the woods. Crows gawk at their presence and follow them by flying from tree to tree. When the envoy arrives to the border of Amina, they're greeted by a giant wall of poisonous rosebushes and thorns.

"We'll take them from here," says Cynné.

"Agreed," replies Shomari.

"What about the Norm boy?" asks one of Shomari's guards.

Shomari frowns. "What is he even doing out here? We're taking him back to Aypha."

Cynné rests her hand on Shomari's shoulder. "Perhaps he should remain with us," she says. "A gentler face may be more convincing."

Shomari brushes off Cynné's hand. "Negative. He's mine to deal with."

"Fine." Cynné motions for the Aminas to take the Yazu.

Asher hugs Free and little Yondi. "Stay strong. Better days are yet to come," he says.

"Likewise," says Free.

Smiling, Yondi squeezes Asher's hand before two Aypha guards drag him away.

The crows from the surrounding trees begin to gawk louder. What was once a few has now become a murder of crows. Black feathers fall from the sky as hundreds of crows descend over the group and peck away at the guards. Many crows swarm over Asher as they're interested in a scent intentionally sprinkled on him. As chaos swarms, smoke bombs explode and release a massive plume of haze. Eventually, the Ayphas and Aminas fight off the crows, but when the smoke settles, many crows are seen pecking away at Asher's clothes.

Shomari turns to Cynné. "You planned this, didn't you?" he snarls while swiping at a crow.

Cynné beats back a pecking crow. "How absurd!" Her hair is frazzled and her face bleeds from many scratches. "This was Petune's doing!"

Shomari shakes his head. "Something's not right. I'm taking the Yazu back. It's not clear who can be trusted."

"No, you will give me the Yazu!" snaps Cynné. "The general ordered you to do it."

Shomari shrugs. "Take it up with him." He then orders his Ayphas to seize the Yazu and return to Aypha.

Cynné seethes but hides it well from Shomari. Without the Yazu, her mother becomes her only option to unlocking the secrets behind the Eye of Truth.

***

An overcast sky helps conceal Rose and Asher as they dash away from Amina territory. Their adrenaline pumps high, but neither say a word until reaching the north region of Beta.

Rose removes the hood on her black cloak and tucks her hair behind her ears. "You're finally putting on some weight," she says.

Wearing only underwear and black boots, Asher is practically naked. "I'll take that as a compliment." He tries hugging Rose, but she instead tosses him a dusty black jumpsuit.

Rose chuckles. "It's the smallest one I could find."

Asher slips on his jumpsuit and the two climb a tree to gather their bearings. "We're dead when they catch us." Asher lies out across a branch.

Rose sighs while surveying the area. "They were going to kill us anyways."

"Us?"

Rose looks to the sky. "I was given an ultimatum. Betray my friends or be killed." She tightens her grip onto a tree branch. "The rumor isn't true, is it? There's no way Marcus would betray Aypha...right?"

"No, but the truth no longer matters." Asher takes a hard swallow. "I'm worried for Marcus. They're going to hunt him down and kill him."

Rose clenches her teeth and hands three daggers to Asher. "We don't have time to worry, there's only time to act, and hopefully stay alive."

Asher nods and looks to the stars. "Any idea where Chance Island is located?"

"Yea, why do you ask?"

"We should hurry. Our friend needs us."

Allegiance

As he sleeps his final days away, General X knows his time is soon to expire. Once a mighty man, he's now nothing more than a bag of bones. His arms are as thin as twigs and his face has sunken in. By all accounts, it's a miracle he's still breathing. Inside his chambers, he lies on a gold-framed bed of wool. Over his headboard is a painting of his younger self and his friend, King Rayne. In the portrait, the two men have their arms crossed with their backs pressed against each other. To General X, King Rayne was more than a friend. He was like a brother. From their youthful days in Eden to their last battle together, General X and Rayne were inseparable. Unfortunately, he could not save his friend from the perils of war.

The ill man cracks open his eyes and reflects on the things he regrets in life. Recalling his shortcomings, he reminisces on old times and lets a few tears form in his eyes.

Unexpectedly, Cynné Bonet enters his bedroom and opens up his silk curtains, bringing in much needed light. The general's rancid odor causes her to gag and cough. She covers her nose with a scarf but the smell of death permeates right through it. She approaches the frail general, takes his cane, and pokes him in the stomach.

"Someone from your command attacked us during the Yazu transfer," she says.

General X releases a heavy wheeze before sitting up. "Shomari tells me it was you."

"Crow spit! Your lapdogs know I'm going to unlock the eye…they're afraid of losing power."

The general scratches his wrinkled throat. "Look at me, Cynné. I don't have the energy for this. You two need to work this out."

Cynné tightly clenches the general's cane. "That wasn't the agreement. You promised me a Phoenix if I delivered."

"That I did and which of them do you desire?"

"The Ice Phoenix." Cynné turns away from the general. "I need it to defeat her."

General X chuckles and hacks up blood into a nearby bucket. "Your mother isn't a threat."

"Seems old age has caught up to you. Mother is regaining her strength. Soon, she'll want to reclaim Amina and to defend my authority, I'll need the Ice Phoenix."

General X clutches his chest before spitting again into a bucket. "Shomari too wants the Ice Phoenix. Like you, he believes he can't defeat his target without it."

Cynné shakes her head and stares out the glass window. "He and I are nothing alike. He's only motivated to kill a man. What I seek is the world you promised me, to open the Book of Pure and obtain all its glory!"

General X glances at the portrait of him and Rayne. He too longs for revenge, but at his age, he's no match for the young King of Kamara. "Shomari was so young when his father was killed. Vengeance is all he knows."

Cynné taps the general's cane against his gold bedframe. "Look, you need my help to collect the keys. To do it, I need a Phoenix. Order Shomari to give me the Yazu, and I promise the Eye will be unlocked!"

General X pulls a feather from his pillow and rips it in half. "Just split the Yazu up. Whoever can get the information out of them will have the first choice in picking their Phoenix."

Cynné squeezes the general's cane and by the rage in her eyes, she's contemplating bashing it against the general's skull. He's reneged on his promise, a common theme of his. Cynné unveils her decision coin and places it onto her twitching fingers. She flips the coin and lucky for the general, it lands face down.

"Keep the Yazu." Cynné's face turns sour. "I'll figure this out on my own." Cynné sets out to leave but the general reaches out for her. His grip is shaky and weak but his touch is filled with sympathy.

"At least let me leave you with some final advice," says General X.

Cynné folds her arms and parks herself at the foot of the general's bed.

General X turns to the painting of him and King Rayne. "I've decided to make Shomari my successor. He's young, but like his father, a good man. His age is a hinderance, and I fear the other commanders will not accept him. However, if the Queen of the Aminas supports him, so too will all others."

Cynné grimaces at the thought. "Placing Shomari in command is a mistake. Petune will sabotage him and ruin our vision."

"Then it's up to you to ensure that doesn't happen. You must work out your differences with Shomari. Your success is tied to one another." General X places his hand on Cynné's. "Just consider it."

Cynné pries the general's hand off of hers and exits his bedroom without a word. It isn't until she returns to her mansion that she reflects on the general's request. Like Shomari, she too is young. Together they must lead their people, for it is the only way the Book shall ever be unsealed. As she heads to the top floor of her mansion, Cynné orders a guard to fetch Loreen. Covered by a glass ceiling, the top floor is a sacred hall to the Aminas. The walls are encrusted in diamonds and the white marble floor is polished to perfection. Sunrays pierce through the glass ceiling and illuminate a corridor where displayed along the sparkling walls are portraits of former Amina queens.

Cynné proceeds down the illustrious hall and stops upon reaching Sinclair's portrait. She slips a dagger into her hand and gradually slashes her sister's canvas until all the pieces lie stripped onto the marble floor.

"Sinclair, you were a disgrace to the Bonet name," Cynné says while grinding her suede boots into the shredded canvas. She paces a few steps back and gazes at Queen Kissandra's painting. "Mother, one day I shall be on this wall and under my name it shall read 'the Last Amina Queen.'"

"Everything all right, Cynné?" asks Loreen while approaching from down the hall.

Cynné's eyes remained fixed on her mother's portrait. "I need your help, Loreen. I'm going to see my mother and need you by my side. She's offering to help me unlock the Eye in exchange for killing General X."

Loreen stares at the tattered pieces of Sinclair's painting. "Did you kill him?"

"I won't have to. He's days away from dying." Cynné places her hand against Kissandra's portrait. "Mother will be happy to hear the news. She'll want to return home, but that I cannot allow."

Loreen's lips remain tight in anticipation of Cynné's next question.

"Who is your allegiance to?" asks Cynné.

Having served under the last three Bonets, Loreen has been a trusted confidant for decades. She's seen the lies and the betrayals, and through it all, she has maintained her loyalty to each queen.

Loreen takes a knee before Cynné. "There can only be one queen, my lady, and that is you. My duty is to carry out your wishes, even if the order is to kill Kissandra." Twice as old as Cynné, Loreen is truly a dying breed among Aminas.

Cynné smiles, delighted by Loreen's absolute loyalty. She rolls her decision coin across her delicate fingers and places it onto her thumb. She flips the coin and it lands faceup, a sign to proceed forward.

"Let us prepare to see my mother."

Things Aren't Always As They Seem

After trekking across the southern desert of Beta, Asher and Rose have finally reached Zell territory. Before them is a dreary swamp that will lead them into the heart of Zell. As Asher moves toward the swamp, Rose grabs his arm.

"We can't go this way," she says. "If the Zells spot us, they'll kill me."

Asher tugs away from Rose. "You're being paranoid. We'll just tell them why we're here."

Rose parks herself underneath a tree. "You don't get it. We need to take a different route to pass through their border security. We can't afford to be spotted."

"Okay, then I'll scout ahead and let you know what I find," says Asher.

Entering the wetlands, he sloshes through thick and murky water. Afraid of nothing, he travels a mile in when he's stopped by Nyree's command of Zells. Poking their heads from the surrounding trees, the girls are on high alert.

"Seems you're lost, little boy," says Nyree, emerging from below the murky waters. She ties Asher's hands behind his back.

"Hey, no need for all that," says Asher. "I'm just looking for a friend of mine. His name is Marcus Azure."

"Just like I told the others, he's not here," says Nyree. "Now turn around and leave."

In no position to argue with the Zells, Asher nods and with his hands still tied together, he waddles back through the swamp and returns to find Rose settled under a tree.

"You were right." Asher slumps next to Rose.

She takes her knife and cuts the strings from Asher's wrist. "Good job, now they know we're here."

"At least it wasn't a total waste." Asher leans back and yawns. "Seems someone else is looking for Marcus."

"What!" Rose springs to her feet. "C'mon. We need to find a way in before the others catch Marcus."

"You're right. What do you propose?" Asher closes his eyes. He hasn't rested in several days.

"Well, there's two ways we can get in. The first…"

Asher begins to snore and drool pours from his mouth.

Rose rubs her forehead before resting beside Asher. She releases and exhaustive breath and looks to the skies wondering what lies ahead.

Fate

MARCUS

After staying up nearly all night, Zyniah now sleeps peacefully in a bed across from me. Though she's quite tiny, she snores like a giant. The air is cold this morning, so I place my wool blanket over her. My stomach growls in need of food but it will be hours before Zyniah is up.

Not wanting to wake her, I slip on a blue cloak and travel to the mess hall. Last time I was bombarded by young hearted Zells, but this time things are different. As I enter the mess hall, the atmosphere is tense. Dynas sit segregated on one side of the room while Zells are seated on the other end. Neither group speaks, they simple snarl and throw dirty looks at each other. They're supposed to be allies but the divide between them remains wide. Unity will be hard. Centuries of past wars proceed their alliance.

I grab a few apples from a fruit basket and spot Hazel with the other Dynas. When I approach the table, many guards grumble and rise to their feet.

"Hazel, can I speak with you?" I ask.

"It's fine, everyone." Hazel weaves between the guards and calms them down. "I'll be right back."

We head outside and a bright smile comes to my face. "I see things are going well between the Dynas and Zells," I say sarcastically.

Hazel rests her head against the exterior wall of the mess hall. "It's been exhausting but I suppose trust takes time. I am worried things may get testy between us." A hint of stress flickers across Hazel's eyes. She's tired and its obvious her mind has been elsewhere.

"Hey, come with me, there's something I want to show you."

Leaving the mess hall, I take Hazel to a shopping corridor and enter a spice shop. Along the walls of the shop are spices used for meats and

241

fowl, but it's toward the back where I show Hazel a delicate yellow orchid attached to green vines.

"What plant is this?" asks Hazel.

"It's called vanilla." In front of the plant are several vanilla sticks. I take one and run it past Hazel's nose. "You can use these to sweeten your desserts." The shop's owner has given me permission to take whatever I need, so I slip a few vanilla sticks into Hazel's hand. "A sweet for a sweetheart."

Hazel smiles and places the sticks into her shoulder pocket. She plays with her Krysanthem leaf necklace. "When you left Dyna, I thought I'd never see you again. Thought this necklace would be the only thing I'd have of you."

I smile. "Guess fate has brought us together."

"Fate, aye?" Hazel examines the spices lining the wooden shelves. "Why would fate bring us together, Marcus Azure?"

Checking my surroundings, I lower my voice. "Fate brought me here to find my parents. What about you?"

Hazel sighs and tightens her jaw. "I'm here to heal the wound of Dyna's heart. My passage to becoming queen starts here and with it shall come Dyna's salvation." Hazel takes a glass jar filled with salt off a shelf. She pores salt into my hand until it overflows. "I'm worried about you though, Marcus. Some burdens you can't contain. Some burdens aren't meant for you to handle and are best left alone."

I pour a handful of salt back into the jar and return it to the shelf. "By burdens you mean my parents?" The muscles in my face tighten as I try to restrain my feelings. "Some burdens are necessary, especially when they have the answer to restoring peace."

"Marcus…"

I tug away and abruptly exit the spice shop, Hazel follows and for several minutes we walk in silence. Her message was disheartening and she can sense it. Her lips part open, perhaps to apologize but she holds the thought as we proceed down a winding stone trail. We pass by a few armor shops as well as some candle stores. Farther down the trail are more eclectic shops, many dedicated to helping Zells with their love life. One shop sells aromas to attract Kamara soldiers. Another shop promotes enhancers guaranteed to help young Zells grow "lady parts."

Beyond the shops, one stone building stands out like a weed among tulips. The shop's glass windows are broken. Where the door should be is merely a tattered "Restricted" sign. Ignoring it, Hazel and I slip in and discover a dim, mold-infested library. A few old books are propped up on the dusty shelves while many others have been chewed away by rats. Toward the back of the library is a section dedicated to foreign authors. Hazel and I chuckle upon seeing a book titled *Whims* by Minnie of Dyna. As Hazel thumbs through Minnie's poems, I peruse the shelf and come across a small black book written by an author named Rayne. The book is stamped with a faded gold lion, indicating Rayne is an Aypha. Titled *Mysteries Beyond the Great Lands*, I thumb through the pages and stop upon spotting a drawing of the Eye of Truth. The relic is a gold amulet of a closed eye surrounded by three colored jewels and two wings. Below the drawing are notes written by Rayne.

According to the old scrolls, when the Eye is activated, it awakens the Phoenixes. A group of people known as the Yazu protect the Eye and obtaining it is nearly impossible.

"You should see some of the wild stuff Minnie writes," Hazel giggles, her face is flushed red. "She's kind of deviant."

"I can only imagine," I say, tucking away Rayne's book. "Let's get out of here before we get in trouble."

Exiting the library, we find Zyniah standing outside with her hands on her hips. "See, Marcus? This is why I can't let you out my sight." From behind Zyniah, Charlotte strides down the shopping corridor and frowns.

"Time's up," she bellows. In her hand, she clutches a Carrier letter. "Commander CQ has intel that someone is on Chance Island. Who is it?"

I shrug. "How am I supposed to know?"

Charlotte grits her teeth. "Don't insult me. You've been wanting to go to the island since you arrived."

I look away, but Charlotte grabs me by my chin so her eyes are dead set on me. "This is serious. Tell me before someone gets killed."

If I tell Charlotte about my parents, there's no guarantee they'll be safe. Especially if they have the Eye of Truth.

"I can't. But I promise there's nothing to fear."

Charlotte squeezes my arm, her grip is incredibly strong. "Commander CQ is preparing a death squad. Whoever you're protecting is going to die unless you speak up. Are you really willing to risk that?"

I stiffen my lips. Charlotte tightens her grip on my arm. "Hazel, talk some sense into your friend. Come morning, I won't be able to help."

Charlotte releases me from her hold, she walks away as does Zyniah. My heart racing, I take a knee to gather myself.

"Crow! This is bad," I say.

Hazel pinches me. "Get up, Marcus. The next decision you make is crucial."

"My parents, I've got to get to Chance Island before the death squad arrives. The problem is the sea water is acidic, making it impossible to cross."

"That's where you're wrong," says Hazel. "My mother has many flaws but warfare is not one of them. When I was younger, she taught me how to infiltrate and extract myself from each Great Land. Marcus, I can get you to that island but…"

"What?"

Hazel frowns. "It may cause greater tension between the Dynas and Zells. They'll likely never trust us."

Seeing her reeling, I clutch Hazel's warm hand and place it on my heart. As it thumps with desperation, I stare in Hazel's eyes. "Please help me. You're the only friend I've got."

Hazel glides my hand onto her Krysanthem necklace. "Guess this is our fate."

The Island of Chance

MARCUS

As I lie awake in the hollow tree that once was home to Queen Zora, I wait for Zyniah to fall asleep before slipping outside to meet Hazel. We mount up on horses and quickly travel undetected to the coast of Zell. A warm full moon shines along the cloudless sky as we arrive to the shore of a black sand beach. The silhouette of Chance Island looms in the distance and the only thing separating me from my parents is a sea of acid.

Ripping off a piece of her scarf, Hazel tosses it into the sea. Instantly the cloth fizzles and dissolves.

"So, the sea really is unsafe for passage," says Hazel as she scans the coastline. Farther north on the shore is a collection of jagged black boulders. Acid waves splash against them, surprisingly to no effect.

"That's the secret to crossing," says Hazel. "Those boulders contain a special metal resistant to acid." She places her hands into the black sand, and her eyes glow with a green frost. The sand beneath our feet shifts and collects around the boulders. One by one, Hazel guides the boulders into the sea and manipulates their shape to form a narrow walkway toward the island. The process takes Hazel over an hour to complete, and the stress of it all has caused black veins to appear along her forehead.

"Done," she says as her eyes return to normal. Panting from exhaustion, she collapses. I quickly grab Hazel and notice her skin is as cold as ice. She shivers and ice crystals form on her eyelashes.

"I've exhausted too much of my Oro," she says.

I take off my shirt and wrap it around her. The shirt does little to keep Hazel from freezing as her hair and skin begin to coat with ice. Her lips turn blue and it's just a matter of time before her body goes into shock.

I wrap Hazel around my arms and call for my Oro. Using my Oroburn technique, I wave my hands just above Hazel's skin to warm her up.

"Thanks." Hazel nestles in closer to me. For the remainder of the night, I hold Hazel in my arms and the feeling is good.

Early in the morning, as the sun peaks above the horizon, Zyniah arrives on shore.

"HEY! WHAT DO YOU THINK YOU'RE DOING?" she says. Out of breath, she rests her hands on her knees. "Don't tell me you're thinking of going to the island. Just tell us what's going on before it's too late."

Zyniah's scratchy voice awakens Hazel, she releases a heavy stretch and hands me back my shirt. Without saying a word to Zyniah, I slip my shirt back on and glance to see Hazel's bridge is still intact. I make a dash onto the bridge and sprint toward Chance Island. Both Zyniah and Hazel follow, but I run nonstop until reaching the shores of the island.

Strange though—there's no life here. No birds chirping or insects buzzing. The island seems inhabitable due to its toxicity.

"Marcus! Marcus Azure, stop right there!" yells Zyniah as she and Hazel catch up.

"Go home, Zyniah. This doesn't involve you," I say.

"You're being rock-headed," she replies. "You don't even know where you're going."

Ignoring Zyniah, I press into a jungle of tropical trees. I'm only a few steps in when a vine wraps around my leg and whips me into the air.

"Meet the island's jealousy vines." Zyniah giggles as I hang upside down. "We use them as traps on the mainland."

I cut myself free with my dagger, only for more vines to wrap around my body.

"You can try freeing yourself, but you won't succeed without me."

"Well, do something then!"

Zyniah folds her arms. "Not until you apologize for being such a meanie."

I continue to wrestle with the vines, but it's no use. "I'm sorry, Zyniah. I'm just nervous about my parents, that's all."

"Your parents?" Zyniah releases a heavy sigh as vines continue to wrap around me. "Tell the vines how beautiful they are."

"Do what?"

"Talk to them. Let them know they're beautiful."

"Jealously vines, yeah? Dear beautiful vines of Chance Island. Oh, how I find your color to be so magnificent. There are no vines prettier than you, and I am in awe of your beauty. Of all the plants in this world you are above them all." After speaking such a ridiculous poem, the vines sprinkle white dust and release me from their grip.

"Why didn't you tell us your parents were on the island?" asks Zyniah.

I grimace, knowing I can no longer hide the truth. "It's because of what they're protecting. They would be killed if the Zells knew what it was."

"And what is it?"

I look away from Zyniah.

"Look, Marcus, I promise not to say anything, but you have to trust me. I'm the only one here who can help you."

"They have the Eye of Truth," I confess.

Zyniah's lower lip hardens. She wants to know more but holds off and leads us deeper into the jungle. Traveling along a path, we become thirsty and our lips turn brittle. Approaching a fork in the path, we arrive at a water well. Etched into the stones of the well are happy and sad faces. A wood bucket dangles above the well with a message.

"Welcome, hope you're enjoying the trip! Want to proceed left, just take a sip. Otherwise head right to where bats stay from sight."

The bucket is filled with water, but as thirsty as we are, we aren't certain it's safe to drink. I take a few strands of grass and try dropping them into the bucket, but a strange gust of wind from the well blows them away.

"So that's why this place is called Chance Island," says Hazel. "Just like the sea, everything here is a gamble."

"Well, should we drink it or not?" I ask.

"Too risky. Let's head right."

"I second that," echoes a chipper Zyniah.

Outnumbered two to one, we veer right, and continue until the trail comes to an abrupt end. Surrounded by tropical trees and thick brush, we're officially lost.

"See, I knew we should've tried the water," I say. "Now what?"

"Take a look," says Zyniah, pointing to the trees. "There's sad faces on the tree trunks heading west and happy faces on the ones heading east."

"Guess we should head toward the smiling ones," says Hazel.

We follow the trees etched with happy faces and arrive at a clear opening. Ahead, a fast-moving river splits into two different caves. Above one cave are the creepy happy and sad faces. Above the other is a black crest of twin trees. As we approach the river, we notice a wooden sign that reads as follows:

"Welcome to Curiosity Rivers! One makes you smile, the other is a quiver. Veer left to see your fortune's best. Prefer life as a guess, choose the one with the crest."

"Definitely we should choose the one on the left," I say. "Can't wait to discover my fortune."

"Or your demise," says Hazel. "Anything that attempts to tell you the future should not be trusted. What do you think, Zyniah?"

"Agreed." Zyniah nods as if she's Hazel's puppet. She takes a few tree leaves and throws them into the river. The leaves don't dissolve, indicating it's safe to travel. Zyniah dives in and veers toward the cave on the right.

It's my turn next, but I'm hesitant.

"What's the matter, Marcus? Need me to hold your hand?"

"Ha, don't be silly."

"Okay. Looks like you missed your chance." Hazel winks at me before diving in.

I too jump in and float into a dark cave. The river picks up speed. I twist and turn around a few curves before blasting out of the cave and into a pool where Hazel and Zyniah await. We climb a ladder and proceed onto a grassy wet field until reaching two massive coconut trees. Beyond the trees is another cave where inside an orange light flickers. Outside the cave is a pair of small pants as well as some tiny boots.

I run toward the cave but the twin coconut trees lean over and form an X.

"They must be warning us of something," says Hazel.

"Either way, I'm going in. You two can stay here if you want."

Hazel approaches and grabs my wrist. "Let's do this together, okay?"

The three of us together move forward causing two coconuts to shoot from the trees and roll to our feet. One coconut is engraved with the word "Big?" the other says "Small?"

"Let's choose big," I say.

Both Zyniah and Hazel grow wrinkles on their foreheads.

"I say small," says Hazel. Naturally, Zyniah concurs.

"What's with you two? Why do you hate my suggestions? Fine, we'll go with small." Out of spite though, I pick up the big coconut and toss it back to the trees. The twin trees shake and each one forms a gigantic coconut. Swelling in size, the coconuts crack open like giant egg hatchlings and reveal two unsightly creatures. According to Zyniah, one of the creatures is a Razorbeast. It's a wooly four-leg animal with spikes protruding from its nose, back, and long sharp tail. The other creature stands on two legs and has scales like a snake. Its head is similar to a lizard, and it's lanky arms stretch to the ground.

"Good job, Marcus," says Zyniah. "You just had to choose big."

Hazel places her hand on the ground. "Spit! I can't use my Legacy for some reason."

Zyniah stretches her short legs. "Guess it's just you and me, Marcus. I got the hairy one!" she shouts while rushing toward the beast.

"Oro release!" I yell. Compressing my Oro, I try forming a sphere, but the lizard's arm stretches forward, forcing me to roll behind a large boulder. Again, I channel my Oro, but the lizard's sticky tongue whips around the boulder and latches onto my arm. I'm flung into the air and then slammed into the ground. The lizard pounces on me, its breath hot and foul. Vile saliva spews from its mouth as it attempts to bite my flesh. I try strangling the odd creature, but it's no use. Switching tactics, I snatch my dagger and stab the lizard in its eye. As it backpedals, I roll away but the lizard wraps its sticky tongue around my chest and constricts tight like a snake. My breathing becomes shallow and my heart pumps with panic until I hear her eloquent voice.

"Focus and stay calm," says Sinclair in the back of my mind.

Closing my eyes, I block out all thoughts and call again for my Oro.

Using Oroburn, my hands ignite with heat, causing the lizard to unravel its tongue. In a dash, I shove my fiery hands into the lizard's face, blinding it completely. The lizard screeches, tumbles over, and curls into a fetal position. A coconut shell forms around it and shrinks to the size of a pea.

Glancing over at Zyniah, she too has just finished slaying her beast.

Hazel claps her hands. "Looks like Marcus was a second faster than you, Zyniah."

Zyniah folds her arms. "Humph, only because I took the bigger one."

Wiggling and rattling, the coconut trees recede into the ground, and from the cave appears an upright walking fox.

"Ah, was counting on you all to die," says the short-statured fox. He puts on his pants and laces up his tiny boots. "You outsiders are becoming a nuisance." By the looks of his gray beard and frail frame, the fox is an old and disgruntled creature. "Most always pick the little option and lose," grumbles the fox.

I nudge Hazel and Zyniah. "See! I made the right choice." They roll their eyes in response.

"Yes, yes, for winning, you're awarded one question and answer. So, what would you like to know?" asks the old fox. After a long and awkward pause, the fox clears his throat and continues. "I suppose I should introduce myself. My name is, well, just call me Francis. I'm the caretaker here who comes up with all the island challenges."

"I'm Marcus Azure. This here is Hazel and Zyniah." I reach out to shake Francis's hand, but instead he strokes his frizzled gray beard.

"Azure?" Francis's ears perk up. "That name sounds familiar."

"Perhaps you've met my parents. Are they currently here?" I ask.

"Ah! That is your one question and now I owe you one answer." The old fox turns his back on us and regurgitates from his mouth a green sphere with swirling white clouds. Francis tells us that the green sphere is known as a *Seeker* and has the ability to locate others. The fox places his hands on the Seeker and asks it to locate who is on the island. The clouds swirl around the Seeker before shooting into the sky. A few minutes go by and the clouds return.

"Besides you all, there are three others on the island. Two are east near the top of a mountain. The other is north wandering through a forest."

"So, what does that mean?" I ask. "Are my parents here or not?"

Francis smiles while rubbing his cotton-white belly. "I've told you all that you need to know."

"No, I asked you a direct question. Why can't you give me a straight answer?"

The fox's silly smile grows wide. "Again, I've told you all you need to know."

Hazel rests her hand on my shoulder. "It's okay, Marcus. Your parents must be the pair on the mountain. We just need to make our way there."

Francis waves goodbye. He then swallows the Seeker but immediately begins to shiver. "Oh dear, this was my biggest fear." Francis's tone has drastically changed. "By releasing the clouds, everyone knows the location of each other. Whoever is north of here is now racing toward the mountains."

"Quick, we must get there before they do!" shouts Zyniah.

"Follow the trail back to the well then take a chance at drinking the spell," rhymes Francis.

"Who knows what will happen by then? You oversee this place. Isn't there a faster way?" I ask.

Francis plays with his paws before releasing a sly grin. "Perhaps...but if you want my help, you're going to have answer a riddle. Get it right and I'll take you by flight. Get it wrong and you must be gone. What do you say?"

"We'll play your stupid game," says Zyniah. "Between me and Marcus, there isn't a game we can't beat."

Francis curls his gray mustache and rubs his paws together. He's delighted to play a silly game while knowing my parents' lives are at stake. "Okay, here it is...This is your greatest enemy as well as your greatest friend. It discourages potential and encourages failure. It can take you to the limits of life or destroy all your dreams. What is it?"

Circling in a huddle, the three of us contemplate the riddle. What could be your friend as well as your enemy? Perhaps a sword? Maybe an animal? Could it be jewelry or clothing? No, Francis's question was much deeper than that. It was something intangible like an emotion or a feeling. It had to be something personal, something we all could relate to.

As I repeat the riddle in my head, the answer finally comes to me. It is something I am quite familiar with. It is both a motivator and a miser. It is something I can confide in at times and hate moments later. It is an easy riddle.

"Yourself," I say. "It is yourself that is your greatest enemy and friend."

Francis's ears turn inward, and his brown nose twitches. "Guess I have to come up with some harder riddles. All right, children, lower your heads and close your eyes."

Upon doing so, we hear what sounds like bones cracking and flesh ripping apart. When we get the clearance to open our eyes, we see Francis has grown ten times in size and bestows gold arched wings. His bushy tail has multiplied by two and on the tip of his nose is the Seeker.

"After all these years, it still hurts to take this form," says Francis. "C'mon. Let's get this over with."

The three of us jump on Francis's back, and with the quickness of light, we blast off into the air. Soaring like a bird, we fly over the island and a warm breeze momentarily breaks our tension.

As we arrive to the peak of a lush green mountain, Francis hovers above and stares at his seeker.

"I don't see the pair, but they're definitely there," he says.

We descend onto the mountain peak. Francis returns to his normal size, his tails become one, and his gold wings simply blow away. He stares at his Seeker intently. "Looks like the third person is closing in, but the other two haven't moved. Apparently, we're right on top of them."

Looking over the edge of the mountaintop, we see no one.

Zyniah places her hand onto the ground. "They're inside the mountain," she says. "It's possible they're trapped."

Laughing hysterically, Francis falls on his back and rolls from side to side. "I love this part." Next to him are two holes in the ground…two holes that weren't there just seconds ago.

"Make a choice," says Francis. "Both choices are quite grand, but I'm certain there's only one you can stand. There's no fun in precision, so hurry, hurry, make a decision!"

Tired of his nonsense, I grab Francis by his dingy beard. "Enough. Now isn't the time for games. People's lives are in danger."

Francis chuckles and enjoys seeing the stress on my face. "Sorry, wish I could help, but I don't make the rules…oops, actually I do, so pick one and choose."

I'm dealing with a miser. But there's no time to argue. Someone's after my parents, and I will not allow them to be harmed.

"Hazel, Zyniah, I'm going down the first hole. You two take the other. If I make the wrong choice, I'm counting on you to protect my parents."

Nodding their heads, we then separate, jumping into the holes of mystery.

I twist down a makeshift slide and quickly realize this was the wrong hole. The slide leads me out to the base of the mountain, I immediately look up and grow anxious. My heart pounds heavy and a knot bulges in my throat. What is happening? Are my parents safe? Please help them Hazel and Zyniah. I wait and wait and wait until…

Two black cloud streams erupt from the side of the mountain and spread across the sky toward the mainland of Zell. Seconds later, a third black stream shoots from the mountain in the same direction. There's a moment of silence before Francis emerges from the mountain carrying Hazel and Zyniah across his back.

"What happened? What did you see?" I ask as they descend to the ground.

Hazel shakes her head. "Sorry, Marcus, they left before we could get to them. All we saw were the trails of black smoke."

I lower my head. "Crow, what a complete waste of time," I say.

Zyniah points to the black clouds which stream toward the mainland. "We should hurry back home," she says.

As we quickly jog back to the island's coast, one question lingers on my mind.

"Francis, who was the other person on the island?"

The fox shrugs. "I could take a guess or even a stance, but it's best you say bye to the Island of Chance."

Tired of his insistent rhyming, I reach out to strangle him, that is until a squad of Zells appear on the coastline. Commander CQ's death squad has arrived.

There's No Place for Children

MARCUS

Commander CQ's death squad is a rough and mangy group of women. Steely-eyed and marked with red scars, the squad members have likely assassinated hundreds of targets. Standing knee deep in the acid seawater, they wear special black bodysuits that are resistant to the acid. A woman of incredible physique waves the other women to the side. She absorbs acid from the sea and hurls it toward us. We roll away just as the acid hits the sandy beach.

"Markel! What are you doing?" yells Zyniah. "They're not the threat."

"Then explain yourself," shouts Markel whose gritty black hair contrasts horribly with her pale skin.

Zyniah looks to the ground. "Um, it's kind of a long story but basically…"

"It's not her fault. I dragged her here," I say.

Markel unsheathes a silver blade. "For what, Aypha boy?"

I think of lying, but before I can, Francis approaches and points to the smoke streaks in the sky. "The answer is back on the mainland," he says. "Three others were just here."

Markel stabs her blade near the fox's feet. "You could've warned us, Francis. Is anyone else here?"

Francis shakes his head. "I must attest, what you see here is all that's left."

Markel shoves her hand into Francis's mouth and yanks his tongue. "You better not be lying. Lying is why you're here in the first place." She releases her grip on Francis's tongue, the old fox grumbles and walks away.

Markel turns her attention back to us. "You all are under arrest for trespassing in a restricted area."

Zyniah drops to her knees and cups her hands together. "But, Markel, we've done nothing wrong."

"Be quiet Zyniah!" snaps Markel. "You're in enough trouble."

As Markel's squad detains us, Francis comes up to me and smiles. "Hope to never see you again, Dark Raven."

His words cause a chill to run up my spine. "Why do you call me that?" I ask.

Francis tilts his head and his pointy ears turn inward. "You're a creepy fellow. Your Oro is disturbing and it makes me uncomfortable. You're like a blend of mystic and hazard, just like a raven."

"All right, all right. Enough of your drivel," says Markel. She pokes Francis in his white fur belly. "Return to your cave and your silly games."

Obliging, Francis departs while singing an awful tune.

Markel and her death squad then take us back to the mainland where on the shore are three massive holes steaming with black smoke. Across the sky are three fresh streams of smoke that lead toward the capital Village of Zenith. We follow the smoke streams and arrive to a catastrophic scene. Nearly everything in the shopping corridor has been destroyed. The spice shops, the food stands, and even the aromatic shops have been obliterated into crumbled stones. Shattered glass and burning wood splinters litter the ground. The few shops that still stand are beyond repair. In the center of the shopping corridor is Charlotte along with several other Zells inspecting the area.

Markel brings us forward and forces us to our knees. "Found these kids on the island," she says. "Just before we arrived, three smoke streams erupted from the mountains and headed in this direction."

Charlotte's eyes immediately fall onto mine. "Witnesses report three unknown entities cloaked in smoke were in a battle here. Who was it, Marcus?"

"I..."

"Commander! There's something you need to see immediately," shouts a Zell soldier.

We follow the soldier behind a damaged armor shop, a cone of black slime is partially covered in the dirt.

"Watch this," says the Zell. She tries poking a stick into the slime, but its immediately propelled away. "Something's inside, but we can't get to it."

As we move closer, my hands tingle and the leaf around Hazel's neck glows hot red.

"I think it's calling for me," I say. "May I try?"

Charlotte grimaces but nods.

I stretch my hand out, the ooze melts away and reveals a gold amulet of a closed eye encrusted with three gems and two gold feathers. I immediately recognize it from Rayne's book—the Eye of Truth. As I reach out for the Eye, it clamps tight around my wrist. I try pulling it off, but its grip is too tight.

Turning to face the Zells they all back away in fear.

"He has the Eye!" yells Markel. "So, this is what you were after." She turns to her death squad. "Seize him immediately."

Several Zells pounce and shove me face-first into the smoldering dirt. Hazel pushes back many of the Zells but she too is eventually brought to the ground.

"Let them up," Charlotte orders. "Queen Annabelle told us to protect this boy. Perhaps it was for this reason."

Markel's pale skin ignites red. "She would never put us in such danger. The Aypha boy is a threat that must be eliminated." Markel eyes fixate on the amulet around my wrist. "Who was on the island? Who gave this to you?"

I puff out my chest and take a step closer to Markel. "It doesn't matter now. What's important is what happens next. I'm going to…"

In one swoop, Markel slides a knife to my throat. "Tell me or I'll kill you right here," she warns.

"Markel, put the knife down!" orders Charlotte.

Markel keeps her knife firm to my throat. "Not until he explains himself."

"My parents were on the island," I finally confess. "They hid there after stealing the Eye from the Ayphas."

Markel grips her knife even tighter. "And the third person?"

"Don't know. But it seems they too were after the Eye. Out of desperation, my parents must've left it for me. I think they want me to finish what they have started and destroy the Eye."

"You take us for fools," says Markel. "For centuries, Divines have sought possession of the Eye. No one would destroy something so coveted. Whoever has the Eye has the power to control Pyris."

"This is why it must be destroyed," I argue. "To do so, the Eye must be reunited with the Yazu. The only problem is they're being held inside an Aypha prison. If I can free them, the Eye can be destroyed."

Markel laughs and taps her knife on my forehead. "You're insane to think we're going to let you leave and return to Aypha with the Eye."

"Come with me then," I offer. "Help me free the Yazu. Together we could do this."

Charlotte steps in between us and lowers Markel's knife. "It's too risky, Marcus. What you have in your possession is extremely powerful."

"We should use it," says Markel. "This is our chance to gain real power. We cannot let an opportunity like this pass us by." Markel sidesteps Charlotte and lunges at me with her knife.

Charlotte intervenes and squeezes Markel by the wrist. "The Eye shall not be used. Doing so will only lead to more harm," she says.

Markel yanks away from Charlotte and throws her knife at my boots. "You're making a mistake, Charlotte." Markel gathers her death squad and proceeds to walk away. "I advise you to reconsider. Would hate for something to happen to Marcus."

Markel flicks me a malicious smile that causes the soles of my feet to go numb and the very air I breathe to cease.

When Children Become Men

MARCUS

Latched tight to my wrist, the Eye of Truth is cold and heavy. Staring at it under the covers of my bed, I'm confounded with what to do. In my possession is a catalyst to death and destruction. I know it should be destroyed, but the Eye taunts me with intrigue. The amulet's red, blue, and purple gems surrounding the closed eye are tantalizing, and the wings that wrap around my wrist are of unblemished gold. The power to wield phoenixes lies with me, as does the heavy burden of what to do.

Across from my bed, Zyniah is asleep as usual. After my encounter with Markel, she vowed to watch over me, good thing I can't sleep tonight. Lighting a candle, I head upstairs to Queen Zora's old study and open Rayne's book. I search for passages about the Eye and one of his notes stands out among them all.

Note #80: The elder scrolls point to evidence the Eye can only be activated through blood. But the blood of who?

Could it be mine? I wonder. Is this the real reason why my parents have given me the Eye? Not to destroy it but to use it against the other Great Lands? I prick my finger with a knife and draw blood. Hovering my finger over the eye, I retract it before blood can make contact. The fear of what might happen is too great.

It's still dark when a knock comes to my door. It's Hazel, dressed in a leather black and red combat uniform. Not wanting to wake Zyniah, I quietly step outside and close the door behind me.

"I know it's early, but I couldn't sleep. Guess I was worried about you," she says.

"Me neither, I'm not certain what to do with the Eye," I say.

Hazel places her hand on my chest. "Follow your instincts. Your heart will guide you to the right answer."

"Thanks, great advice as usual." We embrace and Hazel's delicate hands press nicely onto my firm back. Her touch is reassuring. Much has changed since we first met. She's been there for me in moments of desperation and I promise to one day return the favor.

"Thanks for everything," I say and rest my forehead on hers. "These last few days have been chaotic."

"Don't worry, I'm still here." Hazel looks down at her Krysanthem leaf necklace. "Just as you gave me this to remember you, I have done the same." Hazel hands me a smooth obsidian stone etched with maple leaves.

"I made it from the boulders by Chance Sea." Inscribed on the stone is a phrase:

When like energies connect, happiness and harmony intertwine into an unbreakable bond.

"Beautiful..." My eyes connect with Hazel's and the urge to kiss her becomes irresistible. Our hands interlace and our cheeks softly press together. I close my eyes, going in for a kiss, my mouth yearns for the sweet taste of cinnamon from her lips. But all I taste is salt.

Hazel's fingers rest between her lips and mine.

"Do you still feel incomplete?" she asks. "Does the girl from your dreams still wander your mind?"

Rose. I'm surprised she even remembered; it takes me a moment to respond. "Every time I think of you, peace comes over me like still waters on a summer's eve."

"Aw! How sweet is that?" yells Zyniah, peeking outside the front door. "You gotta kiss him after that line."

"Morning, Zyniah!" greets Hazel. She wipes crust out of Zyniah's eyes. "Since you're up, let's spend some time together, just you and me?"

Zyniah's eyes sparkle, she hugs Hazel like a kid hugs their mother. "Great, let me get dressed. I'll be right back."

As Zyniah returns inside, I take Hazel's hand. "I meant what I said, you know."

Hazel smiles but there's apprehension on her lips. Perhaps rightfully so. "Let's talk later," she says. Zyniah returns and the two depart just as dawn begins to blossom.

Needing to clear my head, I venture to the old mansion on the outskirts of the Village of Zenith. I set up a few straw-man targets in preparation for practice. Having the Eye has created a new sense of pressure and a need to protect myself. My parents have levied a burden on me that I'm uncertain I can bare. They have placed fate of Pyris in the hands of a young man who doesn't even know them anymore. It's been far too long since we've last spoken for them to leave me with such a grave toll. But then again, is this not what I asked for? To become someone, someone worthy of a life? If so, then the time to act is now.

A light whistle from outside the mansion catches my ear. I venture outside and the air in my chest evaporates upon seeing Darius, Rizen, and two other Aypha Divines.

"How did you…what are you doing here?" I ask.

Rizen's smile is devious. "We missed you. Figured we'd pay you a visit."

The four Ayphas fan out around me. The nerves in the tips of my fingers burn but I can't show any fear.

"Truth be told, I was coming home soon anyways," I say.

Rizen points to my arm. "You have the Eye. The only way you're coming home is in a body bag." Rizen snaps his fingers, and the two Ayphas rush forward. My heart pounds. I want to run, but I'm tired— tired of being meek and afraid, tired of pain and failure. Now is the time to rise.

Screaming like a deranged animal, I charge toward the Ayphas. We collide and instantly I shatter the jaw of one of them. We tussle and trade dirty blows. The other Aypha slips his arm around my neck and places me in a choke hold. Desperate for air, I reach for my dagger and stab the Aypha in the thigh. I flip him over my shoulder, and with one punch, he's out cold. There's a spark of energy. The other Aypha clutches an Orosphere and holds it inches before my face.

"Turn off your Oro," commands Rizen. "We have to do this quietly."

Blood trickles from the Aypha's lips. "He broke my jaw. Let me at least repay the favor." The Aypha turns to Rizen. A mistake, for I slice the Aypha's arm clean off, snatching his severed arm, I shove his own Orosphere into his chest. Blood splatters everywhere, and the Aypha drops dead before my feet.

My hands tremble. For the first time ever, I've killed without mercy. It was vicious and cold, yet natural. As I wipe blood from my eyes, Rikari's words now ring true. To survive, there's no mercy in the Divine world.

"So, Marcus, you're not a total weakling," mocks Rizen. "Darius, say your final words to your friend. His life ends now."

Darius sparks an Orosphere. "His life is mine and mine alone to take."

Anger boils within Darius; it's painful seeing my old friend like this. Our friendship is forever destroyed. No longer is it possible to go back to when things were innocent and our cares were none. Pain is all that remains within him. This is different than our last encounter. I can see it in his eyes. He's come to kill and it's either my life or his.

"ORO RELEASE!" I scream. Like the rising of the sun, a burst of Oro fills my hand. With one thunderous squeeze, I form an Orosphere. Struggling to keep it stabilized, I hold it with two hands.

Darius releases his Orosphere, I counter releasing my own, and as our spheres collide, a massive explosion rocks what's left of the old mansion.

Though I've neutralized Darius's attack, it isn't without penalty. Oro spews uncontrollably from my arm. Soon, I'll pass out if I cannot gain control of it. Desperate to quickly end the fight, I channel another Orosphere and hurl it at Darius's feet. He avoids the blast by leaping into the air, but to his surprise, I catch him midjump. My fist connects with his chin, knocking him back to the ground. Standing over him, I prime another Orosphere and pause.

"Well, aren't you going to kill him?" asks Rizen.

Staring at my friend's unconscious body, I'm torn. Although he wishes death upon me, there's nothing in me that wants the same for him. He's still forever my friend.

Rizen sneers and forms an Orosphere. "I take it all back. You're still pathetic." He hurls his Orosphere at me but I counter with my own. White hot Oro continues to spew rapidly from my arm. My vision turns blurry, my arm bleeds like a river, and my heart strains in agony.

I'm seconds away from entering a coma. I must end the fight now, so I feed every last drop of my Oro into a final sphere. Gnashing my teeth, my veins bulge and blood bubbles pop on the surface of my skin. I unleash the sphere with such speed there's no time for Rizen to react. The sphere explodes, decimating everything in its path. It was overkill, but if anyone deserved a merciless death, it was Rizen.

Panting and breathing heavy, I wait for the gray haze to settle. To my horror, Rizen remains unharmed, shielded inside a dome of hardened Oro.

"Playtime is over," says Rizen with a smirk. Retracting the shield, he forms a disc of hot Oro. By the time I notice, it's too late. Warm blood pools around my ankle—Rizen's disc of hot Oro has cut my foot clean off. Yet I refuse to fall down. There's something admirable to die standing up.

As Rizen primes another Oro disc, Darius comes to.

"Just in time," says Rizen. He strengthens his Oro disc and my mind races. I try forming an Orosphere, but my arm seizes up. Drained of energy, I'm good as dead. Taunting me with a wink, Rizen launches his Oro disc.

Swoosh!

The disc splits apart and turns to mist. Charlotte now stands in front of me, four blades strapped to her back and a fifth red-hot one in her hand.

Markel, Hazel, and Zyniah circle around Darius and Rizen.

"Ah, the Seven Blades of Might," says an unshaken Rizen. "Blades so strong they can diffuse all forms of Oro. Seems you're missing two blades, though, so you can't use them to their full potential."

Charlotte says nothing, giving Rizen room to speak.

"Allow me to sincerely apologize. We don't want any problems, we just need to reclaim what is ours. That traitor behind you is an abomination to Aypha and must pay for his crimes."

Charlotte walks toward Rizen, but each step becomes a little faster until she breaks into a sprint. Channeling something in his hand, Rizen releases a bright light, blinding us all.

When our vision returns, all the Ayphas, including the dead one, are now gone.

Relived the battle is over, I collapse to the ground. My leg aches at where my foot has been severed.

"Marcus! Are you okay?" shouts Hazel. Using her Legacy, she quickly sews my foot back to my leg by using thin threads of iron. There's a tingling sensation around my ankle, indicating my wound is beginning to heal.

"Who were those guys?" asks Markel as she stands over me.

I lower my head. "Ayphas. One of them once was a friend."

Markel scoffs. "Some friend."

Hazel helps me up, and with her Legacy, she creates a set of iron crutches and places them under my armpits. "You held your own though."

Reflecting on the battle, I'm relieved to be alive, but the gap in strength between Rizen and me is terrifying.

"They were after the Eye, weren't they?" asks Markel. She checks my wrist to confirm the Eye is still intact. "Those Ayphas know you have the Eye, we must catch them before they escape our borders."

Markel races off and calls for her death squad to scour the woods. Hours pass before we hear news of a capture. The Zells bring them to Zenith's capital square but when we arrive, it's not Darius or Rizen, but Asher and Rose who've been captured. Blindfolded and on their knees, they're being pelted with rocks thrown by an angry mob of Zells.

"Stop!" I yell, jumping in to shield my friends. "These are not the intruders. These are my friends."

Markel enters the circle. "More friends to kill you?" she asks.

Still blindfolded, Asher shakes his head in denial. "Lady, you don't know what you're talking about. We're here to help Marcus."

Markel rips Asher's blindfold off and pokes him in the forehead. "For a shortstop, you sure have a mouth."

Markel cocks back to punch him, but I intervene.

"Leave him be."

Disdain flickers across Markel's dark eyes. "Who do you think you are? You've brought us nothing but chaos. Our shops are destroyed, Ayphas have breached our borders, and now these two are here. All because of you."

Markel turns to the crowd of Zells, "Shout if you're in favor of killing the intruders."

To my surprise, many Zells raucously chant for death before Charlotte steps in and quiets the crowd. She takes a hard swallow and her jawline tightens. "There shall be no killing," she declares. The mob of Zells boo and Charlotte does nothing to stop them.

"What? At least let us hang the Amina!" shouts Markel. She picks up Rose by her collar. "The enemy is right here, yet you do nothing...Annabelle nor CQ would ever allow this."

Charlotte cuts Markel with her eyes and stands nose to nose with her. "They will not be harmed. That's an order."

The air goes silent and there's a long pause before Markel sneers. She bristles past Charlotte; her death squad follows while many other Zells spit on Rose as they disperse. Charlotte grits her teeth and stares at the tips of her boots. Obviously, defending an Amina may come back to haunt her.

"If anyone needs me, I'll be back in my quarters," she says. "Zyniah, watch over them." Charlotte walks away without so much as looking at us.

I help Asher and Rose to their feet. Neither look good. Blood covers them, and their flesh is marked with dark bruises. Of the two, Rose has it worse. Tiny wood stakes are drilled into her fingertips, and her neck is scorched. The Zells were truly planning on torturing them to death.

"Rose," I hesitate, not knowing how to greet her after all these years. "I'm so sorry they did this to you."

Rose wipes blood from her lips. "I'm an Amina, Marcus. I'm the enemy." She falls into my arms and we embrace in a warm hug.

It's hard to see her like this. She was once a delicate flower, her petals are now burned and stained. I wipe dirt from her cheeks, revealing her pretty pink freckles. Under all that dirt and blood is the girl I remember—the one who first touched my heart back in Eden.

"It's been too long," she says softly. "I missed you." Rose stands on her tippy toes to get a good look at me. "You've gotten taller." Her smile turns into a frown. "You were supposed to write me! What happened?"

"I…um."

"You know Marcus has always been lazy," says Asher. His insult is actually a lifesaver. "You should see how he kept his military quarters, just so sloppy and tacky."

"You're one to talk, Asher. Your place smelled like crow piss," I say.

"Least it's not a junkyard. Especially with all those balled up letters…"

I squeeze Asher's lips to shut him up. He returns the favor by twisting my nipples. Rose laughs hysterically and plucks both our foreheads.

"You two haven't changed a bit," she says. "The fighting, the petty antics…it's like we're back in Eden all over again."

I wrap my arms around my friends. "Yeah, I miss home, but I miss you all even more. Say, why don't we catch up over a meal?"

"EXCUSE ME!" yells Zyniah, her arms folded. In the midst of our reunion, we had forgotten all about her.

"Who is this smunchie?" laughs Asher. For once, he is actually taller than someone else.

Zyniah jams her finger up Asher's nose, causing him to wince. "Zyniah's the name, and both of you are in my custody."

264

Asher cocks his head back to stop his nose from bleeding. "Just great. We have a baby watching us."

Zyniah steps on Asher's foot. He tries stepping on hers, but Zyniah is too quick. "Just because you're Marcus's friends doesn't mean you're allowed to wander off unaccompanied. It's my job to watch you, and if at any moment you decide to venture off…I'll kill you."

Asher no longer smiles. In fact all of us are afraid of Zyniah.

"Now let's eat," she says.

Entering the mess hall, I introduce Asher and Rose to Ms. Stussy who affectionately greets them with big hugs. In a hurry, she whips up some bean soup and fire-seared fish. As we gobble down the hearty meal, Zyniah goes to the kitchen to help Ms. Stussy, giving the rest of us a moment to catch up.

"You don't know how glad I am to see you all," I say. "It's been rough these past few days."

"Rough? You left me in a prison," Asher grumbles. "How do you think I've been?"

"Hey, I was coming back for you! I just needed time to come up with a plan."

"A plan?" Asher laughs. "I would've been dead by the time you came up with one. Good thing Rose showed up."

"It wasn't like I had much of a choice," says Rose as she rests her head onto the table. "Because of you two, the Aminas think I was involved in the attack. They're questioning the loyalty of anyone past or present associated with Marcus." Rose raises her head and looks at me. "Marcus, I hope you have a plan."

I huddle closer to Asher and Rose. "My plan is to carry out my parents' wishes. Someone's after them. I don't know who, but I know what they're after." No longer comfortable having the Eye of Truth exposed on my wrist, I now keep it covered by a scarf. Unwrapping the scarf, I reveal the Eye to Asher and Rose. "My parents left this for me. I think they want me to destroy it."

Rose leans in to examine the rare relic. "Marcus…your parents, maybe they want you to have this power. It is everything in this world."

Asher scoffs. "There's more to life than power. Many people live happy lives without it."

"Spoken like a true Norm." Rose props her feet up on Asher's thighs. "Sorry, Asher, but a Divine's life is not filled with happiness. Without power, we cease to exist."

265

Two years ago, Rose would've never said such a thing. The Rose I remember wasn't impressed by power or material things. Her time in the military has changed her. I can only hope she hasn't forgotten her true self.

"The Eye must be destroyed," I say. "It's the only way to end this madness for power."

Rose shrugs her dainty shoulders. "Okay, destroy it then."

"It's not that simple. Only the Yazu can destroy it."

"Ah, that's problematic," says Asher. "Last time we saw them they were being transferred to Amina."

"Then we'll go to Amina and find them."

Asher scratches away at his eyebrows. "Are you insane? We'll be killed the second we're spotted."

Rose nods. "Agreed. It's too risky."

I slam my fists onto the wood table, knocking over Asher and Rose's tin water cups. "Then why are you even here?" It was unfair question to ask my friends. Like me, they're just trying to survive to see another day.

Asher huffs. "C'mon, Marcus. We're with you but wake up. What you're asking for is impossible."

"Well, I can't hide here and wait for death to find me." I point to my wounded leg. "Just like you two were able to find me, so too were Darius and Rizen. They know I have the Eye, and it's just a matter of time before others will come here."

Rose sighs and looks me in the eye. "I get it, Marcus. As crazy as this sounds, I'll help you."

"Me too." Asher slaps my back. "Would be great if we had some more help though."

"You've got one more," says Hazel as she enters the mess hall. She must've been listening from outside the entire time.

I smile. "Asher, Rose, meet Hazel Victoria."

While Asher nods, Rose's upper lip curls in disgust. "You expect me to work with a Dyna? This I cannot do," says Rose.

Hazel sneers. "Careful, Amina, your arrogance is showing."

Rose snatches a dinner knife from the table and flings it at Hazel; she catches the knife and reshapes it into a ball.

"Look, I'm only doing this because Marcus is my friend." Hazel tosses the metal ball to Rose.

"Friend? How? You barely know him," says Rose.

"Hey, all this tension is unnecessary," I say. "If we're going to do this, we've got to have each other's backs. Got it?"

The two grumble before nodding in agreement.

"Check. So what's the plan? We can't go into this blind," says Asher.

Zyniah approaches our table and chomps on a piece of bread. "Sounds like you need Commander Charlotte's help."

Taking Zyniah's advice, we return to Charlotte's quarters. Prior to entering, Zyniah reminds us to stay quiet until Charlotte acknowledges us. Removing our boots, we enter Charlotte's quarters and see her reading a book while sipping tea.

Several minutes of silence pass and Asher can longer take it. He proceeds to examine the many weapons displayed on Charlotte's walls. Impatient, he grabs a sword off the wall and swings it with great ease.

"So, exactly how long before you reach enlightenment? We don't have all day," says Asher. He winks at me, but he's an idiot.

Charlotte slams her book shut and takes a final sip of tea. "That sword, do you know how to use it?"

Asher puffs out his chest with pride. "Absolutely."

Charlotte unsheathes one of her blades. "Show me."

Relishing the opportunity, Asher steps forward while the rest of us move out the way.

"First to be cut loses," says Charlotte.

Asher grins. He lunges forward with his sword, but Charlotte counters and moves gracefully in a circle parrying his strikes.

"Not bad for a Norm, but you'll need a new outfit."

Before Asher realizes it, his baggy pants have been shredded to pieces. Sucking his teeth, he covers himself with a table cloth and takes a seat.

Charlotte sheathes her sword and a slight grin emerges. "Now that's out the way, what do you all want?"

"We're going to destroy the Eye, but we could use your help," I say.

Charlotte sizes us up and chuckles. "Oh? Is this your team? An Aypha, an Amina, a Dyna, and a Norm."

I ignore Charlotte's swipe. "The only way to destroy the Eye is to free the Yazu from the Ayphas and Aminas. We're going back home to save them."

Charlotte sighs and stabs her blade into the polished wood floor. "Marcus, you sure are hard headed." She rests her chin onto the blade's pommel. "Tell you what, you prove to me that you can control your Oro and I'll help you." She points to Rose. "You there, Amina, why don't you work with Marcus on controlling his Oro while I show the norm how to really use a sword."

Hazel frowns but hides it well from the others. "What should I practice?"

Charlotte chuckles. "You're a Victoria. You need not practice. Why don't you keep Zyniah occupied?"

Hazel rolls her eyes as she goes with Zyniah. Charlotte takes Asher, while Rose and I travel to a field of cherry blossom trees to practice.

"Well, Ms. Rose, teach me how to control my Oro," I playfully say.

Rose sits underneath one of the trees. "Easy, Marcus, let's talk first." She pats the ground, wanting me to sit beside her. "Asher told me what happened between you and Darius. About his father…I know it's not your fault." Rose pauses. "In time, I'm certain Darius will see that as well."

I pluck a cherry blossom petal and rip it in two. "Only thing certain is one of us is going to die."

"Don't say that!" Rose pinches my shoulder. "He's still your friend. Don't give up on him."

As much as I wish things were different, hope is no longer possible. Rose clings to a fantasy our friendship can be made whole. But she hasn't seen Darius. She hasn't witnessed the pain and strife he carries.

Rose runs her fingers up my neck. "You know when we were in Eden, Darius told me he'll never lose to you in anything. Why do you think he would say that?"

I shrug. "Darius has always been competitive."

"Perhaps, but I think it was for another reason…when you all left Eden, I received many letters from him, but it was yours I always waited for."

I look to the soil beneath my feet, still regretting not telling her. "It's not that I didn't write you. I just didn't know how to tell you."

Rose cups my chin, turning me to her. "Tell me what?"

Like old times, our eyes connect with ease and all types of past feelings emerge like goosebumps on skin.

Reaching into my boot, I hand Rose the letter I had written her many months ago. "Promise you won't read it till we complete our mission," I say.

Rose slips the letter into her sleeve pocket and smiles. "Promise." Her cheeks briefly go red before she stands to her feet. "Well, let's begin. Show me your Orosphere."

I call for my Oro and form a small Orosphere, but as usual, excess Oro spews from my arm. "Happens every time."

Rose strokes her chin. "Seems your Oro doesn't properly funnel into your hand." She caresses my arm and fingers. "You're too tense, Marcus. Just relax." As her fingertips glide softly over my skin, the runoff Oro dissipates and flows completely into my hand.

"See the more you relax, the better off you'll be. It's that simple."

It hadn't dawned on me the amount of stress I was placing on my body. Straining my muscles with such force must have been causing my Oro to leak.

Rose forms two Orospheres simultaneously. "The more control you have over your body and your emotions, the more Orospheres you can create."

For several hours, Rose and I continue to practice controlling my Oro. Enjoying our time together, all the moments of life's stress begin to vanish and a warm bond rekindles old feelings.

PART 4

It's Not Mother You Should Fear

Though she doesn't want her mother's help, Cynné recognizes Kissandra may be her only option to unlocking the mysteries behind the Eye of Truth. For Cynné though, it is also an opportunity to reconnect to a mother who was quite distant. To a mother who abruptly left her during the fragile years of her young life. Abandonment is a harsh reality, it opens hidden wounds of vulnerability and brightens the insecurities of what shapes us. Most Divines are callous by nature, but a bond between mother and daughter should be unbreakable. Unfortunately, a shattered ego can make even the most prodigious of Divines falter.

Few Divines talk about the Last Great War, for it had taken a toll on many of them but none more than on Kissandra Bonet. She was nearly killed by Queen Zora of Zell and lost nearly all her strength. Desperate to reclaim it, she left Amina, and her two children all in hope of finding a way to recover her power. Before Kissandra left though, she told Cynné a secret that haunts her to this day.

Having received a gold Carrier message from who she presumed was her mother, Cynné travels with Loreen to the northern lands and arrives at the Village of Champi. A heavy fog hovers over the abandoned village. Though dilapidated, a few stone huts remain as does a defaced bronze monument of Yona, a Yazu queen of the ancient era. Climbing the steps of Yona's monument, Cynné scans the village, imagining what once was.

"Is it true my mother massacred these people?"

Loreen sighs, recalling the evils of Kissandra. "The Champies were known as a healing tribe. Many Divines would come here when they could no longer heal themselves. After your mother's fight with Queen

Zora, she came here in search for a cure, but the Champies refused to help her. They said by her dying, thousands of Divines would be saved." Loreen clenches her teeth and fights back tears. "Enraged by their refusal, Kissandra used what power she had left to massacre the Champies."

Cynné takes a heavy swallow as the sun peaks through the clouds and onto the green forest hills. It isn't until the fog burns off that Cynné sees the horror her mother inflicted. Bordered by rows of white flowers is a grave site of over five hundred Champies.

"Mother was ruthless," says Cynné. "This too is how I shall be remembered."

Loreen nods as she turns away from the graves. "So, what's the plan here? Kissandra is expecting you to have killed General X."

"I have a better offer." Pulling from her cleavage, Cynné reveals a small vial of blood with the name "Nandi Bonet" etched into it. Nandi Bonet was a direct ancestor to Cynné and also one of the Noble Eight.

"Mother would do anything for this," says Cynné.

Loreen's eyebrows rise as she observes the vial. "Her blood should be destroyed. You know what can be done with that, right?"

"I'm aware, but that's not what she'll use it for. This is the cure she's been seeking all along. According to Rayne's book, consuming our ancestor's blood replenishes our health and strengthens our power."

"But…" Loreen bites her tongue, knowing Cynné won't listen. Being a young queen, Cynné will have to learn the consequences of her decisions.

Several hours pass, and as the sun beams over them, a lone individual enters the abandoned village. As the figure comes closer, Cynné and Loreen brace themselves, for it is not Kissandra but Annabelle the Ghost.

"Thank you for being the fools that you are," says Annabelle. A bloodlust grin spreads across her face. "Today, all your silly plans come to an end. You've disgraced your ancestors, the Doctrine, even your own family."

Cynné frowns. "Kissandra put you up to this?"

Annabelle smiles, in reality, it was Sinclair who has fooled her sister. "I'm doing her a favor." Annabelle unties her robe and unsheathes a thin blade. "Guess it's too hard for a mother to kill her weakest."

Loreen shakes her head. "Why are you helping Kissandra? In the end, she'll kill you too."

"Wrong, but I'd welcome the challenge. Too bad neither of you shall see it." Annabelle rushes forward.

Loreen launches an Orosphere, but Annabelle absorbs it, converting Loreen's Oro into her own, she now clutches a blue Orosphere and propels it back at the Aminas. Cynné and Loreen shield themselves behind a hardened Oro barrier. The two release smoke bombs and retreat into the forest hills.

"Is it true she can teleport?" Cynné frantically asks Loreen.

Loreen nods. "There are limitations on how and when she can do it. What we see is a past projection of herself. To strike, she must appear in the present, but even then…"

Daggers thrown by Annabelle whistle past Loreen and Cynné. The two dash deeper into the forest and separate. Annabelle focuses her attention on Cynné. Placing her hand against a tree, she absorbs water from its roots and turns the water into arrowheads of ice. She releases the icy arrowheads, Cynné dodges and weaves between trees to escape. Countering, Cynné forms a small Orosphere at her fingertip and flicks the sphere with such speed, it burns a hole right through Annabelle's head causing her to turn into smoke.

Annabelle reappears unharmed, but stands several yards back from where she once was. Unable to dodge Cynné's lightning-fast spheres, Annabelle is hit again, she turns into a cloud of smoke, and reappears even farther away.

"You're not a Ghost. You're a coward," says Cynné. "I've figured out your secret. First you rush toward your opponent to make them react. If the outcome is in your favor, you appear in the present time. But if the outcome is less desirable, you retract yourself to a past image to escape injury."

Annabelle tilts her head. "Is that what you believe? Then how did I get behind you?"

"WHAT?"

Annabelle's blade pierces clean through Cynné's back as her old image dissipates and her new image appears behind Cynné. Annabelle sends an ice arrowhead clean through Cynné's throat. From behind, Loreen unleashes a series of Orospheres, forcing Annabelle to backflip out of harm's way.

A massive mistake. Annabelle is now stuck to an enormous spiderweb made of sticky Oro.

"You were a true legend," says Loreen. "But legends aren't real and neither are ghosts." Loreen unleashes a volley of Orospheres that ignite the web of Oro.

Bursting through the smoke, a bloody Annabelle grabs Loreen by the throat. "Told you next time we met I'd kill you." Annabelle tightens her grip, blood drains from Loreen's nose.

WHOOSH!

A burst of hot air rushes toward the skies as Cynné releases a vicious scream. As she rises to her feet, her sleeves disintegrate into nothing and her arms ignite with burning yellow energy. The heat radiating off Cynné is so hyper hot, it forces Annabelle to release her grip on Loreen. She's seen this Legacy technique before. Similar to Kissandra's ultimate Legacy, this technique can scorch flesh with a single hand wave. Annabelle scratches her brow confused by how Cynné is even alive. Around Cynné's neck is an empty vial of Nandi Bonet's blood. Cynné swings her arms, causing a blast of heat to sear Annabelle's entire body.

Cynné releases another heat wave. Annabelle disappears and emerges behind Cynné to deliver a fatal strike, but an Orosphere slams into her and explodes. Annabelle's arm has been blown off and half her body is scorched. Young Nova has saved Cynné's life.

"I remember you," says a smoldering Annabelle. "You're the pup who pissed on herself. So, you too have come to die."

"Let her be. The battle is over," says Cynné who holds an Orosphere to Annabelle's head.

Annabelle releases an uneasy laugh. "The battle is over when your entire clan is erased. As long as I live, you shall never obtain our key."

"Yet you work with my mother. What has she promised you in exchange?"

"Working with her is not a term I would use," says Annabelle, her image begins to dim. "Truthfully, you're all repulsive." As Annabelle turns to mist, she delivers her final message. "It's not your mother you should fear!"

In an ominous departure, the Ghost vanishes and the Aminas hunch over in relief. Breathing heavy, Cynné nods to Nova. "Many thanks, young one. I owe you. Whatever you seek, it is yours."

Nova smiles, happy to have made an impression on her queen. Though she could've asked to become a squad leader, rank and title are no longer her priorities. "I have a simple request," she says. "Teach me how to use the soul."

Loreen's jaw tightens. "You know that's forbidden. Come up with another request," she says.

Cynné slings her arm around Nova's shoulder. "So, it's power you seek. Let us discuss more on our way home."

Nova bows and grins. "Indeed, my lady."

The Soul

After a day's journey across the northern lands; Queen Cynné, Loreen, and the young Nova approach the outskirts of Amina territory. Seeing a familiar spot, Cynné veers down a grassy hill toward a large pink lake. Removing her robe and combat attire, Cynné slides her thin shaved legs into the warm water.

"I've been made a fool of," she says and stares at her reflection in the lake. Loreen and Nova remain silent. "What do you think Annabelle meant when she said Mother isn't the one to fear?"

"Who knows? Maybe she was just referring to herself," says Loreen.

Cynné swirls her fingers in the pink lake. "Perhaps, but it seemed quite odd. Even more strange, why would my mother send the Ghost after me?"

Witnessing firsthand Annabelle's incredible power, Cynné knows she's no match for her, nor are her young beauties ready for war. Fading from her reflection was the vision of becoming legendary. Her dreams of infamy were slowly beginning to sink to the bottom of the lake. Being a young queen, she was naïve to think the Aminas were superior to their rivals. That may have been true during Kissandra's reign, but those days are no more. Such a title must be earned.

"Fighting Annabelle has taught me a lesson. We should never underestimate our opponents," says Cynné. "Perhaps its pride that's been blinding me, but we can no longer fight our battles off sheer talent alone. We must fight with purpose and strategy."

Loreen rolls her eyes. She's warned Cynné of this many of times but it wasn't until the bubble of delusion popped that Cynné finally sees reality.

"It'll take two years to get the girls trained and ready for their first war," says Loreen.

Cynne scoops water into her hand and lets it slide down her forearm. "Too long. Annabelle knows we're coming; we must strike soon."

Nova casually moves closer to her queen. "My lady, if you teach us the power of the soul, we could be ready for war in days not years."

Cynné glances at Nova before returning her gaze to the lake. "The last time I saw my mother was at this very spot. I remember her telling me about the power of using the soul." Cynné pulls out her decision coin and rolls it back and forth across her fingers. "But she also revealed an unspoken secret as to why using the soul is forbidden." Cynné curls the gold coin into her pointer finger and rests it on the tip of her thumb.

Loreen covers Cynné's hand. "You're not serious, are you?" she asks. "It's reckless and suicidal. Just look at Ophelia—she hasn't been stable in years because she abuses the soul."

Cynné pries back Loreen's hand and stares at her coin. Her thumb trembles. She seeks a sign for guidance. Her mother gave her this coin to guide Cynné and it was the last thing she ever did. Cynné knows the soul would increase their power but doing so could lead to their own peril. She flips her coin and catches it. Without looking, she tosses the coin into the lake.

"No longer shall I rely on signs." Cynné watches her trusted coin sink to the bottom of the lake. "To become legendary, I must go with my heart." She retracts her legs from the lake and cups Nova's soft face into her hands. "The soul is forbidden for a reason. Using it will kill you and everything you love."

Nova bows. "I don't care. I just want to defeat our enemies and serve you, my queen. You deserve this world. Allow me to become a vessel so all your desires and dreams become reality."

Cynné smiles at Nova's ultimate obedience. But only a fool fails to see the pearls of envy in Nova's eyes.

"Loyalty to me is everything." Cynné gives Nova a light squeeze to her shoulders. "But the soul is not the answer to our success. To become great, we cannot take shortcuts. Like every great dynasty, we must work hard to achieve success."

"But, my lady, using the soul is our best chance of winning."

Cynné's mood turns ugly, she squeezes Nova's wrist and fractures it. "Now is the time to shut up and yield. I am willing to make you my apprentice but don't be mistaken. You and I are not equal."

Nova's wrist turns purple as she lowers her head. "Understood, my lady."

"Good, now leave us be."

Being dismissed, Nova leaves the pink lake upset and confused. Unable to convince her queen to use the soul, she wanders to a home where other Aminas dare not go. While Cynné is queen, Ophelia is the one all Aminas fear.

Approaching Ophelia's black stone quarters, Nova examines the cracked human skulls hanging above a blood-stained door. She hesitates before knocking, the door creaks open, and a thick cloud of smoke escapes from the quarters. Inside, Ophelia hangs upside down on an iron beam. A long ivory pipe rests in her mouth and the potent smoke coming from it causes the skulls on the walls to appear psychedelic to Nova.

"What do we have here?" Ophelia growls as smoke funnels through her nose.

"Teach me how to use the soul," Nova asks in haste.

Ophelia's head ticks sideways. "What's a pup like you interested in such a nasty thing?"

Nova treads lightly and moves further into the smoke laced room. "I just want to prove to the queen we can use the soul to defeat our enemies."

Still hanging upside down, Ophelia further twists her head. "Such a dangerous thing to suggest. Your ambitions sound treasonous and against the Doctrine."

Nova twitches and lowers her head. "No, I'm just passionate about my land and my queen."

"Liar. If that were true, you wouldn't have gone behind the queen's back." Twisting her head to a normal position, Ophelia unhinges from the bar and lands upright. She takes the ashes from her pipe and swallows them whole. "Say it. Why do you really want to use the soul?"

Nova grits her teeth and balls up her fists. "I want to be like you. I want to be feared, I want real power."

Ophelia pulls back Nova's gritty hair and stares deep into her eyes. There's something Ophelia is looking for. It isn't beauty or integrity. It is something far more fascinating. A glimpse of recklessness.

"Using the soul is prohibited and punishable by death," says Ophelia. "They say it destroys the user. Do you think that's true?"

Staring at the pupils of a mad woman, Nova's lips part with a hint of pride. "Whoever believes that lacks ambition. They're afraid of their own self-worth. Afraid to shatter the limits of their power."

Ophelia continues to pull back Nova's hair causing strands to break from her roots. "What is your name, young beauty?"

"Nova. I have no last name for I am an orphan."

Suddenly, a dark orange and black hole appears in Ophelia's chest. "Ah, Nova, I may not be your mother, but I can provide what you seek." Ophelia's eyes become amber like a snake's. The entire room trembles, and the candles on the wall turn to liquid. Ophelia grabs Nova's hand and forces it inside the orange and black hole, bonding their souls in unison.

King No More

The stench of blood and vomit flows thick in the air of General X's bedroom. Frail and sick, his body is a heavy breath away from becoming a corpse. Preparing for his last call, he drags himself from bed and stands before a mirror. A shell of his former self, his skin sags and his lips have gone colorless. He chuckles at his sight and reflects on his youthful days. At age thirteen, he was one of the youngest to ever lead a squad in war. As a commander, his success rate in battle was near perfect. Under his tenure as general, a rank only second to a king, Aypha Divines have grown three-fold in size and strength. But alas, his final chapter is not complete until he knows Aypha's future is secure.

The time has come for General X to make plans for his successor. Across Aypha, there are eight commanders and all are worthy of becoming the next general. But of the eight, only two are of good balance to lead. While his commanders in the north are strong, they lack restraint. His commanders in the east are wise but old. Those in the west are smart but lack charisma. Of all his commanders, only Shomari and Petune have the balance to lead the great nation. And of the two, only one is fitting to become a king.

Receiving a message from General X, Shomari returns to the general's quarters. Since their last encounter, the general has become frailer and his eye sockets have sunken inward.

"How are you?" asks Shomari. He slides a scarf over his nose to block out the room's repugnant odor.

"Dying," the general replies. He hacks up a glob of blood and staggers to his bedroom dresser. Sliding open a drawer, he pulls out a sealed papyrus scroll with King Rayne's crest.

"This is from my father?" asks a confused Shomari.

The general nods and points to the red tattoos on Shomari's arms. "Your father sealed them onto you when you were young. Those tattoos were his gifts to you, and the scroll explains everything." General X hands Shomari the scroll. "Your tattoos will give you all the tools needed to find and unlock the Eye."

Shomari examines the scroll, his fingers tremble over his father's crest. "Why didn't you tell me about this sooner, when we had the Eye?"

General X breathes a heavy sigh. "Greed and glory," he admits. "I was to be the one to open the Book of Pure. But as I reflect back and think of your father, perhaps it was always meant to be that his legacy would be fulfilled through you."

Shomari breaks the scroll's seal and sees drawings of a scorpion, fowl, and a lion. The drawings match the tattoos on his tongue and arms. The same ones he's seen many times in his father's study. A private message written by his father reveals the origin and purpose of the tattoos.

"Am I to become…"

The general nods. "When I die, my Carrier will spread word to every Aypha naming you as my successor. But not as the next general but as the king. In honor of your father, I refused to be called such." The general's frail lips part with a smile. "The title as king should be reserved for Rayne's legacy, for his son. Even with this title, the other commanders may resent you and even seek your demise. But with the Phoenixes, all will bow to your lead."

Shomari's eyebrows rise. "General, are you certain about this? King or not, killing Aikia remains my priority."

"Revenge is as old as time," says General X. "Be warned, even with the Phoenixes, killing Aikia will not be easy."

Shomari looks at his tattoos. "Killing him is my resolve and my father's gift shall ensure I see it through."

General X releases a rare smile. "Indeed, but remember, as much as your father would want you to avenge him, opening the Book was his true desire. He spent decades researching old artifacts and excavating ancient villages to understand the mysteries behind the Book. When he discovered the Book of Pure was the source of ultimate Divine power, he became obsessed with it. He believed for our people to survive, we must claim its power. Before he died, I promised to carry on his work, and soon I shall pass it to you."

Shomari stares at a portrait of his father and the general, his whole perspective on life beginning to take form. Soon he would be king and inherit all the great pressures that come with it.

"What should I do about Petune?" asks Shomari.

"Embrace him as a brother. Keep him close."

"But he cannot be trusted."

"They once said the same of your father. Don't give up on Petune, for he may become your greatest ally. Take what your father has given you and lead the next generation. Fulfill the dreams of your father." Kissing Shomari on the forehead, General X staggers to his bed and falls into a deep sleep.

Shomari places his hand on the general's chest. "Father, your friend is coming home but worry not, for your legacy is safe."

***

Inside an Aypha prison, cramped in a single cell sits the Yazu clan. The guards watching over them bang pots and pans to prevent the Yazu from sleeping. The goal was to break them psychologically, but the Yazu are resilient and have unwavering hearts; they cannot be broken by such trivial means.

To drown out the banging noises, Free sings a melody. Her voice is so angelic, not even a bird could mimic such grace. She sings an ancient song passed down to them by their ancestors. Her voice uplifts the Yazu. The sweet melodies carry throughout the prison and even catch Shomari's ear as he arrives. Admiring their resistance, he knows the sorrow his land has caused them, but without pain there can be no progress.

Shomari smiles upon approaching the Yazu. "Your courage and resolve to preserve what is sacred is admirable," he admits. "Soon, I will set you free and there will be no more struggle or pain. I will ensure that no Divine shall ever bother you again."

The Yazu look at one another confused.

Free grabs Yondi by the hand. "At what cost?" she asks. "Your heart doesn't bleed with generosity."

Shomari slips inside the Yazu cell and leans in to Free's ear. "Part of me feels guilty for what I must do." He squeezes Free's arm and presses her against the cell bars. He opens his mouth, the red scorpion tattoo on his tongue bleeds and transforms into a real scorpion. Shomari kisses Free, transferring the scorpion from his mouth to hers. She gags and twitches as her eyes roll to the back of her head.

Discovered by King Rayne, the red scorpion has the ability to extract information from any target.

"How is the Eye of Truth unlocked?" Shomari asks.

Entering Free's mind, he sees a statue of a woman surrounded by flocking crows. Cupped in the statue's hands is a vial of blood. As the vision fades, the scorpion crawls from Free's mouth and dies. Shomari's tongue now burns. It'll be awhile before the scorpion tattoo reappears.

"You're going to take me there," he orders and yanks Free from the prison cell. Little Yondi cries out to her mother. Tears form in her eyes.

"My child, everything will be fine," says Free.

Nodding, Yondi blinks away her tears.

"If you kill her, we will never forgive you!" shouts an old Yazu man.

Shomari smirks. "Forgiveness is overrated."

Leaving the prison with Free, the two head north toward the Land of Yazu. It is there Shomari will find the secret to unlocking the Eye—and while he doesn't have it in his possession, the tattoos on his arms have the power to lead him right to Marcus Azure.

The Eye of Truth

Sinclair Bonet peers over the edge of a white stone bridge. Taking a handful of worms, she drops them into a pond to feed the fish below. No longer wearing her mother's mask, she waits patiently for her guest. In unusual fashion, Sinclair's hair is imperfect, her skin is coated in dirt, and the robe she wears is stained with blood.

"Snakes can only slither for so long!" yells Petune as he emerges from a forest of trees.

Sinclair drops a few more worms into the pond. "Take it the Dynas told you where to find me," she says.

Stepping onto the stone bridge, Petune takes note of the dried bloodstains across Sinclair's face and robe. "They couldn't resist my charm. Plus, I had something that belonged to them. In return, they've given me you."

Sinclair yawns. "Surely you didn't come here to fight? Losing to a woman would surely wither your ego."

"By the bloodstains on your robe, seems you've been doing the fighting." Petune lights a small Orosphere and tosses it into the pond, killing several fish.

Sinclair frowns as dead fish float atop the water. "Sometimes, blood must be spilled to quench the thirst of conquerors."

Petune unties his black cloak and tosses it into the pond. "Is that what you said when you killed the general's son?"

The ugly truth of Sinclair's past lights a fire in her eyes. Sinclair Bonet was a traitor to the Ayphas and Aminas for many reasons, but none more infamous than murdering General X's son. Lying to herself for so long, she had nearly forgotten about it. She was no victim. More so a demon who killed a little boy in retaliation for the sins of his father.

"You're one to talk," Sinclair sneers. "How many Yazu have you killed?"

Petune moves closer to Sinclair and licks the front of his teeth. "For a dead woman, you sure do have great ears. Tell me, my beautiful corpse, what else do you know?"

"I know you lost the Eye but don't worry, it's safe." Sinclair lifts her sleeve and reveals the Eye of Truth. The gold amulet glistens with an immaculate shine of envy. "Amazing you had this for so long yet no clue how to activate it."

Petune combs his fingers through his honey blond hair, he only does so when anxious. "The blood on your robe—is it from Gail and Saphron Azure?"

Sinclair remains expressionless. "I have a proposition." She tosses Petune a scroll. He unrolls it and finds the familiar handwriting of King Rayne. Drawn on the scroll is an image of the Eye of Truth, along with a note.

According to the stone tablet found near Lucky Caverns, the Eye is protected and isolated inside of Yazu. Since the land is shielded from Divines, getting inside will be difficult. Second, even with the Eye, unique blood is needed to activate it.

Petune discards the scroll.

"We've tried this already. We used our blood, Yazu blood, even animal blood—none of them opened the Eye."

"It's Yona's blood you need," says Sinclair. "The Yazu queen who created the Phoenixes."

Petune's perfectly arched eyebrows rise. "Yona is dead, has been dead for a long time. Even if one dug up her grave, there wouldn't be any remnants of her blood."

"Wrong. Her blood has been preserved inside the Land of Yazu. Unfortunately, the only people who know how to pass through the Yazu barrier are you and General X."

Petune sneers. "You're lying. We searched everywhere. We would have found it."

"Even the underground tomb?" asks Sinclair. "Perhaps we should look for it together."

Petune's jaw tightens. "You're delusional, Sinclair. Working with a traitor is a sin against all of humanity."

"Shall a tiger mock the stripes of a zebra?" rebuffs Sinclair. "You and I both have committed evils. That's why you're the perfect candidate for this. Find Yona's blood and we shall battle one another. Whoever survives will have the power to change this world."

Petune forms an Orosphere. "Or I can kill you now and take what's mine."

Sinclair shrugs and points to the surrounding forest. "You're being watched by Dynas. By my command, they will kill you."

"Your command?"

Sinclair flicks a coin of herself to Petune. "Show this to the Dynas on your way out. When you find Yona's blood, we'll see who kills who."

Yona the Yazu Queen

With Free as his hostage, Shomari is steps away from Yazu territory. Peering into Free's mind with his red scorpion tattoo has led him here. His quest for the secret to unlocking the Eye of Truth is near. As they walk through an open field of tall grass, the hair on Shomari's skin rises and his body turns cold. A semitranslucent barrier appears before them. Placing his hand onto the barrier, Shomari's entire arm ices over.

"Open the barrier," he says, retracting his frost coated hand.

Free smirks. "Your superior, the one who calls himself General. He never told you how?"

Shomari grabs Free's arm. He opens his mouth and the scorpion tattoo on his tongue pulsates. "Just do it or I'll force it out of you."

Free's face turns sour. She cups her hands over her eyes and weeps.

"Calm down," sighs Shomari. "I just…"

Free shakes her head, crying not in fear, but to collect tears in her hands. She throws her tears against the barrier creating a hole for them to pass through.

"So, Yazu tears open the barrier…how simple," says Shomari.

After passing through the barrier, Free leads Shomari to the Village of Yamo which was once a large settlement of Yazu. Many of the Yazu who lived here were artist and musicians. Most of the homes in Yamo are made of limestones and painted with pastel colors. Unusual animal sculptures decorate the tops of the roofs. It's silent in the village as not a single Yazu remains after General X and Petune ripped them from their homes.

As they move toward the center of the village, Shomari takes note of the many crystal sculptures lined along unmanicured tulip gardens. Intrigued by the art work, he ventures to a museum made of black glass. The museum is a dedication to the Spirit Weapons crafted by the Yazu. Displayed on a red painted wall is a replica of the Seven Blades of Might as well as the Aurora Blade. In a glass case, there's a collection of eight iridescent arrows and a long staff with blades on both ends. Shomari's fingers tremble upon seeing the metallic staff. He smashes the glass case and grabs the weapon.

"Did the Yazu create all of these?" asks Shomari.

"Yes, but they're only replicas," says Free. "Divines robbed us of the real ones."

Shomari snaps the staff in two. "My father's killer wields the real staff, a man named Aikia of the Wind."

Free cautiously removes the broken staff from Shomari's coarse hands. "This man, is he the reason you seek the Phoenixes?"

Shomari's jaw tightens as he looks away. "Where are the Phoenix replicas? I want to see them."

"They were destroyed in fear someone would want to resurrect them." Free glances at an empty case and leans against it hoping Shomari does not notice. Missing from the case is a replica of the Eye of Truth.

Shomari continues to peruse the museum. "Shame, guess it will have to wait till I unlock the Eye," he says.

Free continues to lean against the empty case. "While the Eye summons the Phoenixes, controlling them is another matter."

Shomari grins and points to the red lion and fowl tattoos on his forearms. "I can restrain any beast with these." He loses interest in the museum and returns outside.

Free follows and examines Shomari's tattoos. "Out of curiosity, how did you obtain those?"

Shomari tugs away from Free. "Just take me to the statue I saw in your head. Show me the answer to unlocking the Eye of Truth!"

Free grimaces but nods. She escorts Shomari to the Village of Yallon. Once home to hundreds of Yazu, the village has been decimated. Brick homes surrounding the village have been burned to rubble. Debris and glass shards from blown-out windows litter the ground. The village square was once a place where Yazu artists would sing melodies and perform plays. Once a place of laughter and joy, the square is now a pile of skulls and bones.

Shomari stares at the mountain of the deceased. "Was this…" his voice cracks, unable to finish upon seeing the massacre.

Free kneels beside the collection of bones. "Your leader and Petune destroyed this place seeking the Eye. In a single night, they killed hundreds of my people and dumped them here like trash. Within this pile are some of my closest family and friends." Tears of anguish fall from Free's eyes. "Let us move past this place."

The two continue beyond the village square and approach a cemetery surrounded by statues of crows. In the center of the cemetery, a large willow tree looms over the dead. Nailed to the tree trunk are two skeletons, Free's eyes fixate on them as she sheds a few more tears.

"Who were they?" asks Shomari.

"My father and son." Free rests her hand onto the tree trunk. "They revolted and attacked General X. As punishment, he nailed them to the tree, burned the soles of their feet, and forced us to watch them suffer."

Shomari looks away as his face turns bitter. "Your father and son died honorably. Rest in knowing they died as brave men."

Free continues to look upon her father and son. "Your words mean nothing."

"You're right, but I share your pain. I know that cruel feeling of anger and hopelessness. The insufferable feeling as your throat burns in anguish from the knot of rage that cannot be swallowed." Shomari leans against the tree and sighs. "I was fairly young when Aikia killed my father. Ever since, I've been conjuring ways to become strong enough to confront him."

"You seek vengeance."

"Indeed. That is why I must obtain a Phoenix."

Free shakes her head. "Using such a powerful weapon to kill a single man is unnecessary."

"You don't understand. There's no Divine alive who can kill Aikia of the Wind." Shomari removes his shirt and exposes the jagged scar across his chest. "I confronted Aikia after he killed my father. Instead of killing me, he gave me an unhealable scar as a reminder of my pain." Shomari slides his shirt back on. "A Phoenix is the only way to kill him and reclaim my father's honor."

Free climbs the tree and removes the stakes from her son's bones. "Is that all you seek? Once you kill this man, then what? Will you do as all others and abuse the power of the Phoenixes?"

Shomari sighs before helping Free remove the remaining stakes from her son and father's bones. "There's other dreams my father wanted, but I'm not certain it's worth it."

"At some point you'll have to follow your own dreams." Free places her family's remains inside an open grave. She covers them with dirt before leading Shomari to a headstone with no name. Using a shovel, she digs up the grave and reaches the casket below.

"The answers you seek are inside this casket but it can only be opened when the sun shines directly over it," says Free.

Not believing her, Shomari tries to pry open the casket but to no avail. With dusk soon to arrive, opening the casket will have to wait until tomorrow.

***

The next day, the two return to the graveyard and exactly when the sun reaches its apex, the casket begins to rattle and glow.

"What you seek is inside, but death may follow you," warns Free.

Unmoved, Shomari opens the casket and discovers an underground tomb. He grabs Free by the hip and descends inside. The walls of the tomb are made of gold and inextinguishable blue flames from lanterns provide shallow light. As they continue deeper into the tomb, soft white sand sifts beneath their boots. The air turns misty and cold. Before them are white crows swarming around an onyx statue of a woman. Cupped into the hands of the statue is a vial of blood and the answer to activating the Eye of Truth.

"Who is this woman?" asks Shomari.

"She is Yona, an ancient Yazu queen," says Free. "She created the Spirit Weapons to protect us from Divines like you."

As Shomari proceeds toward Yona's statue, a white crow darts right through his shoulder. He doesn't bleed, but there's a gaping hole where the crow has entered. Designed to protect Yona's blood, these birds have the ability to erase Divine flesh.

As more crows dart toward Shomari, the lion tattoo on his arm illuminates and summons before him. The mighty lion roars causing all the crows to drop dead before it too dies and turns to smoke. Shomari's arm burns as the lion tattoo begins to regenerate. He proceeds toward the statue of Yona and reaches for the vial of blood.

"If you do this, you'll be setting off the rebirth of a tragic war," says Free.

Shomari hesitates before snatching the vial. "War is a circle. It has no beginning or end, just moments of stability and moments of chaos. Your queen knew this. That is why she created the Phoenixes to protect you in times of war."

CLAP! CLAP! CLAP! "That was quite poetic," says Petune as he approaches from behind. "Power is an addictive thing, you know. Those who fail to control power are doomed to be consumed by it. Do you truly think that if you killed Aikia, your thirst for vengeance would end?"

Shomari takes a harsh swallow, his eyes lock onto the vial of blood within his hand "And what do you desire?" he asks.

"My desire is just like yours," says Petune. "I, too, want to eradicate our enemies. But you think small, while I think grand. You said war is like a circle, but once the Book of Pure is opened, there will no longer be war. There will only be us, Ayphas and Aminas, united. And the one who shall lead us to this destiny is me!"

Oro seeps from Shomari's hands. His veins grow larger and his eyes shift into pure gold.

"Oh, you're taking this seriously." Petune's eyes turn gold as well. "Don't worry. I'll tell Sinclair you died an honorable death."

Shomari's gold eyes widen. "Sinclair?"

Petune smirks. "She's alive and just as pretty as the day she left you."

"Crow Spit!" Shomari forms a powerful Orosphere, causing the underground tomb to rattle and shake dust from the ceiling. Petune lights his Orosphere, and just as he's set to release it, a Carrier bird lands on his shoulder with a message. Petune's Orosphere fades and his eyes return to normal upon reading the letter.

Shomari grits his teeth, insisting they fight, but it serves no purpose.

"Marcus Azure has the Eye of Truth," announces Petune, he tugs away at his once pristine hair. "If that's true, then what does Sinclair have?"

Free smiles in the corner of the chamber. "Only one of them has the real thing. The other has a replica."

Petune eyes the vial of Yona's blood. "That clever Twixie set me up."

Shomari opens the vial of blood and places a few drops on his tongue. "It's old wine," he says, spitting it out.

For the first time in a while, Free releases a hearty laugh. "Soon the Eye will be unlocked," she says. "Hope whoever has it is smarter than you two."

What Am I?

MARCUS

Back at Charlotte's quarters, I demonstrate to her that I can control my Oro by forming several Orospheres. Previously, excess Oro would spew from the pores of my arm but training with Rose has helped me refocus. Rose sits patiently in the corner of Charlotte's training room along with Zyniah, Hazel, and Asher.

"Well, Charlotte, I've proven that I can control my Oro, now are you willing to help us?"

Charlotte sucks her teeth. "A deal is a deal. Still, we'll need to come up with a plan and to do so…"

A large Carrier bird enters Charlotte's quarters and lands before me. The bird glows and transforms into a small box. My heart burns with a sense of uneasiness. I open the box but quickly slam it shut and drop to my knees. I can't help the tears that fall from my eyes, for inside the box is the bloody head of Yondi. As my friends corral around me, my veins boil with anger and disgust. *Who would do something so heinous to a little girl?* On the top of the box is a message written in blood:

Bring the Eye to the Valleys or I'll kill them all.

Wiping away tears, I gather myself before my friends telling them of what's inside.

Asher runs to the box to see Yondi's head for himself. His face is as serious as death. "We're going to kill whoever did this," he declares.

Hazel rests her hand on my shoulder. "Marcus, we'll do whatever it takes to make this right." Hazel's touch is much needed but my tears continue to shed.

I try ripping off the Eye of Truth from my wrist but it won't budge. "These savages, they killed a little girl all for this!"

Charlotte heads to her closet and unwinds a ribbon from a Seeker. "Show me the Yazu," she orders. The clouds from the Seeker disperse.

Many hours pass before the Seeker clouds return with information. "More than forty Yazu are on the move toward the Valleys," says Charlotte. "Among them is a powerful Divine with an uncanny level of Oro." Charlotte gnashes her teeth. "Whoever is with the Yazu, isn't just any Divine."

"Regardless, we must help them," I say.

As though staring through my soul, Charlotte remains unconvinced. "This Divine has the power of an entire army."

"So what are you saying? We should just let the Yazu die? Can't you order some of the Zells to help us?"

Charlotte shakes her head and gives me a hard stare. "Zyniah, take the others outside while I talk with Marcus."

As the others leave, Charlotte's eyes show signs of restraint. There's something she's been hiding and it's written on her lips.

"Marcus, by going to the Valleys, you put all of us in jeopardy," she says. "If the Eye is relinquished, the Phoenixes will be unearthed and used to terrorize the other lands for their keys. And once collected, the most sacred rule of the Doctrine will be broken."

"The opening of the Book of Pure," I say.

"Indeed." Charlotte asks that I take a seat beside her on a wool blanket. She then turns and faces me. "Designed by the Noble Eight, the Book was created as a consequence of the relentless wars between Divines. Its creation brought peace to a world plagued with savagery. In the ancient era, war was all Divines knew. Thousands of them died, poisoned by a curse to kill. The Noble Eight recognized their hazardous ways would eventually lead to their extinction." Charlotte grabs a wood staff and asks me to hold one end of it. "To alter the fate of Divines, a decision was made to fracture Divine power. A call was ordered for all Divines to gather and place their hands into a special book." Charlotte snaps the staff in half. "By touching its pages, half of a Divine's power was taken, weakening their strength and the lust to kill. After every single Divine had touched the Book, it was sealed and forbidden to be opened. With its creation, the Noble Eight successfully brought unity across the lands." Charlotte breaks the staff into several tiny pieces. "However, having reduced power created successive generations of Divines with less strength and greater flaws than their previous generations. Divines today are nothing compared to our ancestors. That is why it's called the Book of Pure—because it contains the power of our ancestors' blood. Pure, free of flaws, and the pinnacle a Divine can reach."

So, this is the history of Divines. Born with incredible power yet cursed with bloodthirst. To think Divines were once stronger than today troubles me. I have seen the evils of men like Petune and Rizen. They exploit their power to terrorize and destroy. More power only leads to more chaos and anarchy. This curse is in my blood, it is my heritage, but it does not define my fate.

"I understand the implications. But together we shall not fail," I tell Charlotte. "The Yazu must be freed. Only they can destroy the Eye and end this cycle for power."

Charlotte sighs. "I never had any intentions of letting you leave here with the Eye. Doing so would be suicide if anyone else were to attempt this. But you're not just anyone, Marcus. It was no coincidence for us to meet. We were brought together so that I may help you. I've been reluctant up until this point, but things have changed." Charlotte raises my chin, we're now eye to eye. "Marcus, you're the closest thing there is to a Pure Divine, and once mastered, you'll have power like no other."

My heart thumps heavy as it all begins to sink in. The Krysanthem leaf that never withered away, Sinclair's obsession of me, even my parents desire to keep me from Awakening—it was all because of what I am.

"How?" My voice trembles, I try to hold my composure. "How do you know this?"

Charlotte taps the back of my hands. "The first thing I noticed were your blemished skin marks. Many think it's a curse but it's actually a sign of a blessing. Second, back when you were training with Zyniah, she absorbed your Oro and told me she felt two sides. One-part Aypha, another part Zell. The only explanation of this would be if you were a Pure Divine." Charlotte places her hand on my chest. "To defeat whoever has the Yazu, you're going to need to access the power within you. To do so requires breaking through your internal suppression seals."

Thinking back to my training with Sinclair, I thought my seal had been broken after Awakening.

"The seals inside of me, are they not broken already?"

Charlotte shakes her head. "Inside of you are six seals, all designed to suppress your Oro. Only the seal of pain has been broken which allowed you to Awaken and access some of your Aypha power. The next one is the seal of sense. Breaking this seal will allow you to feel your surroundings and use the power of a Zell."

"It took weeks to break my previous seal. I don't have time to do this again."

Charlotte unsheathes one of her Blades of Might. "Close your eyes, Marcus. This is going to hurt." She pierces my stomach with her blade causing black mist from my body to engulf the weapon. After a moment, Charlotte retracts the blade and on it are many weird symbols and odd shapes. According to Charlotte, she has extracted the seal and bound it to her blade. As my stomach wound begins to heal, light seems brighter and colors are more vibrant. My hands tingle and my body constantly fluctuates between hot and cold.

"Give it a few, Marcus. Your body is trying to adjust to your new power."

"Have you broken all the seals?" I ask as my teeth chatter and sweat drips from my forehead.

"No, the remaining seals inside of you were formed using more than Oro which I cannot unseal. Worry not though, for you have all the power you need. Besides, Zyniah and I will be with you. Only she and I know what you are, and it's best you keep this a secret, even from your friends."

I nod as my body temperature begins to stabilize. "Okay and now what?" I ask.

Charlotte pats my shoulder. "I hate to tell you this, Marcus, but only through trauma will you be able to fully tap into your new power. The only thing we can do now is make sure you can control your Oro for when it happens."

Charlotte and I head outside where Zyniah, Asher, Hazel, and Rose await. Cherry blossom petals fly by as a warm breeze fills the air. Charlotte calls the others over. "Attention, everyone, Zyniah and I will be accompanying you to the Valleys…"

Markel along with several members of her death squad approach us. They wear armor threaded with silver and forged blue silk. Marching towards us at a steady beat, they unsheathe their black swords.

"Why are you here?" asks Charlotte.

Markel bends her neck, popping the bones in her spine. "I've come to claim what should be ours. The Eye is too valuable to be left in the hands of a child. This is our only chance to save our people from destruction."

Charlotte unsheathes two of her Blades of Might. "The Eye is not the way, Markel. We don't need it to defeat the Aminas."

Markel sucks her teeth. "Forget the Aminas. The Eye gives us dominion over the Great Lands. With the Phoenixes, every land shall bow before us!"

Disappointment fills Charlotte's eyes. "Then we would be no better than the Aminas. Our ancestors sought unity not supremacy across the Great Lands."

Markel laughs and moves closer. "You're blind! Everything we've ever wanted is within reach. No longer shall we live in fear of our enemies but thrive in power."

"You're wrong," Charlotte says as she looks to me. "There's another way we can achieve peace."

Markel's eyebrows fold in confusion. "You talk foolish. Peace is a dream that will never be fulfilled. Power and dominion shall always be the way of Divines." Markel grits her teeth and her pale skin boils red. "We must do this for Zell!" She signals to her death squad. The murderous Zells race forward, but Charlotte quickly strikes them down with her blades.

Markel stares at Charlotte's blood-coated blades. "When we first met, I never understood why you used those blades. Wasn't till later that I realized you're nothing without them. You can't use your Oro, can you?" Markel's eyes turn black and so do the veins in her body. Her body swells and black tar oozes from her pores creating a pool of tar at her feet. Unsheathing a rusted blade, Markel races towards Charlotte. The two clash and ignite sparks from their blades. Markel spits tar from her mouth blinding Charlotte. She then hugs her causing the black tar to quickly engulf Charlotte.

Zyniah screams and runs to help, Markel hurls tar in her direction, a dirt wall formed by Hazel shields Zyniah. The tar quickly consumes the wall and flows towards us like a river. Covering our legs, the tar burns and binds us in place. Seeking the Eye, Markel dashes toward me. Rose and I launch Orospheres, but Markel absorbs them with no impact.

"The Eye is mine!" shouts Markel.

The tar rises to my torso and creeps toward my arm. I must do something. The Eye has to be protected, even if I must sacrifice my body. "Oroburn!" I yell and stick my burning hands into the tar causing it to vaporize into a black toxic steam. One inhale will burn our lungs but at

296

least we're free. Markel grabs Rose by the throat and hoists her into the air. Asher stabs Markel, but the tar covering her body acts as a shield.

"Give me the Eye or I'll kill her, Marcus," orders Markel.

A hint of terror glides across Rose's eyes. My heartbeat spikes. I can't lose her. I can't lose the one who saved me. If the world were to end, I'd rather it be together, holding each other as disaster swallows us whole.

To cut off the eye, I take my dagger and press it to my arm. As I break flesh, Markel releases a bloody scream. Inserted in the back of her stomach is one of the Blades of Might. Charlotte is hard to kill. Her skin severely burned, she thrusts another blade through Markel's chest. Markel falls face-first into her own tar. Blood and oil cover Charlotte. Skin has melted off her face as she struggles to breathe.

She reaches for her Seeker and tosses it to Zyniah. "Use this to track the Yazu," says Charlotte, her voice shallow and weak, she collapses onto her back.

Zyniah squeezes her eyes tight, holding back tears. "No! You have to get up. We need you."

Charlotte trembles as her face begins to sink in. "No, you all just need one another." Her hand shaking, she unsheathes one of her blades and directs Asher towards her. "This is one of the Seven Blades of Might. Use this to protect yourself against the Divines."

Asher bows and takes the blade with honor.

Charlotte calls for Rose and Hazel. Her voice now faint. "Aminas and Dynas have been enemies since the ancient wars. Yet you two stand side by side, bringing hope that one day our lands shall not be enemies but friends." Charlotte coughs up tar and orders me to come closer.

"Marcus, it's time for you to lead. Remember what I told you and you shall not fail. Have no fear and do not waver when the time comes to destroy the Eye. Divine life must continue." Black blood oozes from Charlotte's mouth; the tar has eaten away at her jawline.

"You can't die," moans Zyniah as she sits by Charlotte's side.

Charlotte raises her hand and plucks Zyniah's forehead. "There's something I must prepare for, now go."

Not understanding her cryptic phrase, we leave Charlotte to die and set course for the Valleys of Hope.

Peace
MARCUS

The call to lead is now. Hazel, Asher, Rose, Zyniah—they all look to me for guidance. I cannot fail them. I'm terrified of what lies ahead, but they must not see it. My fears shall be stifled and my resolve must be hardened if we're to free the Yazu. We've just entered the southern desert of Beta. The air is cold, and the clear skies of the night give us a perfect view of the moon.

As we trek across the red sand hills, Asher proudly holds Charlotte's blade. He walks with confidence and shows no fear. Hazel is steely eyed and focused; she stays by my side, never letting more than a few feet separate us. Zyniah walks in silence, her mood not the same since leaving Charlotte. Still it's Rose I worry about most. Solemn is written across her face. By helping me, she knows she can never go home. Like me, she's forever marked a traitor. I want to tell her it will be okay, but why speak with false promises? All I can offer is hope that our efforts shall not be in vain. The desert hills of Beta seem steeper than I remember. Perhaps it's my nerves or maybe it's the weight of knowing our mortality is at stake.

When dawn arrives, we reach a familiar location. We're on the outskirts of Lucky Caverns, and it was here where I last saw Rikari. *A Divine's life isn't filled with bliss*, I can hear her say. *To survive, one must be prepared to kill.* Oh how true her words have become.

We move toward the caverns to briefly rest but the idea quickly vanishes as Zyniah grabs my arm. "Can you feel them?" Her body shivers. "The rest of Markel's death squad is tracking us. We must keep going."

Scrambling to maintain distance, we press forward, and jog for several hours across many sand dunes. Being a Norm, Asher cannot keep pace.

"Go on," he huffs. "I'll catch up." Wincing in pain, he takes a knee in the hot sand.

"Fool, we're not leaving you." I give him the last of my water and help him to his feet.

"We need to slow them down," says Hazel. She digs her hands into the sand, and her eyes glow green. Astonishingly, across the desert appear hundreds of gaping holes. Blood streams from Hazel's eyes as they return to normal. Using so much Oro must come at a price.

"You okay?" I ask.

Hazel breathes heavy and wipes blood from her eyes. "Let's keep going."

We press onward, but I know it's inevitable Markel's death squad will eventually catch up. I need to devise a plan.

"Zyniah, if Zells can absorb Oro, how does one defeat them?" I ask.

Zyniah strokes her chin. "Hmm, well, there's only so much Oro we can absorb. Too much of it causes us to pass out."

I come to a halt. My team looks at me with incredulity.

"What are you doing, Marcus? The Zells are steadily approaching," says Zyniah.

Running will do us no good; now is the time to act. "Prepare yourselves. Here, we shall take our stand." I draw up a plan and give everyone instructions to form a line.

As we stand firm, fifteen members of Markel's death squad march toward us. The Zells form clear spheres of liquid in their hands.

"Careful," warns Zyniah. "Those are acid spheres. All it takes is a splash to dissolve flesh."

The Zells release their spheres. Hazel shields us by forming pillars of sand. As the acid dissolves the pillars, the Zells release more spheres. Acid splashes in my face, I lose sight in one eye. Rose slices the palm of her hand and drenches blood over my eye to dilute the effects. The Zells rush forward. Rose and I fire Orospheres to keep them at distance. The Zells absorb our spheres and release them back at us. Countering, Zyniah absorbs the Orospheres as does Asher by using Charlotte's blade.

Their bodies shaking, Zyniah and Asher can only contain the Oro for so long.

The Zells form a massive cloud of acid that spews from their mouths. One breath will instantly kill us. As the cloud advances, I race toward it and ignite my Oroburn, causing the acid cloud to evaporate. The Zells grab me, their acidic hands burn my arms. Breaking free from their grip, I leap into the air just as Hazel encases the Zells into a ball of sand.

"Now!" I shout.

In unison, we all release Oro into the ball. Cocooned inside, the Zells attempt to absorb the Oro, but it's too much as they all pass out. My plan has worked.

"They'll be out for days," says Zyniah as she checks the Zells' pulses.

Still half blind, I survey the team. The smiles on their faces give me joy in our victory. But it wasn't without consequence. Having to use so much energy has exhausted the team.

"We need a place to recover," I say. Fiddling in my pocket, I remove Rikari's map and locate an area marked as "Peace."

"What type of place is Peace?" I ask the group.

Hazel smiles. "Best you see it with your own eyes."

With the help of Rikari's map, we travel to what is known as Peace. Much to my amazement, Peace is a large monument dedicated to the Noble Eight Ancestors. Before me in a circle are giant marble and gold statues of four men and four women. At the feet of the statues, engraved in large marble stones are their names. King Arius Ulta of Aypha, Queen Nandi Bonet of Amina, King Naasir Braven of Kamara, Queen Nitocris Sinfall of Zell, King Fate Everlast of Quinn, Queen Vanya Victoria of Dyna, King Dyren Linksan of Syren, and Queen Lucia Karna of Tyna.

In the center of the monument, etched into the marble floor, is a quote:

"Let us cast down our infirmities and let go of our wicked past. Open your hearts to others and seek the bonds of unity. Through unity comes love and through love comes peace."

"They did everything in their power to bring peace to this world," says Hazel, she stares at her ancestor, Vanya Victoria of Dyna. "I can't help but think they would be ashamed of us today."

"They were fools to think peace was everlasting," says Rose. "Markel was right about one thing. Peace is nothing but a fantasy."

"It wasn't just for them," says Zyniah as she looks up at the statue of Queen Nitocris. "In their lifetime, they were able to unify the Eight Great Lands. They left us a legacy to uphold."

Staring at the Noble Eight, I wonder what challenges they faced in their lifetime. What scrutiny did they endure? What sacrifices did they make to achieve peace?

Exhausted, I notice several little wood huts surround the monument.

"Hey, let's get some rest," I say. "Tomorrow, we shall make our ancestors proud."

Saying goodnight to the others, I venture to a hut and plop down on a wool rug. Raising my arm, I stare at the Eye of Truth. Are we truly ready for this? We haven't even reached the Valleys and half my team is already wounded. Was Markel, right? Is it better to use the Eye than risk losing it to the hands of evil? If it is my blood that unlocks the Eye, now would be the time to find out for tomorrow we face a formidable foe. As I contemplate what to do, a knock comes to my door.

"Want some company?" asks Rose as she enters the quaint hut. She rests beside me, her warm back presses against mine. "Am I wrong to think peace cannot exist?"

"Anger or happiness? Which one drives you?" I ask.

Rose's back tenses before she releases a heavy sigh. "Happiness, I guess."

I smile, thankful not all is lost between us. "To embrace happiness means to embrace the opposite of hate. While peace may be a dream, it's something we must strive for." I pause reflecting on something Rose once said. "Life is nothing without dreams, remember?"

Rose turns to me, her teeth clenched. "Dreams—haven't had one of those in a while. I've had nightmares though, and they all end in tragedy."

I whisk Rose's hair behind her ear. "That can't be right. What happened to the dream and promise to your sister, the promise to me?"

Rose's eyes fill with sadness. "Like Scarlett, that dream is dead. I miss her and can only imagine what could've been." Rose caresses my arm. "Seeing your skin, the blemished marks and patterns, they remind me so much of her and it hurts just thinking about it."

This is not the Rose I once knew. I miss the girl who always found a way to laugh. What happened to the girl who lived with purpose and inspiration? She used to have dreams just as I did but seems something has corrupted her mind. Perhaps it's just a matter of time before the same happens to me.

I rest my hand on Rose's cheek. "Well, I had a dream about you and me. In the dream, I'm trying to tell you something, but I can't quite say it. If I could, something tells me it wouldn't end in tragedy."

301

The tears in Rose's eyes dry and her lips part with a smile. "Well, I'm here now, why don't you say it?"

I slide my fingers between Rose's. "The letter I gave you. Everything I've ever wanted to tell you is in it."

Rose takes my hand and places it over her heart. "I don't know what's going to happen tomorrow, but if we survive, I think you're right about that dream."

There Is No Love

On the outskirts of the Valleys, Marcus and his team arrive at a small pond and stare at their reflections. Knowing death may soon follow, they collect their thoughts and prepare themselves for battle. What lies ahead is unknown. A mysterious Divine awaits them. This is a day of collision, where triumph and agony must crash, and burn into a nightmare of reality. Sensing the somber mood, Marcus gathers his team.

"I've never been happier than today," he says. "To stand here with you means everything to me. Today, we make history. No longer are we just kids from different lands, instead we are the hope that unity can one day be reclaimed. To make it happen, it starts with us. It is our generation that can break this cycle of war." Marcus raises his arm to the sky. "Ahead is a foe that seeks the Eye of Truth. But they must not obtain it. No matter how powerful they may be, we will clench victory. Let us unify ourselves. Let us make our ancestors proud and reclaim what the Noble Eight inspired. Let peace return to the world. Let us preserve what is left of Divine love!"

Galvanized by his words, Hazel, Rose, Asher, and Zyniah circle around Marcus and place their fists over their hearts. Overwhelmed by the moment, Rose sheds a few tears before wiping them away.

Armed with purpose and conviction, Marcus and his team march proudly into the base of the Valleys. With the hearts of the legends before them, they pass through a twisted trail of green hills and rocky cliffs. Above them, tucked between the peaks of the mountains, misty clouds turn gray. As they move higher in elevation, a drizzle falls and a gust of wind greets them with a chill. Cold and piercing, the air is ripe for violence.

As they enter into a wider section of the Valleys, blocking their path forward are nine Ayphas from Petune's command.

"So this is why the commander sent us," says one of the Ayphas. "Marcus Azure, hand over the Eye or be killed." The Aypha charges an Orosphere and points it at the group.

Wanting to prove himself, Asher leans over to Marcus. "Cover me."

With no regard for his life, Asher rushes forward. Barrel rolling to avoid an Orosphere, he strikes the Aypha with Charlotte's blade and kills him instantly. Like mad dogs, the Ayphas attempt to pounce on Asher, but Marcus fires off several Orospheres to push them back. Hazel forms an iron twist around the Ayphas' legs. Rose releases her Orospheres and kills two more Ayphas. Zyniah zips toward an Aypha and places her hand on his forehead. She activates her Legacy and absorbs all the water within the Aypha's body, causing him to turn brittle and die.

Now five against five, the match is more even. But in reality, it isn't, as Hazel brutally finishes them off by smashing their bodies between two massive iron slabs.

Marcus wipes sweat from his eyebrows. "Everyone okay?" he asks.

The team nods and smiles.

"Aw, what a cute crew you have here," mocks Rizen. Alongside him is Darius. The two are perched on a grass hill overlooking the team.

Darius frowns. "Rose? So you too have joined the traitor? Never thought the ones I grew up with would become such disloyal people."

Rose crosses her arms. "You should be thanking him, not wasting your breath on insults."

Darius's eyes twitch. "Thank him? Should I thank him for being a coward? For his lies? Ah, I know, I should thank him for my father's death!"

Marcus looks to his old friend. "We've been through this too many times, Darius. No matter what I say, I cannot bring back your father. What my parents did has nothing to do with you and me. No matter what you think of me, you will always be my friend."

Darius's forearm begins to bulge as he forms an Orosphere. He shows Marcus his inner bicep—the tattoo of forever friends is no more. "No, Marcus. There's no such thing as friends, just people to hate and people to kill." Darius unloads his Orosphere. Marcus counters with his own.

"Our bond may be broken, but there's still time for you to see the truth. If you continue down this path, thousands of Divines will die. But we can stop it by destroying the Eye," says Marcus.

Darius unleashes another sphere, and again Marcus counters.

"Stop playing and kill him," threatens Rizen. "Finish him now!"

But it is too late. Over a hundred Aminas swoop down onto the sides of the hills. As their leader stands before them, Marcus takes note of her resemblance to Sinclair.

"Who is she?" he asks Rose.

"That is my queen, Cynné Bonet…forgive me, Marcus."

Hope Is Gone When Valleys Cry

Shedding tears of pain, Rose proceeds toward Cynné and bows before her queen.

"My beauty, I know it hurts, but you've done well," says Cynné as she pats Rose's shoulder.

Rose stares at the ground. A part of her might die if she were to look Marcus in the eye.

Marcus's hands tremble and his heart shatters into pieces. "*See what happiness gets you,*" echoes Sinclair's voice in his head.

Ophelia, who is beside Cynné giggles, taking pleasure in Marcus's sorrow. "Aw, look at this hapless pup. Guarantee he's going to cry."

"No need to torture the boy," says Cynné as she extends her hand. "Dear Marcus, there's no shame in yielding to see another day. Give me the Eye and you shall live."

With Darius and Rizen flanked on one side and Cynné's legion of Aminas on the other, Marcus plants his legs firmly into the ground. Staring at Rose, he fights back tears as pain unleashes deep inside. The agony of betrayal sparks something ugly within him.

"ORO RELEASE!" Marcus shouts. Oro spews uncontrollably from every pore of his body. Compacting an immense Orosphere, he prepares to unleash it, but Zyniah absorbs it.

"You're going to kill yourself before the battle even begins," she snaps.

Cynné chuckles and leans over to Rose. "Who's the Dyna? Those eyes look familiar."

Rose continues to stare at the ground. "Hazel…Hazel Victoria," she whimpers.

Cynné clasps her hands. "Valencia's daughter? Oh, this is something rare! It isn't every day I get to kill royalty."

"You're mistaken," retorts Hazel. Her eyes glow green as she stares at Cynné. "For centuries, Victorias have lived by one creed, a creed to destroy anyone who threatens our existence. My ancestors would never forgive me if I died by your filthy hands. By my word, none of you shall survive!"

Hazel slams her hand into the ground causing a great divide to split across the valley. Many Aminas plummet to their doom. From the sides of the cliffs, she forms hundreds of iron daggers that shower over the Aminas, shredding and piercing many of them to death. As the Aminas release Orospheres, Hazel forms a series of iron walls to protect the team. When the barrage ends, only a single wall remains.

"Asher, Marcus, find the Yazu and end this. Zyniah and I will cover you!" shouts Hazel.

Marcus turns to Hazel in disbelief. "What! No, we stay together."

Zyniah tosses the Seeker to Marcus. "Change of plans. Now go!"

As the iron wall crumbles around them, Marcus and Asher race up the green hills and into a canopy of trees. Darius and Rizen move in pursuit.

Hazel forms a second wave of iron arrows from the cliffsides and releases them upon the Aminas.

"Enough of this!" shouts Cynné. Raising her hands to the sky, Cynné's hands illuminate a white glow as she forms a hardened Oro dome shielding the Aminas from the incoming arrows.

"Ophelia, take care of Valencia's seed. I'm going to fetch the Eye," instructs Cynné as the Oro dome dissipates.

As Cynné gives chase to Marcus, Ophelia forms a dark orange Oro whip and whirls it over her head. Salivating for blood, she bites down on her lip. "Valencia's offspring, I promise to sip your blood slowly, for yours is a delicacy." Ophelia cracks her whip, the tip of which explodes.

"Zyniah, can you absorb that?" asks Hazel.

Zyniah shakes her head. "I'll die trying. That whip has been infused with her soul."

Hazel forms an iron wall as Ophelia unleashes her whip. The tip of the whip strikes the wall, disintegrating it into pieces. Zyniah grabs a handful of rocks and feeds her Oro into them. She launches the rocks at

Ophelia, which magnify twenty times in size. Ophelia slashes her whip, destroying the colossal rocks.

"You can magnify objects!" says a shocked Hazel. She forms several iron arrows which Zyniah then infuses with her Oro. Hurling the arrows, they magnify in size. Ophelia leaps high and with a crack of her whip, destroys them. But upon landing, a thick iron rod wraps tight around her like a snake constricting its prey.

"Now!" shouts Hazel.

Zyniah heaves a single arrow at Ophelia, and as it expands in size, there's no escape…her saving grace are the surviving Aminas who destroy the arrow with their Orospheres.

Breaking free from the twisted iron rod, Ophelia releases a volley of hot Oro needles that rip through Zyniah and Hazel. As blood spills from their bodies, the Aminas advance toward them and prime their Orospheres.

Covered in blood, Hazel tries forming a wall, but something greater interferes.

The ground trembles and a massive gold wall rises from the ground, protecting Hazel and Zyniah. Standing at the top of the wall with her arms crossed is Rikari Niacin.

From opposite ends of the Valleys, two massive gold hands collide together, splattering nearly all the Aminas. Only Rose, Ophelia, and a handful of Aminas remain.

"Ah, Rikari! I'm so glad you're alive," says Ophelia. "Let's finish our battle in proper form."

Ophelia darts into the eastern hills of the Valleys. As Rikari pursues, Rose retreats farther north into higher elevation. Hazel gives chase, leaving Zyniah to deal with the remaining Aminas.

***

In the eastern valley hills, both Rikari and Ophelia yearn for this moment. Being apex competitors, they love testing their skills among the strongest. But while Rikari views this as revenge, Ophelia simply enjoys the sport of fighting to the death.

"Hope this goes better than last time," says Ophelia. "You were such a disappointment." She unleashes her Oro whip, and as the tip nears Rikari, she erects a solid gold wall blocking the explosion. Ophelia leaps on top of the wall and rains down many Orospheres, forcing Rikari to activate her diamond-armored skin.

"You can't hide behind your armor forever!" says a bloodthirsty Ophelia as she continues to hammer Rikari with Orospheres. Rikari pounds her fists into the ground and forms a gigantic gold snake that rises from the soil and into the air.

"This is what I came to see!" shouts Ophelia. Her face flushes red, she unleashes her whip against the gold snake, but it has no effect. The colossal metal snake opens its mouth and crashes over Ophelia, swallowing her whole.

There's immediate silence. It lasts but a second as the snake explodes, sending bits of gold everywhere.

Her body soaked in blood, Ophelia yearns for more punishment. "Do you have any more attacks like that?" she asks. "Please, give me more."

Rikari's jaw tightens. Forming such an enormous metal creation has strained her body. Not fully healed from her previous fight, Rikari grows dizzy, swaying on her feet. Slamming her hands into the ground, she creates two misplaced gold spears behind Ophelia.

"Weak!" Ophelia laughs, destroying the spears with a swipe of her hand.

Exhausted, Rikari falls to her knees. Digging her hand into the soil, she forms a blade behind Ophelia. The blade swipes across Ophelia's neck, nearly separating her head from her shoulders. But a red and black hole appears in Ophelia's chest, and her eyes glow red as she activates her soul. Before a single drop of blood hits the ground, tissue strands quickly sow her neck back to her body.

"What a thrill!" laughs a maniacal Ophelia.

Staring at the psychotic woman, Rikari ponders what will it take to kill Ophelia?

***

In the western hills of the Valleys, Cynné chases after Marcus Azure. She nearly catches up to Darius and Rizen when an Orosphere flashes from her peripheral. Dodging it at the last second, she tumbles to the ground. Like a cat, she springs to her feet, but her jaw drops as a masked woman stands before her.

"Mother?" Cynné asks. "Why are you doing this? Have I not been loyal to you?"

"Loyal? You weren't even loyal to your own sister."

Cynné frowns in confusion. Sinclair slowly removes her mother's ivory snow leopard mask, causing all the blood in Cynné's face to collect at the soles of her feet.

Cynné trembles at the sight of her sister. "You're dead. I saw it myself," she says.

"You saw what you wanted to see, what you wanted to believe. You should be ashamed of yourself." Sinclair gnashes her teeth. "You sent the women I once led to kill me, and for that, you're a coward."

Orospheres spark in both Cynné's and Sinclair's hands. As they scream for all in the Valleys to hear, they release their spheres, causing a great blast. Both women gambled on a single, powerful strike, and as the haze around them diminishes, only one remains standing.

***

Farther north, the battle between Hazel and Rose has just begun. It's fitting their battle takes place here. Since the inception of Divines, Aminas and Dynas have used the Valleys of Hope to settle past wars. Filled with the blood and pride of their ancestors, the two unleash their fury. Rose releases her Orospheres as Hazel forms an iron wall. Advancing forward, Rose blasts a hole through the wall and lands a solid blow to Hazel's jaw.

Unsheathing her sword, Rose slashes at Hazel's jugular who catches the sword to protect her neck.

Eye to eye with each other, Hazel smiles. "I see why Marcus liked you. You have the face of an angel." Warm blood drips from Hazel's impaled hand. "If he only knew you had the heart of a demon and the coldest of souls, he would've seen how disgusting you really are."

Hazel twists Rose's sword, shattering it instantly. She then summons a giant iron pillar, rocketing Rose into the sky. The pillar turns to dust, Rose descends into a free fall toward a bed of jagged iron spikes below. Desperate, Rose sets off an Orosphere to propel herself away from instant death. While she avoids being impaled, her arm is badly crippled. Feeling the ground shift beneath her feet, Rose sprints away while spikes of iron follow her every step.

Hazel forms a massive curve-shaped wall to trap Rose. Too high to jump over, Rose blasts the wall with an Orosphere, but the wall is simply too thick. Slowly curving all around Rose, the wall cocoons her into a deadly trap. Now encapsulated, iron arrows dart toward Rose, forcing her to dodge and weave. Relentless arrows shoot from the wall until one pierces her calf. Four more arrows impale her thighs and arms. She pulls the arrows from her flesh, and blood gushes down her legs. She drops to her knees. The match is over.

"What do you want me to tell, Marcus?" asks Hazel as she emerges from the iron cocoon.

Rose looks to the pool of blood surrounding her. "I'm certain he cares nothing of me at this point."

Hazel shrugs. "Fair enough. I'll tell him you died a miserable and brutal death. Perhaps that will give him comfort."

BOOM! Hazel's iron cocoon crumbles to pieces destroyed by a powerful Orosphere.

"I knew you would need me," says Nova as she helps Rose to her feet. A dark orange and black hole swirls in Nova's chest for she is using the power of her soul. "See, the problem with fighting Dynas is they always use tricks. They never fight like real warriors."

Hazel tries impaling the girls with iron spikes, but Nova grabs Rose and leaps over Hazel.

"Get to a safe spot. I'll take it from here," says Nova.

Rose waves Nova off and staggers to her feet. She's badly injured, but pride won't let her run. "The Dyna dies here," she declares.

Simultaneously, Rose and Nova release Orospheres that Hazel easily evades.

"I have to get close to kill her," says a light-headed Rose. "Cover me."

Nova smirks. "Nah, I can end this now." She forms an intense black and orange Orosphere.

Hazel attempts to shield herself behind an iron wall, but the powerful sphere breaks right through and blasts Hazel in her back. Her ribs and organs exposed, blood drools from Hazel's lips. She places her hand on her back and seals her wounds with hot melting iron. Stunned she's even alive, Nova releases several more Orospheres, but Hazel encases herself inside of a giant iron ball. She breathes heavy and tries to regain her composure as Nova channels her most powerful strike yet. Nova fires her soul-infused Orosphere. The immense blast eviscerates the iron ball. Hazel lies unconscious.

"She was tougher than I thought," says Nova as she watches Hazel's blood seep into the soil.

Rose takes note of the gold Krysanthem leaf necklace still resting on Hazel's chest. Shining bright and unblemished, the leaf symbolized unity between Hazel and Marcus.

"Say, is that Marcus?" asks Nova. Across the valleys, Marcus and Asher scramble up a hill in search of the Yazu. Nova charges an Orosphere. "Bet I can snipe him from here."

Rose lowers Nova's hand. "That's not our battle."

"Oh, what's the matter? Scared to see your friend die?"

Rose returns to Hazel and reaches for the Krysanthem necklace, only for someone to snatch her by the wrist. Looking up, Rose sees the cracked snow leopard mask worn by Sinclair, her lips quiver and she stumbles backward.

"This won't be like last time," says a prideful Nova.

Sinclair laughs. "You think the soul makes you stronger. You should be careful, for abusing the soul only leads to one thing."

"You're right—it leads to your death!" Nova releases six soul-infused spheres. Sinclair counters with just as many.

"Shame on whoever taught you the soul," says Sinclair. She then flicks a small Orosphere into Nova's chest, which causes the orange and black hole to close. Nova gasps for air, she clutches her chest, and collapses. Rose charges an Orosphere but is waved off by Sinclair.

"That won't be necessary. It would be a shame to kill you now. In fact, I applaud you." Sinclair snatches the Krysanthem necklace off Hazel and places it on herself. "Because of you, Rose, Marcus knows real pain."

***

In the western valleys, Marcus and Asher continue their search for the Yazu. Using the Seeker to guide them, the two dash through a narrow trail where above them are rocky cliffs. Not far behind them are Darius and Rizen. As Marcus and Asher sweep around a bend, they spot the Yazu encased inside an Oro shield at the peak of a hill.

"Time to end this!" Marcus rolls up his sleeve, exposing the Eye. As he bolts toward the Yazu, Rizen releases an Orosphere at the cliffs above. Boulders rain down on Marcus. He dodges many but is caught by one that crushes his leg.

The opportunity to kill Marcus is now. Darius races toward him, and as he leaps forward, Asher tackles Darius, causing them to tumble down the cliffside below. Their fall broken by the hard ground, the two dust themselves off and stare down one another.

"I'm disappointed in you the most," says Darius. "You chose a traitor over your friend."

"A traitor he is not. He is our friend," says Asher. "Your pain, your vengeance—it is sorely misplaced in him. He feels awful about what his parents have done, but he is not to blame."

Darius gnashes his teeth. "Crow spit! Marcus is just as guilty as his parents. He knew about the attack yet he did nothing!"

Asher shakes his head. "You're wrong, but I can tell no matter what he or I say, you have made up your mind. You've chosen to stay blind to what Aypha is becoming."

Darius forms an Orosphere. "Asher, get out of my way or I'll kill you."

Asher unsheathes his blade. "I'm sorry. I can't, my friend."

"This isn't a fair match. Don't make me do this." Darius raises his Orosphere but Asher remains firm, clenching his blade.

"Forgive me, Asher. I'm sorry for what I must do." Darius closes his eyes and fires.

Using his blade, Asher absorbs the sphere, causing the blade to brighten with a multitude of colors. Unbeknownst to Darius, Asher was carrying one of the Seven Blades of Might. Pointing his iridescent blade at Darius, Asher winks. "I'd say we're pretty evenly matched."

***

Above Darius and Asher, near the peak of a mountain, Marcus frees himself from a boulder. Though his leg is shattered, he hobbles toward the Yazu.

"And here it ends," says Rizen as he leaps in front and blocks Marcus's path. "This is where you shall die." Rizen charges an Orosphere.

The cold rage of anger burns in Marcus's eyes as he too charges an Orosphere. "You no longer intimidate me," says Marcus as his sphere intensifies. "I no longer know the meaning of fear."

Rizen smiles. "Then allow me to reintroduce you."

In a great spectacle, both Ayphas release a barrage of Orospheres. Evenly matched, the two battle until their Oro levels reach near zero. Unable to form Orospheres, Rizen and Marcus trade blows, landing vicious punches to each other's skulls. They refuse to quit; their hearts pump pure adrenaline. Their eyes swollen and heads throbbing, both are willing to die here. Digging deep, Rizen lands a vicious uppercut, levitating Marcus off the ground. He then strikes him with such force, Marcus's jaw dislocates, and teeth fly from his mouth.

"I'll make this quick," says an exasperated Rizen as he stands over Marcus.

Marcus breathes heavy. He tries forming an Orosphere, but it fizzles into nothing.

Rizen chuckles. "Just like your entire life, you go out just as pathetic as you came." Rizen takes a jagged stone shard from the ground and jabs it hard into Marcus's belly.

Marcus screams. His body convulses as blood spreads across his stomach.

"Stay still and die!" Rizen takes another shard and hacks away at Marcus's arm in an attempt to cut off the Eye of Truth.

As blood splatters everywhere, Marcus looks toward the Yazu. He's mere feet from his goal; disappointment fills his eyes. He's failed his parents, his friends. Himself.

Everything Rizen said was coming to pass. Tears burn behind his eyes as Sinclair's voice rings out in his mind. *"Is this the happiness you seek? To die in vain?"* Marcus shakes his head trying to block out Sinclair's taunting words. *"Shame, if only you had embraced anger. I wonder if Rose will even cry when she finds out you're dead."*

"SHUT UP! SHUT UP! SHUT UP!" Marcus screams. Gritting his teeth, he pulls the shard from his stomach and stabs Rizen in his chest. Marcus struggles to his feet. There's no feeling in his butchered, mangled arm. He approaches Rizen but comes to a halt as a squad of Divine Ayphas arrive.

Rizen smirks, knowing he's avoided death. "It's judgment time," he declares. He pulls the shard from his chest and raises his arm. "My fellow Ayphas, I present to you, Marcus Azure, traitor of Aypha. He and his family are a black stain on the royal name of Aypha. Let his death be painful and without mercy."

As fifty Ayphas charge their Orospheres, Marcus stands tall. Bloody and bruised, he's proud of himself and ready for this moment. All his ideals and impossible dreams have faded. Gone are thoughts of a blissful life. Wishes for a taste of his childhood are no more. Thoughts of a time where Asher, Darius, Rose, and he were together turn into glitter. There was a time when everything was innocent, simple, and filled with happiness. Seeing all his friends together was the last image he wanted to see…but Marcus was no longer a child.

The Ayphas release an unrelenting barrage of Orospheres upon Marcus. As each sphere collides into his body, he embraces them, yet not a single one explodes. Instead, Marcus absorbs their Orospheres—just like a Zell.

The Ayphas stare in disbelief. Unbeknownst to them, Marcus is indeed special. He has a secret, a secret that only a handful know about. Marcus has the blood of a Pure Divine, the power of both Aypha and Zell. Secretly born for this purpose, Marcus is a weapon of destruction.

As his eyes radiate a crystal blue, the Ayphas tremble, astonished at what they've witnessed. Placing his hands into the air, Marcus forms a massive blue Orosphere so large, it casts a shadow over the Ayphas. He's filled with rage, and his skin begins to peel and crack due to the strain of the colossal sphere.

"Embrace your anger. Kill them all." Sinclair's voice creeps into Marcus's head.

As Marcus continues to channel the immense sphere, the Ayphas drop to their knees, recognizing their demise. With the immense blue sphere of death whirling above, Zyniah arrives.

"You'll kill us all if you release that!" she shouts.

Seeing the fear among the Ayphas, Marcus grins at the thought. Bloodthirst bleeds into his heart and mind. "No mercy for the weak," he says. "To them, I am nothing. They deserve to die."

"You're better than them," pleads Zyniah. She points to the Yazu, who stare in horror. "Remember what you came here for."

On the verge of a psychotic rage, it takes every ounce of strength in his heart not to release the colossal Orosphere. Slowly, Marcus relinquishes, and the massive sphere fizzles. He proceeds toward the Yazu and destroys the Oro shield surrounding them.

"Young lad, it's so good to see you," says an old Yazu man.

Marcus extends his arm. "Quickly, destroy the Eye," he commands.

Yet the Yazu turn silent. A familiar face appears. It is the little child Yondi.

Wrinkles appear across Marcus's forehead. "How? How are you alive?"

The girl who never uttered a word finally speaks. "Kill me," she says. "Only the one with the Eye can kill me, and by doing so will destroy the Eye."

Marcus stares at Yondi's innocent brown eyes. "But you're just a baby," Marcus whispers. "Killing you would be beyond heartless."

Yondi shakes her head. "I am not what you think I am for I have died many times and have been reborn. Do what is necessary to save your people."

Marcus forms an Orosphere and holds it to Yondi's face. His arm shakes, and tears glisten in his eyes as he grits his teeth. "Forgive me for what I must do."

"That I cannot allow," says Sinclair as she appears in the flesh.

Marcus holds the sphere closer to Yondi's head. "I have to do this. Isn't this what my parents and you wanted?" As the sphere intensifies, Marcus presses forward, prepared to complete his grim task.

Sinclair takes the Krysanthem leaf necklace and swallows it whole. Just a trace of Marcus's blood allows her to control his body and mind. The seals she placed in Marcus enables her to bend him to her will. She places Marcus in a state of unconsciousness and rips the Eye from his wrist.

Now with the Eye, Sinclair attaches it to her own wrist and reveals a mysterious vial of blood. The blood of Yona.

"So it was you," says Yondi as she takes note of the vial.

Sinclair smiles, dropping Yona's blood onto the amulet. The Eye suddenly opens, and a bright white light shoots toward the heavens. As the others in the Valleys see the light, their battles abruptly come to a halt. They now scramble toward the light.

There's a reason Sinclair needed Marcus to bring the Eye to the Valleys. It was during her battle against Rose and Nova, she realized something powerful was here. Her Oro sensing ability had been blocked and the only thing powerful enough to do that is a Phoenix!

Running north, Sinclair ascends to the top of a valley peak and arrives at a shimmering blue lake. As she approaches, the water within the lake bubbles, the surrounding trees sway back and forth, and the air turns frightening cold. Below the lake, a scream erupts and shakes the ground. The moment has arrived where a Phoenix shall be reborn.

"Come to me," says Sinclair as raises the Eye of Truth. Her eyes fill with pride and her lips quiver in desire for the Phoenix. As the Phoenix's crown rises above the water, a dagger slices across Sinclair's knees and a blade cuts her arm clean off. No longer connected to a host, the Eye deactivates and the water ceases to boil. Sinclair desperately crawls toward her severed arm. But it's no use—General X slowly approaches.

"And the dead shall rise," he says. He takes Sinclair's detached arm, peels off the Eye, and attaches it to his wrist. Now connected to the power of the Eye, General X's body transforms. The Eye returns his strength and cleanses his illness. His hair reverts to black, the spots on his body disappear, and the yellow vanishes from his eyes. His once wrinkled skin melts away and reveals a Divine of magnificent physique.

Sinclair releases an Orosphere, but the revitalized general easily counters.

"You haven't changed a bit," says General X. "Only you would take what belongs to me."

Marcus and Zyniah arrive, followed by Rose, Nova, Hazel, Cynné, Ophelia, Rikari, Asher, Darius, and now Petune.

"Rise!" General X raises his arm. The ground shakes violently. Geysers spring from the lake as a colossal Phoenix of colorful crystals and ice emerges from the boiling waters. Looming over them, the Divines watch in awe as the Legendary Phoenix of Ice is reborn.

"Let it be remembered, that it was I who restored the glory of our past and have obtained such magnificent power." The general points to Cynné and Petune. "For too many years now, Ayphas and Aminas have gone astray. Our division has made us weak. It's time we reunite the flock. As the keeper of the Eye, it is my duty to solidify our bond. Give up your past deceitfulness, your hate, and old ways of thinking. Embrace what is destined for us as a family. As your leader, I vow we shall reclaim the power of our true, purest form."

General X takes a sword and forms a line within the soil. "Stand by my side and admit your transgressions or be killed," he declares.

As the Divines gaze at the Phoenix above them, the first to pledge allegiance is Petune.

"I have sinned, great General. I have been selfish and deceitful. Please forgive me," he says, kneeling before the revitalized General X. Darius follows and kneels as well.

Cynné reluctantly stands beside General X and declares her misdeeds. Ophelia and Nova also concede and stand beside their queen.

"Never shall I join the wicked," says a defiant Marcus. "You represent all that is wrong with this world. You seek greed and power. But your efforts are fleeting. In the end, none of it you can take with you."

"Little boys with little thoughts know very little," says the general. "What do you know of life and death? When we return to our purest forms, death will no longer have power over us. Only the pure can sit beside the throne." The general extends his hand. "What shall it be, Sinclair? Your family is willing to look past your transgressions."

Sinclair scowls at General X as she hobbles beside Marcus. Rikari, Zyniah, Asher and Hazel all stand beside him as well.

The only one left is Rose Cross. Her heart teeters with many emotions. Her nerves wrecked, she holds her head low and approaches Marcus. Grabbing his hand, she returns the letter he had given her. Without a word, she turns her back on him and stands by Cynné.

"General X, I ask that you spare Marcus Azure," says Cynné. "He does not deserve death for the sins of his parents."

General X releases a maniacal laugh. "Cynné, you of all people know there's no mercy in this world. Still, I will ensure his name and those who stood with him will be written in the pages of history as the first martyrs of the Final Great War!"

A teary-eyed Rose turns to her queen. "My lady, you promised. You promised he wouldn't be harmed!"

General X lifts the Eye of Truth and calls for his Phoenix to strike. Flapping its mighty icy wings, hundreds of jagged ice crystals form around the Phoenix. The Phoenix towers over Marcus and the others, they stare helplessly, knowing their resistance is futile against such a remarkable creation. From the Phoenix's mouth, a concentrated ball of ice forms. The wind blows fiercely and the air turns frightening cold before the Phoenix releases a painful shriek. The ice from its mouth dissipates, and slowly, the Phoenix pulls away from the group. Raising the Eye, General X commands the Phoenix to return, but a more powerful force draws it away. Taming its power, across the lake, two figures in red cloaks emerge from a forest. As the Phoenix moves toward them, it shrinks and seals itself inside one of the cloaked individuals.

Sinclair squints her eyes. "Gail, Saphron—is that you?"

The one who has sealed the Phoenix extends their hand and releases a catastrophic blast, causing everything to turn to ice and snow. The lake is now frozen, trees are covered in frost, and every creature and Divine are encased in ice—everyone except Marcus Azure.

Staring across the glistening frozen lake, he shouts to his parents, yet they turn their backs and disappear within the ice-coated trees.

His heart beats uncontrollably, his breath visible to the air. Once again, mere feet from his parents, he's been abandoned, leaving him to wonder why.

Suddenly, the icy atmosphere shatters like glass restoring life to everyone.

A relieved Sinclair can't help but take a shot at General X. "Looks like even you didn't foresee this one."

General X grinds his teeth and looks to the sky. "Appears favor from above has spared you. Nevertheless, the Eye is mine, and there are more Phoenixes to be had. Enjoy this moment, for a day will come when all lands must submit to me or be laid to waste. Soon a time will come when blood fills the rivers of this world, and in the end, only those loyal to me shall remain." The general's ominous declaration has officially sparked war against the other Great Lands. As the Divines peer into the souls of one another, they know agony will soon rain over them.

And like a never-ending vicious cycle, just as their ancestors once waged war, the greatest Divines of this generation will once again decide the fate not of themselves, but of life itself.

Author's Note

I hope you enjoyed *May A Divine Awaken,* the first novel in the *The Divine* series. The journey to writing my first novel has been long, but not without promise and a lot of encouragement from family and friends. Special shout out to Zevie G! Your support for this project helped push me to publication.

Also thanks to my cover designer, Franzi Stern © Cover design: Franziska Stern - www.coverdungeon.com - Instagram: @coverdungeonrabbit

To the readers, I'm excited about the future of this series and hope you join me on this magical ride. Book two is on the way and will explore deeper into the minds of some of your favorite characters.

Interested in learning more? Follow me on social media or feel free to send me an email.

About the Author

Michael A. Tinsley is a 2022 debut author and a graduate of North Carolina A&T State University. He currently resides in Bowie, Maryland with his lovely wife and beautiful daughter. He can be reached on social media or by email.

Instagram: AffinityAuthor
Twitter: @AffinityAuthor
Email: Tinsleyaffinity@gmail.com

9 781087 968162